MIRANDA SILVER

FROM THE AUTHOR OF *PRICELESS*

Contents

This is a work of fiction. Names, characters, businesses, places, events, locales, and incidents are either the product of the author's imagination or used in a fictitious manner. Any resemblance to actual persons, living or dead, or actual events is purely coincidental.

Editing by Mackenzie at Nice Girl, Naughty Edits

Cover Design and Formatting by Mayhem Cover Creations

ISBN: 9781005505219

Manufactured in the United States of America

First Edition May 2022

Content Notes

This story contains explicit sexual content, profanity, and topics that may be sensitive for some readers. For a detailed list, click here or scan the code below:

PLAYLIST

Music has played a tremendous part in writing Daisy, Reeve, Nate, Evan, and Blake's story, and this book owes so much to the artists who have inspired it. Each chapter is named for the title or lyrics of a song.

1. Fly Like An Eagle - Larkin Poe
2. Dark Eyes - Beast
3. All Day And All Of The Night - The Kinks
4. Crescent City - I'm With Her
5. Mystery Of Love - Sufjan Stevens
6. Take What You Want From Me - Larkin Poe
7. Cornflake Girl - Tori Amos
8. Ladder - Joan Osborne
9. Revelator - Gillian Welch
10. Wait For The Sun - Ollabelle
11. Pangaea - I'm With Her
12. Old Man - The Wailin' Jennys
13. Nowhere To Run - Laura Nyro and Labelle
14. I-89 - I'm With Her
15. Holy Ghost Fire - Larkin Poe
16. Dracula Moon - Joan Osborne
17. Mantras - Ellen Winter
18. Q.U.E.E.N. - Janelle Monáe ft. Erykah Badu
19. Hypnotic - Samantha Fish
20. Air - Toru Takemitsu
21. Twisted Ambition - Samantha Fish
22. The Fall Tonight - We're No Gentlemen
23. Hell On Wheels - Betty Blowtorch
24. Mr. Hurricane - Beast
25. Can't Find My Way Home - Ellen McIlwaine
26. Nothing Else - Angus & Julia Stone
27. Only For You - Heartless Bastards

28. Glowing Heart - Aoife O'Donovan

29. Tempest - Jesse Cook

30. I Still Haven't Found What I'm Looking For - Sarah Jarosz

31. Girl On The Wing - The Shins

32. Shining Star - Earth, Wind & Fire

Desire: to wish or long for. Can be traced to Latin *desiderare,* originally meaning "await what the stars will bring," from the phrase *de sidere* "from the stars."

Deliver: to hand over to the proper recipient; to provide something promised; to save, rescue, or set someone free from. From Latin *de liberare, de* meaning "away" and *liberare* meaning "to set free."

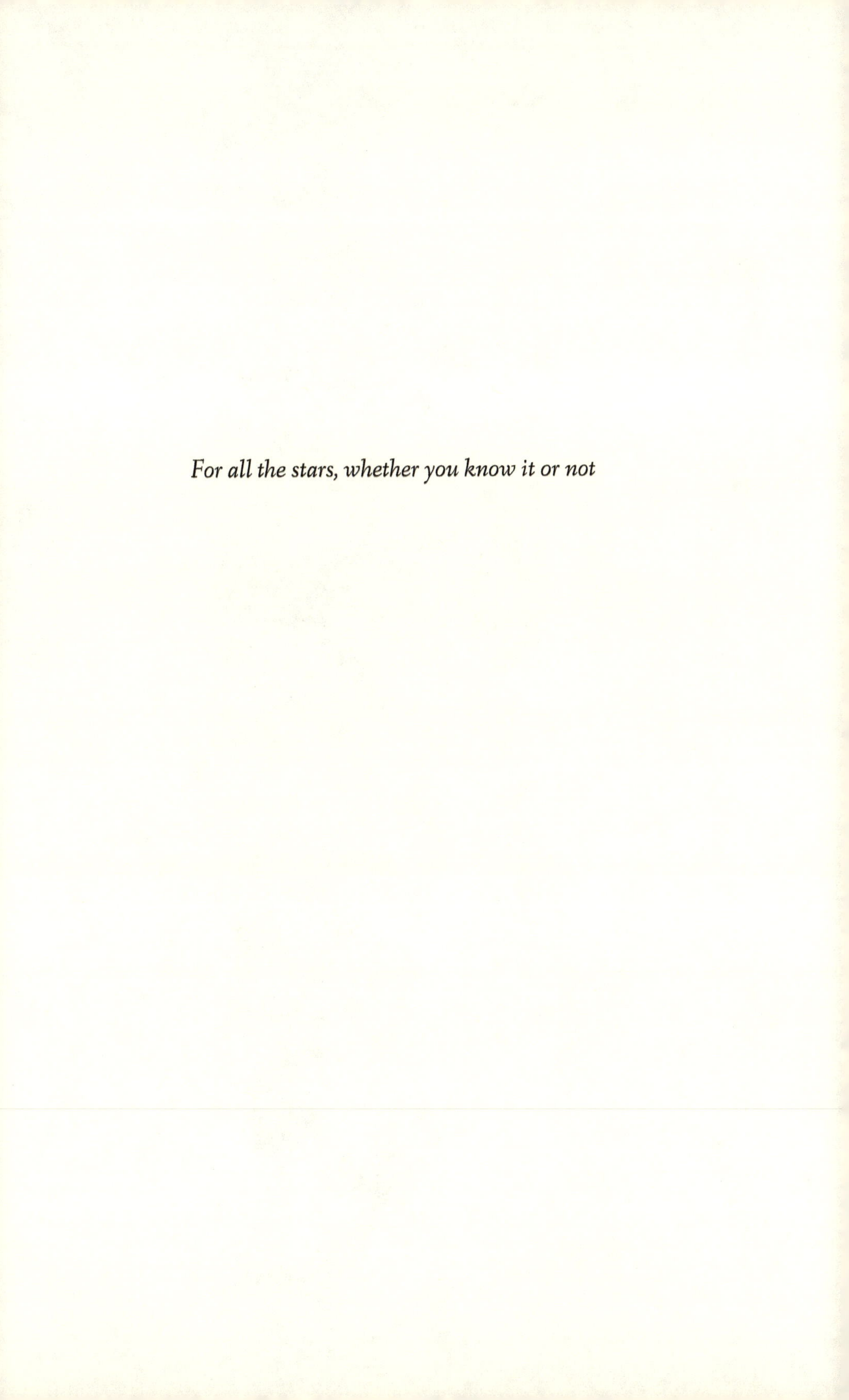

For all the stars, whether you know it or not

1

Fly Like An Eagle

Reeve

R*iches, power, fame…what would you do if you lost it all?*

Daisy's words echoed in the wind around me as I rushed up the dark path on Greer Hill. The sky was empty; the moon was almost new; and the stars hid themselves, as if they couldn't bear to see what happened on earth.

I didn't give a fuck right now about riches, about power or fame. All I wanted was her.

The Star of the Cosmos.

Daisy.

My Daze.

I'd lost her, maybe forever.

But after the hisses that filled my head this evening, interrupting my studies, I'd be damned if I let her slip away without a fight.

The Star is in danger.

Go to her.

Go to the hill.

"Help me," I'd snarled at the serpent, shoving away my laptop.

But desire was a capricious master, and the serpent never acted when it could use humans to do its will.

As I sprinted up the shrouded hill, my flashlight sending its beam over the grass and bushes, the prophecy of the Star pounded through my head.

Once in a century, a woman came along, ambitious, unpredictable, and explosive. If the serpent's devotees could find her and harness her power, our futures would blaze brighter than we'd ever imagined. But sharing power with the Star was dangerous, and finding her was like searching for a pinpoint in a galaxy.

Over the past days, Daisy had passed every test to prove that she was the Star. Stunned that she'd dropped into our laps just weeks before the Joining, I'd carefully planned our seduction of her. I'd trusted that we could make her ours, though magic kept us from speaking of our intentions.

But all I wanted to know right now was that Daisy was safe.

Alive.

I should have brought the others, but they were scattered — Blake at his restaurant, Nate at the gym, Evan in the recording studio I'd built onto the House. There hadn't been time.

Sweat soaked my shirt, wilting the fabric. My hair fell over my forehead, damp and distracting. My heart thudded like a bass drum.

"I'm coming, Daze," I muttered.

Above me, past the crest of the hill, a scream pierced the night.

"Daisy!" A burst of speed took over as I ran even faster toward the sound. "I'm almost there—"

I rounded the crest, and the woods came into view. On the grass, outside the line of trees, a woman slowly got to her feet.

Her hair flamed red in the beam of my flashlight, and she held one arm at an angle to her body, wincing with pain. When she saw me, her heart-shaped face twisted with loathing.

My jaw set. "Where is she, Tara?"

The look of loathing vanished, and Tara let out a whimper.

"Reeve! Help me! I think my arm is broken... She's a monster, she's evil, she's unnatural. You can't trust her. I tried—"

I crossed swiftly to her, dropped the flashlight, and gripped her shoulders. "Where...is...Daisy?"

Fear crossed Tara's face, exquisitely sculpted by magic. Mascara was smudged beneath her eyes.

"Reeve, I know you have *some* heart. I'm injured...you have to take care of me...we've known each other so long..."

I shook her, and she let out a squeak. "Where is she? What have you done?"

Her eyes turned to slits. "She's where you'll never find her. And she's not coming out."

My hand went to her throat, and she gasped. "In the woods? Why?"

"She wears the collar," Tara sneered. "She answers to me now, Reeve. Not you."

Her pulse pounded against my hand. Fury made my vision swim in a haze of red. "You're the monster here."

Tara shook her head, glaring, and I dug my fingers into her neck. She clawed at my face, raking my cheeks, to no avail.

"She threw you out of that forest, didn't she?" I spat. "You tried to make her your puppet, your doll. But she's much too strong for that."

Her breath came in pants, but she laughed, wheezing, until she coughed. "That's exactly why *you* want your precious Star. But if you're the one using her — it's okay. If it's me — it's wrong."

I shoved her away, and she staggered back, gulping for air.

"You hypocrite," she railed. "You fucker, you money-grubbing bastard. I know you'll stop at nothing to get to the top. Don't make yourself into a savior."

I scrubbed my hands on my slacks, erasing the feel of Tara's skin. My voice dropped to a rasp. "I would never hurt Daisy. I want only the best for her. That happens to coincide with my needs and the needs of my friends."

Tara stared at me, her hair hanging in her face. Her hands fluttered to the diamond four-leaf clover necklace at her bruised throat, bought with the hush money I'd paid her.

I remembered that stare, coming from a face that used to be ordinary, neither beautiful nor hideous. The girl from down the road, spying on me through the trees, following me like a shadow for years, startling me as I spoke to the serpent in the woodland that bordered my family's property.

Reeve, you have to help me. I have dreams too. If you don't, I'll MAKE you help me.

Unbelievably, she was coming toward me, closing the distance between us. I recoiled when she clutched my shirt. Unlike Daisy's passion, her grasp was greedy and clinging, a vine that would always shoot out another tendril.

"You won't hurt me either," she coaxed. "Not badly. You need me too much. It should have always been me. Me! Not her. She's a loose cannon you met two weeks ago. She's fucking dangerous. Better the devil you know than the devil you don't. You're safer without her."

"I'll take my risks," I said coldly.

"You think she'd want you if she knew the truth?" Tara scoffed. "No woman could handle your true form. I'm the only one who isn't afraid. She'd run away, because you'd disgust her."

I thought of Daze, of her curse that drove others away as soon as their lips touched hers.

"She wouldn't," I rasped. "She'd think we're beautiful."

"You're delusional, Reeve. *I'm* beautiful. Snake-men aren't."

I thrust Tara away from me, and she lurched backward with a cry. "Don't let me see you again. Don't even think about coming near Daisy. If you do, you'll suffer the consequences, and I don't know which one of us you should fear more."

"You look like shit, Reeve," she muttered sullenly, backing away. "That pretty face is a mess. You've been drinking, haven't you? Sleepless nights — she's wrecking you. She's going to be the ruin of you all."

She stumbled over the other side of the hill, her clothes hanging in rags.

My head pounded, and I rubbed my eyes. Tara was right. I'd been drinking, as much to keep the serpent at bay as to numb the loss of Daisy.

I staggered toward the woods. Power buzzed outward, sparking in a glowing line that surged and pulled back, an electric ocean that tried to tug me in.

I didn't know if Daisy could see that energy. But apparently, she could scamper in and out of the woods without a care in the world.

Moving as close as I dared, I raised my voice: "Daisy!"

The leaves rustled, but that was all.

"I'm here to help," I shouted.

Was I?

I heard her accusing voice. *You see me as a thing.*

"I'm here, Daze." I tried to throw my voice into the woods, but it was strained and dry. "I shouldn't have kept my books from you. You're not a thing to me."

The wind picked up, battling my efforts to be heard.

"Can you hear me?" I called. "I promise I'll do better."

A stick snapped in the woods.

I managed to take a step closer. "You're the one that I want. You. Only you."

There was a great crackling of branches. The wind on the hill picked up, rushing and swirling. The trees bent back, widening, and a lone girl staggered out of the woods.

Her blonde-streaked hair hung in tangled pigtails, filled with leaves and ragged at the ends. Her mouth was a smear of purple lipstick. Dirt smudged her arms and legs. Her black tank top and jeans were ripped, and she had a glazed, sweaty look, as though sleep, showering, and food hadn't come into play recently. She gripped a leather collar tightly in one hand, and a tote bag swung from her shoulder.

"Daze," I whispered.

"Reeve?" she said incredulously, her eyes widening as she caught sight of me. "You came. Oh God, you came. And she hasn't hurt you. I hoped — I didn't know —"

She ran forward and wrapped her arms around me.

The power in her body almost knocked me over. Steadying myself, I hugged her close and buried my face in her hair. I didn't care that the pale strands were lank and smelled of smoke and dirt. It was *her* hair. Daisy's.

Pulling back, she ran her fingers over my scratched cheeks. "Who did this to you?"

"Tara," I said gruffly. "She's gone now."

"How dare she?" Her voice was hoarse.

"Daze, it's nothing. You're the one who matters. You thought she could truly hurt me?"

"She wanted to." Daisy shivered like a leaf in the autumn wind. "She was going to hurt all of you and use me to do it."

"But you overcame her." I kissed her forehead, which felt cold and clammy under my lips. "Let's get you off the hill. I'll take you home, Star."

"Don't. Please don't call me that." She lifted her eyes to mine. "I'm not a star. And there's no place that feels like home right now."

"Daisy, then." My hands tightened on her back.

"But will you stay with me? Just to make sure you're safe," she added in a rush, and my grip relaxed.

I was a hell of a lot more worried about her safety than mine. But I'd take it. She wanted me close; that was all that mattered.

"Lee Tower?"

"Lee Tower," she agreed, slumping into my embrace.

I scooped her up, her long legs draped over the crook of my elbow. As I carried her down the hill, I called on the serpent — silent through this all — for strength.

2

Dark Eyes

Reeve

In Lee Tower, Daisy fumbled with the door to her suite. I reached for her keys to help her, but she shook her head. Finally, she got it open.

I hadn't been in a dorm since freshman year. That time seemed very far away. How could Daisy live like this? The barren common room filled with shitty beige furniture, the cheap posters tacked on the walls...it wasn't the place for the Star. She belonged in the House, enthroned and worshiped.

When she glanced back, tugging me down the hall, I tried to see her as simply Daisy. The way she wanted to be seen.

But it wasn't easy. A glow clung to her, dusty but unmistakable. Every time she came out of those woods, she shone brighter.

She pushed open the last door in the hallway, and I followed her in, closing it behind us.

"My room." Her eyes darted to meet mine.

Entering Daisy's room was like stepping into a different world. She'd done what she could with the small, plain space. Colorful scarves hung in garlands across the ceiling and over the window. Tapestries unfurled above her bed, and twinkle lights decorated the walls.

The room overflowed with signs of witchcraft. Candles in every color of the rainbow covered her dresser, surrounded by crystals. Dried herbs crowded a shelf in the bookcase and hung in bunches from the walls.

The roses I'd given her dangled upside down over the head of her bed, the lush petals dried to near-black. Snakes that swallowed their tails covered the pages of an open sketchbook. She'd tried to draw our tattoo from memory, but she hadn't been able to get it right.

My books — my beloved, precious magic books — sat on her wooden desk.

Could I trust her?

I'd concluded she was innocent, unaware of her power. This scene told me otherwise.

She turned on the twinkle lights with a hesitant smile. Her hands shook as she tried to strike a match.

"I'll do it." I took the matches from her and lit the central group of votives on her dresser. Beside them, an arrangement caught my eye: dried, scattered rose petals, bits of burnt paper, and chunks of pink quartz arranged around a half-melted red candle.

A love spell.

Cast some time ago, judging from the coating of dust on the candle.

The materials were simple, basic. But in Daisy's hands—

With a sudden wrench, I remembered the thunderclap of magic the night we met. The forces in the earth, disturbed. The searing pain in my tattoo. My unreasonable obsession, wanting this woman day and night.

I'd assumed that was due to her being the Star. That I was more susceptible than Evan, Blake, even Nate, because I'd played host to the serpent the longest.

Now, I wasn't so sure.

I turned swiftly to face her. Right now, she looked fragile, a willow that could only bend so far before it would break. Twisting her fingers together, she flushed under my stare.

"Reeve?" she said tentatively. "Tell me what's going on. This *thing*, this collar" — she held up the leather circlet, heavily embossed with silver — "it's wrong. It needs to be destroyed."

"Give it to me." I held out my hand.

She blinked rapidly, her eyes moving over my face. Finally, she extended the collar.

I curled my fist around it. Magic pulsed beneath the surface, restless without a soul to encircle. Snakes flowed over the chased silver.

The collar was a relic from centuries ago, when those who worshiped the serpent needed objects to manifest its presence. The marble snakes in my room served a similar purpose, as did the golden ropes.

But at some point, the collar had become tainted. Instead of calling the serpent, it bound the wearer to the desires of the one who put it in place.

Our first year at Pacific Crest, guided by the serpent, my friends and I had retrieved the collar from the woods on Greer Hill, along with the ropes, the marble snakes, the herbs that summoned and contained the serpent, and a small red book that explained the magic.

We didn't ask how long those artifacts had been there, or what had happened to the serpent's previous hosts, though Evan joked about finding their bones in the woods.

I'd kept the collar hidden in my library ever since.

Tara must have stolen it the night of the party. She'd known of its existence, because in the beginning, like a fool, I'd told her too much.

Daisy watched warily as I examined the collar. I wanted to take care of her. But what if her fragile state was an act? A means to ensnare me, along with that love spell on her dresser?

"You're right," I said slowly. "But the collar isn't simple or safe to destroy."

Messy and dangerous was more like it. It could compromise our connection to the serpent — our lifeline, coiling around our hearts.

"I'll destroy it," she said shakily. "I'll do whatever it takes."

I made my voice firm. "No. There's a safe in the House. I'll put it there and decide what to do next."

She hugged herself. "As long as no one can get to it."

"Don't worry." I dropped the collar in my jacket pocket, then slipped off the jacket and hung it over her desk chair. The simple act brought me into Daisy's room.

I needed to be on my guard. But when she shivered more violently, I couldn't keep my distance. Swiftly, I went to her and took her in my arms.

"Tell me what happened."

She tucked her face into the crook of my neck. "You first, Reeve."

There was so little I could say. I cursed my blood oath of silence, the tendrils of Tara's scheming that had driven me to tie my tongue.

"I never anticipated you, Daze." I forced the words out. "I can't say more than that. Not yet."

She raised her eyes to mine. "Then when? You say you want me to receive, but how can I when you refuse to give?" Her voice, normally so determined and playful by turns, was hoarse and scratchy, as if the collar had diminished it.

I pressed my lips together. I hated seeing her like this.

"Tara's from my hometown," I divulged abruptly. "Her family owns property down the road from mine. I've known her for years. Just like you and Nate, except not."

Daisy pressed her hands against my chest. "You were friends?"

"No." I laughed humorlessly. "Not lovers, either. But she was desperate to get out of that town, like I was. She wanted to be famous. Beautiful. Celebrated and influential, without lifting a finger. Those are Tara's dreams. Like hollow eggs with a gorgeous exterior and nothing inside."

"Go on," Daisy said softly.

"She latched onto me because she saw my determination. She

decided I was her ticket to leave, instead of standing on her own two feet." I curled my fingers under Daisy's chin. "How'd she get the collar on you? Tell me."

She averted her eyes. "I went to an herbal shop downtown. I wanted supplies for a spell to — heal my hand. I'd found one in the book I stole from you." She took a deep breath. "Tara followed me there. I was pissed-off and uncomfortable, but she convinced me to try the collar on. Like a challenge. Maybe I just wanted the attention, because I felt so alone. I thought, why not? Obviously it backfired."

She tried to laugh, but her voice cracked, and the tremors began again in her hands. Guilt, sudden and unfamiliar, washed over me for pushing her too hard.

"It's all right," I murmured. "We don't need to talk about it right now. Come on, let's get you off your feet."

She let me ease her onto the flowered quilt that covered her bed.

"Reeve, I have leaves in my hair." She ran her hands through her pigtails, staring in bewilderment at the ragged ends. "I'm covered with dirt. God, my knee is bleeding, and my hands...." Kneeling in front of her, I turned her hands palm-up, examining the scrapes and ingrained bits of soil. "Ugh, I *smell.*"

Her eyes were metallic blue in the dim candlelight of her room, wide and dazed. She looked exhausted, and the cracked, peeling purple lipstick smudged around her mouth made her seem vulnerable and defenseless. She had every reason to be disillusioned right now, but she was trusting me.

"We'll get you cleaned up." I stroked my thumb over her wrist, and her eyelids fluttered. "Are you hungry?"

Daisy jerked a nod, and a dry, curled leaf fell from her hair — a souvenir of the woods. It glowed faintly, but she didn't seem to notice.

"I didn't eat much the past couple of days," she confessed. "At all, really."

I took her face in my hands. "Then you're going to eat right now."

"I missed you." She turned her face so her soft lips brushed my palm. Fuck, the kiss flared through my tattoo and concentrated in my cock. "I thought if I could heal my hand — I'm sorry. I'm so sorry, Reeve."

I moved my hand away before she pulled me into a danger zone. Even if that love spell was a naïve mistake, she had far too much power.

And what if this was all a ruse? What if she was in league with Tara, and they were playing a long game, broken arm and all, to conspire against me?

"You need to eat," I repeated stubbornly. "Tell me where you keep food."

"But—"

"You still have your ambitions. I wouldn't expect you to forget about them. I don't blame you for making a bargain about my books."

"I hurt you," she said softly. "I see it in your face. I've never gotten close enough to anyone—"

"I don't hurt," I responded harshly.

She caught my hand. "I know you do."

I meant to free myself. To find her some food, because ruse or no, she was the Star and needed her strength. Instead, I took one look at her dirt-streaked, vulnerable, beautiful face and buried my head in her lap.

"Reeve!" She breathed in sharply, thrusting her hands into my hair. "It's all right. You found me. We're together now."

What was wrong with me? I was throwing myself on her mercy when she'd just been abducted and collared. In my bones, I knew — I hoped — Daisy wouldn't have staged that.

I tried to lift my head, but when she stroked the back of my neck, her fingers unbearably gentle in a place no one else had touched, I pressed my face more deeply into her thighs. She quivered as I breathed her in. Sweat and sweetness and wood-soaked magic permeated the legs that flexed in my grasp.

I should let her go. She'd been attacked; she was frightened. I should tread carefully with her. But as soon as her hands moved downward, sliding inside my shirt, I lost my mind. I kissed her thighs, sucking on the faded denim that covered them, biting her innocent flesh.

"Reeve, oh God," she gasped.

I breathed in another scent as I nuzzled upward like an animal: the fresh, tangy musk of her arousal. I pressed my face to it, kissing her pussy through her dirt-stained jeans.

Get up, I ordered myself.

I didn't.

Daisy sucked in short, frantic breaths, holding my head close. Pushing her thighs apart, I rubbed my mouth roughly against her crotch until I was rewarded by sweet, spreading dampness. When I caught myself licking her jeans like a starving man, I came to my senses.

"Lie back," I commanded, struggling for control. "You're a mess from the woods. I'm going to feed you, and then I'll take those ripped clothes off of you and check if you're injured."

She sprawled on her quilt with a sigh that mingled frustration and relief. I found a crushed granola bar and a bottle of water in the bag she pointed to, and watched her like a hawk until she finished both. But as I reached for her shirt, she flinched.

My chest tightened. "Are you afraid to be naked with me, Daisy? I know you just went through hell."

She shook her head. "This is different." Her voice came out faintly as she searched my face. "I want you."

"Are you sure?"

A spark of life flared in her glazed eyes. "Reeve, don't ever ask me if I'm sure about what I want. I am."

I had to restrain myself as I lifted her shirt, which had a long rip at the neckline.

"Did Tara do this?" I gritted.

"No." Daisy's voice was barely audible. "She kissed me. So I threw her out of the woods."

I could imagine the power that had flooded Daisy through the earth. If she was unprepared for it, the experience would have been terrifying.

I forced myself to be gentle as I pulled the shirt over her head, exposing the smooth expanse of her skin and her small, teardrop-shaped breasts. A pink stain circled her neck where the collar had been. Scratches crisscrossed her arms, and a bruise bloomed on her shoulder.

She followed my eyes. "I must have banged into something when I was crawling. A log, or a tree."

The bruise was oddly ring-shaped, like a snake swallowing its tail. I ran my fingers carefully over it, and Daisy shuddered.

"Reeve — it got hot when you touched it."

Without answering, I moved my palms over her breasts, down the slight curve of her stomach to her jeans. I unbuttoned them, and she whimpered. I eased them down her softly rounded hips, along with her sky-blue panties.

When she lay naked beneath me, long and golden, I caught her ankles. "Tell me if anything hurts."

Goosebumps spread over her skin as my hands roamed up her calves. I stopped when I came to her knee, crusted with dried blood.

"I'll clean your wound," I promised.

"Later," she breathed, catching my eye.

Heat rushed through me. I'd told her *later* countless times, playing with her desire like a puppet on a string, until I was as sick of the game as she was.

Exhaling, I slid my palms in circles up the inside of her thighs, which burned and pulsed. Parting them, I stroked her silky pussy as gently as I could. She gasped when I pressed my face to the soft, closed lips.

"Reeve!" She clutched my hair, self-conscious now. I wanted so badly to lap at her sweet opening and taste her juices, but I'd promised myself I'd wait for that pleasure. "I need to feel you."

Dragging my head up, I peeled her apart to expose her glistening pink slit. "I'm going to touch you," I rasped. "Until you come. And then I'm going to wash you and get you clean and make you fucking mine."

Pretty words had deserted me. Pet names, seduction — all gone. There was only Daisy, scared and trusting and barely able to contain her own power, capable of hurting me more than anyone else, piercing my heart with those gray-blue eyes.

And the only way I could trust her in return was to take a leap of faith.

"Please touch me," she whispered. "Even if I cry. Especially if I cry. If I'm shy or turn away — keep going."

I pulled her cunt open like the petals of a newly bloomed flower, growling when she showed me everything. I kept her spread wide as I pinched her clit, making it stiffen into a proud little bud. When I pulled back the hood to expose it, stroking the tiny bulb lightly, she stiffened like an electric shock had seized her.

Sharp, shared pleasure lanced through me. My cock ached to thrust, to plunder, to take. Her eyes shimmered with tears, and she blinked rapidly as they spilled down her cheeks.

"Mine," I growled, caressing her clit until it was flushed and swollen and stood out from her dripping cunt. "You're mine, Daisy. Not hers."

She buried her face in the pillow, arching the slopes of her thighs toward me. "Never hers."

Her orgasm came sooner than I expected. I held her down, blowing across her rosy folds as I massaged her clit, never stopping as she bucked and writhed beneath me. She moaned my name like a benediction.

"That's it," I husked. "Give me all your orgasms, baby."

"Reeve—"

"What is it? Are you afraid?"

She caught my wrist, squeezing it with strong, slender fingers. "In the woods — Tara told me I'm an attention whore. I'm afraid — that she's right. She saw the ugliest parts of me and they're all true."

I growled. "You're *my* attention whore. You hear that? You're going to receive and soak up and drink in absolutely everything I give you. That's not ugly, Daisy. It's beautiful, it's between us, and I want it."

"I want *you,*" she breathed, right before her body contracted again and she arched off the bed. "God — baby, I can't —"

I stiffened. Daisy had rarely used endearments with me. I'd been the one to heap them on her. Hearing the pet name fall from her lips in an unguarded moment — it made me feel good. It was the simplest thing in the world, and the most intoxicating.

Drunk on her, I stroked her through her climax, letting her ride it out until she slumped to the bed. Finally, I closed her quaking thighs.

"That's just the beginning," I rasped. "No holding back for you tonight."

Her eyes were saucers as I helped her to her feet. She squeezed my hand, dirt-streaked and scratched, naked and alive. Opening the door, I led her into the darkened hall, but she froze on the threshold.

"My roommates—"

"They're not home."

"I don't think so either, but can you check? How are you sure?"

Because I sensed people when they were nearby. Felt their heat, the beat of their hearts, their fears and desires. It wasn't as intense as what Nate, Blake, Evan and I experienced with each other, nor as overwhelming as the week of the Binding last year when we'd deepened our dedication to the serpent. But that awareness was always there.

Daisy and I were alone in her suite.

But because I couldn't explain, because I wanted to put her at ease, I went through the motions of knocking on her roommates' closed doors. When no response came, I guided Daisy to an open door and turned on the light.

The bathroom.

It was a standard dorm bathroom, in decent shape, but sad-looking and pale compared to what I could offer Daisy at the House. Still, I pulled her in and closed the door behind us.

I undid her pigtails, allowing her ragged hair to fall free above her waist, as she ran her palms down my sweat-stained shirt.

"Did you mean it when you said I'm yours?" she whispered.

"Hell yes."

And I'm yours.

But I couldn't say it. The love spell in her room flickered in front of my eyes.

She tried to unbutton my shirt, but I moved her hands away. "You're the one who needs a shower."

"You need one too." A fleeting spark of humor lit her eyes, and I ached to see her smile. "Reeve, I want you to help me wash it all away." She touched her throat, still encircled by a faint red ring.

"Come here," I said gruffly.

She pressed her body into mine. I inhaled sharply at her softness against my painfully hard cock, confined in my slacks. When she arched her neck, I kissed her above and below the cruel trace of the collar. She trembled in my arms.

"Good girl," I soothed. "I'm going to get you all clean." Daisy tensed, pulling back. Immediately, I understood. "Did Tara call you a good girl too? Did she dare?"

Daisy's eyes darted around the bathroom. Bending her head so the pale strands of hair fell over her face, she nodded.

"Do you want me to reclaim it?"

She looked up at me suddenly and violently.

"I do." Her eyes blazed. "I want you to reclaim it so hard that I'll forget all about her. And if she ever comes near me again, I'll have the strength to resist."

"*That's* my good girl." My voice roughened. Her sudden, quick smile was all I could want. "I'm going to cleanse you of everything."

I guided her to the shower stall, where a clear plastic door led to a white-tiled cubicle. When I turned the water on, Daisy gave the faucet a hard twist, raising the temperature until steam rose.

"You're scratched up," I warned. "Hot water will sting."

"I don't care," she replied recklessly. "I want it as hot as I can stand it." When I stepped into the shower with her, she tugged my shirt collar. "You're coming in fully dressed? That's ridiculous, Reeve. Even for you."

"Even for me, huh?" I raised an eyebrow, and a faint laugh escaped her — the sweetest music. "Guess I'm ridiculous, Daze, because my clothes aren't coming off."

I didn't trust myself naked around her. She'd shown every characteristic of the Star, including the ability to take my cum without taking my powers. But there were no guarantees, and I needed to stay in control.

When the spray soaked us both, she gasped, backing into me. I held her close. Heat didn't bother me; my body temperature ran a few degrees higher from the serpent's energy. But the water was undeniably hot.

Quick and sudden, she wrapped her arms around my neck. "Help me, Reeve," she whispered. "Get me clean."

Pressing her against the tiled wall, I lathered my hands with a bar of soap and ran them over her soft skin, going easy on the scratches. She allowed me to clean the cut on her knee, then yielded with a sigh when I told her to turn and face the wall. I lingered over the arch of her back, her gently rounded ass, her supple thighs.

Dirt swirled down the drain, filling the steam-cloaked space with the earthy, wild scent of our magic. As I washed it from Daisy's body, she glowed brighter. Her eyes were closed, her hands pressed against the tile.

"That feels so good," she breathed.

"You deserve it."

"No, Reeve. I don't."

"Didn't I tell you that you're a good girl?" Seizing her waist, I turned her to face the shower door and pinned her there, watching her reaction closely.

She gasped. "Yes, but I'm not. I'm bad."

"Mmm." Choosing a shampoo from the assortment of bright plastic bottles, I lathered up her hair and rubbed her scalp with sensual strokes. As her breathing quickened, I wrapped her hair, wet and foamy, around my hand. "Why so bad, Daze? Because you stole my books? Ran from me? Lied to me? Yearned for attention?" I pressed her against the shower door firmly, relishing the way her back arched into my chest.

"All those reasons and more," she breathed.

My free hand slid down the curve of her hip and over her mound. I wanted her to confess to the love spell. To take responsibility for roping me in, hijacking my mind. She was close to making an admission; I could taste it.

"Reeve..." Her head fell back to my shoulder. Rivulets of water ran down her collarbones, the faint pink stain around her throat. "Are you upset?"

"I just want to know if there's something you'd like to tell me."

Confused, she looked up. "Only that even though I've done bad things — I really am yours. It was your face that got me out of the woods. The others, too, but I kept seeing you. Otherwise, I'd still be lost."

I groaned. I was defenseless against her. And this, this was what I fucking hungered to hear, more than any admission of guilt.

"You're here." I rubbed her clit in slow, firm circles until she puddled in my arms. "I've got you."

"Oh God — oh God —" she panted.

"That's it, baby. I'm going to cleanse you, but it's going to take all night."

When I penetrated her with the tip of a finger, she shuddered. "I want you to fill me up."

Trying to restrain myself, I stretched her slowly open with two fingers pressed together, massaging her gently.

"More, please, more — oh God." She threw her head back when I added a third, barely able to cram it into her soft, tight entrance.

Urgently, she rubbed her ass against my throbbing cock as I thrust into her, plastered against the shower door. For a second, I saw us from the outside, cloaked in mist: her tall, naked figure, caught in my arms. My white shirt, soaked and translucent. My dark hair bent against her fair head, my hand disappearing between her legs.

I'd learned the taste of her excitement early, the slick, honeyed feel of it, but a gush of wetness startled me. When I eased my fingers out of her, they were etched with blood.

Fear, sudden and alien, ripped at my chest. "Did I hurt you? Tear at you? Or —" Fury made my vision swim. "Did *she?*"

Daisy turned, staring at my fingers. "No, no." She laughed a little, her cheeks coloring. "That's just my period starting. It's due today. If you don't want to go on, I understand."

The fury vanished. Animal desire replaced it, squeezing me with its claws. I didn't know what to do with all this goddamn emotion, except let it out with her.

I scraped her delicate neck with my teeth, and she gasped. "Do *you* want, Daisy? Do you want me to take you in every way? Do you want my fingers wet with your blood while I make you come? Don't hide your fucking desires. I want to taste every one of them."

Her body went tense between mine and the shower door. "Yessss. But we're here to get clean, and we're just going to get messier."

I gripped her long hair, still full of lather, exploring her pussy deliberately. She curved backward in my arms, breasts rubbing the glass door, eyes going wide and unfocused.

"I want all your mess." My voice was soft but threatening, and she moaned louder. "I'm going to give you mine in return."

Daisy whipped her head to the side as I stroked her clit. She was deliciously hot and wet, and when I sank two fingers inside her and held them there, a cry left her mouth.

I pressed my lips to her ear. "You're good. You're mine. And I'm going to get you clean. All you need to do tonight is believe those three things."

She shook as I worked a third finger back in. "Reeve, oh God — you feel big in this position — it hurts a little, and I need it —" As she spoke, she bucked her hips in tiny thrusts toward my hand.

"Do you want it to hurt, sweet flower? Or do you want me to take care of you?"

"Both." Her lips fastened on my neck.

When I withdrew my fingers from her silky pussy, dripping with blood, I almost lost my mind. Confined by wet fabric, my cock thrust against her ass.

"Turn around," I ordered. "Watch what I do to you."

She hurried to obey, flattening her bare back against the shower door. The ring around her neck had faded almost completely. I hoped that with a few more minutes of my attention, it would be gone.

My hands ran down her body, squeezing and taking. When she reached for me, I ordered her to keep her palms on the shower door. She whimpered as I dipped my fingers into her cunt, drawing out a slippery brew of her blood and juices, painting swirls on her inner thighs as my thumb kept flicking her clit.

"Filthy and pure, Daze. My perfect, naughty girl," I hissed, dropping to a crouch. A cry flew from her as I sucked on her thigh, licking the reddened streaks.

"Reeve, Jesus, you're *tasting* me." She grabbed my head, and I savored the sight of her eyes going wide as I sucked.

The metallic taste coated my tongue, edged with the tang of magic and Daisy's essence. The flavor I'd tasted in the air that first night, like tart, almost-ripe fruit. Her sweetness was heavier now, closer to readiness.

"I told you I want your blood. Fucking Star, I want everything about you." I bit her thigh. She shrieked, pushing her pussy toward my face.

Outside the bathroom, a door slammed. Daisy stiffened, her face flushing with nerves, and I gripped her thighs.

"Hush. Someday, I'll indulge your penchant for exhibitionism. But tonight, I don't want us to be disturbed."

"*My* penchant?" she countered.

"Do you deny that you love to be watched?" I asked. Slowly, she shook her head. I ran my thumbs down her cunt. "Would you like it if I fucked you in the middle of campus where everyone could see?"

She held my gaze, her eyes going wide. Jerkily, she nodded. "Honestly, if I was turned on enough, I think I would."

I smiled up at her. "My sweet attention whore. Understand, Daisy, that I mean it as a compliment in every way."

Her lips parted in disbelief. "You really don't think there's anything bad about me."

"Or maybe, it's that everything you consider bad about yourself, I love."

"Love?" she repeated, her breath coming faster.

The power she had over me was beyond comprehension. I stared up into her glazed eyes and said nothing. Just gently stroked her pussy until her thighs ran scarlet.

Her head bowed. "Reeve, can you lick me? Please stop teasing...I want your mouth there."

"No."

"Why not?" She clutched my wet hair savagely with her left hand, then dropped it with a wince.

Because deep in my mind, even after Nate's betrayal, lived the thought of sharing Daisy with him. I wanted to save just one of her firsts for the man she'd wanted for so many years.

When I thought of his face between her thighs, sucking on the exquisite pink shell of her cunt, giving in because he couldn't deny his urges any longer, my head went light, and my cock throbbed like a rod of fire.

Rising to my feet, I covered her mouth with mine.

"Because I'm going to get you clean now." I slapped her ass lightly. "Rinse that beautiful hair and kneel for me, Daze."

Bubbles streamed down her long strands as she washed her hair clean. Her breath came faster as she dropped to her knees, flushed with heat.

I couldn't contain myself any longer. She drugged my senses, flooded my mind. When she knelt obediently before me, I unzipped my soaked slacks.

She reached out eagerly, then pulled her hands back.

"Very good, sweet flower," I said steadily, desperate for control. "You'll touch me when and how I tell you."

She inhaled sharply when my cock sprang free, running her pink tongue over her swollen lower lip.

"God, you're gorgeous," she breathed.

I wanted to fill her until she couldn't hold any more of me. Precum oozed from the tip of my cock, and my balls ached for her gentle, hungry touch.

But I took her face in my hands, searching it. "I'm going to give you so much, baby. I'm going to cleanse you with my cum. If it's too much for you, tell me, okay?"

"Reeve, I want all of you too," she panted. "You want my blood? I want your cum. It's only fair."

I grinned. "I suppose you're right, my sweet slut."

She blinked at the word, and I wondered if I'd misstepped, if Tara had the gall to use it too. But the pink glow that deepened in Daisy's cheeks signaled *yes*.

"Take me in your mouth, Daze," I hissed. "Take as much as you can."

Daisy let out a low moan, but she didn't move. "Can I use my hands?"

"Such a good girl for asking." I smoothed wet locks of hair from her face, turned dark gold by the water. "You may."

Quickly, as if she feared I'd change my mind, she wrapped one hand around my shaft. I hissed louder at the relief of her soft skin. With her other hand, she cupped my balls, stroking them lightly.

As she opened her lips tentatively to lick my crown, I jerked forward.

At first, she took her time, excitement and disbelief mingling in her eyes as I gave her free rein. She lapped at my shaft and tongued spirals around my head until I grunted and pulled her toward me by her hair. When her lips engulfed my cock, I lost all control.

"Fuck, Daze." I thrust deeper.

She sucked and licked frantically, trying to keep up with my plunges. Her eyes locked on mine, the color of a stormy cloud-ridden sea. She wanted to know if she was pleasing me, and I reassured her with a firm hand on the back of her head.

It had been so long, and never like this. I fucked her hot mouth with abandon, harder than I meant to. Her rhythm was jerky, her tongue exploratory and inexperienced, but it was her mouth. *Hers.* I didn't want anyone else's.

I wanted us, here, forever. Spinning together, inextricably entwined, hurtling into the endless abyss of wanting and taking...

Wavering, I braced myself against the shower wall, dizzy not from the steaming water, but from the beastly strength of desire.

Is this good? her eyes asked. *Do you want me?*

"You're everything I've ever wanted," I told her huskily. "You're what I need, what I've been looking for all my life. You're my Star. My goddess. My slut. You're on your knees for me, and together... we'll rise."

Her eyes glowed. She buried her head in my crotch, her tongue working magic until I knew I'd explode. Her hand flew between her legs to rub her clit, and this time, I didn't stop her.

Ripping the buttons from their holes, I tore off my shirt. My eyes half-closed in agonized need as she pleasured us both. I towered over her, but I was at her mercy. I filled her world, yet she bounded mine.

"Sweet flower," I growled. "Take my cum."

She startled in my grasp, her eyes flying open as my essence spurted into her soft, hot mouth. She wouldn't be able to take it all — not tonight, not her first time. But she hungrily sucked and swallowed, a rainbow of emotions flickering across her face, until she pulled away and I slipped free.

Jets of cum spattered her cheeks, her rosy lips, and the column of her throat. She gasped, laughing as it caught on her eyelashes. "Reeve, it's so much."

"Stand up, baby," I rasped. "Lean against the wall. Lift your beautiful leg for me."

She obeyed, angling her knee out to the side. Grasping her ass, I pointed my spurting cock at her exposed pussy, lashing it with hot white ropes. She gasped, bucking her hips toward me until the head bumped her clit.

"Oh God, *yes,*" she moaned. "Don't leave..."

I had no fucking intention of leaving. I rubbed the head of my cock all over the bud of her clit, oozing cum onto her flushed lips. The pearly strands ran down her pussy and slicked her tight back hole.

"You feel amazing," she moaned. "How can you keep coming?"

"Don't you like it, sweet?" I sucked hard on her neck as I pushed two fingers into her clutching sheath, coaxing my cum inside her. I knew it amplified her pleasure, sizzling her sensitive skin.

When I withdrew, relishing the mix of blood, cum, and pussy juice, the head of my cock slid down until it lodged at her entrance.

"Please," she breathed, pushing against me.

"Sshhh, sweet Daisy," I growled, oozing my seed into her tender cunt. My cock strained against her cherry, slippery with all our fluids. "Just take my cum."

She gasped, lifting her leg farther, trying to hump the fat head of my cock, lust driving her to take me in. I held her hip firmly against the shower wall to prevent her from going too far. Despite all the experiences her sweet cunt had had over the past two weeks — my fingers, Blake's, Evan's, the marble snakes I'd inserted to such an eager welcome — she was still very tight. I doubted we'd fuck by accident. But I wasn't taking any chances.

Inside me, the serpent constricted, forcing out our shared essence. It wanted to possess Daisy as badly as I did. It squeezed out all reason, replacing it with the primal need to come endlessly on and in the Star, filling her unprotected cunt with my seed.

Unprotected.

I jerked away, spraying her hips. She was on her period, but I didn't want to take a single chance with her.

"Reeve!" She grabbed me, pulling me back. "Don't leave."

"Too risky," I ground out. "No protection—"

Her glazed eyes widened. Unbelievably, she laughed. *"That's* it? I'm on the pill. I got a prescription after the first night with you, in the tower. The curse was broken, and I wanted to be safe. You're clean, aren't you? It's been so long for you..."

I jerked a nod, allowing my cock to nestle against her entrance again. "Safe," I managed. "Good girl."

Shaking with restraint, I pressed my thumb to her swollen clit, massaging it firmly as my cum ran down her thighs. She quivered, burying her face in my neck, until I drove her over the edge.

Her pussy tightened like an echoing thunderclap. She contracted in a flurry of need, pushing her opening desperately against the tip of my cock. Light flared from her, bathing the white-tiled shower in a dazzling flash.

"Reeve — Reeve — Reeve." My name and her cries blended together. I rubbed her clit steadily, pressing into the exposed tip until she trembled and came again in a rush.

I held her to me under the shower's spray. I wanted to feel her heart beat against mine forever, her cheek pressed to my jaw, our arms wrapped around each other as the water washed us new.

Afterward, wrapped in towels, she perched on my lap while I sat on the closed toilet seat. Snip by snip, I trimmed the ends of her hair with the sharpest scissors she'd been able to find.

An open box of tampons sat on the counter. After the shower, she'd finished cleaning up, unashamed in front of me.

She didn't explain the ragged state of her hair, but I could guess: she'd offered it up in her failed spell. At least she hadn't chopped it all to make a sacrifice with nothing in return.

Small curls, wet and shining, fell to the floor. When Daisy bent her head, I tugged her hair lightly. "Look straight ahead."

She gave a little laugh. "You seem to know what you're doing. I'm glad you offered."

"I gave my brothers and sisters haircuts when we were young," I said quietly. "My parents, too. I was the best at it. The steadiest with a blade. It meant something that they trusted me." I looked at my scarred left hand, crossed with the evidence of offerings to the serpent.

After another snip, she turned and stroked the precise edge of stubble along my jaw. "You took care of everyone."

"In some ways, yes. Until I couldn't."

She opened her mouth to ask more, but I shook my head. Facing forward, she allowed me to continue.

"What does music mean to you?" I asked abruptly. "I need to understand."

Her shoulder blades drew together, and I regretted pressing her. But as I worked patiently, combing out the next wet section of her hair and cutting the ends even, she spoke.

"It's transportive. When I listen to music, I'm carried away to another place. A better place. And when I played..." She hesitated, swallowing. "I liked telling stories. Creating an atmosphere. Giving people happiness. But most of all, from the time I was young, I felt powerful. With my flute, I was the mistress of — everything, really. The queen of my castle."

She laughed a little, pulling a strand of hair between her fingers.

"The other motivations came later. Playing with other people — I loved that so much. And competing, which was more of a love-hate thing, but I took pride in it. What came first, though, was being in charge of — I don't know how else to say this — a magical domain. When I was a kid, I'd imagine these scenarios where danger always lurked, but my flute protected me. Sometimes, it even saved the day." She ducked her head. "Does that sound silly?"

"Not at all," I said quietly.

When the haircut was finished, I rubbed her hair dry with a towel. Loose, the waves reached just above her waist. They'd been down to her hips before she hacked off the ends. I'd angled the front, giving her a few shorter strands that curled inward.

She studied herself in the mirror, a slight smile curving her lips. "I think you missed your calling. You're really good at this."

"You like it?"

She nodded. "If the stock market ever crashes, you've got a backup career. I guess you have that degree in history coming up too, but I feel like this could make you more money."

I ran my fingers through her thick waves, smiled, and said nothing. If the stock market ever crashed, I'd reap the benefits, not sink with it. And if all went according to plan, I wouldn't be at Pacific Crest for graduation in May.

None of us would.

Unexpectedly, I felt a pang. I wanted a degree, an education. I'd been proud to be the first McClellan to go to college, even if the location was due to dark magic.

You can have it all, the serpent hissed.

But I knew its trickery.

In Daisy's bed, we curled up in exhaustion. Her mattress was narrow, creaking on a spartan wooden frame. Her purple tie-dyed sheets were a far cry from the black silk I slept on. Naked, we were molded together with little room to turn or move.

It was exactly where I wanted to be.

"Better?" I asked.

"Better." She pressed her face into my chest. "You really did wash me clean. And you?"

"I'm the best I've ever been," I whispered, and fuck, I meant it. For now, I didn't doubt her. Whatever she'd intended with that love spell, it hadn't been malicious. "My sweet Star."

She snuggled against me, her eyes drifting closed, but a distinct growl issued from her stomach.

"I should eat," she murmured. "That granola bar wasn't enough."

"Let me take care of you," I said. "I'll order all the food you can eat. A banquet, because you deserve it."

She laughed. "All right. Thai food? I'll even let you pay."

"Of course I will." I smoothed her hair. "I'm going to give you everything you could ever want."

"Don't make promises you can't keep," she teased.

"I don't." Kissing her cheek, I climbed out of bed to get my phone, then paused. I looked down at her, puddled on her purple sheets, her long legs tangled in the blanket. She was tired, unguarded, gorgeous. "Believe me, Star. You're worth it."

3

All Day and All of the Night

Reeve

Take her.
Use her.
Bring her to me.

I bolted awake. The serpent slithered over my skin, squeezing me tight, pinning me to the wall.

Where was I?

A beam of faint fluorescent light filtered through the darkness, illuminating a bunch of dried lavender, a slice of an art deco poster, and a hanging fringed scarf, ghostly in the night.

Daisy's room.

I wasn't caught in the serpent's coils; I was mashed against her warm body in a twin-size bed. She'd rolled over, pushing me against the wall and capturing my leg between hers.

She stirred, peaceful in my arms, as I drew my thumb gently beneath a scratch on her shoulder. The pink circle on her neck — the souvenir from the despicable collar — had finally faded.

On her desk sat a small city of open takeout containers. Maybe I'd gone overboard, ordering every single one of her favorites off the menu.

The strain of the day had worked up an appetite. Between the two of us, we'd finished every bite, then collapsed in bed.

Now, she stretched against me, wrinkling her nose and yawning. Her eyes opened, reflecting the streetlights outside in tiny pinpoints on her luminous irises.

She broke into a sleepy smile. "You're here."

I kissed her forehead. "I'm not going anywhere."

"But the collar —" She touched her throat, wincing.

"I'll take it to the House first thing in the morning."

"Could you..." She trailed off uneasily.

"Say it, Daze."

"Could you do it now? I know it's the middle of the night," she added hastily. "I wouldn't ask normally. But I absolutely hate having it here. Knowing it's close by makes me so anxious all of a sudden." She shivered. "I don't know why it's bothering me now. We had such a good evening, and I was able to push away the thought of it, but now, I just...can't."

I climbed swiftly out of bed. My clothes were hanging up in the bathroom. A few hours had passed since our shower; they'd be damp or even dry by now.

"Consider it done. You won't have to think about it for another minute. I'll be back before you know it. Unless you want to come too?" I hated the thought of leaving her alone.

She looked away, bunching the comforter in her right hand. "No. I don't want to see Nathan. I'm pretty upset with him right now. I called him before Tara attacked, asking for answers, and he hung up on me."

Jesus. I knew that Nate had been trying to protect Daisy, in his convoluted way, but this was going too far. He could have prevented the entire attack if he'd taken the time to listen.

Should I worry about him? Along with his physical changes, he'd become increasingly impatient and moody, his fuse shorter by the day.

But the Joining was coming in less than two weeks. Once we undertook the necessary rituals, Nate would be fine. Better than fine. He just needed to hang in there.

I kissed the top of Daisy's head. "I'll be back very soon, sweet."

"What happened to you?" Evan demanded. "You look like you got fucked up, and I can't tell if it's in a good way or a bad way."

He was draped naked across one of the plush couches in the great living room of the House, idly sipping a drink. Blake paused from chopping something up in the kitchen, his silver knives ceasing to flash. Nate leaned against the black marble table, shirtless and glaring at me. Sweat gleamed on his bare skin, illuminated by the flickering flames in the fireplace.

"It's been a night," I muttered. My friends eyed my stained clothes and scratched face in disbelief.

Evan cocked his head, nostrils flaring. "You smell different. She's inside you now. You tasted her blood, didn't you?"

Nate blanched, the color draining from his face, and Blake dropped his knives. "How can you tell from there, Ev?"

Evan smirked. "I pay attention. What's that beauty doing in your hand, McClellan? Don't tell me you changed her mind with it."

I tossed the collar on the table. It landed with a clatter. "Tara got to her."

Three blank stares met mine, then converged on the collar.

Evan rose from the couch and stalked to the table. Picking the collar up, he ran caressing fingers over the silver designs. His pale eyes were too curious, too eager.

"Don't touch that," I ordered. Evan shrugged and let it fall.

In a clipped voice, I filled them in. Their faces turned to thunderclouds as the story unfolded.

"So you hung up on her, Nate? Right when she called you for help?" Blake stared at him, disappointment etched on his face.

Folding his arms across his chest, Nate jerked a nod.

"How could you abandon her like that?" Blake stormed. "I thought you had some human feeling left."

Nate turned wounded eyes in his direction. "I was trying to protect her."

Their gazes caught and held. Usually, Nate was the one to avoid looking at Blake for too long. Since the Binding a year ago, when we became celibate, he'd created distance between them.

But this time, Blake turned away first. "There are other ways to protect her."

I lifted the collar carefully from the table. "Exactly. That's why I'm going back to Lee Tower for the night. She needs someone to keep her safe. "

It sounded convincing. But did Daisy really need my protection? She'd fought Tara off, pushed her way out of the woods. I was the one who felt naked and lost, away from her side.

My friends stared at me.

Evan let out a long, low whistle. "You've lost it, man. You expect us to believe you're going to turn your back on all of this" — he gestured around at the grandeur of the living room — "to sleep on a crappy dorm mattress? Or on her *floor?*"

"We should bring her here," Blake said. "This is where she belongs. We can protect her better if we're all looking out for her."

I shook my head. "Not yet. She needs to recover. And frankly, she has no interest in encountering Nate."

Pushing away from the table, Nate crossed to the fireplace, glaring into the flickering flames.

"Put this in the safe." I handed Blake the collar, and he took it gingerly between two fingers. "Do it now," I snapped, when he hesitated. He hurried out of the living room, glancing back at me.

"Evan, look into Tara. Find out if she has any more surprises up her sleeve."

"How about I do more than look into her," Evan drawled, draining his drink. "I'll give her a taste of the Beast."

I held up a warning hand. "We don't want trouble on campus. Gather information only. Give her a wide berth."

Evan snorted. "Don't tell me you feel *sorry* for her. Did you forget our principles? Your past means nothing. Your future means everything. Forget the little neighbor girl who followed you everywhere like a clinging vine. No weakness, brother. No mercy. She sure as hell wouldn't have shown it to us."

I shoved my hands through my hair. "I feel what I feel."

"Since when do you feel anything besides hunger?" Evan questioned, his eyes narrowing.

"Do what Reeve says, Ev." Nate turned from the fireplace, his massive arms still held tightly against his chest. Finally, he looked me full in the face. "Do you have an assignment for me too?"

My jaw tightened. "Yes. Earn my trust back and don't fucking interfere."

He swung away, pacing across the room until he stopped in front of a velvet-draped window. "You're obsessed with her."

"You heard your assignment," I said coldly. "I expect you to obey."

Red crept over his cheeks. Nate flushed easily. I'd always enjoyed that about him, that even after the change, he showed his emotions so readily.

Ducking his head, he walked stiffly out of the room.

I went upstairs quickly. In my bedroom, I shoved a week's worth of clothes in a leather duffel bag and hurried downstairs.

Evan was still in the living room, alone. He'd put on a pair of black boxers. As I entered, he pulled out the piano bench and sat down in front of the instrument with a flourish.

"Taking a suitcase?" He arched a blond eyebrow. "How long are you planning to stay?"

"As long as she needs me."

"She's ours, Reeve." His teeth bared, the faintest hint of a threat lacing his voice. "Not yours."

My nightmare echoed through my mind. "She's not any of ours, brother. She belongs to the serpent."

Evan's eyes flared bright green, the pupils lengthening to slits. Purposefully, he stroked the erection that tented his boxers. Heat spiked through my arm, leaping straight to my cock, when he pressed his fingers to his serpent tattoo.

His eyes dared me to groan, and I pressed my lips together in protest. Holding my gaze, he rubbed the snake's head, squeezing his monster erection with his other hand, until the pleasure was almost unbearable.

"Remember that," he said softly. "Remember who she belongs to."

But as I eased my car away from the House with a low purr of the engine, I tried my hardest to forget.

4

Strange Bird

Reeve

When I opened the door to her suite, Daisy looked up at me from the couch.

She was huddled under a woven blanket with her computer on her lap. In the dark room, the flickering screen cast blue and gold splashes over her face.

"Reeve, what did you bring?" She started to laugh. "Look at all this. I don't believe it."

I dumped everything from my laden arms onto the couch. A heating pad, a bottle of painkillers, and a stash of the nearest drugstore's finest chocolate. "I just want to take care of you."

"So you're trying to take me to period heaven?" She shook her head, smiling. "How do you even know what to do? Living with those boys, I wouldn't expect this to be on your radar."

"I grew up with sisters." I tossed my duffel bag onto an armchair. As always when I thought of my family, the serpent tattoo throbbed dully. "How are you feeling?"

"Crampy." The blanket slid down as she put a hand on her belly.

"Let me." I plugged in the heating pad and arranged it over her. Dropping next to her on the couch, I put my arm around her and waved at the array of chocolate. "Milk or dark?"

"You're really pampering me." After everything I'd offered her these past two weeks, she still looked incredulous.

"Expect it, Daze. I want to." My voice was firm.

"Dark," she said finally, a smile sneaking across her face. "But I won't say no to milk, either."

I tore open a bar of dark chocolate with toffee and offered her a square. "Painkillers?"

She shook her head. "No to those."

I rubbed a second square of chocolate over her lips. She laughed and snapped it up. "Why?" I asked. "I wouldn't have taken you for *that* much of a masochist."

Her cheeks turned pink, and she sprawled against me, adjusting the heating pad. "Reeve, I took so many painkillers after my accident that I just can't right now. I'd rather be uncomfortable than numb."

I looked at her left hand resting on the blanket. She'd put on sweatpants and a faded tank top that said *Felt Cute, Might Curse You Later*.

"Nice shirt," I remarked.

"Sasha gave it to me. You know, Nathan's sister."

"I know." I offered more chocolate.

"After the accident, she bought me a stack of funny shirts. She worked so hard to cheer me up." Daisy sighed.

"It's good to have a friend." I stroked her cheek, my hand lingering

I didn't want to think about any of the Davises right now. Nate, with his twisted attempts at protecting Daisy. Sasha, complicating Daisy's loyalties. Their absent, self-absorbed parents, who had never given Nate the attention he needed.

"Not that this applies to you." She traced the letters on her shirt. "That particular curse doesn't seem to be a problem. You've never run away after I've kissed you. But I'm starting to think I'm cursed in other ways." She touched the pink stain around her throat.

"You're not," I said gruffly.

Yet, in a way, she spoke the truth. There were burdens to being the Star. Power always came with burdens.

I kissed her jaw, pulling the blanket over us both.

"It feels good when you hold me." Her eyelids fluttered as I wrapped my arms around her securely, following her gaze to the computer as she pressed *play*.

On the screen, dancers cavorted in a grassy meadow, spliced with images of a rock band.

"What are we watching?" I asked.

The "we" felt strange. For four years, "we" had meant my friends and me. Blake, Evan, Nate. No one else.

Daisy took out one of her earbuds and offered it to me. "My dad used to direct music videos. He hasn't done it for a while, though. Now he's all about cheesy horror films. This is from when I was ten."

A young girl skipped into the circle of dancers, and they fanned out into a line. She lifted a flute to her lips as her pale hair streamed behind her.

I recognized her immediately. Even at ten, Daisy had presence. Tall and coltish, she commanded the screen as soon as she began to play.

Daisy laughed a little. "The band thought my dad was crazy, bringing his kid on set. He was like, 'Trust me, she's a professional. She's just what you need.' You'd never guess how many arguments he and my mom had about all the hours I spent on the flute. She encouraged it, but he thought I should have a normal childhood. Play with other kids after school, run around outside, watch cartoons."

"What changed his mind?"

"I guess *I* did, eventually. I told him I was doing exactly what I wanted to do." She pointed to one of the dancers, a tall, graceful blonde who moved with the same determined force as Daisy. "That's my mom. She and my dad fought constantly during the shooting. He told her she could choreograph, then the band wanted to bring in one of their friends to do it. My mom thought my dad should back her up, and he didn't. He said she was too intense, as usual. God, what didn't my parents fight over? I was happy to escape it all by practicing. I'd hunker down in my bedroom. If I played loud enough, I could drown them out."

"I'm sorry." I reached across to grip her right hand.

Daisy squeezed back. "See that crown of flowers?" She pointed to the circlet of rosebuds and daisies on her younger self's head. "Itchy as hell. But I loved the way it looked."

"Why now?" I pointed to the screen. "What made you want to watch this?"

She pursed her lips, then retrieved her phone from the coffee table. "I just got some news from my dad. He called right around the time I was in the woods. I guess I was a little preoccupied."

She gave me a twisted smile and showed me her phone.

Hey, D! Carmen and I are engaged! I popped the question tonight and she said YES! I'm the happiest man in L.A. Carmen can't wait to become your stepmom.

I raised my eyebrows, unsure of how she was feeling about the news. "Congratulations."

"Yeah, I'm happy for them. I really am. But I'm turning twenty next month. I don't need a stepmom. Carmen's, like, thirteen years older than I am. Then he sends me *these.*"

She scrolled down the chat until two pictures appeared.

The first featured a row of formal gowns hanging in a closet. The space was stuffed with overflowing boxes, old coats, dusty hats, and rolled-up posters. In the midst of the mess, the dresses were a bright rainbow of color, showing a slice of satin, a flash of rhinestones, a peek at a rosette.

The second photo showed a shelf covered with trophies and framed certificates. Some said "Daisy DiCosmo," and others said

"Daisy Fisher," but every trophy and certificate celebrated some achievement on the flute, spanning over a decade.

"My dad's a pack rat." Daisy tried to smile, but her lower lip twitched, and her nails dug into my hand. "When Mom and I moved to New York, he held onto all this stuff. He even brought it with him when he moved into a smaller apartment. Now Carmen's moving in, and she's the exact opposite of a pack rat. She wants to clean the whole place out and redecorate. It'll look like something out of a magazine when she's done. So Dad asked me what I want to do with all my old concert dresses and — and these." She pointed to the trophies. "Because he's chucking them."

"He can mail them to me," I said firmly. "There's plenty of room at the House. I'll pay for shipping."

"Reeve—" She half-laughed. "I don't even — God, I don't even know if I want to keep them."

"But you don't want to get rid of them."

"I'm not ready," she murmured.

She fiddled with the blanket, her eyes darting. I waited for her to go on.

"Those dresses — they're all second-hand. In high school, Sasha and I would go shopping at vintage stores in L.A. It's what we could afford, but I also loved that the dress I'd wear to perform had been someone else's prom gown, or special occasion dress, or even a costume on a set. Maybe I should just give up and sell all the dresses back to those stores. Someone else can give them life."

"Daisy, your career isn't over." The words burst from me before I could stop them.

"How can you say that?" She stared at me, surprised and angry. "You know it is. I can never play the way I used to. I can't practice long enough to build up those skills again. The healing spell didn't work, and I was stupid to expect it to. Don't tell me pretty lies, Reeve. I expect more from you than that."

My face blazed with answering anger. If I could just fucking *tell* her, if I could stop her pain...

"I'm not lying." The serpent tightened its coils inside me, forcing out my breath, and my head went light.

"Reeve?" Worried, she took my shoulders in her hands. "What's wrong?"

Slowly, the pressure eased until I could breathe normally.

"Nothing's wrong, sweet." I smiled, hating myself for telling a pretty lie after she'd forbidden exactly that. I couldn't go any further. But soon, I'd find a way. And she'd know everything.

Concern creased her forehead, but she relaxed in my embrace as I petted her hair. The music video had ended, and she closed her laptop, dropping the earbuds on the table beside her phone.

"Tell me more about your family." She stroked my forearm, her touch as soft as a swan's wing. "Now that I've talked your ear off about mine. I carry your mom's tarot cards around, you know. I use them every day."

I forced another smile. "That means a lot to me, Daze."

"Are you up for talking?" she ventured. "I want to know about your past. How you grew up."

The past. Exactly what I'd rejected all these years. Evan was right; disowning it was the first principle of our brotherhood. Yet Daisy, with her mere presence, stirred it up.

I pulled the blanket more tightly over us. "You probably want to hear about life on the farm. How we frolicked in the fields, and swam in a water hole in the summer, and it was fucking idyllic."

Her face turned serious. "I want to hear whatever you'll tell me."

"Do you really, Daze?"

"*Yes,*" she replied firmly. "I'm not afraid of pain."

I stood, throwing off the blanket.

The door to the suite opened. Her roommates tumbled in — Michelle and Amy, I remembered. Laughing, talking in bursts. They stopped abruptly when they saw me standing at their coffee table. Their eyes flickered to Daisy on the couch.

"Well, hello there." I smiled, remembering a beat too late to be charming.

"Are we interrupting? Sorry, um—" Michelle and Amy stood frozen by the open door.

"We're just hanging out," Daisy assured them. "Do you want the common room?"

"No, uh, that's totally fine. You guys keep on doing — whatever you're doing." The two girls hurried down the hall, glancing over their shoulders. *"Reeve fucking McClellan is in our suite,"* Amy whispered to Michelle, not quietly enough.

I waited until their doors closed. Daisy looked up at me from the couch, knotting the blanket in her hand.

"I'm listening," she said quietly.

Crossing to the window, I yanked the slatted blinds open and stared down nine stories to the street below.

"My dad died when I was sixteen," I stated abruptly. "Worked himself to death. He'd always had a weak heart, and our farm was failing for years. But hey, hard work. That's what my parents valued more than anything else." I smiled mirthlessly. "Doesn't matter what you accomplish, or whether you succeed, as long as you're working hard. The land was shit — still is — and they should have sold it years ago. I told them to cut their losses and get out of that town. But they're fucking proud and stubborn as hell and as they always said, 'If we leave you with one lesson, son, it's never to quit.' Idiots." I swiveled to face Daisy. "I could help them so much now. My mother's alone with four kids at home. She can barely make ends meet. She's gotten old before her time. All I want to do — all I've ever wanted to do — is raise them up. But she refuses. I can't tell you how fucking powerless I feel."

Daisy's arms lifted and dropped at her sides. "She won't accept your money?"

"She doesn't trust it. It's all smoke and mirrors to her. She only trusts what a person earns with their hands." I stared up at the ceiling. "You and I, we were both raised to believe hard work will get you places. But you can be the hardest worker and get fucking nowhere." I shook my head. "From the time I was a kid, I tried to help. Day and night, I thought of ways to lift my family up. I wanted to be somebody. I wanted that for all of us."

"I understand," she whispered.

"When Dad got sick, my mom switched so fast to depending on me. I tried, but now I've finally succeeded, and I can't help them. The last time I saw them, I was so proud. I drove home in my new car, ready to impress them and save them all. Instead, it was..."

Daisy waited, unmoving, as if she would break the spell of my confession with a single motion. I was raw, unmasked before her.

"It was awful," I admitted in a low voice. "I was a stranger to them."

My mother hadn't allowed me in the house. She'd simply brought out the last remaining box of my possessions and dumped them on the porch.

"I know this isn't you, Reeve Junior," she'd muttered, backing away. "It's not — *just* you. I see it in your eyes — the evil inside. Whatever foul thing you've done, don't darken my door until you've undone it."

The serpent had lashed inside me as I walked with leaden feet to my gleaming car. *Forget her. Forget your family. They'll only weaken you.*

"Leave me alone," I'd snarled. It was the first time I'd ever been angry with the serpent.

"I'm sorry," Daisy said swiftly, squeezing my arm. "You've been so patient, listening to me whine about concert gowns and new stepmoms when my problems are nothing compared to yours."

I took her face in my hands. "Daze, it's not a contest." Managing a smile, I stroked her cheeks with my thumbs. "Sorry to puncture your farm fantasy...city girl."

"Did you like anything at all about growing up there?"

I shook my head. "That life was never for me. I lived through reading — anything I could get my hands on. Books were the best friends I had."

She leaned closer, her head tilted. "What about people friends? Did you have those too?"

I looked away. "I was always different, Daze. A strange bird. I never fit in and never wanted to."

"I believe it."

My gaze snapped back to hers. She deserved as much truth as I could give. "You want to know about the past? I made choices that I regret. I saw people as pawns. I was with women and had no feeling for them. I was reckless and greedy. When I found Blake, when Evan and Nate came to me, I finally focused. But everyone else? They were still pieces to move around on a game board. I can't do that anymore. I don't want to."

"What do you want?"

"You," I answered, without an ounce of hesitation.

Her gray-blue eyes flared, wide and electric. A beat passed. Then she grabbed me in a hard, fierce hug.

"I'm here," she whispered. "What happened with your books — I won't ever do that again. I won't leave you. I promise, Reeve."

My grip tightened. I was shaking — *shaking,* my heart thumping against hers, crushing her sweet body to mine.

"Are you afraid?" Her voice was a murmur into my neck.

I pulled back and took her face in my hands. "Not with you, Daze. Nothing can go wrong tonight."

5

Mystery of Love

Reeve

Throughout my life, all I'd known was hunger. Whether I fought, appeased, or harnessed it, hunger drove me.

For the first time, I felt something different.

Happiness.

Over the next week, Daisy and I spent every free minute together, and I never tired of gazing into her face. When we spooned in her narrow bed each night, legs entwined, I didn't miss the long nights alone on my king-size mattress, with its silk sheets and nest of down pillows. Her warm skin, flowery scent, and sweet breath were all I wanted.

I'd always used my tongue to flatter, to persuade, to coax, to distract, to spin stories, to seduce. For the first time in my damn life, I used it just to talk.

We talked for hours. About everything — almost.

Her face turned wistful when she mentioned music, but she brightened when she told me stories about her friends at conservatory. She took out her phone and played me recordings of the pieces that had meant the most to her when she was growing up.

I'd always thought music was fine, nothing more. But Daisy loved it, and when she described or listened to a favorite piece, her face glowing, I loved it too.

"I wish I could hear you play." As soon as the words came out, I cursed them. They'd only hurt her. I'd spoken impulsively, when before now, I was never impulsive.

A shadow crossed her face. "I wish I could play for you."

"You can." I rushed on, still unthinking. "You said you could play a little, right? I know you haven't, but if you ever want to try...I'd love it."

She gazed at me, considering. "I'd sound terrible."

"I don't care about that. You could never sound terrible to me."

Her smile was a tentative sunbeam.

Each day, when Nate's sister Sasha texted Daisy a photo of her travels in Morocco, she shared it with me. And instead of calculating how I could use Nate — or his sister — as a tool to reel Daisy in, I looked at the photos with her and dreamed of traveling together.

"You've really never left California?" she asked.

"Never. But I want nothing more than to see the world with you. Soon, Daze."

"We'll go everywhere," she sighed, rolling against me and tangling her legs with mine.

Later, she talked on the phone with Sasha while I stretched out on her bed, working on a history paper. Daisy had refused to believe that I did any schoolwork until she saw me studying. But it was important to me. As I'd told her, I wanted an education.

"This feels real, Sash," she said quietly into the phone, glancing at me. "I've never spent so much time with someone. Romantically, I mean," she added quickly. "Where is he?" She laughed. "Oh, he's right here on my bed, listening to every word."

I beckoned her over, and she curled up against me as she talked. Far from a distraction, her voice and presence soothed me while I worked. When she held out the phone, asking me to say hello to Sasha with a teasing smile, I took it from her.

"So this is the great Reeve," came a slightly hoarse voice through the phone, sounding like it was about to break into a laugh.

"None other." I tickled Daisy's stomach, sliding my hand under her shirt. "It's a pleasure to talk to the great Sasha."

I'd heard about Nate's sister, but had never met her. To hear Nate tell it, she was scornful, self-absorbed, and arrogant, hogging the lion's share of the little attention their parents doled out. But when Daisy spoke about Sasha, her eyes softened, and a smile broke across her face.

"Be good to her, okay? To Daisy. She's..." Sasha trailed off.

"I know." I pulled Daisy even closer. "She's special."

"Consider this the obligatory best-friend threat that if you break her heart, I can and will come for you." Sasha spoke lightly, but there was an edge to her voice.

Daisy sat up. "What's she saying to you? Give me that." She made a grab for the phone, but I held it out of her reach.

"No threats necessary." I matched Sasha's joking tone. But I suspected that she and Daisy had practiced witchcraft together, and for a moment, I wondered about their combined fury if anything went wrong.

But nothing would. I was with Daisy, who tackled me as soon as I hung up the phone to cover my face with kisses. She made me want to do better. Be better.

"Are you human?" she asked one morning, when we were cuddling in bed.

The question startled me. "Yes."

"*Completely* human?"

What could I say? I was both more and less than human. But this week, for the first time, I felt like a fucking person.

"I don't know," I said, surprising myself. She nodded a few times, thinking this over, but didn't push.

"Do you miss Blake and Evan?" she asked. "And Nathan? You were always together."

"Do *you* miss them?" I countered.

She looked wistful, then gave me a sly smile. "Sure," she teased, pouncing on me and rolling me over. "But you're keeping me pretty busy."

I ran my hands over her body, savoring every touch.

Day by day, I watched myself unravel my own carefully laid efforts: the plans, the seductions and tests, my goddamn *grooming* of her. Deep down, I knew she was meant for the Joining. Our Star of the Cosmos, our uncontainable power source.

But I didn't give a fuck about the Joining right now. I barely crossed paths with my friends throughout the week, though I felt their power ebb. I didn't check my stocks; didn't care if they rose or fell. The serpent lay dormant inside me without a murmur.

I didn't want Daisy hungry; I wanted her happy.

All this led to the afternoon when we were tangled up in her bed, my thigh between hers, her head on my chest, my arms wrapped around her as we watched old movies on her laptop.

"Reeve," she said dreamily, as the black and white images of *La Dolce Vita* flickered in front of us, "I want you to be my first."

I lifted my head.

"I know I asked you to fuck me before, back at the beginning," she continued, breathless. "I was horny and you were beautiful and I was in this huge rush because it was all so new and exciting. But now I mean it in every way. This isn't about wanting to get off. This is about you and me. *Us.* I want to be with you that way. I want you inside me—"

She cut herself off, kissing me so sweetly that it almost broke me in half. Her kisses got deeper, hotter, as she climbed on top of me. Desire for her clouded my mind, crowding out everything else.

Desire — and love.

I couldn't love. This wasn't possible.

But it was happening.

My palms ran over her back, possessing every inch of soft skin. I squeezed her ass, giving it a little slap, and she squealed and tickled me under my arms. When I caught her right wrist, she pushed her mound, covered only by a silky pair of panties, onto my throbbing cock. She kissed me again and pulled back.

"Do you want to?" she whispered.

"Hell yes."

"Then take my panties off." She giggled, and I rolled her over onto her back in a burst of playfulness, her laughter kindling mine.

I kissed her, licking her collarbone, tasting her breasts. When I sucked her nipple into my mouth, she cried out and grabbed my hair.

"Please, Reeve. You've teased me so much, I'm always wet for you. I'm ready. I need you *now*."

Warning bells rang in my mind, but fuck it, I didn't care. To hell with the snake and the Joining. To hell with everything I'd thought I'd wanted for the last six years and beyond.

I wanted Daisy. I wanted to be human.

Grasping her panties, I pulled the silky fabric down her thighs. I parted her legs to stroke her wet folds until she cried out.

"Now, baby," she panted.

I lowered my body over hers, groaning as she took my cock in her hand. When the head pressed against the sweet heaven of her pussy, I braced myself to fill her in one long plunge.

Before I could, pain flared in my left arm — sudden, cruel, and red-hot.

Leaping off her, I doubled over, gripping my biceps where the inked serpent writhed.

"Reeve!" Daisy shot out of bed. She was holding me, her head bent over mine. "What's wrong?"

The serpent was waking up.

It shifted inside me, coiling and arching. Sharp hunger spiked through my body. Shaking Daisy off, I gripped the edge of her dresser.

"I have to go," I gritted.

"But we were just about to—"

"Later."

Use her.

Take her.

Devour her.

I summoned the strength to put as much distance between us as possible, yanking on my clothes.

"This isn't you, Daze. I promise. We'll have our first time together."

"At least tell me what's going on," she said, her voice sharp and worried. "Are you hurt?"

"I'll be fine. I'll call you tonight. I just need to get home."

She crossed her arms over her naked body. Her eyes were huge with concern as she watched me.

Jesus, she probably thought it was that curse. Driving me away as soon as we were about to consummate our relationship.

Relationship.

I must have lost my mind.

I was fucking up everything, absolutely everything I'd worked for.

This was madness.

The serpent tore at my insides. I muttered words under my breath, bringing it to heel. I knew the effect would be temporary.

"It's not the curse, Daisy." I made my voice as gentle as possible. "You're my beautiful Star. We'll have our first time together, don't worry."

As I shoved my feet into my shoes, she walked over to the dresser and drummed her fingers on one of the packs of tarot cards.

"Reeve, if you don't want to have sex with me, at least do me a favor and tell it to me straight."

With one hand on the doorknob, I looked directly at her. She truly didn't know the strength of the hold she had on me.

"I want it more than anything. I want to push you onto that bed, sink into you, and never leave. And if I do, it'll be the end of us both." A stab of pain through my arm made me gasp.

She rushed toward me. "Something's very wrong. Please, let me help you."

"No, Daze," I said firmly. "I need to handle this alone. I'll call you tonight."

6

Take What You Want From Me

Reeve

I staggered to the parking lot by Lee Tower. Under the merciless sun, my car was covered with dust. I'd driven to campus only for class, and a couple of perfunctory visits to the House. The rest of the week had been Daisy, all Daisy.

Sweat poured down my forehead, stinging my eyes as I gripped the steering wheel. The House reeled me in with an invisible tether until I entered the private driveway. Then, finally, the crushing pressure on my chest eased.

The security guard nodded politely as he patrolled the front courtyard. I managed a greeting, but my tattoo throbbed in an insistent warning.

When I entered the living room, the three of them were waiting for me. Their skin was sallow, their eyes dull, their hair lank. Guilt hit me like a tidal wave.

Nate rose from his armchair. "Where have you been all week?"

"You know where I've been." I unbuttoned my shirt halfway and pulled it up to mop the sweat off my forehead.

"Locked in Lee Tower, sleeping in a cramped twin bed, when you should have been here," Blake mused. "She really is powerful."

Evan folded his arms. "Sharing is caring, Reeve."

"I've been with my girlfriend," I stated calmly, though I'd never used that word with Daisy.

"*Girlfriend?*" Nate stormed. "Are you out of your mind?"

I turned to look out the tall back windows, where sunlight played over the sparkling fountain in the pool.

"You almost fucked her!" he spat. "We all felt it. Do you know what that would have done to us?"

"Nate, he knows," Blake said.

"He just didn't care," Evan growled.

Facing them, I pointed to the snake on my arm. "So you called me back with this?"

In the heavy silence, I saw their bare arms, their exposed tattoos. On each, a drop of blood welled where the serpent swallowed its tail.

We'd always been careful with the serpent's mark, because one touch would echo through all four of us. The three of them must have simultaneously pricked themselves. They'd put their bodies through the same pain they'd inflicted on me, so they could pull me away from Daisy.

"We couldn't let it happen." Blake's voice was at its most reasonable. "We gave you a chance to reconsider, and you did."

"Did you think about Daisy?" I asked quietly. "She stripped herself bare for me, and I ran from her."

Evan shoved an armchair across the floor in a burst of savage strength. "Did *we* think about *her?* Fucking hell, Reeve, we've thought about nothing *but* her for the past week, and you made it worse. I mean, look. What the hell is this about?"

He gestured to two cardboard shipping boxes that sat on the carpet. The larger one was slit open to show a glimpse of rhinestones and brightly colored satin. The smaller held a jumble of trophies, framed certificates, and a couple of classical music magazines. Daisy's face peeked at me from a cover. *Players to Watch: The Next Generation.*

The return address said "Jon Fisher," but in a bubbly handwriting I suspected was Carmen's.

"They're her concert dresses," Nate growled. "What are they doing here?"

Trying to control my temper, I answered evenly, "She needed a place for them. That place is here."

"So where is *she?*" Blake demanded, his voice rising. "Both of you should be here, along with her dresses and trophies and whatever the hell else is arriving in the mail. I've been advocating for her to join us here for weeks."

Nate cast him an angry glance. Blake crossed his arms.

"Obviously, we've been thinking about her," Evan said, his voice low and menacing. "But the real question is, did you think about us? No, you fucking well did not. Nate collapsed again at the game on Saturday. He won, yeah, but he was struggling. Blake's food was off this weekend—"

Blake dug the heels of his hands into his eyes. "A customer sent a dish back to the kitchen," he muttered. "Said it was 'just okay' and he expected better."

"You should have seen Blakey." Evan stepped swiftly in front of me. "He was a mess."

Blake shook his head. "I got quiet, that's all."

Evan gripped my shoulders. I let him. If I tried to restrain him right now, his aggression could erupt elsewhere, with catastrophic results.

"I'm just grateful," he hissed, his nose an inch from mine, "that I didn't have any shows scheduled this week, because they would have been a disaster. For the past three years, you've drummed it into our heads that we fucking depend on each other. But you? You let us down."

I held up my hands. "You're right. I stayed away too long."

Nate glared at me over his shoulder. "Have you forgotten who you owe allegiance to? We've tied our futures to yours. You promised to take care of us."

"The Joining's in four days," Evan cut in. "Everything you've done this week has pushed the Star away from us, not brought her closer."

I closed my eyes. "I did this for all of you. My time with Daisy was part of the plan."

A roar of incredulous laughter forced my eyes open. My friends stared at me, united in their disbelief.

Blake strode over, bumping Evan aside, and clapped me on the back. "Brother," he said, "you are so full of shit."

"Blake..." I warned.

"Lie to yourself, lie to her if you have to, but don't lie to us. You can't."

"Do you really want me to lie to Daisy?"

"Fuck no," he snapped. I'd never seen Blake so agitated. "But our tongues are tied. Bring her here and we have a chance of convincing her. You've screwed everything up, because you've been selfish."

Nate crossed to the marble table, pushing his fingers into the puddle of melted wax that dripped from the lit tapers. "That's what we are, Blake."

Blake whirled. "Not with each other!"

Evan jabbed a finger at my chest. "Fix this. Or I will. You're dragging out this game. I want her naked on that table in four days, where she belongs. I'm not letting the Star get away."

"That's a lot of *I*, Ev," Blake cautioned. "How about *we*. That's what we need to get back to. We, all four of us, working together."

I walked to a velvet-draped window that looked out at the side lawn. Statues presided over the flawless grass, and a grapevine-covered trellis arched overhead. Everything I'd dreamed of, everything I'd worked to create, was here.

Exhaling, I turned to face my friends. "You're right. If we work together, everything will fall into place. Daisy will be ours, as she's meant to be. Willing and eager."

"Exactly," Blake said, relieved. "We're not judging you for wanting her. You just need to share."

Evan loped across the room, stretching his shoulders. "You can fuck all you want after the Joining. I know I will. She's going to taste so good..."

"Enough!" Nate swept the burning tapers off the marble table, startling us. Candlesticks fell to the floor, splattering hot wax. He glared around at us, a vein throbbing in his forehead. "I refuse. Daisy's off the table. We'll find another girl; I don't care who. But try to use Daisy for the Joining and I won't do it."

"Then why were you in such a hurry to keep Reeve from fucking her?" Evan drawled, poking Nate in the chest.

"Evan," I warned.

Blake put a sympathetic hand on Nate's shoulder, but Nate shook him off. "Why are you fighting so hard?" he asked gently. "Daisy's the one."

Evan snorted. "Let the knight charge, Blakey. He needs a battle. Some game he knows he can't win."

Nate glared at him. "Shut up, Ev."

"Don't argue." Blake held up his hands. "Remember what binds us. Think of everything we've done with her, everything *Reeve's* done, yet we still bear the mark of our lord." Pointing to the snake on his arm, his voice deepened reverently. "She's passed every test. The Star of the Cosmos, named in the prophecy. She comes along—"

"Once in a century." I pressed my fingers to my temples. "And there's no guarantee our paths would have crossed."

"We need Daisy, Nate," Blake said softly. "She needs us. Don't you want to give that to her?"

"You know the rest of the prophecy." Evan bared his teeth in an animal grin. "Stars can be volatile. Explosive. The greater the power, the greater the risk. I'm here for it. You should be, too."

Nate pushed open the tall doors to the back lawn and stalked out, slamming them behind him.

Evan shook his head. "See? Too emotional. A few years of history with her, a couple of little kisses, and he's all fucked up. Probably still thinking about his sister, too. He should cut that tie."

Shaking his head at Evan, Blake draped an arm around me. I flinched, and he stepped back. "We trust you, Reeve. You've got our lives in your hands. Don't let our trust be misplaced."

Leaving my shirt on the couch, I followed Nate outside. My phone buzzed in my pocket with a message from Daisy.

Are you okay?

After everything I'd put her through, she was only thinking of me.

Quickly, I texted back, bringing my shaking fingers under control. My tattoo itched in a constant warning.

I'm much better, sweetheart. Don't worry. I'll see you later tonight like we planned, all right?

Somewhere outside our romantic bubble, she was working tonight. A campus catering job that she'd signed up for this week, because she was starting to let go of her dreams of music. "Facing reality," she'd called it.

I had a meeting that would run until ten. A campus advisory board that worked with donors, because I liked to keep a hand in the monetary affairs of Pacific Crest. It was one aspect I could control, one means of leverage of this land I was tied to.

The pause that followed my text lasted seconds, but it felt like years.

All right.

I found Nate on the floor of the pool house, his head in his hands. He was slumped in the exact spot where the couple had had sex at our party a few weeks ago. They'd moaned in ecstasy, and Daisy's eyes had gotten twice as big.

Ever since that moment, she'd expanded to fill my whole world, and I was slipping. My leadership, my vision, my control — all slipping.

Leaving the door open, I sat down beside Nate. The early evening air, scented with orange blossoms, wafted into the pool house.

He pillowed his head on his knees, turning to speak to me.

"You weren't there, but Evan was right. At my last game, I collapsed again." Despite his hulking size, he suddenly looked vulnerable. As though the closer we got to our goal, the more the magic took its toll.

I put my hand on his shoulder. "I won't miss another game."

"After the Joining..." he began.

"Nothing will ever hurt you again."

"What do you want with Daisy?" He sounded so tired. "Forget the prophecy. Why her?"

"Because I love her."

We stared at each other. It was hard to tell who was more shocked.

I pushed my hair off my forehead. "I just said that out loud, didn't I."

Nathan nodded, his jaw set.

In the silence that followed, a war raged inside me. I wanted the simplicity of being with Daisy. Yet I burned with the promise of the serpent, the ache to share her with my friends.

Blake was right. She was destined for us. The five of us should feast and rise as one.

But love — the fragile, human kind — had no place in that feast.

I shook my head to clear it. "She loved you when she was younger. Did you love her back?"

Nate raked his fingers through his hair until it stood up. "Hell, Reeve, I don't know. I'm not who I was anymore."

"Are you sure about that?"

He stretched out his arms, cracking his knuckles. "When I look back — I really hate that guy. He was just a shell. A fucking pathetic soul. I'm done with him."

"Don't be hard on yourself." I squeezed his shoulder.

Nate was so brittle, I was afraid he'd snap before the Joining. After the Binding a year ago, we'd all experienced physical changes, but Nate's were by far the most drastic. He was struggling. With his body, with fame.

"I'd like you to have some time with Daisy," I said abruptly. "Alone."

"Don't make me do that," he muttered. "I'm trying to protect her."

"I'm not *making* you do anything," I said patiently. "It would be good for both of you."

He barked an incredulous laugh. "You can let go of control for that long?"

"Turn around."

He held his breath, then let it out and swiveled so his back faced me.

Taking his shoulders in my hands, I kneaded his muscles through his T-shirt with long, slow strokes. He groaned softly.

"You've sacrificed so much, Nate. But it's all paying off. Soon we'll be free, and the world will be ours. We'll be able to leave Pacific Crest and achieve the fame that's coming to us." His eyes closed as I massaged his neck. Color rose on his skin. "Take your shirt off."

He tensed. But I wouldn't have given the order if I hadn't sensed that he wanted to. After a minute, he pulled his shirt over his head and tossed it to the side.

I dug into his tight, knotted muscles, and his breath came faster.

His desires were so strong, so twisted up, that they pulled at mine. I could help him. I could find the dangling end of that tortured knot and yank it until he felt nothing but pleasure.

There was no reason on earth for him to be so miserable.

Not with our power.

I felt the moment he melted into my hands, savoring the rush of answering pleasure. His cock rose in his loose sweatpants.

"Fuck, Reeve," he hissed.

"Won't it feel good when you let your inhibitions go?"

I brushed my thumbs over his flat, beaded nipples, and he jerked sharply. His erection pointed upward, tenting his pants, and my own dick throbbed in sympathy. When I imagined Daisy naked and flushed between us, caressing both our cocks as we overwhelmed her sweet body, I cursed under my breath.

"You need her, Nate," I coaxed. "She needs you. There's too much between you for any of us to ignore. It's going to eat away at you until you're with her."

He groaned as I palmed his abs, exploring the map of grooves and ridges. The hard muscles jerked under my hand. "And you're too involved with her. We both know that."

"I'm giving you permission to do everything that I have. Just make things right with her. Believe me," I whispered, "she'll want you to."

Grasping his upper arm, I pressed my fingers to the scarlet head of his inked serpent. He moaned, his biceps flexing in my grip. When a damp spot painted his sweatpants, I rubbed the head of the tattoo more firmly, brushing my lips against the softness of his earlobe to inflame his lust.

"Go ahead," I murmured. "Refuse to fuck Daisy. Resist taking her in the Joining. But don't deny your needs. You deserve to see the Star naked. To give her the privilege of your cum. You deserve to let her kneel and worship your cock. To make her come until her light floods your vision and you both see stars. You can do that much without repercussions. Do you expect to leave this campus without ever touching Daisy again?"

"Don't — tempt — me." He shuddered, his head lolling against my chest. His groin thrust toward the ceiling, begging for attention.

"Nate, I'm just asking you to think," I crooned.

Deep inside me, my desires fought a battle. I wanted to keep Daisy for myself; I wanted to take care of Nate and fix everything for him; I wanted them to finally be together like they'd yearned for all these years.

I wanted to pave the way for the Joining to take place.

The serpent writhed inside me, insisting we could have it all if I only offered my trust. Stroking Nate's chest, I let the words take over.

"Think about how gorgeous she would look, spread open and glistening with all the power you've saved for her," I whispered. "Think about the trust in her eyes as she kneels for you, inviting you to touch her wherever, *however* you want."

Drunk on our mingled lust, I let my hand slide over his abs and down his waistband. When he lifted his groin, I squeezed his cock firmly through his sweatpants.

He let out a strangled groan, bucking into my palm. Goddamn, he felt good in my hand, thick and hungry. Sliding lower, I cupped his heavy balls, fondling them as he writhed.

"Think of her," I rasped, "because it's all I can do. Take some of that from me."

He gripped my wrist.

"Stop," he panted. "Or I'll come."

I wrenched my hand free. He leapt to his feet and bolted across the pool house. Gripping the doorframe, he stared out at the fountain splashing in the pool, breathing hard.

His desires were dangerously close to the surface. It could be a grave mistake to trust him with Daisy alone.

But intuition said otherwise.

I came to his side. Heat surged from his skin.

"You can't love her, Reeve." He pointed to the snake on my arm. "That won't let you."

"Daisy seems to be the exception to the rule."

"If you break her heart, I'll kill you," he muttered.

"You can't." I nodded toward his own tattoo. "That won't let you."

Despite his size, he suddenly looked vulnerable, his eyes darting as he pressed his forehead against the doorframe.

"I love you also, brother," I said softly. "I'm telling you to enjoy yourself because you deserve it. There was a time when Daisy wanted to give you all her firsts. She still has some for you."

He let a strangled noise. "Which ones?"

"Find out."

He shook his head.

"Why, Nate? You feel guilty because she's your little sister's friend? Because she was naïve and trusted you once? Or are you afraid of her power? Putting all the 'shoulds' aside...all the guilt... what do you really want?"

His face contorted, dark energy swirling as he clenched his fists.

"I want..." His shoulders trembled.

"Go on," I encouraged.

His massive body contracted as the words rushed out.

"I want to kiss her until her taste is so deep inside me, it won't ever get out. I want to strip her naked and possess her completely. Those long legs, those soft tits... I want to suck on her hot pussy, fuck her little cherry with my tongue, lash her clit until she screams. I want to make her come all over my mouth and fingers, I want to feed her my cock, teach her to take it deeper and deeper..."

I rested my hand on his back. Desire gripped him, strong and potent, flooding my own body.

"Let it all out, Nate. She still has those firsts for you. She's waiting."

7

The Other Side

Daisy

Pulling my denim jacket close, I picked my way along the outer campus road. The evening was cool and smoky with a promise of autumn.

This was usually my favorite time of year. But as I walked along the sidewalk, my eyes stung, and my chest felt hollow.

My body throbbed from the afternoon. I kept seeing Reeve running out of my room. He couldn't leave fast enough.

"Cursed," I whispered. "First kissing, then sex."

And it was worse than before. Reeve hadn't just run; he was in pain.

Whenever I tried to concentrate on the question of the four men, the pieces of the puzzle slid away from me. As if they couldn't stand to be examined.

When Reeve had looked at me with those brilliant green eyes, I'd seen Nathan, Blake, and Evan in the room with us. My desire had roared up in a blaze. I'd wanted all of them, and guilt pierced me for being only with Reeve.

I needed to understand.

I turned right onto Jacaranda Row, where faculty homes overlooked manicured lawns. I'd sent my resume off to Campus Dining Services earlier this week, and received my first job today: serving hors d'oeuvres at a party at Chancellor Weston's house.

Maybe the Chancellor knew something. If Reeve had truly paid him off to protect Greer Hill, there were secrets at play. Secrets someone might allow to slip during the party tonight...

I touched the hollow between my breasts. Beneath my black shirt was an amulet I'd made this afternoon. When Reeve left, I'd pulled on my clothes and rushed after him, only to see his car leaving the dorm parking lot. He took ages to respond to my text. So, angry and frustrated, I'd turned to his stolen books, which had sat on my desk all week.

Using an old locket I'd bought from a street vendor in New York, I did my best to create an amulet with the materials I had — the herbs in my room, candle wax to seal it, and an incantation from Reeve's book on amulets and wards.

I had no idea whether it would work. But if, by some miracle, it did, it would protect me from magic, while also detecting magic nearby.

The serpent was real. It had looked out at me from Reeve's eyes in my bedroom. And in that moment, it wasn't my friend.

As I walked down Jacaranda Row, something didn't feel right. I squinted down the road. The streetlights turned to haloes in my vision, and the quiet street sounds were dulled.

The ground was humming.

It wasn't as though it had started just then. No, it had been humming for a long time, longer than any of us had been around, and I was only noticing it now. These weren't the quakes I'd felt on Greer Hill; this was a deeper, more constant music. Vibrations rose through my black ballet flats, rippling my body.

The ground...wanted something.

My eyes snapped open. The third home on the left, glowing like a beacon in the dark, was Chancellor Weston's house. Buttoning my shirt to the collar, I went to the side service door and knocked.

"Start by circulating the tuna wontons." Louise, the kitchen head, thrust a platter into my hands. "Come back for a refill when the tray is mostly empty."

I smoothed my apron with one hand. Balancing the loaded tray, I edged into the hall.

Heels clicked on the hardwood floor, and I stepped aside to avoid a collision. Coming around the corner, dressed in black with a white catering apron, was a red-haired woman.

Her curls were scooped into a bun, and her right arm was in a sling. She was ordinary-looking, her freckled face neither beautiful nor ugly. With a smile, she'd be cute in a girl-next-door kind of way. But her jaw was set, and her mouth was sullen.

When she saw me, she turned pale and scuttled away.

"Wait," I called. "Do I know you?"

She glanced over her shoulder, looking both furious and terrified.

She seemed vaguely familiar. Something about her made me sweat, driving a lump to my throat. Did she remind me of Tara? Because of the red hair and freckles? They were about the same height and age; they could pass for distant cousins.

Suddenly, Tara's words crept into my head from the day she'd tried to abduct me: *You like my face? Someday, if you're a good girl, I'll tell you how I got it.*

A shiver ran through me.

Checking that the hall was empty, I lifted the amulet over my head and tucked it in my pocket. The amulet could only wield its power, protecting me and showing magic in the vicinity, if it touched my skin.

Edging down the hallway, I peered at the guests mingling in the living room. Circulating through the crowd with a tray of appetizers was Tara: graceful, angelically beautiful, her heart-shaped face lit from within. Her curls were glossy, her body curved and shapely.

Quickly, I pulled the amulet from my pocket and held it tightly in my hand. As soon as I touched it, Tara wavered into the sullen, hard-faced girl whom I'd seen in the hall.

A glamour.

Tara had glamoured herself.

How could she? That was magic from fairy stories, not the craft I practiced. To alter the fabric of reality...it stunned me. And she'd confessed she didn't have any power of her own.

But on a campus where men had the eyes of a snake and marble statues moved by themselves, where the woods opened or closed at whim, and strange talents catapulted unknown students to the brink of fame — I shouldn't be surprised.

Tara caught me staring, and her eyes roamed over me with a glare of hatred.

I backed against the wall, holding one hand over my rocketing pulse. She was here. I should leave. It wasn't a coincidence; I was positive about that. She'd freely admitted to stalking me once she had the collar around my throat.

But the look in her eyes was all fear now.

If she was following me, she was afraid to come close. And I had protection in the form of the amulet.

I touched my shirt pocket, where I'd stashed my card of the day: the Six of Swords. I'd taken to picking from Reeve's mother's tarot deck, and he'd enjoyed seeing me do it each morning as we cuddled in my bed. The cards carried a strange energy, like the ash of old dreams.

The Six of Swords indicated a change or ending due to moving in a different direction. It was about making a conscious decision to chart a new course so I could ensure my survival. Maybe I was meant to be here tonight, moving away from music, figuring out a brand-new path.

The card felt like a talisman, sitting over my heart.

"No, Tara," I said softly. "You won't hurt me. I'm not running away from this job."

Carrying the tuna wontons, I walked into Chancellor Weston's living room.

The space was gracious and welcoming, all warm wood and rich leather. A fire crackled in the fireplace, casting a glow over the crowd that chatted and mingled.

A student string quartet in the corner caught my eye. They were tuning their instruments by a potted palm tree, setting up their sheet music and metal folding stands, and joking with the easy camaraderie that comes with playing together.

The violist leaned over to whisper to the cellist, pointing at the thick binder of music on her stand, and they both burst out laughing.

My heart squeezed.

I'd loved playing with my chamber group for events at Siderio. Performing onstage was exhilarating, but playing with a small ensemble while a roomful of people laughed and mingled was low-key and relaxed. You could focus on the people you were playing with, smile at each other, weave in and out like partners in a dance.

Tonight's party looked very similar: glasses clinking, appetizers circulating, polite conversation interrupted by animated stories and laughter. I was dressed in black from head to toe, as I would be to perform. But instead of playing, I was serving.

Not worthy, the serpent had hissed.

I gritted my teeth. Hadn't I told Reeve I was accepting reality?

"Wontons?" Stopping by a group where someone was telling a story, I flashed a dazzling smile all around. They smiled in return and plucked the appetizers from the tray. One person wanted to know every ingredient, and I listed them off effortlessly.

The next group beamed at the sight of food. As I focused on the job at hand, shutting out all the questions, I began to enjoy myself. It felt good to be gainfully employed. And there was something satisfying about offering delicious bite-sized appetizers, arranged neatly on a square white plate, and making people happy. It was exactly the distraction I needed right now. I smiled at the guests as I made my way around the room, offering seconds.

The string ensemble began a Haydn quartet, one that my friend Jessamyn had performed at Siderio, and the memory brought a bittersweet smile to my lips. My tray emptied rapidly as the wontons were gobbled up.

But when Tara passed close by, carrying her own tray one-handed, I tensed. Abruptly, she turned away.

As she moved through the room, stopping curtly to allow guests to take canapés, I glimpsed a middle-aged man built like a former linebacker at the edge of the crowd. He chatted affably with the people surrounding him.

Chancellor Weston. I recognized the salt-and-pepper hair, the square jaw and easy, jokey manner.

Before I could study him further, he excused himself and disappeared into the hall. A moment later, Tara followed.

Impulsively, I whirled to hurry after them.

"Whoa, whoa, slow down," chuckled a younger guy in a navy blazer and slicked-back hair. "Don't rush the wontons."

"Sorry!" Gritting my teeth in a smile, I held out the tray.

"What's a beautiful girl like you doing serving hors d'oeuvres at the chancellor's house?" asked his older companion.

Shrugging, I kept the smile plastered patiently on my face as he took a wonton, ready to throw the entire tray at him so I could slip into the hall and spy on Tara and the Chancellor.

Fortunately, two women came over and joined the conversation, allowing me to steal away.

I stashed the tray in the kitchen and hurried out before Louise caught sight of me.

The hallway was dark and empty. Choosing a direction, I

rounded the corner. A crack of light emerged from a door that stood slightly ajar.

Approaching the door on tiptoe, I opened it an inch, then another.

It led to a flight of carpeted stairs that spiraled downward, leading to a dimly lit underground space lined with shelves of bottles.

The chancellor's wine cellar.

Two voices floated up: a high-pitched, strident female, and a low, genial-sounding male.

"So you screwed up the collar," the lower voice drawled. "And now she has it. I'm disappointed in you, Tara. Very disappointed."

"I'm sorry," Tara panted, her voice pleading. "But there are other ways..."

My throat went dry. Moving as quietly as I could, I angled closer to hear more.

"This has gone too far already," the man grumbled. "The parking garage issue is a farce. I'm reverting to the original plans. We'll tunnel into Greer Hill as soon as possible."

"No!" Tara sounded desperate. "There's still time. Don't destroy the hill. I can get to the boys."

"They want nothing to do with you now." The man's tone sharpened to brittle dismissal. "You've proved useless to me."

"Let me try. If something happens to her...let's just say they need me." Her voice grew heavy with malicious satisfaction. "Watch, Charles. They'll come slithering back if they don't have an alternative. Their lives depend on it."

"I see a whole lot of benefit to you in that scenario, Tara, and none at all for me."

"So put the squeeze on Reeve. He'll pay whatever you demand to get what he wants. Isn't that all you need?"

Cold laughter issued from the wine cellar, nothing like the chancellor's affable chuckle. "I need more, but that's a start. They won't ever leave this school if I have anything to say about it. You deal with the girl."

Tara blew out a frustrated breath. "Me? I'm not going near her again. She's fucking dangerous!"

"You lost control."

"I couldn't help it! It was like she was controlling me! She's a freak. Do you know how hard she pushed me? I flew through the air like a doll. It's unnatural."

"The woods helped her." Shoes scuffed the cellar floor as the chancellor paced. "Corner her away from them and she'll be powerless."

I stiffened. My fingers gripped the door, my mind whirling. I caught a glimpse, through the stairway railing, of Tara's sullen face.

"Reeve's obsessed with her," Tara muttered. "He barely left her dorm for a week. I don't know what she put in his coffee, but she's got him wrapped around her little finger. It's like she cast a spell on him. She's a full-on witch."

Cast a spell.

The words lodged in my mind. I saw the remnants of the love spell I'd cast the night of The Crush, which I hadn't bothered to clean off my dresser.

Was Tara right? Had Reeve only stayed with me all week because of a love spell gone awry?

No. It couldn't be. What we'd felt was real. Jagged, soft, imperfect...loving...

Please be real, I prayed.

And if I hadn't cast that spell? Would Nathan want me after all?

I gripped the tarot card in my shirt pocket. *Give me answers.*

The chancellor chuckled. "Don't worry about that. A minor distraction, that's all. Come here."

He ran a finger along her jaw, and she flinched before pasting on a smile. I knew he saw Tara the gorgeous angel, not the ordinary, irritated-looking woman the amulet showed me. Maybe he didn't see the truth of her feelings either. How little she cared for his touch.

She patted his hand and twisted away. "Not now."

"Are you really still holding out hope?"

She shrugged. "I'll take care of the boys. You take care of the rest. Hold the hill over Reeve's head if you want more cash."

High heels clicked a staccato pattern toward the stairs, accompanied by shuffling soles. Letting go of the door, I shot upright. I tiptoed the first few steps down the hall, then hustled the rest of the way and zoomed into the kitchen.

"Where were you?" Louise glared at me from the oven as I hung onto the counter, panting. "People have been asking for the tuna. One gentleman asked for you — 'the very charming wonton server.' I had to send Amber out with more."

"I'm so sorry. I'll bring out another plate right now."

"We're done with them. Go bring out those drinks, and don't disappear again." She nodded curtly toward a tray of cranberry cocktails.

I apologized profusely and took the cocktails to the living room. The string quartet was playing Eine Kleine Nachtmusik. Guests laughed and chatted as Mozart's bouncy music buoyed the conversation.

My mind chased itself in circles as I crisscrossed the room, offering drinks. With two left, I approached Chancellor Weston. He stood by the fireplace, collar pressed and tie neatly knotted, surveying the room with a satisfied expression.

"Would you like a drink, Chancellor?" I asked politely.

He smiled at me, his eyes lingering. "Only if you'll have one with me."

I inhaled, startled.

"I'm working." I smiled apologetically. "I really can't."

"You really must. My wife's out of town, and I hate to drink alone." He gave me a meaningful look.

His wife. He had a wife. And he was telling the nineteen-year-old server — a student at his school — that she was off the premises. Did he want to lose his job? Or did he care more about whatever nefarious plans he had with Tara than any risk to his position?

"I'd be happy to bring you a glass of water, then."

He roared with laughter and took a cocktail. "That won't be necessary. What's your name?"

"Daisy Fisher."

"And you're a student here, Daisy Fisher. Is that right?"

"Yes. I'm a sophomore."

"You look so familiar," he said affably. "I'm sure we've met before. What's your major?"

My arms prickled. In the cellar, the chancellor hadn't mentioned my name. I was simply "the girl." But he had to know. And I was sure he remembered meeting me at Blake's restaurant when I'd come there with Reeve a couple of weeks ago. He'd approached our table, making me uncomfortable from the start, and told me I was lucky to be with Reeve.

What else did he know about me? Could I find out by playing this elaborate game of pretend?

"I'm undecided," I answered lightly.

"Is that so?" He seized the shoulder of another man passing by. "This is Andrew Gates Hall, one of our law professors. Andrew, meet Daisy Fisher. She hasn't declared her major yet and is just waiting for the right path to unleash her charms."

Andrew Gates Hall looked me up and down. The prickling intensified. "What are you interested in, Daisy?"

I smiled at him. "Anything and everything."

"I think you'd be perfect for the law."

"But would the law be perfect for me?"

The three of us laughed as I handed him the last cocktail. Over his shoulder, I caught Tara's narrowed gaze.

"So nice to meet you," I said quickly. "I should refill this tray."

I nodded at Andrew Hall, smiled at the chancellor, and turned to go. A touch on my arm froze me in place.

"After you're done cleaning up, Daisy, feel free to stay." The chancellor's voice was low, meant for only me to hear. "There's a nice pool out back."

"Thank you." I pulled free and hurried to the kitchen with my empty tray.

After we cleaned up and Louise told the catering staff that we could go, I hung back. The living room was quiet and empty. All the guests were gone. The string quartet had packed up their instruments and left with their music stands. The only movement was the flicker of the fire in the grate.

When I heard Louise leave, I crossed the living room to look out at the landscaped backyard. An inviting pool sparkled in the moonlight. The house made an L-shape around the pool, and the lights in the rest of the windows were off.

It was late. The chancellor was nowhere in sight.

What were he and Tara plotting? What did he know about the men that I didn't? Or — about me?

The ground vibrated slightly beneath my feet.

"You're so sure I'm powerless away from Greer Hill, Chancellor Weston," I murmured. "Should you be?"

As though agreeing, the ground gave a gentle shudder. When I pressed my amulet against my chest, the grass gave off a faint glow. It gave me courage to investigate.

Glancing over my shoulder to make sure I was alone, I tiptoed through the door to the courtyard.

The night air was warm and heavy with the scent of oleander. The pool lapped quietly at my feet.

I pulled my phone out of my pocket. One message from Reeve.

Missing you, Daze. Wish I didn't have this meeting tonight.
See you afterwards, around midnight?
I'll make everything up to you.

"What's your story, Reeve McClellan?" I wondered. "How much truth have you been telling me?"

I called him. No answer. My head spun with too many emotions and rumors.

At my feet, the pool beckoned with its own glow. The rhythm of the breeze rippling the water, the palm trees waving overhead, seemed to say *Come here, come here.*

Fuck it. Why not? Why not do something a little naughty and crazy? I deserved a swim in the chancellor's pool. And he was nowhere to be seen. I could take a private night dip and clear my mind.

As the water and the trees combined in a siren song, I stepped closer to the pool's edge.

Of course I could go for a swim. The amulet protected me. The ground had helped me during Tara's attack. She feared me now, the chancellor was just a man, and I — I was starting to like the taste of power.

Kicking off my ballet flats, I wriggled out of my black pants, then my black blouse. I bundled all my clothes in a pile by the pool. Cool night air swept my skin with goosebumps, kissing my neck, my stomach, the crevices behind my knees — all the sensitive spots. Reeve had found every one.

I texted him:

Miss you too
About to go skinny-dipping in the chancellor's pool
See you at midnight

Let him wonder.

In my bra and panties, I dove into the pool.

Warm water enveloped me, splashing cheerfully as I swam a lap. It felt so good to relax, alone and buoyed by the water.

The sliding glass door opened.

I froze. Then I flattened myself against the pool's wall, in a dark corner, out of the path of lights that illuminated the chancellor's backyard.

Chancellor Weston walked out of his house and stood on the deck with a bottle of wine in one hand. He wore swim trunks. He was in decent shape for a man in his fifties. There were other women out there who'd appreciate that, women like his wife.

"Where are you, Daisy?" he called softly. "I know you're out here."

Fuck, fuck, fuck. My throat squeezed, and I tried to slow my breath. What had I been thinking, jumping in the pool?

"I see your clothes on the ground." Arching his neck, he brandished the wine bottle like a club. "You didn't hide yourself well at all."

My breath caught. Swiftly, I lifted the amulet from my neck, holding the chain away from my skin, then slipped it back on.

No change. The chancellor wasn't using magic. All he had on his side was brute strength, and the amulet would do nothing to protect me against that.

What did he want?

"It's only a matter of time, Daisy." He stalked across the lawn. "You walked right into my house. Not so bright, are you? Our admission standards have never been very high here at Pacific Crest. That's all going to change. This school will become something very different if I have anything to say about it." He chuckled, swinging the wine bottle, looking less like the respected bedrock of the university and more like an animal on the hunt. "Now, where are you? You want to play games? Okay, we'll play games. But the winner gets everything."

"Reeve," I whispered soundlessly. But he wouldn't come. He knew where I was, but he was in his endless meetings and had no reason to think I was in danger.

"McClellan will do anything for you, won't he?" the chancellor said pleasantly. "That makes you the most valuable thing on this campus to me. With you as leverage, what won't he give? And his friends would be pretty worried if you're unavoidably detained here. All their access to you cut off... I know they have something pretty important coming up. What is it, Daisy? What do those boys want you so badly for?"

I don't know. I clenched my fists underwater. Terror strengthened my anger. A "valuable thing?" I was done being anyone's *thing.*

I'd fought off Tara, but I had no idea if that burst of strength would come again.

I dug my fingertips into the tiles that lined the pool, and a faint quiver in the ground gave me hope.

Leave, damn you, I thought fiercely at Chancellor Weston, my fear narrowing into a laser beam of will. *Go inside your house. Forget me.*

He blinked. "Daisy? You are out here, right?"

Leave. Leave. Leave.

His gaze shifted, confused. Then his teeth bared in a grin that made me shiver. "Oh, you're out here all right. I can smell you."

He stalked toward the pool, and my mind went blank.

A huge, dark shape bounded over the fence, landing cat-like on its feet.

"What the hell?" The chancellor whirled, halting. The figure moved swiftly on the lawn, stopping a few feet from the chancellor. Overhead, the spotlights showed massive, tensed shoulders, sinews standing out on the bulging arms, a messy thatch of brown hair, and narrowed eyes.

"Good evening, Chancellor Weston," Nathan said mildly.

"Well, look at this. It's Nate Davis." The chancellor forced a smile, but kept his grip on the wine bottle. "Always a pleasure, but this is a private backyard."

"I heard a friend of mine might be back here. Can you tell me anything about that?"

The chancellor laughed heartily. "Well, for their sake, I hope they're not. I'd have to call the police, have them arrested for trespassing."

My thoughts raced, searching for the words to some spell, any spell. Nathan's eyes flitted to the pile of black clothes beneath a tree.

"Where is she, Weston?" he hissed. His shoulders twitched, and for a moment, his eyes glowed brilliant green in the dark.

"I don't know what you're talking about." The chancellor hefted the wine bottle. From my hiding spot in the pool, I saw a bead of sweat run down his brow. "But I think it's time for you to run along now. You wouldn't want trespassing on your record, would you, Davis? Or worse? Not when you have such a bright future."

Nathan let out a low growl as they circled each other. He could take the chancellor in a fight; they both knew that. But what about the consequences? He'd be kicked out of school. His career could be ruined.

I wracked my brain. *Do something, anything, Daisy.* Treading water, I tried to stay noiseless.

"You certainly wouldn't want anything to threaten your next game," the chancellor added. "You've already had two unfortunate incidents. Collapsing on the field...we can't have that happening to our star athlete."

Nathan gripped his hands into fists. "What do you know about that?"

The chancellor chuckled, but his eyes never left Nathan. "Life's boring when you always win, isn't it, Davis? People are that much more invested in our team now. Pacific Crest is making its place on the map like never before. Do you have any idea how much is riding on you? On your back, boy?" Nathan flinched. "A killing came in on that game we lost, and now everyone will be dying to see what happens next time. That's what your friend McClellan does, isn't it? He bets against the market, expects companies to lose, and it's made him a very wealthy man. This school has racked up debt, and I'd like to see it gone. I'm going to turn this third-rate school into a place of prestige. The most desired university in America. Don't worry, Davis. Everyone loves an underdog. A hero who rises from the ashes."

Nathan's jaw clenched. "After this season, I'm done here."

"I own you, Davis."

Nathan barked a laugh. "Whatever owns me, Weston, it's not you. And you'd run screaming in the night if you ever met it."

The chancellor's face paled, but he shook his head. "I know

there's something here you boys want. You don't leave this campus. You've done workarounds for away games to make sure you're never gone too long, and your friends travel with you because you can't stand to be apart. I've been watching all of you. You could be conquering the world, but you're stuck here because you need this place. And I think you'll be paying your debts to Pacific Crest for a long, long time. Starting with that friend who you're looking for. She's important to you boys, isn't she?"

Nathan's eyes darted back and forth. I could sense his thoughts. He wished Reeve was here, or Evan, or Blake. He needed their charmed words, their quick thinking. Reeve could talk his way out of this situation, even turn it to his advantage.

But Nathan was too straightforward for intrigue. He was floundering.

"You're going to tell me what's here, Davis, at this school. You're going to funnel all the benefits to me in perpetuity. You're going to tell me why Greer Hill is so very precious that it can't possibly be destroyed. The girl is mine, whatever she's worth, until you guarantee I have everything I want—"

Fury twisted Nathan's face. He leapt on the chancellor, grappling with him.

I gasped when he shoved his face into the ground and punched him. Visions of a very bad fight, of repercussions that could never be fixed, flashed through my mind.

Desperately, I pressed my palms against the wall of the pool and tuned into the earth.

I asked for help. I fucking begged; I imagined pressing my face in homage to the ground; I pictured the serpent and offered it my fear and need. I saw the abyss and promised to jump.

I opened myself to receiving, and the vibrations grew stronger.

Thoughts came into focus:

Forget this, Weston.

The ground trembled slightly. Both men started.

Forget this and go inside.

The ground shook harder. Nathan rolled off the chancellor and leapt back.

The chancellor stumbled to his feet, clutching his nose. "What's going on? This an earthquake?"

Nathan cast one swift glance at the dark corner of the pool where I huddled. Sparks streamed through my arms and legs, and the water felt like needles against my skin. Quickly, Nathan stepped into the shadows as more vibrations ran through the ground.

Forget this, go inside, and leave us alone.

Chancellor Weston shook his head as if he were clearing away cobwebs. He peered at the yard, then the bottle of wine that lay in the grass.

"Senior moment," he muttered, sounding a lot more like the affable guy who'd welcomed new students a few weeks ago. "No clue what I came out here for. Must have walked into a door..." Gingerly, he rubbed a smear of blood from his nose. "And that wine? Jesus."

He picked up the bottle. Looking down at his swim trunks, he shrugged and shuffled back to the house. The sliding glass door closed behind him.

I expelled a breath.

Adrenaline pumped through my body, driving me halfway down the pool. I was swimming again, kicking through the heated water, because I could.

The banishment had worked. I wanted to jump up and down and squeal. The land at Pacific Crest truly did hold power...

There was a resounding splash behind me.

I whirled around. Nathan had shed his shirt. Waves sluiced from his dark head and shoulders. He swam so swiftly that by the time I caught my breath, he was in front of me.

His eyes were honey-colored in the lights of the yard. Water dripped from his massive chest as he backed me against the side of the pool.

"You and I," he said roughly, "are long overdue for a talk."

8

Ladder

Daisy

I grabbed Nathan's shoulders. "How'd you find me? Did Reeve tell you?"

"What the fuck are you doing in the chancellor's pool?" he shot back. "What's happened to you? You're reckless, taking crazy risks—"

"What's happened to *you*? All this..." I ran my fingers over the swells of his muscles. "It's unnatural."

"You're unnatural. You shouldn't be here."

"Fuck you, Nathan." Anger surged inside me. "You mean at this school? You think I wanted to be?"

His hands burned my cheeks as he cupped my face, bringing my eyes back to his. "Just answer my question. What the hell were you thinking, coming out here?"

His clean, masculine fragrance surrounded me — his wet hair, his familiar shampoo. And underneath, the scent of the men, wild and earthy and decadent.

I shook my head. "I wanted a swim! The water called to me. Yes, it was reckless. But look at us! We're safe. We're fine now."

His hands left my body to grip the edge of the pool, and the serpent writhed crimson on his inner arm. "This is what you do, isn't it? You go where you're not supposed to. You show up in my family's backyard. Break into the House, crash our party. You haul Blake and Evan into the woods. Jump in the chancellor's pool."

I dragged my eyes away from the serpent tattoo to look straight at him. "Anything else?"

His voice dropped. "Sleep in Reeve's bed. Invite him into yours." As I stared, he went on in a rasp. "You took him in, Daisy. You opened your world to him. You shouldn't have done that."

"I guess that's what happens when you don't belong anywhere. You care a lot less about breaking in."

"Spare me the pity party, okay? Your life isn't over."

"What about yours? What did Weston mean when he said that you don't leave this campus?"

"Daisy, I can't —" Nathan's face twisted, and he forced out the final words. "Tell you."

"It's because of this, isn't it?" I stroked the tattooed snake's head, and Nathan twitched as if dosed with electricity. "The snake that eats itself. The circle with no end."

Nathan laughed, harsh and humorless. "You have no idea what you're getting into, Daisy."

"I've *met* it, Nathan. I've summoned it, spoken to it. It picked me up and dangled me over the abyss. It showed you to me." He went pale, his face working. "But I want the truth from *you*. Not the serpent."

He gripped my wet braid. "Is there anywhere Reeve hasn't touched you? Blake, Evan?"

When he pressed his body to mine. I gasped and pulled him closer so I could feel his unyielding chest against my breasts. The water lapped around us.

"No," I breathed. "They've touched me everywhere, Nathan."

Nathan's eyes flickered, his lashes thick and dark. "Their mouths. Have they used their mouths?"

I shuddered. "Not to make me come. Not there."

"Be grateful."

"What the hell?" I exploded, my patience at an end. "Where do you get off glowering at me and giving me warnings and trying to cockblock me when I finally, *finally* have a sex life? You hate me, but you're trying to protect me?"

Unbelievably, a smile flashed across his face. "*Cockblock?*"

"Goddammit, Nathan, I loved you. I really did. And now you don't give a damn about me, except to hound me about your friends and shame me for enjoying other people's company. You walk around looking all intimidating with your writhing snake tattoo and your giant muscles and your constant bad mood—"

"Well, how do you think I felt in high school? You and Sasha, with your successes, and your superiority complexes, and looking down your nose at everyone else."

"I never looked down on you. I liked that you were so normal."

"*Normal,*" he scoffed. "You mean boring, Daisy. Worthless. Forgettable."

Water swirled around us. The sky spun overhead. I took a deep breath.

"Nathan, some of the best moments of my life were our secret nights on the patio swing. When we talked and shared ice cream...I was so excited, I couldn't sleep afterwards."

"You just wanted me to listen to all your plans."

"No! I cared about you."

"Did you?" His hands closed over my shoulders. "Did you even know me?"

We could only stare at each other for a moment, our heavy breaths mingling, as I searched for the answer in his eyes.

"Maybe I didn't know you," I replied quietly, "but I definitely had feelings for you. No one else ever came close."

A strange expression passed over his face.

"Daisy," he whispered, and when he said my name, I saw the sweet, shy boy I'd loved.

Impulsively, I stroked his wet hair off his forehead. Such a simple gesture, but I'd wanted to do it for years. When he didn't stop me, I gently threaded my fingers through the thick, soft strands, smoothing them back.

Nathan leaned down. His lips came closer and closer. When they were about to touch mine, I came to my senses and pulled back sharply.

"I need to talk to Reeve first."

Nathan shook his head. "Believe me, he won't care."

The words made me feel hollow. I put my hands on Nathan's hard chest. "*I* care. And I'd like to hear how he feels from him."

His eyes narrowed to slits. "Reeve isn't what you think he is, Daisy. He's not a good guy. He has a lot of darkness inside him."

I felt ropes coiling around my breasts. I saw the changing colors in Reeve's eyes, heard his rough whispers as he and his friends spanked me.

"I know. I've seen it. I like it."

"No, Daisy. You haven't seen it yet." Pulling my head back by my braid, he dragged his knuckles over my cheek. "And you haven't seen mine."

"I want to see you," I whispered. "Exactly as you are."

Slowly, I leaned forward. I was falling off a cliff, and Nathan was about to fall with me.

Our lips touched, and a spark leapt between us.

Nathan groaned and pulled me up hard against him. At the throb of his cock against my thigh, the closeness with him that I'd craved for so long, I flashed to Reeve in my bed, mere hours ago, and jerked back.

"Wait."

"You want to talk to Reeve? I'll call him."

"We're in the chancellor's backyard. He could come out again."

"He won't. What you did, Daisy..." Nathan gestured to the air, and a smile sneaked across his face. "It'll last for hours. Trust me, Weston's not coming back out tonight."

I stared into his amber eyes, sparking with greenish gold at the edges. "Okay. Make the call."

Nathan vaulted out of the pool and sprinted to the fence. He was naked, gorgeous in his speed and size. He moved so quickly that I couldn't make out many details of his body, but the lights shone on the water streaming down his broad, furrowed back. His tightly muscled ass. The arrow of his gleaming cock.

He was back a second later with his phone, dialing and handing it to me. It rang once and picked up.

"Nate?" Reeve answered briskly.

"It's Daisy." I felt suddenly, inexplicably shy.

"Hi, sweetheart." His voice softened, and my insides turned to mush at that one little word. "Are you with Nate right now?"

I took a deep breath. "Yes."

Nathan lowered himself noiselessly into the water and caressed the back of my head.

"In the chancellor's pool?" Reeve asked teasingly.

Jesus. I closed my eyes. Of its own accord, my body arched into Nathan's touch. "Mm-hm."

"Naked?" His velvet voice deepened to a growl.

Nathan stroked my neck, closing his hand around the nape, and I let out an involuntary moan. His free arm wrapped around my waist as he nuzzled my jaw.

"Almost," I whispered. "And Nathan is."

Reeve inhaled sharply. I knew those sudden breaks in his control, when he threatened to come apart at his smooth, polished seams. "He's doing things to you, isn't he?"

Nathan's palm slid around to my throat, pulling me against him. I shuddered. My body was hot, pulsing, aching between my legs. My free hand came up to cover Nathan's. For once in my life, I felt fragile, pulled up close to his huge body.

"Yesssss. Are you picturing it, baby? Do you care?" I wanted to sound sultry, but my voice came out a dry, throaty rasp.

"Always."

"Then—"

"I want you to enjoy yourself to the fullest, naughty girl. I'll see you back at the House."

"Enjoy myself," I repeated. "You mean..."

"Daze." His voice was a caress, lapping at me like the waves of the pool. "You deserve to get everything — *everything* — that you want."

He hung up.

Stunned, I handed Nathan the phone. He pitched it across the lawn. I tensed, expecting it to crash and break, but it landed precisely in the middle of my pile of clothes.

"Shit, Nathan," I whispered. "Your aim is perfect."

A cocky grin broke across his face. He closed in on me, bracing both hands on the edge of the pool.

"*You're* perfect," he whispered back, his gaze tracing my features.

"Oh God, no, I'm not." I shook my head slightly, but his fingers gripped my chin to stop the motion.

"Daisy, we both need this. I can't fight it anymore."

"I stopped fighting it a long time ago," I whispered, almost breathless.

Was there any reason not to kiss him right now?

He was here.

I was here.

Reeve had given us his blessing.

Sasha was thousands of miles away, pursuing her own dreams.

I grabbed the back of Nathan's head and pulled him to me.

The kiss was nothing like Reeve's velvet seduction. It was harsh and raw and burning hot. Our tongues chased each other, our lips battling until they were bruised and swollen. He bit my neck eagerly, and I sobbed. His big hands squeezed my breasts, crushing my nipples. I moaned his name over and over again, making this moment real, as I buried my hands in his wet hair and pulled.

I couldn't touch him enough. My palms needed to be everywhere, all over his body. When he squeezed my ass, I shrieked, and I didn't care who heard.

His hand slid inside my panties, exploring me roughly, giving me what I needed. When he pressed on my clit, I kicked in the water. I sucked hard on his lower lip, panting for breath, grasping his massive shoulders as he worked a finger inside my pussy.

"I need you there, Nathan," I panted. "I've thought about you inside me so many times."

He grunted with pleasure and thrust deeper. It stung a little, but God, I wanted that from him right now. I wanted everything from him, all the built-up longing of the past five years. When his thumb rubbed my clit, tormenting the little bud, the longing threatened to explode into climax right there in the pool.

I couldn't leave him behind. Stroking his hard abs, I soaked up his groans of pure need, until my fingers brushed his cock and I grasped it firmly in both hands.

"Fuck," he gasped, his face glowing with agonized bliss. "Daisy — oh God."

I squeezed his thick shaft, staring into his honeyed eyes, until the last word I wanted to hear fell from his lips.

"Stop."

"Are you kidding—"

"Daisy," he gritted. "Get out of the pool. I want your mouth."

I shivered at his tone. On the surface, it demanded, but beneath it was an ocean of barely suppressed desire.

When I grabbed the side of the pool, a twinge in my left wrist stopped me, so I swam for the ladder. Nathan had already climbed out. As I reached the top, he scooped me up, carrying me to a patch of grass in a shadowed corner of the yard.

Breathless, I glanced at the dark house. "Are you sure the chancellor—"

Nathan set me down. "He won't be a problem. On your knees."

I scrambled to obey. Grass pressed into my skin.

"Take my cock in your mouth," he grated.

I wrapped my fingers around his hot, pulsing cock. I'd spent years longing for this exact moment. I wanted to take my time.

But his big body quivered with need. Had he been holding back like the others? Denying himself touch and release?

Giving the head of his cock quick little licks, I breathed in his musky, woodsy scent. When he trembled and moaned, I opened my mouth to suck on his thickness. He swore, gripping my wet hair. His cock was hot, the skin satiny smooth, and he held the back of my head firmly as he sank deeper between my lips.

"Fucking hell, baby. Cup my balls."

Eagerly, I stroked his balls, large and firm in my hand. When I rolled them lightly, Nathan thrust hard, nudging my throat. Caught off-guard, I tried to keep up with him.

"Don't be gentle," he groaned. "Don't be so sweet with me, Daisy, I can't take it...Oh *fuck*. Shit, girl, I can't..."

Salty cum flooded my mouth. I tried to swallow, but as with Reeve, there was so much. Nathan's cum dripped deliciously from my lips and down my breasts.

But I refused to let go of his cock. I kept it stubbornly in my mouth, hungry for his pleasure, letting him ride his climax. His growls were all I heard, and every drop lit my skin on fire.

Finally, I pulled away, panting, gazing up at him. His eyes flared green with pure lust as he took in my appearance.

With a sharp turn, his hand twisted in my hair, making me moan. He gestured to his still-hard cock.

"Continue."

My jaw ached, but all I wanted to do right now was please him.

"Anything for you," I whispered, my admission making him groan.

I took him in my mouth again, swirling my tongue over his silky skin, and lost track of time as he fucked my face.

We were connected, and I was drunk on it. His cock, my breath, in a constant push and pull. Never-ending, like a snake swallowing its tail.

His voice deepened to the rattle of rocks. "Relax. Open. Trust. I'm your everything right now. Your world. Your air. Filling you up, little girl. You're going to take my cum again and again and again..."

His release filled my mouth, and my nails scratched his thighs in excitement. All I knew was his cock, thick and veined and sliding over my tongue, as Nathan loomed over me, blotting out the moon.

When I pulled free, his hand closed on mine, pulling his cock with quick jerks. More spurts of cum soaked my face and neck, sizzling my skin, until Nathan let out a last raw groan and dropped to his knees in front of me.

"Daisy," he breathed. "Are you okay?"

My throat was hoarse, but a laugh emerged. "I'm so not okay. I don't want to be okay. This — us — belongs to a whole different realm than 'okay.'"

A slow grin spread over Nathan's face. "Then lie back. I'm going to make you even more not okay. And you're going to love every fucking minute of it."

Gently, he wiped me clean with his T-shirt and tossed it aside. Naked and panting, I stretched out on the chancellor's lawn.

Kisses burned my neck, my collarbone, my breasts. I thrashed when he sucked hard on my nipple, and he gripped my hips with firm hands to hold me down. When his tongue trailed over my stomach and down to my pussy, I gasped.

"Let me get this straight," he rasped. "The others have never kissed you here?"

"No."

"Reeve's never licked your sweet little pussy."

"No..." My thighs were starting to shake.

"Never sucked your hot clit."

"No."

"Never pushed his tongue into your tight hole."

"No, God, Nathan!" I thrust my crotch toward his face.

"How much do you want it?"

"Please," I gasped. "I want you to do all of that."

He buried his face between my legs.

Oh Jesus, it was complete overload. His tongue roamed everywhere, invading my most secret places. He sucked hard on my clit and I bit my fist to keep from screaming. He licked my opening over and over while he rubbed my clit to a swollen peak. I shook, pulling his hair, bucking like crazy underneath him.

When I couldn't take it anymore, he lifted his head, lips glazed with my juices.

"Do you want to come?"

"Yes, oh God, yes," I babbled.

"Say it. Look at me and say my fucking name."

I stared into his eyes. Looking out at me was the serpent. Nathan's eyes were as shimmering and green, as animalistic, as beautiful and deadly as Reeve's had been when he tied me up.

When he ran from my room.

My thighs trembled. "Nathan, I want you to make me come."

Deliberately, his eyes never leaving mine, he licked my pussy juice from his upper lip. "Mm. Beg for it."

"Yes, yes, whatever you say. I want you, God, I *need* you to make me come. Please, Nathan, please..."

He groaned. Putting his face between my legs, he tongued my clit until sweet fire spread through me. I cried out when his big fingers sank into my pussy, thrusting and curving, sparking twinges of hot and cold.

I came for him. Need flooded me as he swept me away. My whole body was in his hands, and my mind winged upward. A bird, flying far overhead.

When I fluttered back into my body, Nathan was licking lazy circles over my clit, his fingers still buried inside me. If he licked just a little higher, in one particular spot...I was so close to coming again.

Arching my hips, I met his gaze.

"Continue."

His eyes widened. Then he laughed quietly. That was the only warning I got before his tongue lashed my clit. I clapped my palm over my mouth to stifle my shrieks as he fingered me, stinging and soothing me at the same time.

I came in a rush, soaring even higher than the last time. My whole world narrowed to Nathan's hands and mouth, then expanded outward in a bright flash that lit the yard like a streak of lightning.

"Damn," Nathan breathed. "You really are a star."

We lay in the grass together as my racing heart slowed. My legs were carelessly spread, his head between them. My skin was sticky with his cum and mine.

He eased his fingers out of me and rested his head on my thigh, planting a soft kiss there.

"And you're my knight," I whispered.

As I stroked his hair, a window opened above us.

"Hello?" called a grouchy male voice.

I froze. Nathan smiled up at me, completely at ease. He held a finger to his lips.

"Who's out here?" grumbled the Chancellor. "What was that bright light?"

My eyes darted to the window, then to Nathan. He had the nerve to wink at me. Lifting his head, he blew a soft stream of air over my clit.

I let out a yelp before I could help myself and glared at Nathan.

"I hear you," the Chancellor growled. "You think this is some kind of game?"

Nathan treated me to a cocky grin and tickled me behind the knees. I burst out laughing and grabbed his wrists.

"Very funny," boomed the voice from above. "I'm coming down now and I'm calling the—" There was a thump overhead. "Oh hell," he muttered. "What was that doing on the floor? Why am I out of bed? And the window... Must have been a dream." There was a grunt, followed by the window banging shut.

Nathan raised an eyebrow. "You see? He won't bother us tonight. All because of you."

I laughed, giddy at the power and the possibilities and the sensations still buzzing through my body from Nathan Davis's tongue.

"And because of you," I whispered, stroking his damp hair. "You really are my knight in shining armor."

He snorted, but that cocky grin was back. The light by the pool caught his honey-colored eyes. Traces of greenish-yellow flickered as he bent and pressed his lips to my forehead.

"Let me take care of you like I should have all along," he said softly. "Come back to the House. Spend the night with me."

I sat up, and the real world came back into focus. My clothes lay in a heap a few feet away, with Nathan's phone and my amulet on top. The light in the chancellor's living room cast a dim glow through the sheer curtains.

"Reeve..." Guilt washed over me.

Nathan put his arm around my shoulders and ruffled my drying hair. "It's okay, Daisy. Don't worry about him."

"Don't *worry* about him?" I buried my head in my hands. "I know he gave us permission, but it still feels strange. Things are different now."

His lips twisted. "Trust me, he won't be upset."

"What about me? What about *you?* Nathan, I really — I — he means a lot to me. It feels like a relationship. I don't want to fuck this up. And there is some seriously weird shit going on with the Chancellor and Tara, and I think we all need to sit down and talk —"

Nathan's arms tightened around me, but he said nothing.

"What does he want?" I demanded.

"Reeve wants a lot of things." He rubbed my back. "Come back to the House with me, okay? We'll all talk when he gets home."

Nathan's eyes were warm amber, sincere and open. His carved shoulders and thick arms were more relaxed than I'd seen them since arriving at Pacific Crest.

I let out a breath. "Okay."

Rising, Nathan bounded across the lawn and came back with my clothes and his before I could blink. His eyes slitted as he gazed at me.

"Nathan?" I stepped toward him.

A smile tugged his lips. "You're bright, that's all."

9

Revelator

Daisy

The white stucco buildings of campus streaked past, ghostly beneath the moon. Nathan held me to his chest, his arms locking me in place as he raced down the back roads of Pacific Crest.

Though I'd witnessed him on the football field, his speed and strength stunned me. The night was calm, but wind whistled in my ears.

When we reached the tall hedges surrounding the House, he burst down the curving path. The security guard gave us a curious glance, then looked away as we approached the columned front porch.

"What's made you such a star athlete?" I demanded. "It's not drugs."

"Nope." Nathan kicked the door open.

We flew through the living room, passing the black marble table. Under the low lights, the white veins threading its surface blazed with cold fire.

Lush chords reverberated through the air. Evan turned from the piano bench, shaking back his hair with a knowing smile. Before he could speak, Nathan bounded up the stairs two at a time. I jostled in his arms, and he tightened his hold.

"What the hell is going on with you, Nathan?"

"Figure it out, Daisy." That cocky grin was back on his face. "If you guess right, you get a prize."

"All of this — your talents, the House, Tara — are related to the serpent. Am I right?"

As I spoke, the inked scales shifted on his skin.

"No hints. You come to me with a complete theory, or you get nothing."

We passed Reeve's closed door, and two more doors that must be Evan's and Blake's. At the end of the hall, Nathan opened the last door. We burst through and he tossed me on the bed.

"Nathan!" I bounced on the mattress, breathless.

Large windows looked out on the pool. Beneath me, a blue plaid comforter spilled over white sheets. Pillows were scattered everywhere, on and off the bed. The floor was polished wood, and the thick blue rug was rumpled. A painting of a speeding sailboat hung over the desk. There were no cabinets of curios or strange figurines to be seen.

Spotting a small brass bowl on the desk, I climbed off the bed for a closer look. Piled in the bowl was the same reddish herb I'd seen in Reeve's room, which I'd used to accidentally summon the serpent. Beside it was a second bowl in hammered silver that held the other type of dried leaf, dark green and tightly curled. The herb that Sasha hadn't been able to identify.

I reached out to touch them.

"Don't," Nathan said from the center of the room.

Beside him stood a huge fish tank, fitted into a column that ran from floor to ceiling. He'd had fish in high school, too — a colorful array that he took good care of. This tank was at least twice that size, featuring elaborate plants that waved in the water and a dazzling assortment of fish.

"Did Reeve pay for all this?" I gestured around the room, and Nathan nodded. "How do you feel about that?"

"Reeve likes taking care of people."

"I asked how *you* feel about it."

He exhaled. "It's part of the package."

"The *package?*"

"Our friendship," he corrected quickly. "I won't be hurting for money next year. I'll offer to pay him back, but I doubt he'll want me to."

Right. Nathan's career would start next year. He was already on the brink of fame.

My black server's outfit, damp from pool water, stuck to my back and breasts. I crossed my arms, shivering with a sudden chill.

"Hey." He crossed the room and lifted my chin with his finger. "Are you okay?"

The tenderness took me by surprise. "Not at all. Remember? You were going to make me not okay, and you succeeded."

He smiled slightly, keeping hold of my chin. "I remember one of our talks on the patio. You said you never wanted to be just okay. You wanted to be great."

"God, I really did say that, didn't I? I can't believe you spent all that time listening to me."

His eyes flicked down, lashes long against his cheeks. In this unguarded moment, even with his thick neck and massive arms, Nathan was still pretty.

"I listened to you, Daisy, because I wanted to be great too."

The admission hung in the air.

"And now you are," I said quietly. "You're the big football star."

"I'm the most wanted college player in the nation. NFL scouts are at every game. It basically happened overnight."

"You don't sound happy," I murmured. "You sound like you're reciting a grocery list."

"I don't do grocery lists, Daisy. Blake takes care of that."

"You know what I mean." He cocked his head and didn't respond. "Why are you looking at me like that?"

"Like what, baby?" He wasn't glowering anymore. A smile hovered around his lips, and his eyes were all hunger.

I shivered. "Like you want to eat me."

"Because I do. You know what it's like to always be hungry?" His heat smoked around us both.

"Yes," I whispered. "Very much."

"Hungry for success. Hungry for fame. Hungry for the world. Keeps you up at night, doesn't it?" He lifted my chin in his hand, seizing me with the intensity of his stare. "I always knew you'd be awake, those nights we talked on the patio. I heard you pacing the house like a hungry ghost. You still do that, don't you? When was the last time you really slept?"

I stretched up on tiptoe to whisper in his ear. "With Reeve."

He barked a laugh. "You're joking."

"Nope. Deep, dream-filled sleep. He has a very relaxing effect on me."

He scooped me up and threw me on the bed again.

"Nathan!" I laughed uncontrollably as he crouched over me, tickling my sides. "I'm not —" I panted for breath. "I'm not used to being thrown around."

"Do you like it?"

"Yes!"

"I can help you relax better than Reeve can."

"It's not a competition."

A firm hand covered my mouth. His lips brushed my ear, making me suck in a breath against his palm.

"I," he whispered, "am very competitive. However hard Reeve's made you come, I'll make you come harder. If he haunts your dreams, I'll haunt them every night. And if he gives you the sleep you need... you'll get it even more with me."

I was panting, licking his palm as he loomed over me.

"I've known you for years," he whispered. "I know who you are from the inside out. I know your dreams, your desires. All the little hints you'd drop, trying to flirt during our talks." I flushed hot. "I knew long before Reeve that you're an exhibitionist. You need to be watched. Performing is like sex for you. When you played, you made love to your flute and everyone in the room, and they all fell under your spell."

I pushed his hand up so I could speak. "What else do you know about me?"

"Hmmm." The tilt of his head was playful, but his eyes held danger. He covered my mouth again, the pressure driving my pulse through the roof. "There was the time that you told me you thought tickling was hot. Did you hope I'd reach over and try? Just like this?"

Teasing fingers wandered over my neck, my breasts, under my arms. I shivered, goosebumps popping out on my skin.

"You love control," he whispered, "but I think you love losing it even more. You know how many times I've thought about tying you up and tickling you while I fuck you? Picture it: you, helpless, squeezing my cock, soaking wet, laughing and crying. And coming. Uncontrollably. So turned on, you can't think."

I cried out, the sound muffled again by his heavy hand, as he pinched my nipple through my blouse.

"Why didn't you ever touch me?" I asked, wrenching my head from his grip.

"Because you belonged to—" His face contorted, and he took a deep breath. "To Sasha."

I gripped his shoulders. "Nathan, were you *jealous* of Sasha? Of us?"

He looked away, his lips twisting. "My sister and I have never been close, Daisy. You were just one part of it."

"But I wanted you. We could have—"

He shook his head. "You kept our talks a secret. You avoided me when she was around."

I traced his jaw. "I'm sorry. I didn't know how to have you both."

Silently, he stroked the loose wisps of hair from my forehead, damp and curling from the pool.

"That time is over," I said more urgently. "We're together. Tonight. You and me. Nathan and Daisy."

When he looked up, his eyes were pure, brilliant green. There was no trace of the whites. The pupils were cold, implacable slits.

I shivered. "Nathan? Is it you?"

He didn't respond, just stared at me.

My voice fell to a whisper, and what came next surprised me. "Am I worthy?"

I felt the sting of the serpent's rejection in the woods, of Reeve running from me today. It made no fucking sense, and yet it all made sense on a level I couldn't quite grasp, like a dream slightly out of focus.

Nathan shook himself, his eyes fading to warm honey brown. He pressed his lips to my neck.

"*Yes.* In every way, yes. You're absolutely worthy. And it's us, Daisy. The Knight and the Star."

Marking my throat with kisses, he unbuttoned my blouse.

This time, he went slow.

I tried to keep quiet. Evan was downstairs; Blake might be home too. And Reeve... But Nathan stoked my need until my moans filled the room.

"Can I tie your wrists, baby?" He nuzzled my bare stomach, working me up so much that every touch burned. "Or will it strain your hand?"

I wanted him to, so badly, but I shook my head. "Not tonight."

He must have seen the pain in my eyes, because he peppered my stomach with kisses. "Then I need you to be very good for me and hold on to the headboard. Don't move. Don't even think about letting go."

I did. When he began tickling me, I dissolved into giggles. One hand squeezed my pussy through my panties, the only clothing I still had on. The other roved over my ribs, tickling mercilessly under my arms, easing up to tease my throat, my breasts, my belly.

"So naughty," he whispered. "You're hoping I'll take your panties off, aren't you? You want me to touch your pussy while you giggle and squirm."

I curled up, breathless with laughter, clamping his hand between my thighs.

"Such a bad little girl," he hissed. "Serves you right if I feel you up just like this."

"Nathan, please..."

I shook as he rubbed my clit through the soaked fabric. I buried my face in the pillow, but I couldn't look away for long. I couldn't hide from the face I'd loved for so many years, darkened with lust and focused on my every reaction.

Finally, the sweet torment ceased. Hooking his thumbs in my underwear, he yanked the lacy purple fabric down my thighs and gripped my ass in both hands.

I moaned as he ate me out. His mouth was doing the tickling now, nibbling my pussy, tonguing me with a featherlight touch that grew firmer and rougher until his lips fastened on my clit. Pleasure shot through me. It was so much, almost too much. When I bucked and squirmed, his hands joined in, roving over my body and tickling my most sensitive places. I writhed on his bed, clutching the headboard.

"Nathan, oh my God!"

"Fuck, you're wet," he groaned.

I giggled uncontrollably. The more I moved, the harder he sucked on my clit. "Hold me down. Please..."

His huge forearms pinned my thighs, spreading me open so he could lash my pussy with his tongue.

When he lifted his head, his brown hair was a mess. His gaze was feral, his mouth smeared with my juices.

"Reeve liked to play games with you," he hissed. "'You can't come unless I say so. Don't touch yourself or you'll be punished. Give me your panties. Be my good girl. Stay away from my junk.'

How about we play a different game? The one where I make you come until you can't take it anymore. Because it's fun, and I feel like it."

I opened my mouth to reply, but a knock on the door interrupted me. From the sound of it, quiet and measured, I knew it was Reeve.

My gaze locked onto the door, unmoving.

Nathan raised his eyebrows. "I think that knock excited you." I managed a nod. "Do you want the Devil in here too?"

I stared at him. "Do *you?*"

His face turned serious. "Daisy, it's up to you. I tried to control the outcome and I fucked up. I hurt you; I hurt Reeve. So right now, all of this — it's about what you want."

My body trembled, my thighs captive beneath his arms. He didn't move. Didn't release his hold or lean down to give me relief.

"Okay," I whispered. At the very least, the three of us should talk. I raised my voice to call out tentatively, "Come in."

The door swung open. Reeve walked in and shut it behind him, carrying a glass of red wine. As usual, he was impeccably dressed. His eyes were black and shining, his lips a heartbreaking curve, his dark stubble perfectly shaped. But his eyes were shadowed above hollow cheeks, and a vein throbbed in his forehead.

"Are you all right?" The words leapt from my lips.

"I am, Daze," he replied quietly. "I'm sorry I ran from you."

I flushed, naked in Nathan's grip under Reeve's intent gaze. "I know we're together. I—"

His voice was steady, his eyes flicking from me to Nathan. "You don't have to choose. In this House, you can have everything you want."

"That's not possible." My throat went dry.

He smiled. "Let us show you. What was Nate doing that got you so worked up?"

I swallowed. "He suggested we play a game. The kind where he makes me come until I can't take it anymore."

Nathan flashed a cocky grin at Reeve, who set the wine down on the bedside table. He took his time unbuttoning his sleeves and rolling them up over his forearms.

"I like the sound of this game," he said calmly. "And if it's all right with you, I'd like to watch."

"Are you sure?"

"Very. Do you want that, Star? Do you want me to be the audience while Nate pleasures your hot little cunt over and over until you're begging for a reprieve?"

This was unreal. It was crazy. It was everything I wanted.

"Do you, baby? Tell us." Nathan's face hovered between my thighs.

"Let's play," I breathed.

Nathan dove in, licking my swollen clit. I cried out as fire flared between my legs. An orgasm tumbled over me, fast and sudden, stealing my breath away. I was coming for Nathan uncontrollably, just as he'd said, and a glow so bright bathed his room that my eyes squeezed shut.

"Oh!" I gasped.

When my head rolled to the side, I saw Reeve pulling up a chair a few feet from the bed and making himself comfortable. He arched his neck sinuously, his wineglass in his hand, his dimple flickering in his cheek.

Nathan snarled as my pussy tightened on his fingers. "That's right, baby. Put on a good show for Reeve, okay? Let him see how hard you come when you're treated right."

I let out a sound between a laugh and a groan. It died on my lips when Nathan sucked my clit into his mouth. Another explosion built, faster, faster... The second orgasm chased the first, sending me down a rollercoaster.

"So wet," Nathan hissed. The noises he made as he feasted on my pussy were outright obscene. "What a horny little girl you are for us."

"He's not wrong," Reeve chuckled. An erection tented his perfect slacks, but he made no move to touch it.

I stared at the bulge of his cock as Nathan relentlessly pushed me to another climax. My pussy was oversensitive now, so turned on that it hurt.

Reeve the detached, Reeve the observer, Reeve the voyeur. The man who stood on the sidelines of his own party, his own damn life, and enjoyed it vicariously through his guests. The man who wanted to experience my feelings, yet evaded his.

For a week, I'd seen him feel.

Had I?

He took a leisurely sip of wine. "Nice, Nate. You're getting her so aroused. I like the way her thighs are uncontrollably shaking."

"It's cute, right?" Nathan pushed his stiffened tongue inside me, rubbing my clit mercilessly. The pleasure was so intense that tears oozed out of my eyes. I arched, stiffening, my toes curling as yet another orgasm seized my body.

I collapsed to the bed, crying softly, as Nathan pushed my legs open even farther.

"That's it, Daisy," he murmured. "We're just getting started. I owe you for all those nights on the swing, when you were so close and I couldn't fucking touch you."

Daring to let go of the headboard, I thrust my hands into Nathan's hair, the hair I'd longed to pull and stroke so many times.

Reeve cocked his head, staring at my pussy. He crossed his ankles, cool and calm, and suddenly I wondered how much of a show he was putting on himself.

"How does her little cherry taste, Nate?"

As Nathan grinned, his lips shone with my juices. "Incredible."

"And how many times do you plan to make our virgin Star come tonight?" Reeve sipped his wine.

I moaned. It angered me when Reeve fetishized my virginity. Especially now, after he'd run away from having sex with me this afternoon, in pain and afraid. Yet I couldn't deny that every time he did, it made me hot and needy.

Nathan laughed, his honey-brown eyes cast in green. Holding Reeve's gaze, he sank two big fingers inside me. I moaned at the fullness, squirming as he worked his way deeper until he was buried to his last knuckle. "Let's find out."

When I thrashed, Nathan held my thighs down firmly and began licking again. Reeve's gaze heated my body with a prickling flush. I turned my head to bury my face in Nathan's pillow, taking comfort in his clean, familiar scent as he pushed my body to its limits.

"Too much, baby?" Nathan teased, lifting his head. "Does your little pussy need a break?"

I made inarticulate noises, shaking my head, trying to shove my pussy toward his face.

I could stop Nathan with a word, I knew. But I wanted to find out what would happen if I didn't. How far this would go, how far *we* would go.

I tried to look at Reeve, but tears of need blurred my eyes.

"Trust her, Nate," Reeve said silkily. "She wants to be yours tonight. She needs you to use her hard."

I groaned, another peak building between my thighs. Nathan's massive arms didn't allow my legs to move. So I grabbed his hair, pulling with all the strength in my right hand, desperate for an outlet.

Nathan growled. "Pin her," he grunted to Reeve. "Grab her arms. She needs to be completely restrained."

Reeve raised his eyebrows, swirling the wine in his glass. "I'm just watching, Nate. This is your and Daisy's show."

I moaned as Nathan swiped my pussy with long, hot licks. "Please, Reeve."

"Are you sure?" His eyes, hot and dark, moved from me to Nathan's gleaming, muscular body. Reeve McClellan wasn't used to asking for permission.

We stared at each other. Suddenly, he looked younger. His beautiful lips parted. In this moment, he was unguarded, and I could slay or soothe him with one word.

"Yes." My voice was stronger now. "I'm sure."

Reeve set down his wineglass and rose from his chair. "Nate? You're sure too?"

Looking between the two of us, Nathan grinned and smacked the mattress. "Get on the bed."

Reeve's brows lifted at the order, but he climbed gracefully behind me.

"Hold your right wrist with your left hand, Daze." Pinning my right hand above my head, he slid his free hand down to pinch my nipples sensually.

"I'm so close," I gasped.

"Come for us both," Nathan growled, burying his face between my legs.

"No mercy, Star," Reeve hissed. "You belong to us."

Leaning over me, his face upside down, his lips covered mine. His kiss was what I needed. It sent me tumbling over the edge again, clasping Nathan's head between my thighs.

When the waves of pleasure subsided, I collapsed to the bed, panting. The men released me, pulling me into an embrace that tangled our arms and legs.

"Reeve," I murmured. "What about you and me?"

"Nothing's changed, Daze. You and Nate have needed each other for a long time."

I shook my head. "Nothing's *changed?* We really do need to talk."

He stroked my sweat-dampened hair. "You want this. I want it. Nate wants it. Is there anything else to talk about?"

Their hard cocks pressed against me. I felt their need, tugging at my desire to give to them.

"Do you want it, Nathan?" I whispered. "Do you want Reeve here?"

He met my eyes and nodded once. It felt so good, being with both of them. How could it be wrong?

"All right," I murmured. "We'll talk later."

Nathan lifted his head. "Kiss him again, Daisy. This time, I want to watch."

I wrapped my hand around the back of Reeve's head. His hair

was so soft under my fingers. Inch by inch, I pulled him down until our lips fit together.

When our tongues tangled, I gasped. Reeve didn't give me room to catch my breath. He sucked hard on my lower lip. His tongue was everywhere, hot and hungry.

He grasped my braid, undoing it roughly and quickly, his composure cracked.

"Take your clothes off," Nathan said in a low voice, and I realized he was talking to Reeve. "Daisy's humping your leg, making a mess of your pants, and I know you hate a mess. We can't have that."

Reeve stiffened, and I expected him to refuse. Then he lifted his mouth from mine. "You do it, Nate. I'm kissing our girl right now."

I flushed with pleasure at *our girl,* even though a stubborn part of me also wanted to hear Reeve say *mine.*

Nathan grunted, his eyes going smoky as he stared at Reeve still fully dressed in my arms. Crouching over me, pinning me tightly between them, he went to work on Reeve's crisp button-down shirt. I moaned as the shirt fell open, exposing Reeve's coppery chest.

"Are you going to touch each other?" I whispered. Nathan's cock pulsed against my ass.

Reeve raised an eyebrow. "Do you want that?"

My eyes widened. It was up to me? Quickly, I nodded.

Nathan ran his hands over Reeve's chest and shoulders as he eased off Reeve's shirt. Reeve was breathing rapidly now, his hands tightening on me until I squeaked.

"Is this okay, man?" Nathan murmured. "I know it's hard for you to be touched."

"It's okay," Reeve gritted. "It feels good."

"Daisy's helped with that, hasn't she?"

"In every way. Our sweet Star." Reeve's eyes were fixed on mine.

Nathan's palm moved down Reeve's abs, the movement so erotically charged that I moaned. When he reached his pants, he unbuckled the thick leather belt, undid the button, and slowly pulled the zipper down.

Reeve's fingers dug into my tender skin. I wanted to tumble into the darkness of his stare, but I needed to watch Nathan peeling off Reeve's slacks, then his boxers. His carved erection sprang free.

"Fuck," Nathan muttered, grazing Reeve's cock with his fingers. Reeve jerked and groaned.

"I can't believe I'm seeing this," I breathed.

"Don't worry, Daisy." Nathan bent to nuzzle my neck. "I'm just getting him ready for you."

Nathan's gentleness surprised me as he fondled Reeve's heavy balls. He knew what he was doing, which only aroused me more. His hand glided over Reeve's cock with ease, but his face held a look of wonder, his eyes wide with raw emotion. He'd done this with Blake and Evan, I guessed, but never with Reeve.

I buried my hands in Reeve's hair. "Is this the first time Nathan's touched you?"

Reeve managed a nod.

First times have power.

"It's all right, brother," Nathan murmured, and it stunned me to hear this role reversal, where he was comforting Reeve, reassuring him. "We're here for you. I know I betrayed your trust, but I won't ever do that again. We all belong to each other now."

Reeve groaned, holding me close.

"Look how hard he is." Nathan flashed a grin at me and circled Reeve's cock with his fingers, pulling softly on the flared head. Reeve swore, a pearly drop clinging to the tip. Wiping it with his thumb, Nathan brought his hand to his mouth and licked it clean.

When he met my eyes, his smile belonged to the sweet boy I loved, not the arrogant, angry jock. But his words were pure filth.

"Suck Reeve now, baby. Do him as good as you did me tonight. Take him deep."

A shudder ran through Reeve as Nathan squeezed his cock one last time and let go.

Climbing over me, Reeve clasped my face in his hands and let his cock brush my lips. Nathan moved to my side, stroking himself, his flushed head emerging from his fist. I arched toward them both. When Nathan took my hand and wrapped it around his shaft, I moaned, allowing Reeve's cock to sink into my mouth.

He felt huge looming above me, fucking my lips, my tongue sliding over his pulsing veins. Nathan caged me in, one palm covering my breast, moving my hand firmly over his cock.

"Fuck yes, Daisy," he grunted. "Take care of Reeve the way he takes care of all of us. You're going to make him feel really good, aren't you?"

I nodded as I let out muffled moans.

Reeve praised me as I frantically sucked, stroking my hair, telling me how beautiful I looked as I pleasured them both.

"Deeper," Nathan hissed, and I gasped, my mouth full, seeing the serpent's flat chartreuse stare regarding me from Nathan's face. Reeve thrust in response, plunging in to nudge my throat. When I sought his gaze, nervous and aroused, the same eyes looked out at me. "Take him all the way in. I want to see you choke on his cock."

The crude words made me tremble. I obeyed, driven by the need to surround Reeve, squeeze him, swallow him, as his thickness probed my throat.

For a moment, I felt intensely fulfilled. Then I coughed, my eyes watering, and he eased back to let me breathe. Murmuring endearments, he sank in again. Repeating the cycle, guiding me to open for him as he filled my throat again and again.

I was slipping under a warm, dark tide, surrendering to Reeve and Nathan. Only their cocks were real, and our shared need, and the light behind Reeve that sparkled and coruscated until it formed a writhing scarlet knot that bit its own tail.

I moaned with desire, my throat constricting around Reeve's cock. The serpent was here. It approved of me. It was pleased.

It was the one fucking my mouth in a cycle of infinite pleasure, and all I wanted to do was swallow it forever, until Nathan's voice pulled me out of the reverie.

"You've been taking Reeve's cock in your mouth all week." He thrust roughly, smearing my palm with precum. "And you were such a good girl, sucking mine tonight. You love it, don't you? Having two cocks to play with. Think about licking us both together. Trying to fit both our dicks in your sweet mouth. Can you do it?"

Oh God. I needed this more than I could say. I nodded eagerly, and Reeve pulled free, letting me grasp his shaft. Nathan rose to his knees, massive, blocking out the light as he leaned forward to rub his head against my lips.

It felt deliciously submissive to lie beneath them and stroke both their cocks. Hemmed in by their sweaty bodies, breathing in their male musk. My tongue danced between them. When I tried to close my lips over both their tips, pressing them together, both men gritted a curse.

I took my time, snaking my tongue over every sensitive spot and soaking up their reactions.

"You're going to make us come," Nathan growled.

"I can taste your longing, Star," Reeve crooned. "For me, for Nate." Those velvet tones roughened to gravel. "Isn't it right to get what you want after waiting so long?"

"Yesss..."

"I want you to have that, Daze. Every dream, every fucking desire. We're going to grant them."

"I want to make your dreams come true too," I panted.

Their hands closed over their cocks, jerking as I lost myself in their taste. When they climaxed, it was eerily synchronized, as if a switch flipped, propelling them over the brink.

Nathan moved down my body, his cum spurting over my breasts and belly, each spray sending sweet, searing need through me.

I breathed in Reeve's woodsy scent, burying my face in his crotch, taking his cock as deep as I dared. He hissed words I didn't understand as his essence spurted onto my tongue. All I knew was the thick cock filling my mouth, the hot cum soaking my flesh, my body splayed out and bared to them both, my secrets revealed.

At their mercy. In their hands. Theirs.

I tried to swallow as Reeve came. He was hot and salty and everything I wanted. But, as with Nathan, it was too much. He withdrew, erupting in a stream of lust-fueled profanity when Nathan firmly gripped his cock, pointing it at my breasts, stroking him hard and fast through his release.

"That's so sexy," I panted. "I — oh Jesus."

"Take it, baby," Nathan gritted. "All over you, everywhere."

"Fuck, yes," Reeve hissed. "Soak her. Claim that sweet flesh."

The two men held me down, rubbing their cum into my skin as I writhed. Until it felt like they'd touched every part of me, indelibly coating me with their essence.

When the blunt head of Nathan's cock pressed against my entrance, I gripped his waist, seeking his eyes, but he didn't penetrate me. Steady pulses throbbed against me as he kept climaxing.

"More." I spread my legs wider, rubbing frantically against him. "Give me everything."

"Keep going," Reeve urged. "She's hungry for it."

Finally, Nathan groaned and collapsed on top of me. Kissing me softly, he pushed himself up onto his arms and smiled.

Overwhelmed, I smiled back and touched his face. A river of warmth ran down my cunt and between my cheeks. I flexed my thighs, straining toward Nathan, but he rocked back on his knees and lay down by my side.

As Nathan squeezed my breasts, Reeve pounced between my legs, pushing them apart. Finally, for the first time, his mouth descended on my pussy.

It seemed like I'd been waiting years for this. When he licked, I rose off the bed, electrified.

Nathan swore softly. "That's beautiful."

I gazed into his eyes, every swipe from Reeve sending sparks through my body.

"Why did you wait so long?" I panted. Reeve lifted his head, his sensual lips smeared with my juices.

"Sweet Star, I wanted to hold off until I could taste Nate dripping out of you."

"He wanted us to have a first together," Nathan murmured.

"Thank you," I breathed.

Then I cried out when Reeve lapped in earnest, his tongue hot and determined. He really was drinking Nathan's cum. My juices. Nathan crouched over me, massaging my breasts.

"Look at him," he hissed. "Look at what a slut you are for us."

"The two of you taste so good," Reeve purred. "All mixed together. All desire."

"Reeve..."

"We're going to make you come, Daisy. Together. Can you be a good girl and come one more time for us?"

I nodded jerkily.

"If it's too much, say so." Reeve spread me open, exposing my folds to the cool air. "But I want you to try. To trust."

"Okay..."

The men's eyes met. As if he could read Reeve's mind, Nathan let go of me and lay back on the bed, chuckling at my sounds of protest.

"Straddle Nate, sweet girl." Reeve's order penetrated the marrow of my bones. "You're ours now."

Sticky with both men's cum, I obeyed. They were right. I was a slut for them both. All I could think about was pleasure. Desire consumed me, immolating me, and I wanted more, more, more.

Kneeling above Nathan, I yielded to his fingers opening my cunt, his thumb caressing my clit, and the sudden, cool shock of gel between my cheeks.

My ass. Reeve was touching my ass, teasing my tight back hole, lubing the sensitive skin.

"Do you want us both, Daze?" Reeve's voice was silk. "Men, where you once had toys?"

"Yes," I gasped.

Every touch made my knees quake. I braced my weight on my

right arm, and Nathan swiftly supported me with a hand on my waist. My awareness narrowed to his big fingers sinking inside me, his thumb stroking my throbbing clit, Reeve's finger penetrating my ass. He eased back, then slowly, patiently filled me with more thickness.

"Unnnh," I groaned.

"I've got two fingers in your ass now, sweetheart," Reeve crooned. "You like that?"

"God, yes. Nathan?"

"Three," he growled.

"I'm so full..."

"It's hard, isn't it, Daisy? To have so much intensity and no place for it to go? Let it out on us. Come all over our hands, sweet flower. It's okay if you're overwhelmed. We'll take care of you."

I rocked back and forth, caught between them. Leaning forward, I sought Nathan's lips. He kissed me hungrily, and the overpowering lust almost frightened me. Nathan had never been so close, yet the boy I loved felt so far away.

"Reeve, help me," I gasped.

"Almost there, honey. We know how badly you need this." As he probed my fluttering ass, his free hand caressed my pussy, spreading the silky wetness. "Mmmm, that's right. Soak us both. Get us drenched."

Inexorably, Reeve eased the tip of his finger in to join Nathan's, filling my cunt until I gasped at the brew of discomfort and pleasure and intense satisfaction.

"Reeve!" I moaned. "Nathan..."

"Trust," they both whispered.

I was beyond full. They were calling me all kinds of names, sweet, dirty, loving, and cruel, and the sensations were too much, climbing and climbing and climbing, and they were so big and a little scary and God, I wanted it all.

I peaked and peaked. Gripping their fingers in my pussy and ass, I climaxed until the light that flared in the room made us all gasp.

Time stopped, then rushed in, as they carefully eased out of me and I collapsed into their arms.

There were no words. No sounds. Nothing, in the now-dark room as we held each other close, except the heat of our bodies and the thump of our hearts.

And in the air, a hiss of satisfaction.

10

Wait For the Sun

Nate

The House had a rooftop garden. I hadn't been up here in a while; I preferred to keep my feet on the ground. But Reeve came here often, and so did Blake. They liked to lie back on the lounge chairs, between the potted trees and trailing plants, and look up at the stars.

Now, Reeve and I sat side by side in the shadow of the tower.

After we'd showered, and I'd changed the sheets on my bed, we'd cuddled Daisy between us. She'd fallen asleep almost immediately, which made me smile. I knew how much insomnia she'd dealt with over the years.

Propping myself on one elbow, I'd studied her dark brows, her full lips, and the gentle slopes of her tits. The raised scar on her chin, the splotch of a birthmark on her shoulder — all the details I'd tried not to stare at during our porch swing talks.

Her damp hair was shorter, drying with kinks and waves. Hacked off because of the spell from Reeve's book, I knew.

I'd stroked the ends of her hair and hoped she'd forgive me for that too.

When Daisy rolled over, my eyes met Reeve's. We'd slunk out in silent accord, careful not to wake her, and made our way up here.

It was peaceful under the night sky. For once, I felt relaxed, and Reeve let out a contented sigh. Wearing only boxers, he seemed more at home in his body.

"Can I do this?" I asked, extending my arm above his shoulders.

To my surprise, he laughed. "Go ahead."

I put my arm around him. Reeve was sleek, but his shoulders felt strong and solid. He sighed and rested his head against the lounge chair. I stroked his soft, dark hair.

"That's nice, Nate." He closed his eyes.

My fingers tightened. I gave his hair a tug, and he grunted softly. "But not like when Daisy touches you."

"No," he agreed. "She's like a drug. Sometimes almost too intense; sometimes a safe harbor. I always crave more. But in just a few days—"

"How are you going to tell her?" I eased my grip on his hair, still in a state of disbelief that he was letting me touch him. "How are *we* going to tell her?"

"We'll find a way. We can't rush it — this is delicate. But we're close, Nate." His eyes opened, black as a bottomless pit. Flickers of green curled over the irises. "She's crossed another boundary. Now that she's been with both of us, it'll be so much easier for her to give in to her desire for Evan and Blake. Making her dreams come true will be the cherry on top."

"What about your 'relationship?'" I made air quotes, then wished I hadn't when a shadow passed over Reeve's face.

"It's real, brother. Whether I want it to be or not."

"You still love her."

"I can't stop it any more than I can stop breathing." He pressed his lips together, looking almost angry.

"What's wrong?"

"She — never mind. Everything's on track. And in a few days, everything we want will be ours. No boundaries. No barriers. No more imprisonment. We can have it all."

It was relaxing, running my fingers through Reeve's hair. I liked being able to give to him for once. Gradually, his cock tented his boxers. When he saw me looking, he gave me a slight, knowing smile.

"Not without her here," he warned. "Too dangerous."

"Because of the magic, or your feelings?"

A flush rose on his cheeks. Talking about feelings pushed a button for Reeve.

"Both," he muttered.

I looked up at the glittering night sky. Clear and cloudless, it was salted with stars. Inside the House, Blake was a warm spark, awake and working in the kitchen — his own safe harbor, the place he went to calm down. Evan burned hotter, tossing restlessly in bed, reaching for something nearby. When I felt a dull ache throughout my body, and a throb in my tattoo, I knew he was hitting the bottle.

"Ev's drinking too much," I said. "It worries me. He's always been a partier, but these days, he practically has a bottle attached to his hand."

"He has a lot of demons. You know that." Reeve leaned back, stretching his arms over his head, his dark eyes watchful. "If I hadn't found him that night in downtown L.A., he could have killed someone. His father, or an unlucky stranger."

"He's the one who's always on our case to forget our pasts."

"Because he struggles the most with his. Nate, fuck knows we all have our family problems, but none of us endured the abuse Ev's father subjected him to."

Right. The world-famous conductor who'd stop at nothing to mold his son into a musical prodigy. After months together, Ev had finally told us about the room Rowan locked him in as a child, bare except for a piano, denying him food until he performed to his satisfaction. The constant put-downs, the cruel, belittling comments. Remembering made me stiffen with anger.

Reeve put a reassuring hand on my shoulder. "Trust me, Daisy will help Evan in ways we can't. I don't know how, but I dreamed about it. She's what he needs."

I sighed, letting him massage my neck. I both wanted and didn't want to see Evan with Daisy. He wouldn't be worshipful or playful or loving; he'd be rough and greedy. Taking. It turned me on more than I cared to admit. At least the rest of us would balance him out.

Reeve continued as if he could read my thoughts. "After the Joining, Nate, all those demons will go away. We'll be able to fulfill our principles without sadness or struggle. Everything will be—"

"Fine," I finished. "Because we'll be the demons."

He met my gaze. I leaned toward him, though I didn't know what I meant to say or do.

A point of light grew warm behind us, coming closer. I knew without turning around that it was Blake.

He cleared his throat. "How is she?"

I turned, not meeting his eyes. "Sleeping."

He settled down next to me on an open lounge chair, graceful but cautious. "Did you enjoy yourself?"

I blew out a breath. "Yes."

Blake eyed my arm around Reeve. "Our Devil seems considerably more relaxed."

"Mm-hm." Reeve flashed a grin, but tension still ran between his shoulder blades. I felt it, along with the pulse of his blood. Blake was right; he was more relaxed, yet still vigilant.

And now that Blake had joined us, the space between us hummed with energy. I was aware of every inch of his body. Being with Daisy laid me bare, opening up all the wanting I'd buried.

I didn't dare think about what would happen after the Joining. Whether our feelings would be more or less real. Whether we'd be humans or monsters.

Blake shifted next to me, and I wished that he'd put a shirt on. Those tattoos writhed and beckoned to me. There was a time during that hot-as-hell L.A. summer three years ago that I'd licked every one of them. I thought of Daisy doing the same, her tongue flickering eagerly over his lean chest and arm, and instantly regretted it because a bolt of desire shot through me.

When I pictured her pinned between us while I ravished her from behind, taking her soft pussy — no, her ass — and touching Blake everywhere I could reach...

"Fuck," I muttered.

"You okay, Nate?" Blake looked at me with those summer-blue eyes.

I turned to stare up at the stars. "I'm great."

Reeve reached over me to put a hand on Blake's leg. He gave it a squeeze through his loose olive-green sweatpants, and Blake let out a strained laugh. "Aren't you affectionate tonight."

Reeve chuckled. "Guess Daisy's a bad influence."

"Or a good one." Blake stretched, careful not to touch me. He was hard. We were all fucking hard, and we couldn't do a thing about it. Not without Daisy here to receive and preserve the magic. One misstep, and everything would be lost. "She's powerful, man. When the two of you were with her — I felt everything."

"I'm sorry." The words burst from my mouth. I didn't even know what I was apologizing for. Pushing him away this past year? Fighting the force that dwelled within us? Trying to separate Daisy from my brothers?

"Don't be." Blake's gaze was compassionate, which was the last thing I deserved. "It was heaven and hell, and I don't resent you for a fucking minute." Our eyes held. He broke the contact first. "She'll be with all of us soon. Our Star."

"And she'll belong to the serpent," Reeve said quietly.

"She already does, brother." Blake leaned back, fingers laced behind his head.

The three of us watched the sky until it turned red with dawn.

11

When the Ground Cracks

Daisy

I woke cocooned in heat. My cheek rested on a warm chest, and a hard body spooned me from behind. When my stomach growled, I lifted my head.

Nathan smiled up at me, bathed in a shaft of sunlight, his face sweet and open. His brown hair was rumpled, and his cheek showed creases from the pillow.

"That's how you used to smile." I smoothed his hair off his forehead, surprised when his grin faded. "No, don't put it away. I love your smile."

"Oh, yeah?" He raised his eyebrows.

"It's like a bird I could never catch. Here and gone so quickly."

He laughed and pulled me down for a kiss. "Well, you obviously caught me. How about some breakfast? I bet you worked up an appetite."

"Sounds amazing."

Behind me, Reeve ran his hand over my hip. I lay back in his arms as Nathan climbed naked out of bed.

Last night had really happened. It was no dream.

In the bright morning sunshine, I could fully appreciate Nathan's body. All that masculine bulk, the changes that had made me uneasy a few weeks ago, now roused something deep and primal, feminine and carnal, inside me. In his presence, I felt delicate, girlish, the sweet flower that Reeve had named me.

Impulsively, I turned to bury my face in Reeve's neck. "Thank you," I whispered. "Being with you both — it meant so much to me."

His arms tightened around me. "Anything for you, Daze."

"*Anything?*" I teased.

He loosened his hold and drew his thumbs over my cheeks. "You know I mean it. Don't worry, I enjoyed myself too."

Nathan opened the door, peered into the hallway, and chuckled. "Blake came through."

Bending, he lifted three wooden trays. Balancing them in his arms, he carried them easily to the bed. They were loaded with cups of steaming coffee, plates piled high with French toast, goblets of cut fruit that glistened like jewels, and crystal bowls of whipped cream that reminded me of captured clouds.

The fragrance of the coffee swirled around us as Nathan set the trays on the bed, earthy and deep, touched with cherries and chocolate. I could already tell it would be the best coffee I'd ever drunk.

"He knows." I pointed to the three trays.

Nathan grinned. "Blake? Well, yeah. There aren't any secrets in this House."

Reeve propped himself up on the pillows. His dimple showed, but violet circles shaded his eyes.

Settling in bed, Nathan brought his tray to his lap. "If anyone told him, baby, it was you. Making enough noise last night to raise the dead."

I smacked his arm. "I was not that loud."

Nathan speared an enormous piece of French toast and popped it into his mouth. "You have to try this, Daisy." He waved another bite of French toast on his fork as Reeve lifted his cup of coffee and sipped it meditatively. "Blake infuses it with orange and rum, and it's fucking amazing."

"How indulgent. You know I'm not a breakfast person. Coffee, yes." I lifted my mug.

A memory came to me of drinking cardamom-flavored coffee in the Davises' kitchen the morning after a sleepover, while Sasha tried to tempt me with the pancake recipe she was tweaking. I'd drunk the coffee as slowly as possible, hoping Nathan would make an appearance in the ratty old sweatpants I loved.

I felt a pang, thinking of Sasha. I'd have to work things out with her — soon.

"Come on. Just try it." Nathan danced the bite of puffy bread in front of my mouth. "Open up, little birdie..."

"Nathan!" I grabbed his hand, laughing. "Okay, I will." When I tried to snap at the toast, he zoomed it from side to side, evading me. "I'm going to kill you. Just give me that toast."

Reeve steadied the trays to keep them from falling as I tussled with Nathan. Finally, he relented and fed me the French toast.

"Oh." My eyes fluttered closed. It was the platonic ideal of French toast — everything a fluffy, custardy slab of bread should be. The orange essence took me deep into a sun-soaked grove. The rum, mellow and decadent, danced over my tongue. There was a hint of burnt caramel. I snuggled between the two men, letting Nathan feed me while we joked back and forth.

As I waved Nathan away so I could drink my coffee — which was, in fact, the best I'd ever had — I caught Reeve's eye.

His body was relaxed, his arm draped around my shoulders. But he was too much the detached observer. He'd been quiet this morning, and the shadows under his eyes were more pronounced than ever.

"Are you okay?" I touched his face.

He closed his fingers around mine. "Of course. Busy week, that's all."

"With what?"

Reeve and Nathan exchanged glances.

"This and that," Reeve said smoothly.

"Tell me more. You both look exhausted. Did you sleep at all?"

"Sit back, Daze. Nate's right. We need to give you the full breakfast experience." His hand moved to the back of my neck. "Now close your eyes and open your mouth."

"Hold on."

Reeve wagged his finger. "Your mouth is open, but your eyes aren't closed."

"Shake your finger at me again and I'll bite it," I warned. "What's going on with the chancellor?"

Again, the men exchanged looks.

Nathan squeezed my knee. "Daisy, don't bring that guy in here. We're having a very nice morning."

I turned to Reeve, who caressed my cheek. "Pleasure now, business later, sweet flower."

I sat up straight, jostling the dishes on my breakfast tray. "He and Tara are conspiring against you. He knows about the collar."

Reeve's face darkened. "You saw her?"

"She was working at the party. I heard her talking with Chancellor Weston in his wine cellar. They have something going on, but I think she's playing him. Reeve, I saw her true face."

Both men's eyes widened. "How?" Reeve asked quietly.

I glanced at the pile of my black server's clothes by Nathan's desk, where the amulet was hidden in my pants pocket.

"I just did." I toyed with a fork. "She implied that you — never mind."

"Tara has no power of her own," Reeve said softly. "Neither does Weston. They're all bark and no bite."

I stared into the depths of my coffee cup. It was empty, the swirl of earthy brown at the bottom giving me no answers. Reeve took my cup and handed me his, still half-full.

"Daisy, come on. You're powerful." Nathan tickled me under the chin, trying to get me to smile. "You threw Tara out of the woods. You dismissed the Chancellor from his own backyard. If anyone messes with you, we've got your back, but more than that, you've got your own back."

I stared at their faces. On one side of me, the man I'd tried to win over with a love spell. On the other, the man I may have won.

"And yours." I gulped Reeve's coffee and reached for the goblet of exquisitely cut oranges, kiwi, and strawberries. "If the Chancellor gets in your way and you need me to take care of him, I will. I can send him away. Banish him from campus. Maybe turn him into a toad..." Giddiness surged at the memory of last night's magic.

Reeve's grin creased his dark eyes. "Protect yourself first, Daze. Always. Now let's relax and enjoy our breakfast. Are you going to do what I say?"

His fingertip traced the outline of my lips.

"But Tara," I blurted. "She said you threw her away. She's desperate and angry. That's not a good combination."

Nathan's eyes narrowed. Reeve's finger halted, then drew a slow line down my jaw. "She won't hurt you again. I swear it."

"No," I said softly. "Because she's afraid of me."

"Course she is," Nathan said, returning to cheerfulness. "I'm afraid of you too. You even make me scream in the night."

Reeve laughed.

I wanted to push, to find out exactly what was going on. To cut the tightening knot of intrigue that bound us ever closer. But it was so surprising and sweet to see Nathan happy, so new to be ensconced between him and Reeve. The beautiful breakfast beamed at us from the trays.

Nathan was right. We were having a very nice morning — a fantastic morning. I should savor every moment.

"All right, enough about that." My voice turned teasing. "I'm ready to have the full breakfast experience."

I closed my eyes and opened my mouth. When nothing happened, I stuck out my tongue for extra encouragement. Swiftly, two cold dollops painted my cheeks.

"Reeve, you jerk!" My eyes popped open. "Nathan? Who did that?"

Both men roared with laughter.

"You really are no good at waiting, Daze." Reeve's dimple flashed. "I didn't say anything about tongue."

Then he scooped up the cream from my cheeks, feeding it to me with his fingers. And between the sweet vanilla scent and the French toast from Nathan and the fragrant coffee and the soft sheets and both men...the trays being put aside, the kisses, the caresses...I let it all go. For now.

Side by side, Nathan and I took our seats in the back of the lecture hall for Geology of National Parks. The first day of classes, we'd crackled and snapped with tension. Today, we held hands.

Nap Boy slumbered in his usual seat, his head pillowed on his backpack. When Nathan and I settled in, he cracked an eye open.

"Guess you're friends now," he slurred. "Just don't keep me awake, 'kay?" He buried his head in his backpack with a snore.

The professor turned on his mic and smiled, practically rubbing his hands together. "Before we get into our slides, let's talk about last night's earthquake. The epicenter was at our very own Chancellor's house. As you can imagine, the geology department's pretty worked up." There was a smattering of polite laughter. "For decades we've tried to figure out how to predict an earthquake, especially the ones that can really do damage. But scientists finally know how big earthquakes start: with a series of smaller ones."

"So is a big one coming? Should we be prepared?" a girl asked.

"C'mon, it's California," Nap Boy mumbled. "Earthquakes happen. We're in the middle of fire season. The forests are fucking burning. Someday, this whole state's gonna break off from the rest of the country and fall into the ocean."

"Look at you, shaking up Pacific Crest," Nathan leaned over to whisper in my ear. He squeezed my right hand as the lecture began.

After class, we walked together to the athletic center.

"I know this isn't a dream," I said, swinging his hand. "But I keep wanting to pinch myself."

"This is real, baby." He scooped me up to kiss me. When he set me down, I was breathless.

"I can't believe you picked me up like that. One-handed? Seriously, Nathan?"

"Guess I just want to sweep you off your feet."

I laughed, blushing. When we reached the entrance to the field, I wrapped my arms around his neck and pressed my lips to his. "See you later today?"

He nodded, but his eyes went vague. "I'll call you. Be careful, Daisy. Watch your back." He gave me one last kiss and a squeeze around the waist, then jogged into the athletic center.

Once he was gone, I looked around the emerald lawns and white stucco buildings. Sprinklers played over the grass, wetting it with a glistening sheen. Though I'd slept in the arms of two men last night, I suddenly felt alone. Away from Reeve and Nathan's heady presences, the questions pressed in.

My fingers hovered over my phone, ready to text Michelle and Amy to meet up for lunch. But if I did, I'd just be pushing away everything that crowded my mind.

In the end, my feet took me to Greer Hill. I'd stopped at Lee Tower to change, but I still wore the amulet, rubbing it nervously as I climbed the path. With every step toward the woods, I remembered the clutch of the evil collar around my throat, Tara's grip on my hand.

At least the collar was safely locked away in the House now.

When I reached the forest's edge, I hesitated. I wanted to reclaim this space, but was it even mine to claim?

To my relief, the trees opened, and I felt them sigh as I passed.

The pleasure of entering a place so welcoming washed over me. I inhaled the greenness of the leaves and ferns, the earthiness of the soil underfoot. Putting my hand on the rough bark of a tree, I smiled.

Reeve had called me a city girl. But as much as I loved New York's concrete landscape, there was a profound happiness to being in the wild.

The path seemed more overgrown, the forest floor more lush. But I found my circle of sticks, replacing the ones that had strayed, and dropped to my knees. Closing my eyes, I breathed in and out.

This was my place. Not Tara's, not anyone else's. Mine.

I didn't cast any spells. I rifled through Reeve's mother's tarot deck for reassurance, but I didn't pull a card. I simply let the forest surround me. Eventually, I leaned back until I sprawled on the ground, staring at the canopy of leaves that made patterns against the sky.

"Thank you," I whispered. "For having me back."

Dark coils curled overhead, obscuring my vision.

Do you wish to be worthy? The voice that hissed in my ear was the rush of a waterfall, the rustle of trees, the whisper of flesh on flesh. A voice older than time.

Yes! Every cell in my body wanted to shout. But I hesitated.

"What exactly does worthiness involve?"

Laughter rippled through the earth like the rumble of an avalanche, the susurrus of the ocean.

So cautious, bright one. So full of doubt. Come back tonight, when you've shed those earthly cares.

The inky spirals vanished, and the tranquil afternoon sun filtered through the leaves.

I sat up and rubbed my temples. Why tonight?

And when had I become so comfortable with a disembodied voice hissing at me?

A buzz came from my tote bag. I pulled out my phone to find a message from Sasha. Below the picture of colorful lanterns that she'd texted me this morning, which I'd failed to respond to because

I'd been naked between her brother and Reeve, was a terse command:

Call me. Now.

I dragged my feet as I trudged back to Lee Tower. I needed to tell Sasha the truth eventually, but did it have to be today?

As I took the elevator to the ninth floor, I had a sinking feeling. It was close to midnight in Morocco. My morning-lark friend, up at the crack of dawn to cook and bake, wouldn't normally be awake.

In the privacy of my room, I dropped my bag on my desk, lit a candle, and called her.

"It's about time." She sounded farther away than she ever had.

I collapsed onto my nest of pillows. "Hey, no word of the day?"

She exhaled, and suddenly she sounded much nearer, as if she were on the bed with me. "Daisy, did something happen between you and my brother?"

A horn honked outside my window, followed by a chorus of yells. I hugged a pillow to my chest.

"Yes."

"YES? Goddammit. I knew it! He called me today. He never fucking calls! He was being all weird, like, 'I just called to see how you're doing,' and it was so awkward, and I finally mentioned you, all ignorant and breezy, like 'Daisy's settling in and she seems to be so much happier, and I hear she's even dating one of your friends,' and he got really, really quiet. Then he said, 'Yeah, she told me to call you,' and he tried to change the subject in a painfully obvious, clumsy way. When I asked him straight up, he got mad."

Right. I had told Nathan to call Sasha, the day he helped me steal Reeve's books.

Just do one thing for me, okay? Call Sasha and be her big brother, even if you think she doesn't want that. You need each other.

"What the hell?" Sasha burst out. "What's going on? No matter how bad things are, Nathan never gets mad."

"He does now."

She sucked in a breath. "What happened between you? What? What?"

"A thing."

"What thing? More than kissing. If you'd just kissed, you'd say you kissed and that would be it." She sounded frantic. I squeezed my eyes shut. "One day, you're telling me that everything feels so real with Reeve. The next day, there's...this. Daisy, did you fuck my brother?"

It was so ugly, the way she spat it out.

"No."

"Then what?"

"Sasha, I'm not going to tell you. It's between us."

"Us," she repeated, her voice dripping with contempt. "Us is you and me, Daisy, not you and him!"

I put my head between my knees. "Why are you so angry? I still love you. You're still my Sasha. This doesn't have to change anything."

It was exactly what Reeve had told me. And if I was being honest with myself, I hadn't believed him.

"Oh, really? You really think it won't change anything between us?"

"Sasha, you're six thousand miles away, and I don't—"

"Dammit, this is *Nathan* we're talking about," Sasha said, steamrolling over me. "It's not just that he's my brother. He's so *boring*. So middle-of-the-road. He's not that smart; he has zero aspirations. There's nothing special about him. But you—"

"Sasha, stop."

"Is this, like, you're unsure about yourself because you're not this flute star anymore and so you're aiming for the middle? You're going for total mediocrity?"

My stomach lurched at the pain of her words. Sasha couldn't mean to be this cruel; she just couldn't. Instinct drove me to defend Nathan instead of myself.

"Don't you ever talk about him like that." The words roared through my small dorm room. "How well do you even know him?"

"He's my BROTHER!" Sasha sounded shocked that I was raising my voice.

"That doesn't mean you have any idea who he is," I snapped.

"Well, what happened to Reeve, the one who you were so hot for?" Sasha demanded, changing course. "You were full of heart-eyes for him, what, like three days ago?"

I closed my eyes, a lump growing in my throat. "He was there."

"...*Oh.*" Her voice dropped an octave.

"You said a sandbox with two slides and a jungle gym," I said desperately, grasping at straws. "When I got here, you said this was a giant playground that I should conquer."

"Excluding my relatives! Aren't there about fifteen thousand guys at your school? Why Nathan? Are you trying to hurt me?" Her voice frayed and cracked.

"Never," I said quietly. "I like him, Sasha. I've liked him for years. And now—"

"Now you're hooking up? You're having threesomes? You're *fuck buddies?* Daisy, I know you and I know my brother. Neither of you are casual sex people. You are intense as hell, and he would never lay a hand on someone he couldn't imagine a nice, stable, conventional future with. We're talking ring on the finger, married with two kids, all the way."

My head was beginning to ache with the effort of battering against her anger. "I think you guys have gotten really out of touch," I said between my teeth.

"Promise me nothing will happen between you ever again."

I threw my pillow across the bed. "I can't make that promise."

"Fuck, Daisy! Do you not care about me at all?" Her voice broke, and I could feel her shame through the phone. Sasha hated crying.

"Don't do this, Sasha. Don't make it either-or."

"How can I not? And Reeve? Are you still seeing him too?"

I pressed my forehead to my knees. "Yes. Yes, I am."

"Of all the people," she whispered. "I just — I can't do this right now. You can't have everything, okay? You absolutely fucking cannot."

"Are you *slut-shaming* me?" I broke in furiously. "How dare you."

Her voice dropped, as if my words had gotten through, but not far enough. "I'm friend-shaming you, because you're putting me last. Call me when you've made a choice, when you stop being selfish, when you have your *shit* together, Daisy. Not before."

She hung up.

"When?" I yelled at the dead phone. "When is that going to happen? In twenty years? Are you only friends with people who have their shit together? People who know exactly what they want, and don't take more than you think they should?"

The room seemed to close in on me. When my racing heart slowed, I called her back. But her phone went to voicemail.

12

I'm a Lot Like You Were

Daisy

Gripping my flute case, I approached the Pacific Crest music building.

It looked like every other building on campus: a broad white stucco structure featuring arches and a red Spanish-tile roof. But I'd avoided it since I arrived at Pacific Crest. My heart beat faster as I walked inside, and a trickle of sweat slid down my neck.

I'd tried calling Reeve after Sasha hung up on me. Then Blake. If I'd had Nathan's number, or even Evan's, I would have called them too. But no one answered.

After pacing my room, I'd finally turned to the one friend — the lover, the faithful partner — who had never let me down. No, I was the one who'd left.

"I'm sorry," I whispered, cradling my flute case to my chest.

I held tight to the banister as I climbed the stairs of the music building. On the second floor, practice rooms lined the hallway: soundproofed cubes with doors, furnished with a piano and a music stand.

At the end of the hall, a crowd pressed against the last door on the right. More people hurried up the staircase, edging past me to join the onlookers.

As I approached, clutching my flute, a guy gave me a funny look, and I sighed inwardly. At Siderio, no one would give side-eye to someone hugging their instrument.

"What's happening?" I pointed to the knot of people pushing against the door.

"Evan Hayes," he replied in hushed tones. "That's what's happening. He almost never comes here anymore because of the crowds. Those lucky bastards up front?" He pointed to the door. "They're getting high just from listening."

I eyed the door. "That's *my* practice room."

"Yours? I've never seen you here before."

I shook my head. "Not here. My old school in New York had the same layout. Second floor, sixth room on the right — that's what I always used. The building at Siderio had more concrete, but—"

"You went to Siderio? Damn, that's legit. What are you doing *here?*" He looked down at my flute case.

Right then, the door opened, and the crowd drew back.

Evan's broad frame filled the doorway. His pale jade eyes swung over the crowd and locked unerringly on me. He crooked his finger.

"Are you kidding me?" I muttered.

But my breath came faster. Twenty feet separated us, yet electricity jolted my body. A trail of sparks seemed to part the crowd, melting away the impasse.

I followed the path, walking between people in silence until I reached the practice room and Evan pulled me inside.

The door clicked closed, and as we silently stared at each other, I could feel tension rising in the space between us.

I hadn't seen Evan since he'd waylaid me on campus over a week ago, trying to seduce me into being selfish. Into forgetting my deal with Nathan and pursuing what I wanted.

He gave me his slight smile. Sun-bleached hair brushed his

cheekbones. He folded his arms across his chest, seeming to take up most of the space in the small room.

"So you captured Reeve's heart." He sounded amused. "I didn't think he had one left. But something went wrong, didn't it, Daisy? You wouldn't be here otherwise."

"I don't want to talk about it right now," I muttered.

"Is it those loyalties, pet? Those pesky obligations? Putting other people's needs above your own?"

"Evan, I'm confused. Okay?" I met his eyes, shivering when he curled a finger under my chin. "I don't know the right thing to do right now."

"What if it's not about what's right?" he interrupted. "Only what feels good. That much you know, baby girl. Your body will never lie."

"I don't know the right thing to do right now," I repeated shakily, cutting him off, "except to play."

"Fair enough." Evan gave my jaw a final caress and nodded to my flute case. "Then let's play."

I blinked. "I haven't touched my flute in months."

"So?"

"I'm rusty. My hand..." I glanced down at it. "I won't sound good. I didn't expect to play with anyone else tonight, least of all you."

"You came," he said calmly. "You're obviously ready."

"I don't have sheet music."

He smiled patiently. "We don't need it."

My eyes darted. "All right," I conceded. "But I should take it easy. I don't even know if I can play a scale."

"Do you want to take it easy, Daisy? Is that the kind of girl you are? Or do you want me to help you clear up all this bullshit and get to the heart of your purpose?"

Evan's voice deepened to a growl. I'd never heard him sound so intent.

Slowly, I nodded. I didn't want easy. I wanted to plunge in, splash around in the waters I'd been missing for so long.

"Sit." He patted the piano bench.

I sat beside him on the bench. Heat pulsed from his body. Though I squeezed my thighs together, our legs brushed.

"Just breathe, baby girl." Presumably, he meant to breathe calmly. Deeply. To chill out. My breathing was anything but calm. "I know what you're feeling, trust me. Can I see your hand?"

I hesitated, then held it out to him. "Please be careful."

"I will." He took my left hand in his. Slowly, he stroked my palm, the inside of my wrist. My breath caught.

He looked up, his pale green eyes concerned. "Does that hurt?"

"A little."

"Let's see what we can do about that." Watching me intently, he ran his fingertips over my hand and the soft skin on the inside of my arm. As minutes passed, the pain seeped away.

Oh God. Evan's eyes were shifting, changing, not lazy flickers of brilliant green, but stormy lightning. Though he eased my discomfort, there was a beast inside, waiting to get out.

I inhaled sharply. "It doesn't hurt anymore."

"Good." He didn't take his eyes off me. "Let's play."

As if this were a dream, I stood and opened my flute case, fitted the joints together, and lifted the flute to my lips. All my worries about being clumsy, stiff, and out of practice dissipated until they were gone. When Evan struck the keys, my notes rose and twined with his.

And the music washed us away.

Sweet holy everything, he was good. I'd thought him arrogant, chasing the spotlight. But he was one of those players who wasn't only a gifted soloist; he was such a good accompanist that he elevated whoever he was playing with. His playing was gorgeous, subtle. Not the overwhelming heavenly light from the concert hall, but an experience that was absolutely intimate, as if he knew me from the inside out. He filled my mind, my body, and lifted me up.

I lost all sense of time beyond the beat and tempo. I didn't notice my wrist, the room, anything except the music spiraling around us, speaking its own language.

Then it was over.

And God, I wanted more.

I lowered my flute, and immediately, awareness rushed back in: the gray soundproofed walls of the practice room, the silver wand in my hands. My chest rose and fell with a mix of adrenaline and longing, never wanting this feeling to end.

"Thank you," I said. "So much."

"Hey," Evan said softly, his lips crooked in a smile. "That was just a warmup, right? Let's keep playing." He unbuttoned his shirt.

My response caught in my throat as he shrugged off the pale blue button-down, leaving him in a white tank top. It wasn't such an unusual thing to do. Playing worked up a sweat. I was hot too.

As he hung his shirt on the hook over the door, blocking the small window, I tried not to stare at his broad shoulders, the swells of his muscles, the soft blond hair glinting on his arms... the serpent twisting on his inner biceps.

"It is getting pretty warm in here." I slipped off my black cardigan and draped it over a chair. Evan's eyes roved openly over my clingy red blouse. "Let's go on."

He grinned. "Here's something I wrote. You'll pick it up."

Notes bloomed under his fingers, and I followed. As we played, I was being led down a twisting, turning path, deeper and deeper into the heart of something I couldn't see, but dammit, I would go wherever he took me. The synergy, the lightning-fast connection — it was like we could read each other's minds. I knew where he wanted to take an idea, and he backed me up without missing a beat.

I had never experienced this kind of chemistry when playing with someone else. It was charmed. Eerie.

The tempo picked up, faster and faster, notes flying into the air, until Evan got up from the piano, shoved the bench in, and kissed me.

"Oh — oh God." I gasped between kisses. My right hand still clutched my flute; my left hand slid into his hair as he backed me against the wall of the practice room. Our mouths on each other were hot and hungry and everything was happening so fast. His tongue burned, demanding, his lips closing hard on mine. We sucked and bit and panted. I kissed all over his face and cried out when he took the vulnerable skin of my neck into his mouth. His hands ran down my thin blouse, closing over my breasts, and I thrust them into his palms with a moan.

The energy was unbelievable. I knew the eroticism of being with Reeve, the intensity of Nathan, the excitement of the touches I'd shared with Blake. Evan was another level altogether. Connected, we were lit up and blazing like an overcharged circuit. I couldn't catch my breath, couldn't control my reactions when he pushed up my blouse and captured my breasts in his huge paws.

Where did this connection come from? Was it because we had music in common?

My head spun as he pinched my nipples, crushing the small buds urgently, pushing me toward the edge. It hurt. It was unbelievably exciting. I ran my hand all over his bulky shoulders and back, digging in my nails, my flute pressed between us as I kissed him frantically. My core tightened, need gathering in an insistent coil.

No. It wasn't possible. I was going to come. He hadn't even touched me below the waist.

"Evan," I gasped.

Sensations rushed over me. My skin burned. I couldn't take the anticipation, it was almost too much, it was everything I wanted doubled and tripled.

"Do it, Daisy," he ordered. "Fucking come right now. Take what you want. It's what we do."

He bent and sucked my nipple into his mouth.

I threw my head back as an orgasm overtook me. Evan growled, the sound of a pure beast. When he lifted my leg and ground the ridge of his cock against my jeans, I pulled him close, electrified.

Jesus, he was coming too. He had none of Reeve's restraint. His curses and animal noises drowned out my moans, and his big body covered mine, wracked with pleasure as he came.

Wrapped tight in his arms, I shivered with the aftershocks of climax. His cock was still hard, and God, I couldn't think about anything else right now. He captured my lips with his again, the kiss dominating this time, for his pleasure. Except that his pleasure was my pleasure, and when his hot tongue pushed into my mouth, a fresh wave of need washed over me.

He grunted with approval. And his long thrusts and groans... he couldn't be, but he was coming again already.

"Oh, *yeah,*" he whispered. "Why didn't we do this sooner? Take your clothes off, pet. I've been dying to see you naked. Our bodies together, yours and mine."

The words brought back a memory. That first night, the night of The Crush, when I'd met all the men — Evan had grabbed me and hissed, *Let's keep it our little secret for now. Yours and mine.*

Pushing on his chest, I broke the embrace.

"Evan, I — I — I can't right now."

Jesus, his eyes. "Who gives a fuck about *can't?* Not you, Daisy. Not me. That doesn't apply to us."

I bent over, panting for breath, my hair hanging around my face. My body throbbed, every inch pulled toward him like a magnet, and I backed against the wall for refuge. Adjusting my blouse, I pulled it down over my breasts.

"Things are complicated right now. I don't want to pull you into that."

He came close, heedless of his dark, cum-soaked pants. Arousal poured from every pore. The air in the practice room was thick with sex.

"It doesn't have to be complicated." One big hand covered my cheek, blazing on my skin. "I know you're with Reeve. I know about Nathan."

I clutched his arm, trying to get a grip on myself. "How much did they tell you?"

"We know everything about each other. We're as close as four people can be." He leaned in to whisper. "I knew before I touched you, before Greer Hill, how soft your skin is. How sweet you taste.

How you blush all the way down your chest when you're turned on. How sensitive your nipples are, though I know you've never come just from Reeve or Nate touching them. How much you enjoy having your ass played with, because even though you look innocent, you're a dirty, dirty girl who wants us to be more and more depraved with you. And I'm telling you, Daisy, this is very simple. You can have everything you want. And so can we."

My wrist throbbed, sudden pain lancing up my arm. I'd played too long, pushed too hard. The magic of the practice room had worn off.

"Evan, not now. I need time to think."

Stepping past him, I snatched tissues from a box on the piano and quickly cleaned up. I took my flute apart and put it in its case. I was prickling, electric, needing to grab onto something to ground the sparks. Though I couldn't stay still, Evan stood unmoving, two feet away in the confines of the practice room.

"Greer Hill will be beautiful tonight," he remarked, his face eerily calm under his shaggy hair. "Good time for a walk."

The comment didn't make sense, but I nodded mechanically, backing away. "I'll keep that in mind."

"You don't know everything, Daisy," he called after me. "Reeve's been keeping things from you."

I hurried out, and the door banged shut behind me.

13

Nowhere to Run

Daisy

My wrist hurt. It hurt like hell.

For a brief window of time, Evan had made it feel better. He'd given me a glimpse of another world. Then reality kicked in — pain.

In the dark sky, red-tinged clouds hung their bellies low over the horizon. When I checked my watch, nearly three hours had passed since I entered the music building, though it felt like only minutes.

Too keyed-up to think straight, I fled to Lee Tower to change my clothes. Caving, I opened the bottle of painkillers Reeve had brought when I had my period and swallowed two.

But Advil wouldn't get to the root of my problems. The men had unlocked me. After being numb for months, I felt everything, and it was too much.

In desperation, I combed the campus library for some book, some answer, some fucking solution that would give me back a sense of control. I ignored dinner. I didn't call the men, and they didn't call me. I couldn't get my duet with Evan out of my head. The music twisted around me, calling.

Greer Hill will be beautiful tonight, Evan had said. And the serpent had hissed its own invitation:

Come back tonight, when you've shed those earthly cares.

I waited until the waxing moon rose high in the red-stained heavens. Shortly before midnight, my amulet hanging around my neck, I walked to the hill.

"Sorry, miss." A burly man in a security uniform, looking strangely familiar, blocked my way at the head of the trail. "Greer Hill's closed."

"Closed?"

"Too many stories of weird things happening here. Bad for student safety. Bad for the university rep."

I clenched my right fist. "It's perfectly safe."

The man looked me over, a mean smile on his face. "Haven't I seen you before? Last time we met, you were trying to access Reeve McClellan's house unlawfully."

Right. This was the guard who'd turned me away from the House the night of the Crush.

I blew out a breath. "Are you working for Chancellor Weston now? Because Reeve McClellan wouldn't want this hill to be blocked."

He laughed. "I'm not at liberty to disclose my employer. Just like you aren't at liberty to be here. Now shoo, before I call the cops."

I widened my eyes. "Listen, can I just take a quick look—"

The guard took out his phone. "I'm dialing now. I'll tell them you're a troublemaker."

Huffing out a breath, I stomped away, circling the base of the hill and keeping to the shadows. A guard patrolled the east side too, as well as the north.

When I reached the west side of the hill, it was empty. It was also covered with thick, dry brush, making it completely inaccessible. There was no path.

Who had closed the hill?

I heard Chancellor Weston in the backyard. *I own you. Your time is up.*

Did he know what Greer Hill was? Or simply that it mattered to Reeve, who'd paid him off?

What did the hill mean to the men?

Taking a deep breath, I pushed into the thicket of brush.

Using the flashlight on my phone, I worked my way up, fighting branches and thorns. After ten minutes, I was scratched and exhausted and had made almost no headway.

Something I'd said to Reeve, the night of Evan's concert, came back: *I'm not used to receiving.*

Get used to it, he'd said.

But I wasn't. I pursued, I reached, I strove. It was what I did.

Caught in spiky branches, I closed my eyes. I wanted to extend my thoughts to the woods, far above me on the hill, but instead I simply opened my mind and waited.

I'm here, I thought. *I'm ready.*

Scales slithered across my closed eyelids, but the overgrown brush stayed as stubbornly impenetrable as before.

I'll do whatever you want, I thought.

The branches shivered, though there was no wind.

I'm yours.

The dry, bristly brush slumped before me, opening a tunnel.

Who had I just promised myself to? The hill? The serpent, the men?

Right now, it didn't matter. All that mattered was a way forward.

Tucking my hand against my chest to keep it free of the branches, I climbed up the hill. At any moment, the brush might collapse, closing in on me. If it did, I'd be trapped. I had my phone, but I was already halfway up the slope, and anyone I called for a rescue would have to hack through the brush.

I kept my thoughts fixed, like an incantation.

I'm here.

I'm ready.

I'll do what you want.

I'm yours.

And beneath that, pounding like a drumbeat: *Heal me.*

The branches remained arched: tense and quivering overhead, slouching underfoot. The air was stuffy and close, underscored by the sharp, herbal scent of dried stems and leaves. I picked my way up the hill, coughing.

With every step, I prayed that the woods would welcome me. I had no supplies or offerings, not even a candle. But my flute weighed down my tote bag, and maybe if I laid it at the serpent's feet, it would understand.

Suddenly, a silvery light beamed through the tunnel, and fresh, sweet night air met my face.

I stumbled out of the brush and collapsed on the grass, gulping in deep breaths. I lay yards away from the entrance to the woods.

"Thank you," I whispered.

Getting to my feet, I looked around for guards or interlopers, but I was alone on Greer Hill.

Yet the closer I got to the woods, the more a *feeling* was present. The air was...alive. It grew thicker and heavier with each step. It pushed me away from the woods, making my head want to turn and my feet point in the other direction.

"Not me," I pleaded. "That's for everyone else. I belong here."

My uncertainty grew. Who was I, to think I was special? Tara had taunted me about that. Maybe she was right. Maybe the woods were done with me.

The serpent's words came back: *So cautious, bright one. So full of doubt.*

I straightened. "I'm not cautious anymore. I want it all. Music... the men...I want everything."

The woods stirred, and I took a step closer.

The air carried a strong scent, earthy and mossy, like the dampness after a storm. A darkening fog surrounded the woods, obscuring them with billows of smoky coils.

Holding up my phone to light the way, I walked into the fog until it was impossible to see any farther. Inky, oily, and jet-black, the air swallowed the narrow beam of light. I gave a final jerk forward and reached out my hand.

My palm brushed rough bark. I instantly snatched it away. That trunk was hot. Burning.

Everything about this situation said *get away*. Which made me all the more determined to get in.

Out of sheer instinct, I pulled the amulet from around my neck with my left hand and pressed it hard against the tree.

With a whoosh, I was sucked into the woods.

It happened so fast, it stole my breath. I rolled on the ground, coming to a halt against some gnarled roots. The fall jammed my wrist, and I stifled a cry.

The flashlight from my phone bobbed on the trees. These were my woods. Weren't they? The place I felt safest, serpent or no serpent. But right now, the forest didn't feel like mine. It belonged to somebody else.

Stiffly, I got to my feet and settled the amulet around my neck. As I headed down the path, alert to my surroundings, sounds reached me — low, rasping, and rumbling. I killed my flashlight and focused intently.

The noises sharpened to gravel rubbing, tongues hissing. A language I'd never heard.

Except from Reeve's lips.

I shivered, but heat chased the goosebumps on my skin.

Somehow, I made my way forward in the dark. As I got deeper into the woods, flickering lights illuminated the trees ahead.

Slowing my pace, I trod carefully until I reached a clearing.

Tallow candles marked the edges of a huge circle. The flames threw guttering flashes over four figures that crouched motionless, facing inward at the points of a compass. Shadows played over muscular backs, slithering around sleek shoulders.

The hissing grew louder. Mixed in were words I recognized.

Devil. Beast. Tower. Desire. Serpent.

Candles in the center sent their flames skyward. The air was thick with the scent of the vision-herb.

One figure, his hair dark as night, rose to his feet.

"The Star," he murmured, his velvet voice turned guttural. "The vessel."

I clapped my hand over my mouth. This figure was half-man, half-snake. We weren't talking about top half and bottom half. No, the two were so intimately intertwined that the essence of both permeated every part of his body. He was man-shaped, but a snake lived inside him, flashing its vivid markings through translucent human skin. It coiled along his limbs and knotted around his heart. Its eyes looked through his, its fangs flickered in his mouth, and its forked tongue flashed out.

He was naked. Eerily beautiful. His hard cock pointed upward, thick and pulsing.

He was Reeve.

"The Star," the other men chanted, rising to their feet. "The vessel."

I stifled my cry, biting the palm of my hand, to see the snake inside Nathan, Blake, and Evan. They blazed with beauty, and their tattoos crackled and writhed.

"The key for us all," Reeve rasped. "The path to our freedom." He grasped his cock, and it jumped, fucking *slithered* in his hand.

It was terrifying. It was arousing. I kept my hand clamped over my mouth.

"In her innocence, pure and precious," he chanted, and the others echoed him. "To have...to take...for power beyond our dreams."

Shocked and betrayed, I turned away.

I was just a thing to these snake-men. A thing they planned to use for their own gains.

I'd been so grateful to draw the Star card, to know I had a purpose with them. And this was it?

A *vessel.*

A means to someone else's end.

A hole for these bastards to fuck.

The four of them walked steadily toward the blaze in the center of the circle. It burned scarlet, gold, and black as jet. The flames licked their sleek outlines, flaring up at their groins, their mouths, their hearts.

"Draw in the fire and let it consume you," Reeve intoned. "Know that we will consume her and be consumed by her."

I let out a noise halfway between a snarl and a furious yell.

The central fire went out. Four snake-men turned unnaturally quickly, their eyes glowing.

As one, they surged toward me.

I gasped and took to my heels. But they were fast, too fast. They surrounded me, their hands all over me. I shook, scared and excited, as my clothes were pulled at and hungry mouths slithered over my body, until I broke away.

When a tree bent toward me, I grasped the trunk and shimmied up before I remembered my hand.

It reminded me at the top, with a painful throb. Snakes circled below, surrounding the tree in a fucking nest.

"Ours," one of them hissed. Blond, shaggy headed. Evan, with fangs. "You're ours."

"Get away from me!" My voice trembled. "I see you as you are."

A dark head detached itself from the group. Reeve bent over, gripping his legs. He breathed rapidly, muttering words that reached a crescendo. Sweat poured down his forehead.

Finally, he stood upright and flung his arms out. The snake was still visible, but he was more human, his skin nearly opaque, flickers of scales showing through in translucent patches.

"Stop!" he ordered in the voice I knew. "Control yourselves."

The writhing slowed. The hissing ceased.

"Daisy, come down." Reeve's voice was urgent. "Don't be afraid. We won't hurt you."

I laughed wildly, making the branches rattle. "No. You be afraid, Reeve. Be afraid of what *I* can do to *you*. Because you should be. You all fucking should be."

It was sheer bravado. I was the one up a tree. But my voice reverberated through the forest.

"No one will do anything to you, I swear."

"Except — what? Your grand plan? Where I'm a *vessel?*" My voice cracked. "No wonder you wouldn't tell me anything. All your secrets, all your lies. What's the truth? You're screwing around with sex magic, is that it?"

"I resent the word 'screwing.'" Blake leaned against the tree trunk, his skin flashing with patches of color. Like the others, he was more man than snake now. But when he forced a smile, I saw fangs. "We take our efforts very seriously."

"And I'm the key to your efforts." I was shaking uncontrollably, the branches trembling beneath me. "Don't tell me, there's some kind of ritual. Where you all *take* me."

"Smart girl," Evan said approvingly.

"Shut up, Ev." Nathan glared at him.

"Were you ever going to talk to me about this? Or were you going to let me think it was happening organically? Just some — some sexy times that happened to involve all four of you. Like with Nathan — hey, wait, that was just last night. Was that an audition? A practice run? The final frontier? 'Oh, let's make sure Daisy hooks up with all of us, so we can seduce her into a magic orgy!'"

"It wasn't like that," Nathan muttered. "Not with you and me."

"Did it mean anything to you, Nathan? Or were you just playing a role?"

"Daze..." Reeve said.

"Let her finish." A half-smile twisted Evan's mouth, like he perversely enjoyed seeing the wreckage.

Nathan dropped onto a tree stump and buried his head in his hands.

"This is why you wouldn't have sex," I spat in Reeve's direction. "You want a fucking *virgin* for your vessel. That's the way of it for all these rituals, isn't it?"

"Told you she was smart." Evan nodded in appreciation.

"Shut your mouth, Evan," Nathan muttered.

"You don't give a damn about me. I really am just a thing to you." Clinging to the branch, I looked down at Reeve. "You've lied through your teeth about everything. Everything!"

"I never lied to you, Daisy." Reeve's voice was deathly quiet. "I omitted information because I had to, but I never told you an untruth."

"What do you mean, you had to?"

No one spoke.

I shook with nerves, but I couldn't take being treed like a scared animal. Sliding down the trunk, I dropped to the ground and walked up close to Reeve. Close enough to smell his scent of woods and moss, and the smoke of his desire, and the scorch of his ambition.

I loved him. I hated him.

"You wouldn't ever have told me, would you? You would have let me think it was all my idea. That you were being so good to me. So understanding in our *relationship* — God, what a joke — by letting me live out my fantasies. With Nathan"—I darted one anguished look in his direction, and he stared back at me—"with Blake, with Evan. And we'd all just be having the best time, and oh, don't look, Daisy, we're just sacrificing a cat in the corner, and don't mind the goat's blood or the hissing incantations or the circle of salt—"

"No!" Reeve held up his hands, alarmed. "No sacrifice. No cats. No goats."

"Why so upset, Daisy?" Blake's voice was reasonable, but his fingers drummed his thigh in a restless rhythm. "You want to be with us, we want to be with you. You want power, we want power. We all benefit. We need each other." His voice softened. "Hear Reeve out so he can explain."

It hit me that they were all naked. That I was arguing with snake-men. That my feelings were a tangled mess of need and betrayal.

"Forget it. I'm done." I turned away, too choked to speak.

"I told you so," came Nathan's muffled voice. To his friends, not to me.

I whirled. "You never told *me.*"

His hands parted, showing his agonized face. "I tried. I warned you again and again. I told you to keep away from us."

"But you never said why. You want this too, don't you? This — ritual? With me?"

His eyes met mine, the honey brown I'd loved for so many years. "More than anything."

I turned and ran down the path.

"Daisy, wait," Reeve shouted.

I picked up speed, and as I did, I heard Evan mutter, "She deserved to know."

My flashlight bounced on the trees as I ran from the heart of the forest, toward the border, until I reached my spell circle.

Animals had scattered the sticks. I laid them back in place with shaking fingers and crouched in the center, where fire had burned and a serpent took me into its mouth.

Pounding feet approached. Reeve pulled up short outside my circle, naked and sheened with sweat. In his hand was a small book, bound in a red leather cover. Gold embossed symbols caught the light.

"So this is where the magic happens," he said.

I leapt backward, putting the circle between us. "Don't come any closer."

"How often do you come here alone?"

"Why do you care? I'm just some vessel. Some *thing* you want to use."

"No! Daisy, no one thinks you're a thing." His voice softened, dropping to his old seductive tones, but underneath, it sounded shaky. "All I'm saying is, it's not good to be alone. You can do a lot more with others."

I stared at him. "With you? With Nathan? With Evan and Blake? I've done all kinds of things with you, Reeve, and somehow, I feel more fucking alone than ever."

"Daze, listen to me—"

I backed away. "Don't do that. Don't talk to me in that soft, reasonable voice." His mouth opened, but I rushed on. "You're the first person who didn't run away after kissing me, and I spilled my guts to you about that, about *everything,* and it turns out to be a sham."

"I have a theory about your 'curse,'" he said quietly.

"I'm not interested in hearing your theory."

He stared at me from across the clearing, and I looked away in defeat.

"What's your theory?" I asked sullenly.

"When you kiss someone, it shows them what they really want. They can't avoid that truth. Can't pretend otherwise. If you kiss someone who prefers men, it'll drive them away from you. If it's someone who isn't over their last love, they'll run back to her."

"And Nathan?"

Reeve blew out a breath. "Nate was afraid of what he wanted. So he fought it."

"And I just had bad luck, kissing people who never wanted me?"

He shook his head. "I think you were afraid to be desired. Afraid, Daisy, to invest in anything other than your music. Because people are a fucking mess, and with your flute, you had control. Because your parents were driven by passion, and you don't want their fate. Because wanting more than one thing is a distraction."

"Until you." My voice broke. "I hate you for making me care. I hate you for lying to me and fooling me into thinking you were my friend. Dammit, my *boyfriend*. My first relationship, and it was fake. I really am cursed."

"Well, how do you think I feel?" His shout, sudden and savage, ripped through the woods. "You fucking bewitched me!"

"What?" I gawked at him.

Reeve paced the opposite side of the circle, fury smoking from his body. "You want to talk about fake, Daisy? You started all of this. You made me love you."

My throat seized up. We'd never used the word *love* with each other, though I'd thought it just a few minutes ago. To know he felt the same way I did — it made this even worse.

"Reeve, I—"

"You cast a love spell. I felt it the night of The Crush. That's when you worked your witchcraft, wasn't it? Well, it fucked with the energy here like nothing else. There's power under this campus." His mouth crumpled as he pushed out the words. "You know that now, don't you? But you need your own power to activate it." Sweat stood out on his forehead. "Do you have any idea how it felt for me? It *hurt* when you cast that spell. You threw out bait, and I had to bite. I had no choice."

My throat was dry. "Reeve, listen. I didn't mean any harm. Why are you so sure you had no choice?"

"I saw the evidence in your room. Plain and simple, you made me love you." He lifted his head, his gaze searing me. "Why? Why did you force me to think about you all the damn time, wondering where you were, *how* you were, if you were okay? Hearing your laugh, seeing your face, talking to you in my head with stupid little conversations, making me want to tell you everything, protect you, raise you up, holy fuck, Daisy!"

Heat washed over my face. It was the first declaration of love anyone had ever given me, and it was stained with magic and betrayal.

I couldn't stop my body from shaking, and I clenched my fists to get a grip.

"It was meant for Nathan. I didn't even know you. I saw you in my dreams, but never your face. You weren't in my mind when I cast the spell! Reeve, I didn't use force, I swear. I hoped that if Nathan felt anything for me, this would help it come into the open. The spells I cast, the magic I work — it just brings out what's already there. It amplifies possibilities."

"There is no possibility! I can't love anyone I'm not bound to." His voice cracked. His mouth snapped shut, and anything else he might have said was cut off.

"Because of the serpent," I said, realization dawning as the pieces of this mystery clicked into place. "The four of you are bound to each other and the serpent. And — and to this campus, too. That's why you can't leave, isn't it? The Chancellor said that to Nathan — 'You boys don't leave this place.' You've never travelled, even though you can afford it and you're dying to. You're limited, stuck at this school, though you could be world-famous."

He jerked a nod. "The night we met, I was looking for you. I needed to know who was here, what game you were playing. But it was too late. You already had your hooks in deep. And then you came to me."

"Because of Nathan," I murmured.

"I had to learn more. And what I found out is that you, Daisy Fisher, are sitting on a massive amount of power. You're just starting to scratch the surface. You're—" His face twisted, and he forced the words out. "You're the Star."

"So that's why you want me," I snapped. "Because I have some kind of power pussy that lights up when I come. The dates, the games...the 'save your orgasms for me'...it's all been a goddamn investigation."

He made fists of his hands and pushed them against his thighs.

"You need to understand, Daze. We would never feed off of you. You have power, and we want that. Badly. But you wouldn't be diminished. You'd grow. You'd get something out of it too. You'd get — a lot."

His voice was nothing like velvet or caramel. It was raw. Halting.

I lifted my hand and dropped it. "What's the purpose of the ritual? Does it free you from this place?"

He managed a nod.

"And?"

"I can't tell you more."

"Goddammit—"

"We thought Tara was the one," he burst out. "She followed me around when we were kids. Not because she liked me, but because she smelled ambition and wanted a piece. Years ago, she found me in the woods on my family's property, talking with—" His lips twisted in a sudden contortion, cutting him off. "I made the mistake of telling her the truth. She pleaded and coerced me. She followed us here, and I made a promise to her. But after she threatened to spread our secrets, we swore a blood oath that we would never talk about our magic or the ritual with anyone else. I can't break that for you, Daze."

Tara. Suddenly, all her machinations made sense. She'd been the intended vessel. She'd tried to get rid of me so she could regain her place. Bizarrely, I felt sorry for her: so sure of her position with the boys, yet suddenly cast out.

"You're saying that you can't discuss it at all," I said flatly.

"Only with the woman who's committed to us."

"So you really wouldn't have told me about this ritual. You would have fooled me, or seduced me into it."

He looked away. "We would have found a way. I was sure you'd agree."

"And you want that."

"I want you." His voice was rough, vulnerable.

"No, Reeve. You want what I can give you."

"Daisy, I want *you.* I don't want to do this thing with anyone else." He pressed his lips together. "I want to be your first."

"I don't fucking believe you. You first, your friends following, like you think you have a right to stick your snake-dicks in me?"

He winced. "Look me in the eye and tell me the truth. You don't want us? You're not curious? Hungry?"

Of course I was. And he knew it.

"I feel your desire, Star. Smell it...taste it. You were afraid when you saw our true forms. You were frightened when we came for you, mindless with lust. But you were also aroused. You want what's inside us."

"And that's all you want from me," I whispered. "My power. Whatever you say, I know it's true."

His eyes locked on mine. "Oh, no. I want all of you, Daisy. Every inch of you, inside and out. To taste...to possess...to worship...like I've wanted nothing else. You did that to me, Star of the Cosmos. I don't know if it's your spell, or simply you. But you've ensorcelled me."

Drawn by a tightening thread, I walked slowly around the circle. He came toward me, naked and beautiful, the suggestion of scales whispering on his skin.

His fingers slid into my hair. He leaned in.

"Let me show you," he whispered.

All I wanted was for him to kiss me better, and it scared me. I put my hands on his chest, pushing him back.

My voice was raw. "So you want to have your cake and eat it too? Be together, but share me with your friends? Use me and Nathan like puppets? Have a sweet little relationship with a side of dark magic? Be a man and a snake? Reeve, do you have any idea what the hell you want?"

"I know exactly what I want," he said, low and controlled. "I want power beyond measure. I want to harness the world and give it to you. I want you at my side, in my arms, amidst the four of us where you belong. What do you want, Daisy?"

"I want you to go," I whispered. "Please. Just go."

He lifted his hands and let them fall. Crossing the clearing, he dropped the small red book on a stump.

"If you want to understand, read this," he said quietly. His obsidian eyes flickered with green. "These are our secrets, Daisy. I'm trusting you with them."

I folded my arms, stone-faced. Finally, he walked away, his footsteps fading in the brush, and my heart ached for me to follow.

14

Everybody Wants a Piece of Me

Daisy

When I was certain the woods were empty, I fled Greer Hill, my flute and the red leather book in my tote bag.

For an hour, I paced the Pacific Crest campus. I couldn't stay on the hill. I couldn't go back to Lee Tower. I needed to be outside, connected to the earth.

Finally, I found a deserted corner outside the quad and huddled on a bench.

A couple of drunk guys lurched toward me in the darkness. "Hey, beautiful. Whatcha doing over here by yourself?"

Planting my feet on the earth, I summoned energy. It was easier now. The power practically leapt into my body, as if it longed to be there. A tremor made the guys jump.

"Shoo," I whispered. They skittered away like frightened rabbits.

Only the moon looked on as I took Reeve's book out of my bag.

The crimson leather binding was cracked and worn. Running my fingers over it, I remembered where I'd seen this book before.

The small, slim volume had sat in Reeve's cabinet of curiosities in his bedroom. I'd taken it out and paged through it the night of Evan's concert, while Reeve had left to argue with Nathan downstairs.

In the little red book, there'd been explicit drawings of one woman with four men. Drawings that had to be related to the ritual they wanted me for.

Taking a deep breath, I opened the book to the first page.

Black print, small and ornate, met my eyes. The language was archaic and difficult to follow. But the opening phrases leapt out at me.

On achieving your heart's desire:

Power beyond measure in whatsoever area you choose

Slowly, I began to read, puzzling out the contents. As I did, I filled in the gaps from the visions I'd had, the bits and pieces the men had let drop, making guesses and conjectures, until a story emerged from the instructions on ancient magic that sat in my hands.

Born into a home that struggled to make ends meet, Reeve McClellan IV had chafed at his life for as long as he could remember. Yet he was loyal to his family. He wanted to provide for them. He also wanted to exceed his upbringing, to conquer all obstacles and bring them to his feet. He hungered for wealth and accomplishment, luxury and ease.

He was brilliant, conniving, and trapped by his circumstances.

Perhaps his mother, once a witch, had felt the same way. She'd hidden her magic from her family, and she hadn't practiced it for years. When his father passed away, Reeve — grieving and angry — went through his family's effects. He searched the boxes in the attic, looking for anything he could sell to support his mother and four younger siblings.

Hidden among the dusty clothes and broken furniture was a padlocked box. His mother, embarrassed, told him to burn it. Instead, he hauled it out to the woods, picked the lock, and found all her magic materials and supplies. He was intrigued, to say the least.

Forced to support his family, pressured to drop out of high school, he was desperate to leave. He wanted to learn, to rise, to achieve a life beyond what his parents imagined.

So, sixteen and curious, he'd started working magic. And before long, a serpent came to his dreams.

In its alluring hiss, it promised everything he desired. It treasured his hunger for success, and for the first time, Reeve felt understood.

He began sleepwalking. Sleeptalking in a strange, hissing language. He had precognitive dreams where he saw the other chosen ones before he met them. An abyss opened, and it called for him to jump.

And beneath it all, coiling endlessly, was the serpent. Guiding, tempting, seducing.

The pull was strong. Even when Tara, the sullen neighbor girl with her own dreams of power and celebrity, found Reeve working magic — spying on him, following him to the woods, threatening to tell if he didn't include her in his rise to fortune — Reeve wasn't fazed.

He had a job for her. She would keep his secrets and be the vessel for the final ritual. In return, he would pay for her silence and acquiescence. He'd ensure that she got accepted to Pacific Crest, where the serpent dwelled in Greer Hill. It didn't matter that they couldn't stand each other; all that mattered was that she was willing to play a role.

In his dreams, the serpent showed Reeve visions of power, wealth, and glory — for a price. And when the serpent found Blake, when it found Evan and Nathan, it showed Reeve their faces. It led him to each of them at their lowest moments, when they were ready to renounce their lives and follow him.

There was a name for the four men. The ones who had been called by the serpent, who banded together and took it inside them, who worshipped at its altar in return for the realization of their fiercest ambitions.

The *Desiderata.*

The desired ones.

The serpent lived in the hearts of all people, but it hungered for a group of true hosts to possess. Throughout history, these hosts had almost always been male, which made me wonder about the ambitious women in the world. About their dreams.

When the bond broke, because of death or weakness, the serpent searched for a new group.

It found the leader of that group in Reeve. In his hunger, his ambition, his dissatisfaction. He had the vision to succeed, the charisma to gather the others, and the strength to make the necessary sacrifices.

Once the men bound themselves to the serpent, their hearts were closed. The serpent coiled around each of those hearts, constricting and living off of them. They couldn't love anyone except each other.

Moreover, they were bound to Pacific Crest, as I'd guessed. They'd performed a ritual called the Binding that tied them here a year ago. Since then, they couldn't be apart or leave the campus for more than a day or two.

If they tried...bad things would happen.

Nathan must have been yanking at his tether when I found him in his family's backyard before the semester began. Kissing me was an act of rebellion — or submission to the constant desire that the serpent invoked in its hosts.

The monthly orgies at Reeve's House had an explanation as well. All that lust was a tribute, saturating the air and walls of the House. After each party, the men would gather to summon the serpent, using the herb I'd found in Reeve's room. When it manifested, they fed together off the lingering cloud of desire.

Somehow, the serpent was able to split its presence. It lived in Greer Hill, but it also possessed the men's bodies. Throughout history, its dwelling place had changed, from the site of one rise and fall of an empire to another.

Now, it lived ninety miles south of Los Angeles, the city that was a temple to desires and dreams, making its home in the faultlines of the Southern California earth.

And if the men didn't perform the final rituals at the appointed time — the ones they wanted me for — they'd be trapped here forever. At Pacific Crest. Leashed to the serpent and the hill. Their talents would flounder. They would never be able to go out into the world, to achieve fame and recognition for their gifts.

Heart racing, I read through everything the serpent demanded: the offering of the blood, the judging of the earth, the dedication of the body and its lusts. I skimmed ahead to the middle section, *The Final Rites,* and my head went light.

Four to begin, five to seal, four to end.
One lock with four keys.

The ritual in question actually had two parts: the Joining, which took place first, and the Sealing, which took place seven days later at the full moon.

The Desiderata needed a woman for both rituals — a "pure vessel." My lips twisted as I read the insistence that she must be a virgin.

So Tara, for all her seductiveness, had been saving that particular act for the boys. It must have been part of her agreement with Reeve. I pictured him telling her that she could do whatever she wanted, with whoever she wanted — just don't have sex.

The woman didn't need to have magical abilities. She wasn't required to host the serpent for the rest of her life. But in performing the role of vessel, she received a wish. Whatever her heart desired most would be granted.

Hugging myself, I heard Reeve's raw voice: *You'd get something out of it too. You'd get...a lot.*

I stared at my left hand, feeling my flute keys under my fingers. The siren song of *Syrinx* swirled through the night air.

But all these rules come to naught for the Star.

I almost dropped the book when I read that line.

There was a prophecy. Once a century, a woman came along who channeled the serpent. It visited her with dreams and portents, allowing her to access it through fire and earth. It wanted her as badly as it wanted the Desiderata, and she blazed with enough ambition to feed it for decades.

The word "desire" originally meant "await what the stars would bring." And the Star brought everything that was needed.

If the Desiderata and the Star crossed paths and performed the rituals together, the influx of power was immense. All five would be vaulted into fame and fortune beyond their wildest dreams. There were risks, but they came with an enormous payoff. And the Star took the serpent inside her as well, living in its possessive embrace for the rest of her life.

I shivered.

Me?

I felt ragged and worn out, alone and bewildered. Anything but powerful right now.

But it had to be true. This was why the boys had dropped Tara, why I'd managed to drag Blake and Evan in and out of the woods, maybe even why I'd been drawn to the Davises' backyard and to Nathan all those years ago.

Did it explain why my love spell had pierced Reeve's armor?

I leapt up and paced the dark lawn.

Were any of the feelings between us real, or were they all magic? Was the serpent manipulating us? Or was it our parasite, feeding off our human longings and hopes?

Opening the book again, I turned to an illustration: four nude men standing in a circle, connected by arcs of light and smoke. A drop of blood fell from each of their hands to the earth.

The next page depicted a black altar on which a woman writhed in ecstasy. One man leaned over her, their bodies joined, while the others surrounded them. She reached out to touch them all.

The final illustration showed her on all fours, taking in three men at once while the fourth put his hands on her. This was the drawing I'd seen in Reeve's bedroom.

The pictures were elegant and graceful, drawn in pen and ink. I wondered what it would be like, in the woman's position. The leaves rustled in the trees, and with a rush of energy, I felt myself there.

The impossibly hard, smooth marble table under my back. My bare skin, glowing with magic and slick with the desires of five people. Taking Reeve inside me first, as he'd promised. Locking my legs around Nathan's waist. Tasting Blake, gripping Evan. Welcoming them all, hungry for the pent-up need that matched my own.

Against my better judgment, I turned the page.

The book went on to explain the details of the Joining. The incantations, the arrangements of candles and spell circles, the fasting beforehand, the herbs to be burned and taken in various measures.

And for the seven days leading up to the Sealing, the final ritual — my head spun and I clutched the book, forcing myself to focus on the cramped black letters.

> *For the next seven days, all will drink as deeply as their hearts desire.*

Four men, one woman. The grass blurred in front of me as I imagined the hard bodies, the bruising kisses, the hungry embraces, the cocks. God, all that cock.

It was too much.

It was everything I wanted.

And to be able to play music afterwards... I could feel my flute in my hands. Smooth, cool, welcoming my touch as if I'd never left.

I stumbled away from the bench, clutching the red leather book.

The ritual must happen.

If I didn't fuck the men, Tara would. Bad blood or no, I had no doubt that both she and Reeve were calculating enough to go through the motions. The others would follow, because their lives depended on it. And they'd leap to some higher plane of power and glory, leaving me here.

I walked for hours, crisscrossing Pacific Crest, until I reached the dark, empty quad. The clock tower struck three in the morning.

I could heal my hand, just from being with these men. From welcoming the serpent.

Was it worth it?

For the first time, I dropped my guard and let myself miss the flute with all my heart. Every note, every piece, every emotion rushed in. I fell to my knees as twelve years of memories washed over me.

I could have it all back and more. I'd become a better musician than I'd ever been.

But my ties to everyone outside the Desiderata would be cut, because the serpent was a selfish lover.

I shook my head. That couldn't be true. Reeve still cared for his family; I'd seen his anguish that he couldn't help them. Nathan had called up Sasha when I'd asked him to. Evan hated his father, but hate was most definitely a feeling. And Blake's voice had softened when he spoke of his mother.

There was still love, in whatever form it took; there had to be.

Taking my tarot deck from my purse, I spread the chosen cards on the grass. The Knight, the Ace, the Beast, and the Devil, all surrounding the Star.

What if this was my purpose?

I stared up at the moon, which bathed the silent buildings and trees of the quad in silvery light. Overhead, a bright streak fell to the earth.

A shooting star.

I took it as a sign.

Pulling out my phone, I called Reeve. He answered immediately.

"Daze?" His deep voice was measured, but underneath the cloak of velvet was an eager pulse that broke my heart.

"I want it all back," I confessed in a rush. "Everything."

He let out a breath. "You can have it."

"I want to be the best," I said recklessly. "Better than Evan. I want to be the greatest musician in the world."

"You will be." He let out a laugh of relief. "Daisy, I promise, you can have whatever you want. Did you read the book?"

"Yes."

"All of it?" His voice turned urgent. "Everything? Do you know exactly what you're getting into? You need to come into this with open eyes."

"I do. But I haven't read the third section in-depth, *The Reversal*. Should I?"

"No need."

"And if it goes wrong?" I exhaled. "The book said — with the Star — it's a gamble."

"It won't go wrong. I'm very, very thorough. I'll make sure we're prepared." He sounded incredulous. Overjoyed. "I would never let anything harm you, or them. I'll take care of all of you. *We'll* take care of you."

"Do you really want me?" My voice was suddenly small, my feelings for him creeping into the forefront of my mind. "For more than just my power?"

"Like I've wanted no one and nothing else," he said quietly.

I ached to touch him. "How much?" I whispered.

"More than the House." His voice was charged. "More than money. More than everything I've acquired and every ability I possess."

I closed my eyes, taking a deep breath at this admission. "Will you still want me once the ritual is sealed?"

"Fuck, Daisy, *yes*." His enthusiasm was infectious, and a smile spread across my face.

"What will we do?"

He laughed. "What won't we do? Life will be ours for the feasting. The earth will be our fucking table. Remember how we talked about traveling together?"

"Of course." Giddiness began to overtake me.

"I'll take you all over the world. We'll see everything there is to see. We can settle anywhere you want. New York..." He dangled the promise in front of me. "In a beautiful apartment. We could help your mom. You told me she struggles financially."

It was like Reeve, to offer that. To want to take care of my mom, because he couldn't take care of his.

"And Nathan? Blake and Evan?"

"We'll still be connected. You can have us all. And your music? It'll be the stuff of legends."

The possibilities unrolled like a gorgeous, shining tapestry.

"I want nothing more, Daze, than to see you rise." Every word sizzled through the phone. "I want you to have everything you deserve after it was taken from you."

"Reeve — it was an accident."

"I don't believe in accidents."

I closed my eyes. "God, all four of you..." I pictured what I'd read in the little red book and shuddered.

"We'll make it good for you, sweetheart. I promise, we'll be so careful with you."

"Not *too* careful," I said, and he let out a strained laugh.

"Do you want it?" he murmured. "Say the word. If you agree, come to the House and pledge yourself to us. I swear, you will be absolutely safe. We'll give you pleasure and fortune like you've never known. All of us."

Taking a deep breath, I looked around at the empty quad, the silent trees, and the tarot cards arranged on the grass. I touched my flute case, and the ground seemed to tremble.

"I want it," I assured him quietly. "I'll be your Star."

15

Holy Ghost Fire

Daisy

The half-full moon shone overhead, illuminating the marble statues as I walked down the winding path to the House.

My white cotton dress flowed to my ankles, simple and unadorned. Reeve had sent it over. Per his instructions, I wore nothing underneath.

I hadn't seen the men since coming to the House two nights ago to pledge myself to them. I'd stripped naked on the marble table and accepted their hands on my body while I vowed to be theirs, and theirs alone.

I'd sworn to cut myself off from the past, dedicating myself solely to the serpent, the future, and our desires.

I was afraid, even as I spoke the words. But when eight hands traveled my skin, trust bloomed and certainty increased: this was my path. My purpose. What I was meant for.

Yet nerves held me back from reaching the climax that would seal the pledge.

In the end, it wasn't Reeve's dark passion that drove me over the edge. It wasn't Nathan's playful intensity, nor Blake's patient caresses. It was Evan, a slavering beast who growled filthy words about what a good little toy I was, and all the ways he'd use me like a fucking instrument for the next week.

After that night, I was forbidden to touch myself or see the men until the Joining. We'd fasted today, bathed with herbs to purify ourselves, and chanted incantations of preparation.

Before dawn, I'd taken out my flute. I didn't play; I simply ran my fingers over the smooth joints and curving keys.

"Soon," I whispered.

It was surreal to go about normal life as I prepared. I'd had sushi for lunch with Michelle and Amy yesterday, and we'd chatted about classes and college gossip. I wondered if I would see them again, or if the men and I would break free of Pacific Crest as soon as the week of the Joining ended. Would I care about my roommates after the Sealing?

I called both my parents and told them I loved them. I didn't know how our relationship would change, either.

I thought about Sasha. I thought about her a lot.

In the end, I'd called her, over and over. But she didn't answer.

What if the rituals backfired and left me empty? A husk, a shell? What if the four men drained me of my power and left after they got what they wanted, after I'd served my purpose for them? The red leather book hadn't specified the risks — it simply stated that they existed. And that with the Star, they were higher.

What if *I* took all the power?

Taking a deep breath, I walked down the path to the House. The pavement, still warm from the heat of the day, scraped the bare soles of my feet. The duffel bag I'd packed swung at my side.

A security guard sat in the shed by the driveway, and another patrolled the perimeter of the House. When I came into view, the guard in the shed did a double take. He squinted, shading his eyes as if a spotlight shone on me.

"Daisy DiCosmo Fisher?" he croaked.

I smiled in spite of myself and gave him a nod. So that's how Reeve had written me down.

"You can go on in."

"Thank you." I swept up the path. I was hurrying now, nervous. At the grand entryway, the flagstones were cool and slightly rough under my soles. I wondered if the guard had noticed I was barefoot.

The front door opened at my touch.

Torches lit the foyer. The room yawned before me. The frescoed ceiling suddenly seemed as high as the heavens, and I was only a tiny speck beneath it.

I took a deep breath, letting it fill my lungs.

"I'm going to be great," I said softly.

I walked the length of the hall, parted the velvet curtains, and entered the dark living room. Flames danced on black marble as four figures turned to face me.

My heart raced. I hadn't been sure of what to expect. Would the Desiderata be naked? Wearing hooded robes?

No. They were wreathed in scarlet mists that darted and writhed, obscuring them completely. They were as faceless as they'd been in my dreams.

Swallowing hard, I dropped my bag by the wall and stepped forward to offer myself.

They surrounded me and swept me to the center of the room. Blood rose to my face as we spoke the opening lines of the Joining.

"You're ours," they hissed in one voice. "Our Star, to have and to take."

I lifted my chin. "Your Star, to have and to take."

"Stand before us."

One of them had a knife in his hand. I knew, on a bone-deep level, that it was Reeve — and that he held the jeweled dagger I'd seen in his room.

I sucked in my breath as he slit my gown from neckline to waist. The cotton parted like a cloud under the blade. Behind me, another — Blake, I sensed his energy — twisted my hair out of the way. When

Reeve sliced open the back of my dress, the halves of the gown fell to my waist, exposing my breasts.

The others — Nathan and Evan? — stepped forward, one in front and one behind. Grasping the fragile fabric, they tore it with their bare hands. I stifled a cry as it fell around my feet, leaving me naked. My nipples tight, my muscles taut.

"Part your legs," someone ordered, and I did. "Give us your hand, Star."

It was Reeve's voice, though distorted. He took my right hand in his, gripping my fingers firmly to keep me from jerking as he pressed the point of the knife to my palm.

The metal bit into my flesh. I winced as a bead of blood welled up. He squeezed the fleshy part of my palm, encouraging the scarlet pearl to grow, then turned my palm downward so the drop of blood fell into a bowl.

"Kneel," he commanded. "Accept the bond of the earth and the judgment of the serpent."

I dropped to my knees and bowed my head. My hair fell in a curtain to the floor.

Out of the corner of my eye, I saw one figure take a stone bowl of dirt — from Greer Hill, I knew. Another held up a copper basin of water. Slowly, the dirt was sprinkled with water, then mixed with a copper rod.

The first figure dipped his fingers into the bowl. They came away covered in a rich, reddish mud.

My skin tightened into goosebumps as the cool mud touched my cheeks, streaked across my forehead, and was painted around my breasts.

A moan escaped me.

"Is she worthy, Serpent?" asked the figure standing in front of me. I clung to the knowledge that it was Reeve, though I couldn't see his face.

In my mind, a hissing voice urged, *Hush, Star. All are one.*

I shivered, gripping the carpet. Hands steadied me.

"You're ours," someone whispered in my ear. "Don't doubt it."

"I'm yours," I whispered back, willing myself to believe it.

"Do you accept the Star as your vessel?" Reeve continued. "Pure and blazing? Ours to have and keep?"

There was silence.

The wait was agonizing.

The red book had said nothing about what to expect.

"Please," I whispered.

"Spread your thighs," ordered a third figure who stood over us.

I obeyed, kneeling. Suddenly, I felt a hand between my legs. Patterns were swirled on my open thighs with the cool mud, while a knowing mouth sucked on my neck until I was lightheaded.

I throbbed, digging my hands into the carpet, trying to stay upright.

"Never doubt." The command came from all of them at once, from inside me, from every corner of the vast room. "Trust. Believe."

Finally, I surrendered, melting like wax from the sputtering tapers on the great marble table.

I accept, came a voice that was the hiss of wind, the rumble of earth, the crackle of fire, the rush of water. *She is ready to receive and to give.*

Strong hands helped me into a broad basin and sponged me clean with warm water. Every brush of the sponge burned and teased. Red mud ran down my body in rivulets, until my skin was free of it.

"Take your place on the altar, Star."

Favoring my right side, I gripped the rough-hewn edge of the marble slab. With one knee on the table, I tried to swing myself up, but my palm slipped.

"Dammit," I whispered.

I tried again, and my face burned with frustration as my hand slipped a second time.

Lips pressed against my shoulder.

"You can do this, baby," came the low voice in my ear. "Whatever pain you feel, it'll all go away very soon. Do this for us, and we'll take care of you from here."

Nathan.

Taking a deep breath, I leaned my weight on both hands and climbed onto the table. The jolt through my left wrist made me cry out. A scarlet wraith of mist leapt onto the table behind me.

"Lie back. Hands over your head," he ordered. "I'm going to hold you down." His voice flowed over me, and I could almost make out Blake's calm tones. "I'll go easy for now."

He took both my hands in his, and when he touched my left hand, a rush of sparks ran from his palm to mine, easing the pain.

As the others surrounded the table, the mists dissolved to reveal their forms: man-shaped, with translucent skin that showed the serpent slithering inside.

Reeve climbed over me: naked, beautiful, all sleek, carved muscles.

"Daze," he murmured. "I promised this to you."

Holding Blake's hands, another shiver ran through my body as Reeve kissed me. My hips surged toward his. Shock and need flamed through me as he pushed my thighs apart.

"Look at you glow," Reeve hissed. "You love the attention. You're dying to be fucked by all four of us."

His mouth marked a burning path over my throat, my breasts, my belly.

"Harder," I begged, craning my neck to expose the vulnerable skin. I bucked my pussy toward him, begging silently for his mouth there too, but he only dropped a last kiss below my navel before pushing himself up to cover my body with his.

The blunt head of his cock nudged my tight entrance, driving a gasp from me.

"You want the serpent, sweet flower. You're going to let it fuck you too, aren't you? You'll be our good girl, our slut, our blazing Star."

"And your Daisy." I stared into his golden-green eyes. Seeing the snake aroused me desperately, but I longed for a glimpse of Reeve McClellan, the man.

For a brief flash, I saw him look out at me.

"And my Daisy," he repeated.

Hard flesh pushed at my soaked and sensitive pussy. When I cried out, Blake gripped my hands tighter.

I arched instinctively, raising my hips, and Reeve surged inside me.

"Fuuuuck," he groaned.

My head fell back as he worked his cock in and out, sinking deeper each time. He was so big, so rigid and hot. I heard my own cries as I stared up at Nathan and Evan, their eyes glued to us.

A sudden thrust, stinging, made me sob. The men groaned, the sound heavy with lust.

I wanted to hold Reeve, but I was pinned down for his taking. I felt incredibly vulnerable as he opened my tightness. The initial bite of pain softened into a constant pleasurable ache, driving my need higher.

"You're so deep," I gasped.

Reeve's eyes swallowed mine. "Sweet girl, it's only beginning."

"How does it feel, pet?" Evan's voice was a predatory growl. "Reeve is right. He's going easy on you. You're lucky he's preparing you for the rest of us."

Squeezing Blake's hands for dear life, I writhed on the table as Reeve's cock moved inside me. He plunged in more firmly, staring into my eyes.

When I moaned, the ground quaked. I was suspended in a haze of desire. As Nathan's and Evan's hands moved between us, running possessively over my breasts and throat, I looked into the face of the serpent. It was on top of me now, and its hungry jaws opened, ready to swallow me whole.

Before I could call out for Reeve, he was back, as darkly beautiful as the serpent was scarlet and bright. In the next instant, the serpent took his place again. I shivered uncontrollably as my lover flashed between man and snake. Hard muscle, pressing against all my soft spots, turned to thick writhing coils that fucked every inch of my body.

The serpent struck.

I cried out as its head flashed close. But instead of a bite, Reeve's mouth devoured mine. I kissed him back hungrily, matching every movement. Hisses filled the high-ceilinged room as he came. His cock pulsed inside me, and the hands of the others tightened on my flesh.

My body tried to follow Reeve's as he eased out of me, but he pressed my hips firmly to the table and gave me one last kiss.

He looked almost human, smiling down at me in the flickering light of the candles. Shakily, I smiled back. His cock was smeared with blood. My juices and his cum ran down my ass, puddling on the table.

Blake released my hands and moved to stand before me at the end of the table. He gently spread my legs, and his bright blue eyes roved over my sweaty body.

"Look at you, Star," he murmured. "Sticky with Reeve's cum, all pink and excited. You're absolutely beautiful."

Without warning, he climbed on top of me. I kissed the tattooed arm that braced him up, shuddering with excitement, and he sucked hard on my neck.

Dipping his fingers into my pussy, he pushed them into my mouth. I tasted the blood of my virginity, given to Reeve, returned to me by Blake. It mingled with the tart, musky flavor of my pussy, and as he massaged my clit, I was so close to coming...

His mouth moved down, tasting my breasts, teasing my stomach, until it locked on my cunt. I kicked as he pushed his tongue inside, soothing the place that Reeve had invaded.

"Reach out, Daisy," came the order.

My fingers curled around hard, pulsing cocks. Nathan and Evan groaned.

"Nathan," I whispered, gazing up at him. It was so intimate to hold him this way. A bead of precum oozed from the flushed tip, and he closed his eyes as I slowly pumped his shaft.

"Talk to him." Reeve's voice was a silky command. "Tell him everything. All the need, the longing. Everything that brought you here to us."

I thrashed as Blake sucked on my clit.

"I've wanted you for so long, Nathan," I breathed. "I dreamed about holding you like this." I squeezed his cock, and he grunted. On my other side, Evan thrust ferociously into the circle of my fist. "I thought you were perfect. I dreamed of giving you my firsts."

His eyes opened, flickering between green and amber, dark and dangerous. "Why didn't you?"

"Because —" All the reasons faded from my mind, except one. "Because I was saving them for all of you."

His face flushed, unrecognizable in animal lust. "You did right, girl."

As cocks filled my hands, Blake continued licking my cunt furiously.

"Make her come," came the hissing command. "Her pleasure strengthens us all."

Strong hands gripped my ass as I climaxed. Golden light flooded the room, stained with scarlet and black that swirled around me.

I gasped as the light solidified into slender golden snakes. They curled over my skin, flicking out tiny tongues, lashing me to the table. Coiling around my breasts, they held my thighs open. Electric need followed, lighting me up everywhere they moved.

Then Blake was on top of me, his pierced cock pushing against my cunt.

"Oh," I gasped.

"Relax, Daisy," he coaxed, pressing and easing off. "Open up for me."

I groaned as Blake worked himself inside me with infinite patience. His piercing rubbed against my tender flesh, making me shake in the snake-ropes' embraces.

"You feel so big..." My head fell back.

When he was halfway in, he took my face in his hands. I still grasped Nathan and Evan's cocks.

But where was Reeve?

Blake's tender kisses blotted out my thoughts, soothing me as his cock stretched me open. When his thrusts became deeper, Nathan and Evan matched those thrusts in my hands.

"It's okay, honey," Blake whispered. "You don't need to prove anything right now. Just be here with us."

I stared up at him, caught in golden coils.

I didn't know what that was like.

I didn't know how to just be.

As if he read my mind, he kissed me more deeply. "We'll help you. You're everything we need and want. Just receive us and let it feel good."

My mouth opened to his pierced tongue, my body to his cock. I yielded to Evan and Nathan's frenzied thrusts and the tightening, slithering snakes.

Blake arched above me, slamming his hips into mine. His kiss swallowed my gasp as he plunged deep, cracking me open.

"Fuck, yes," he groaned.

Like Reeve, his eyes were all snake now. He came, flooding my body. I bucked helplessly as he speared me with long thrusts, grinding against my clit with every stroke.

Deep inside me, something uncoiled.

It was powerful. Hungry. Pleased by Blake's cum that oozed out of my pussy and dripped down my ass.

But it wasn't satisfied. It would never be satisfied.

When Blake pulled out and kissed my forehead, I strained at the constricting snakes.

"More," I hissed, squeezing Nathan and Evan's carved cocks.

"All done playing, pet," Evan growled. "Time to really be fucked."

Jade green eyes devoured me as I trembled in the serpents' embrace. With a growl, Evan pounced.

He was so broad, looming above me. He pinched my clit.

"Evan..." I stared up at the damp blond hair brushing his cheeks.

"You scared, baby girl? Afraid I'll be too much?"

As he captured my breasts in his hands, a hard bulb pressed against my entrance. Evan was huge. Bigger than Reeve and Blake. I tensed as the snakes writhed over me.

"Easy, boy." A firm hand circled Evan's cock, gripping the base — Reeve's. "She's not going anywhere."

The move was so fucking hot and wanton that my toes curled.

"Savor her," Reeve continued. Fingers brushed my ass. "You'll have countless opportunities to fuck her senseless later."

I lifted my head, and the voice that came from me, low and gravelly, was barely recognizable.

"Not later. Now."

Savage joy lit up Evan's face.

Growling, he sank his full length inside me, pinning my thighs to the table with his, and I shrieked at the exquisite pain and pleasure. My pussy was tender, and he was so big, so deep.

"Oh God, Evan."

"I've needed you for so damn long. We're finally complete. You and me together."

I squirmed at his relentless invasion, pinned to the marble table by each greedy thrust. Magic was easing the way; it had to be, because I couldn't possibly take him otherwise. Sweat dripped off Evan's forehead, splashing onto mine, as his hands roamed my breasts and face. But it wasn't until I kissed him eagerly that he went rigid on top of me. Gripping my hair, he came in a rush.

I wanted to hold him in return. To dig my fingers into his husky back, understand the savagery that lay inside.

I wanted to awaken the beast that Reeve tried to control.

But the serpents held me firmly in place. All I could do was moan and buck my hips until Evan withdrew, his eyes glazed.

When Nathan replaced him, I could barely breathe.

Nathan took his time, kissing every inch of me until I trembled. He sucked on my nipples, vying with the snake-ropes, until my pleas rose to the ceiling. His stormy eyes never left mine as he parted my thighs.

"Finally," he muttered. "You're all mine to touch."

I shook uncontrollably as his hungry mouth met my pussy. Through a haze, the other men circled us.

"You're driving me crazy," I gasped.

Reeve stroked my hair. "He's going to take all the time he needs with you, Daze. He's wanted you for so long."

"I need — Nathan — I have to —" I thrashed at the snakes, which tightened their hold.

"Sshhh." Blake caressed my breast, rolling my aching nipple between his fingers. "Just let it feel good. Don't you like his tongue on your clit?"

"Yes," I moaned.

"That's all you can do, pet." Evan crushed my other breast in his huge hand. "Feel. Open. Surrender to us."

"Please, Nathan, I'm about to come..."

Nathan chuckled evilly, raising his head. "Oh, you will. When it's time."

In one graceful bound, he landed above me on all fours. My legs were held wide by the others. Nathan rubbed his cock over every fold of my pussy until I was aflame.

His eyes flickered between amber storm and golden snake as I searched them for some trace of my first love.

"I've waited so many years for you," I murmured.

He groaned and entered me with one long glide. Wrapping his arms around me, he fucked me thoroughly, heedless of the snakes that held me down. I lost myself in his skin, his scent. I bit his neck until the salt of his sweat was all I could taste.

When he came, he sighed my name.

"On your hands and knees, Daze." Reeve's deep voice cut through the fog of need. "Climb on top of Nate."

The snake-ropes vanished as I followed his direction.

My limbs were jelly, and I was ready to dissolve. But I managed to turn over and straddle Nathan when he stretched out on his back, bracing my hands on his massive shoulders. My left wrist throbbed, and he gripped my hips in support.

Evan knelt on the table in front of me, Blake crouched to my right, and Reeve moved behind me. His hands ran possessively over my ass, and I shivered.

It was the final stage of the ritual: the joining of us all, the making of my wish.

My awareness flashed between the men surrounding me and my heart's desire. I struggled to keep my intentions focused and pure.

Closing my eyes, I saw myself onstage, my flute in my hands. There was no pain, only joy. The music enchanted the audience, bringing them under my spell.

Time stopped as I played *Syrinx*. As I lowered myself onto Nathan's cock.

When Evan lifted my chin, smooth skin nudged my lips. My eyes fluttered open, and my mouth followed suit. I sank down to engulf Nathan completely in wet heat, taking Evan's broad, flared head into my mouth.

Staring into his narrowed gaze, I focused fiercely on the musician onstage. But Evan, thrusting raggedly, was a constant distraction. Nathan bucked upward, piercing me with every thrust. And the noises the three of us were making...God, the slurping and sucking and *squishing*...they nearly drowned out the seductive silvery notes in my mind.

I shuddered, caught between Evan and Nathan, getting wetter and wetter as Reeve massaged my ass. To my right, Blake rubbed my back reassuringly.

"You can do this, Daisy." Reeve's voice was all velvet seduction. "Trust us. Trust yourself."

He spread my cheeks open, tracing the cleft of my ass. I cried out, my voice muffled as I sucked Evan feverishly, my pussy clinging to Nathan's cock. I was dimly aware of Reeve rubbing cool, slippery lube into my tight back hole.

He worked his finger inside me, praising me softly for taking him so well. Then he added another.

I clenched and fluttered, my ass gripping him like a vise. There was no way he could fill me any further. Nathan's cock was deep inside me, crowding Reeve's fingers. But when Reeve eased out, kissing my shoulder, I missed him immediately.

Focus, Daisy.

The tip of Reeve's cock pushed against my dark, secret pucker. I seized up, then relaxed, opening to him. A wave of profound need ran through me when his slick head opened my ass.

I was no longer fighting the lure of these men. They strengthened me. I received them all, and my mind went aglow with pleasure.

Reeve murmured reassurances as he sank deeper into my ass. The sensation was so intense that I could barely think. Finally, both he and Nathan filled me completely, alternating their thrusts. I sucked Evan eagerly and reached out to grip Blake's cock, trusting my left hand and the men to hold my weight now.

"Deeper, baby girl." Evan's hands twisted cruelly in my hair, his cock surging forward.

Breathing through my nose, I allowed his head to nudge my throat. All I wanted now was to oblige, to yield...to submit. My mouth was his, riding on his pleasure.

"Fuck," Evan panted. "*Fuck!*"

I sucked and swallowed frantically, doing my best to take every drop of the salty cum spurting into my mouth.

When he finally pulled out, he bent, taking my face in his hands, and kissed me hard. I rocked between Reeve and Nathan, overwhelmed, yet welcoming them both deeper.

Blake pushed Evan aside to take his place, his lean body taut with need. Tattoos roiled over his translucent skin as he blazed before me.

I didn't hesitate. I wrapped my hand around the base of Blake's cock and sucked him in as fully as I could.

Heat flared in every place that the men filled me. It spread to my upper arm, where the Desiderata bore the serpent's mark, and raced down to my hand, enfolding my entire left side in a wash of warmth and light.

You're a star. And I can't wait to see you go supernova.

A cascade of notes filled the air: the unearthly tones of a flute — so poignant and promising that they formed a siren's song. My soul held the image of the woman onstage, while my body fucked four men and their desires mingled with mine.

Nathan massaged my clit firmly. "You're a star, Daisy."

"Our Star," Blake groaned, fucking my mouth faster.

"You belong to us," Reeve crooned.

"Ours," Evan rasped.

The notes crescendoed to a peak as light flooded the great room. Reeve and Nathan's cocks were enormous inside me. Blake filled my throat, and Evan's hands were everywhere. I was pinned, caught, filled.

I came.

I saw stars.

When they climaxed, they gave to me until I couldn't hold any more.

The five of us collapsed on the marble altar. Blake, Reeve, and Nathan eased out of me, and the men surrounded me protectively as I curled up in their warm embrace.

A low hiss filled the air.

All are one.

And now, Star — now you are worthy.

16

Dracula Moon

Daisy

I sat up in a warm tangle of arms and legs. The room shimmered with magic — restless, pulsing. The candles sputtered, their flames low.

All four men lay unconscious on the black marble altar, breathing peacefully. According to the book, we'd sleep for hours, recovering while the serpent gained its hold.

An elaborate grandfather clock chimed four. I'd only been asleep for a few hours at the most. Was something wrong? Or was there an exception for the Star?

"Please tell me it worked," I whispered.

The men didn't stir. But my left arm twinged, and the upper area itched. Turning my arm over, I stared at the ink now etched into my skin. Red, black, and gold scales coiled endlessly, and the serpent's mouth opened to swallow its tail.

I touched the head of my new tattoo, and a shiver ran through me.

Stretching, I unkinked my muscles and took stock of my stiffness and soreness. In a daze, I slipped on a black dress I'd brought, took my flute case from my duffel bag, and walked out the front door of the House.

Campus was deserted. I carried my flute to the moonlit, empty quad. With trembling hands, I fitted the joints together and put the instrument to my lips.

From the first note, everything was different. The confidence, the beauty. Playing took no effort at all. I barely had to breathe. My left hand didn't hurt; it was infused with a warm glow.

The notes flew into the night, until a man in a campus security uniform approached.

"Miss, you'll have to stop," he said gruffly. "I'm sorry, it's quiet hours right now."

Looking straight at him, I played a lilting run. My tone was pure as a bell. My fingers were flexible, soaring like never before.

"Are you sure?" I asked calmly.

"Oh. Oh... No. No, of course, you need to play. I understand." His features softened, and his jaw hung slack as I played on. "Don't stop," he pleaded when I paused.

"You have rounds to do," I said gently. "Someone might need your help."

"Not if they hear you. Please, keep playing."

One by one, they began to come. People appeared in the quad, some in pajamas, some dressed, some nearly naked, pulled from their dorms and apartments and nighttime wanderings. They dropped to their knees on the grass and listened. Every face turned toward me as the notes wound over the lawn. More people, and more, until the quad was packed. It was as full as it had been the night of The Crush, but the crowd was motionless.

I marveled at my playing. The grace and ease almost didn't seem like my own. I'd always been an intense performer. Even during the calmest pieces, I'd been laser-focused on each note, each breath. After months away from my flute, I'd expected an awkward reacquaintance process, but this was very easy.

Too easy.

No one danced. No one moved. They simply sat and stared, spellbound.

Pink light crept up the horizon as the sun rose. My hands and arms didn't betray a trace of fatigue. And the hundreds of people in the quad hadn't moved a muscle...God, how long had I been playing? An hour? Two?

Drawing out the last notes, I lowered my flute. A forest of hands reached toward me, just as they had for Evan.

"Don't stop," someone pleaded.

"I'll be back," I assured them. "Tomorrow night."

"No, now."

"It's dawn. You should get some sleep."

A voice hissed in my mind. *Sleep? Who needs sleep? Your sleep is mine now.*

There were grumbles of protest from the crowd. I waved my flute at them like a wand, and it seemed to calm them.

"Tomorrow night," I promised.

As I packed up my flute, people pressed in. I edged through them, overwhelmed by the hands that wanted to touch me, the strangers' arms that reached out for hugs, the faces leaning into mine with breathless congratulations.

Then I saw Michelle and Amy.

They both grabbed me in a hug, and for a second, it all felt so normal. But when I disengaged, they clutched my arms.

"Girl, you can *play,*" said Michelle.

"We can't get enough," giggled Amy.

"You're coming back to Lee, right?" Michelle said. "You'll keep playing for us?"

"Special privileges because we're your roommates," Amy put in. "Your *favorite* roommates."

"Come on." Michelle began to pull me along the main path of the quad.

"You guys, I've missed you," I began, "but I'm going back to the House. The boys are waiting for me, and —"

"The boys!" Amy scoffed. "Who cares about them? We're not sharing. You're ours."

Their hands tightened on my arms. Panic rose as I tried to twist free.

"You're bringing Daisy to me? How thoughtful." Reeve appeared in front of us, blocking our path. He seemed to have materialized out of the early morning fog. He looked into Michelle's eyes, then Amy's. Slowly, they loosened their grip.

He smiled at them, his voice soft and confiding. "I need to take her home now. But don't worry, she'll see you very soon."

Simultaneously, my roommates let go of my arms.

"Bye, guys," I said quickly, as Reeve whisked me away.

He pulled me into the shadow of a building. "It's a lot at first, isn't it?"

My breathing was rapid. "I need to be media-trained or something. People-trained. Are they going to be okay?"

"They'll be fine. You'll get used to the attention, Daze, and you'll handle it like a pro."

"You heard me play?"

"Every note. You're astonishing."

I held my flute case to my chest. "You were right. I got it all back and more, Reeve. I just wish that — you'd heard me before my fall. I wasn't as good, but..."

What to say? That playing had been more difficult, which made it feel more worthwhile?

I took his hand, staring at our fingers laced together. "A few times, I've experienced magic during a piece. It was so perfect, I couldn't bear it. I couldn't believe something this wonderful could exist in the world, that people were capable of composing and playing to create such beauty. It actually hurt. The first time it happened was in the middle of Mozart's Requiem. I was fourteen, and that was when I knew I'd do this for the rest of my life. But now—"

Reeve took my shoulders in his hands. "Now it's all magic."

"Not like that."

"Daze, I don't want you to be in pain." His beautiful face furrowed. "I don't ever want you to experience sorrow or deprivation. Only happiness. You're safe now. You're invincible. You can't be harmed. That's what I've always wanted for all of us. To protect you, to provide for you."

"But if I can't experience sorrow—"

I can't play well. I can't enjoy the good parts of life. I can't love.

"Then what?" He leaned close, and I tumbled headfirst into the starless night of his eyes.

"Never mind," I said, and kissed him.

The kiss was soft and sweet, laced with an intoxicating brew of danger. With every press of our lips, he tugged me into him.

"Reeve—"

He groaned, his cock bursting through his pants. "I'm going to take you, Daze. Right here and now."

"Outside?"

"Fuck, yes. On the ground, because it's ours. This campus is ours. Do you want to be my Star right here on the grass?"

"Yes," I gasped.

I shivered in the cool dawn as he unbuttoned my dress.

There was no restraint this time. No areas that were off-limits. He covered me with his mouth as he stripped my clothes away to let them fall to the ground. Nerves surged through me when I was exposed to the open air. I clung to him, soaking up his heat, as I pulled at his immaculate shirt and perfectly creased slacks.

Reeve didn't tease or toy with me. He didn't coyly hide his nudity. In the rosy light of dawn, the grass was wet and cool. He eased me down in one smooth motion. The dew-coated blades chilled and tickled my back.

Without a word, he pushed my knees to my chest. I was ready. Spread like a butterfly, knowing that while he loomed above me, filling my vision, coming closer as the world faded around him, I was reeling him in.

In the afterglow of the Joining, I felt a twinge of soreness. But hunger accompanied it, hurtling through me at the slightest touch. I bit Reeve's shoulder as his cock sank inside me.

He was so deep in this position, and his cock kept moving, *writhing,* massaging me from all angles. It was unnatural, for Reeve to be snaking inside me, and yet it felt utterly right.

I rocked against him, the sky turning from pink to pale blue overhead, until a murmur of conversation caught my attention.

When I saw curious eyes around us — people staring — I seized up in shock and excitement.

"They're watching, aren't they?" Reeve murmured. "They should. You're the Star and no one will ever doubt it."

I arched against him, riding the thrill, as the circle of onlookers watched with their mouths gaping. Reeve reached between us to rub my clit.

"That's it," he growled. "Let the whole world see me fuck you. Come hard on my cock, my precious slut, my Star of the Cosmos. Come with the pussy that everyone wants."

Waves of need crested and crashed. Clamping down on Reeve's thick cock, I came in ripples. I begged for his hard thrusts, growing deeper and rougher, until he spilled himself inside me.

"Fuck," someone whispered. The exclamation made me groan and pulse one last time.

I held Reeve close, savoring his pounding heart. "Are they going to leave?" I whispered.

"Are you ready for them to?"

"Yes."

"Then tell them," he said simply.

I looked up at the slack-jawed college students who surrounded us — exhausted and glassy-eyed, yet hungry.

"Go." I drew a rumble of energy from the earth. "Go about your business. Leave us now."

They did. It made me giggle, seeing them scurry away. Reeve's chuckle brushed my ear.

We lay locked in an embrace, his skin hot against mine, until he kissed his way down my chest and gently spread my pussy to drink in the view.

"What a beautiful sight," he murmured, his eyes still snakelike. "Let's go get clean, dirty girl."

Holding Reeve's hand, I floated on the walk back to the House, barely touching the ground. As we exited campus, he reached over to take my flute case.

I pulled it close. "Thanks, but I'm not ready to let go of my baby."

He laughed. "Just being a gentleman."

"I like you the way you are," I murmured. "You're no gentleman."

"Not even a little?" He raised his eyebrows. "I want to do right by you, Daze."

I squeezed his right hand with my left, still amazed at the absence of pain. "Oh, you do."

The House was silent when we entered. In the darkened living room, the drapes were closed. Nathan, Blake, and Evan still lay on the marble altar.

They were even more beautiful than they'd been before the ritual, their limbs sculpted like perfect specimens of art. I wondered if my appearance had changed as well. I hadn't looked in a mirror since the Joining.

"Should we wake them?" I whispered.

Reeve shook his head. "Let them recover. When they rise, they'll be more than ready for you. And you, sweet flower — you'll need all your strength."

I shivered, anticipation fizzing inside me.

In Reeve's opulent bathroom, I stared into the enormous mirror as he opened the taps to the tub.

I was brighter. More polished. More refined. My eyes flickered between blue-gray and greenish-gold, wide and arresting. My face looked startlingly symmetrical; one eyebrow had always been a little higher than the other, one eye a little droopier, but now they matched. My cheekbones were exaggerated, my jaw sharper. The scar on my chin from a childhood dive into the shallow end of a pool was erased; the birthmark on my shoulder had vanished. The little hairs that would normally escape my braid and frizz into a halo now lay sleek as silk.

My skin was a smooth satin canvas, each curve and dip pronounced, with only the snake tattoo for variation. It was like my body existed for the sake of the serpent's throne. I looked airbrushed, lit from within.

Every sign of the past, of the human life I'd lived — deleted.

Behind me, Reeve glowed with his own shadowed fire. It almost hurt to see the two of us in the mirror, as it would to look at the sun.

He chuckled. "Admiring yourself? Good. You should."

"I don't look real," I protested, but a grin kept sneaking through. The slight gap between my front teeth was now closed. "My smile looks like a toothpaste commercial."

"It's still the smile I've loved since the moment I saw you. Sudden and sweet, a little innocent and a little naughty."

Behind me, I saw Reeve rub a hand over his own face and turn quickly to pour fragrant oil into the tub. The scent of sandalwood rose through the air.

Loved. We hadn't talked about my love spell, or its effects on Reeve, since the confrontation in the woods.

Did it matter now?

When he beckoned me to the tub, I gave him my right hand, angling my body to protect my left, and we both laughed a little.

"I guess I don't need to do that anymore." I sank in up to my chin.

Reeve pulled me close. Sprawled in his lap, my back to his chest, I ran my finger over the scarlet twists of his snake tattoo. His skin blazed briefly, his cock twitching against my ass, and my own tattoo glowed hot.

"That's amazing," I breathed. "We feel each other through the ink?"

"All five of us can." His sleek arm wrapped around my waist. I sighed as he swirled a sponge over my breasts, washing away the pungent herbal scents of the ritual. "It's the presence of the serpent, Daze. Feel it inside you?"

I stretched. "Yes. It feels — delicious. It's moving, filling me. It knows everything I wish for, and it wants me to have it." I twisted around to meet Reeve's eyes, brilliant green with black slits for pupils. "*You* know everything I want."

"I do." He kissed my neck.

I snuggled up to his chest as the steaming water lapped around us.

"You're really with me now," I murmured to Reeve. "You're not holding back."

A sudden wave of profound exhaustion rolled over me, making me droop in his arms, and he cuddled me against him.

"Sleepy, sweet girl?"

"Mm-hm." I nodded, letting out a yawn, and twisted around to look up at him. "God, last night was indescribable."

"Told you we'd take care of you." Reeve gave me a smug smirk.

"Oh, don't look so pleased with yourself." I sat up and threw the sponge at him.

He stretched his arms above his head with a broad grin. "Why not? I'm completely fucking pleased with myself. We'll celebrate. You see? There was nothing to worry about. No risks at all."

I thrust my fingers into his wet hair. "Reeve...they all came to listen. I was somebody."

The door opened.

Blake stood there, naked, his lean body glowing in the sunrise. He raked a hand through the curls that brushed his shoulders. In the wake of the Joining, his network of tattoos writhed like a briar patch, swirling up his left arm and across his chest. I wondered if the serpent controlled them all.

"You two." He shook his head. "Look at you whispering together. Haven't you had enough one-on-one time, Reeve?"

Reeve's snake eyes darkened. Then he smiled. "You're right. Daisy, why don't you get some rest in Blake's room? I don't think you've seen it yet."

I glanced between him and Blake. This was why I was here, right? What I'd come for.

"I'd love to." I stood up, water streaming between my breasts.

"Make sure she eats and sleeps, Blake," Reeve said, giving him a significant look.

"Of course." Blake offered me a hand to climb out of the tub, and I deliberately gave him my left to get used to using it again.

"Daisy," came Reeve's voice behind me. He sat alone in the deep tub, his arms stretched along the rim. "You were always somebody. Music or no."

I nodded quickly. "You too."

17

Mantras

Blake

In the hallway, I pressed Daisy against the wall. Her body was lithe against mine, sizzling with energy. Gently, I smoothed the wet strands of hair from her face.

"How are you feeling?"

Her eyes were bright. "I don't even know how what to say. Was it this intense when you did your last big ritual? The Binding, a year ago? Will I ever get used to it?"

"You will," I reassured her, cupping her chin in my hand. "You're made for this, Daisy. *Destined* for it. And the Binding was much more challenging."

"Why?"

"Because that's when we became celibate. Think of all that desire, bottled up inside you with no outlet except your talent."

"Were you horny?"

"All the time, chicky. All the damn time."

A rueful smile played over her lips. "That's how I felt with the flute, when I was so frustrated about being cursed. I put all the energy into it that I would have put into another person."

I kissed her forehead. "Then you understand."

"So you're saying you're not horny now?" Laughing, she poked me in the stomach.

"That's not what I'm saying at all." I caught her hand and pressed it against my abs.

She tilted her chin toward me. "I dreamed about you for months before I met you. You were always the bright one, a flame. The Ace."

I drew my thumbs down her cheeks until they met and tugged at her lower lip. Her mouth slipped open, and her breath quickened.

"And you're our goddess." I brushed my thumb against her tongue, and her body arched, caught between mine and the wall. "Our Star."

"Blake—" she gasped, and I bent my head to kiss her.

Her mouth was as sweet as I remembered from Greer Hill. I'd kissed her during the Joining, but this was different, alone in the hallway. Each kiss felt stolen and private and utterly delicious. I nibbled on her full lower lip, grazing her tongue with mine. As she responded, deepening the kiss, I ran my hands reverently over her glowing curves.

"I feel like you're worshiping me," she whispered, twining her arms around my neck.

"Never doubt it." I flicked my tongue piercing against her lower lip, making her sigh, and worked my leg between her thighs. "It's the least you deserve. Are you hungry, sweetheart?"

"Starving in every way," she breathed out between kisses, pushing against me more urgently.

"Then I'll take you to my altar," I murmured in the shell of her ear. "And I'll feed and worship you there."

A smile broke across her face. "The kitchen?"

"Exactly."

Clasping hands, we ran naked down the stairs.

In the living room, Nate and Evan lay unconscious on the marble table. Evan was sprawled on his back, his left arm flung out to the side. His tattoo writhed, and scales shifted over his skin as he hissed and muttered. Nathan lay face down, silent and unmoving.

"Are they all right?" Daisy whispered.

"They'll wake when they're ready," I assured her. "The magic works on everyone in its own time."

I led her into the kitchen, where Daisy blinked under the bright lights. Her skin was radiant against the white-tiled counters, shimmering with the occasional flash of scales.

"What do you want to eat?" I asked, gesturing around at the huge fridge, the shining pots and pans hanging from the ceiling, and the eight-burner range. I swelled with pride at finally having her in my domain. "I can make you anything."

"Anything?" Her eyes widened. "I'd love to take you up on that. But for now, something quick. An omelet? Or — honestly, I'm craving grilled cheese and tomato soup. But the soup would take a while—"

"Not for me," I said simply. As Daisy perched on the countertop, I chopped tomatoes at lightning speed and cooked them down with onions while I started the grilled cheese.

"You're so *fast,*" she exclaimed. "I can't believe you haven't lost a finger yet, going a hundred miles an hour with those knives."

I crooked an eyebrow at her and touched the serpent tattoo on my arm. She bit her lip, feeling the twinge from our shared mark.

"It really is magic," she murmured. "Everything smells incredible already."

Adding homemade broth, I waved a hand over the pot of tomato soup to speed up the cooking. The grilled cheese sandwich sizzled in its pan. In minutes, I was adding a touch of cream to the soup, blitzing it in the blender, tearing in fresh basil, and setting out full bowls and plates for both of us.

"I'm glad you're going to eat with me," Daisy said, perching on her chair and picking up her spoon. "After hanging out with Reeve, who'd rather watch me eat than eat himself, it's refreshing."

I grinned, waiting for her to take her first taste before I dug in. "We all need our strength, Star."

Her eyes closed as she tasted the soup. "It's perfect," she said. "Oh my God, Blake. It's the perfect tomato soup. And the grilled cheese—" She bit into the crisp, buttery crust, and stared at me as she chewed. I chuckled, reaching over to tuck a string of melted cheddar cheese into her mouth. "I can't even," she mumbled. "Please excuse me if I don't talk until this food is gone."

"You're excused." I winked at her.

She was trying to pace herself, but she gulped her soup and devoured the sandwich. Her body was adjusting to so many changes; I knew she needed to satiate it. When her dishes were empty, I whisked them away and refilled them.

"Thanks," she managed, before cleaning them completely again.

I watched her as I ate. She was too focused on the food to be self-conscious, but when she finished, a flush rose on her cheeks.

"I think I'm satisfied now." Quickly, Daisy got up and started to clear the table. I took the dishes from her and put them in the sink, stroking her cheek with a smile. "At least, when it comes to food..."

"Good." Catching her, I whirled her back to me so her ass grazed my cock and she was looking out at the kitchen. "Are you ready to be worshiped?"

"Yes." Her voice spun out in a thin thread, growing taut with excitement.

"Our Star." Lifting her damp hair, I sucked gently on her neck. She shuddered from head to toe. "Our sacred one."

"My Ace," she murmured, and I smiled, scraping my teeth over her delicate neck. "You feel so amazing; I want to make you feel good too. Tell me what you want...please."

A tempting array of filthy acts flashed through my head. Everything I'd dreamed of over the past year — dreamed of doing with Daisy once I met her. But what came out of my mouth was something else altogether.

"Tell me about you and Nate." I pulled her close. "I want to hear about the time when you first knew each other."

"Now, Blake? Why?" She shuddered when I brushed my thumbs over her nipples. Her breasts were delectable little morsels, and I covered them completely with my palms.

"Because Nate's important to me."

She twisted around to look into my eyes. "You love him, don't you?"

I pressed butterfly kisses down her neck until she melted against me. "We're all bound now, Star. We all love each other."

"But he's special to you."

I slid one hand down to tickle her belly. She wriggled in my arms, laughing, and I held her closer.

"You're right," I whispered in her ear. "He is."

"He was always —" She frowned, trying to retrieve the memories, and I wondered if the serpent was already constricting her ties to the past. A trickle of concern ran through me, then vanished. "He was always so patient and kind," she said at last. "He felt like a rock that nothing could ever sway. I told him everything during our midnight talks. Not that I had such big secrets, but I told him things I didn't share with anyone else. Even his sister."

"Like what?"

She bit her lip. "Oh, about my parents fighting horribly before their divorce, and how much I hated it, and that I was sleeping over more often because of that." My arms tightened around her, wanting to take away the remembrance of her pain. "And how I wanted to win my next music competition to show my parents that they should stay together. I honestly don't know how I thought it would accomplish that, but I did. I wanted to win everything. And—" She screwed up her face, chasing memories that I knew must be eluding her. They'd never disappear completely, but they'd feel less important over time. She gave her head a shake. "Anyway, it doesn't matter now. But Nathan was an amazing listener. I only wish he'd talked to me more."

"I believe it." I turned her face up to mine and kissed her.

"His family never paid enough attention to him," she added softly, tugging at the strand of memory.

"I know." I stroked her hair. "But we'll pay enough attention to each other."

"And your parents, Blake? Do you talk to them at all?"

"They're in the past," I answered mildly.

"Completely?"

Should I show her? I was ashamed of the tie I still had to my history. Evan never missed an opportunity to give me shit about it, and even though Reeve said nothing, I knew he thought it was foolish. Nate had understood, but Nate and I hadn't had a real conversation in a year.

The serpent hissed inside me, pushing me to forget, to bend Daisy over the counter and fuck her, because that was our purpose here. Gritting my teeth, I forced it down. *Not yet.*

Daisy's brow furrowed. "Blake, are you all right?"

"Come here." I led her to a tall cupboard and opened it. She stared at the stack of cardboard boxes that rose from floor to ceiling, each labeled with the same name and address.

"Carrie Phillips. That's — your mother?" Daisy peered at the labels. "What do you send her?"

I shrugged, trying to be nonchalant. "A box of treats once a week, that's all. I want her to have a moment of happiness."

"Why do you look embarrassed? That's incredibly sweet."

I scrubbed my hands over my face. The mantra that I told myself daily came to mind: *I'm doing this for the sake of good.*

"Because I want more for her than that. With enough magic — with you here — the happiness might last longer than just a moment. I want to heal her."

Daisy took my hand between hers. "There's nothing wrong with wanting that," she said softly.

I closed the cupboard door with a sigh. The serpent lashed within me, angry that I was putting off my worship of the Star. When it squeezed, pushing out my thoughts, lust surged through me abruptly.

"Enough about that." I pulled Daisy to me again, so that her gently rounded ass pressed against my cock. "It's time for me to feed and revere you as you deserve."

She turned, frowning, and I sensed the battle inside her. She wanted to keep talking, but the same lust hummed through her veins as through mine. I saw her acknowledge it, then succumb to it, her face relaxing and her eyes turning hot with need.

Lifting her chin to kiss me, she arched against my body while our tongues entwined.

"You want this, don't you, baby?" I whispered, stroking her hips.

She inhaled sharply. "So much."

"Mmm, and I can tell you just had Reeve inside you." I ran my fingers through her shimmering hair, making her shiver.

"I did," she confessed. "We were in public."

"Really, chicky? Right in the middle of campus? With an audience watching every move while you soaked up their attention?"

"Mm-hm." Her cheeks reddened, and she let out a giddy laugh.

"That's our Star." I nuzzled her neck.

Swooping her up into my arms, I carried her to the large white kitchen table and settled her on her back. She lay sprawled there, her eyes shining, ready to sanctify this room.

"Is his cum still inside you, baby? Because I want to taste it again." Kneeling before her, I spread her long legs firmly, massaging circles on her thighs. Her ass pressed deliciously against the table as her legs dangled in the air, toes flexing and pointing.

She moaned. "Blake, we took a bath. It's probably all gone...*oh.*"

I lowered my mouth to her pussy. She made soft, pleading noises as I sucked on the tender flesh, stiffening my tongue and pushing it inside her to savor her.

"Not gone." I lifted my head. "I recognize his taste, Star."

She shuddered, her eyes widening. "Did you — taste him back at the beginning? He told me before the Joining that you all used to be together."

"That's true," I admitted, surprised that Reeve had been able to tell her that much. "And yes, I did."

"Were you already here at Pacific Crest?" She lifted her head curiously.

I stroked her clit, trying to keep her focused on our needs, but her eyes narrowed in expectation.

"After Reeve found us," I said softly, "we shared an apartment in L.A. for the summer. Then we came here. We started out rooming together in the dorms, because we were required to for the first year, but that didn't last long. I would've been fine with it, but Reeve didn't have much patience for college life, and it would have been hard to hide that we were dedicating ourselves to the serpent at every full moon." I pushed a finger into her glossy cunt, pulling it out slowly, and she sucked in a breath. "So he managed to move us into an apartment nearby. You know how persuasive he is."

"I do." Her hips thrust toward me as I pressed my thumbs into her thighs.

"And yes, we were involved with each other up until the Binding, which was when Reeve earned enough to buy the House. It was the most intense at the beginning, though, when we were novices. Like you are now."

I tongued her opening, savoring her tart, delicate flavor as her arousal mingled with the trickle of Reeve's cum.

"Tell me more," she pleaded. "Did Reeve actually let you touch him?"

I lapped at her harder, enjoying her little pants and gasps. When she moaned and grabbed my hair, I finally relented and stopped my feast.

"Reeve touched us, but he never let us touch him. I guess he needed total control. Sometimes he'd stroke himself when he couldn't stand the pressure of the magic anymore, and I begged him to allow me to lick up his cum."

She lifted her head, excitement flaring in her eyes. "Did he?"

"Yes." I grinned. "He acted like he was indulging me."

I remembered kneeling before Reeve on the wooden floor in that cramped L.A. apartment at the very beginning, opening my mouth to the fountain of his cum, aroused beyond all reason.

I remembered Nate and I giving into our needs together and holding each other afterwards, talking quietly.

I remembered Evan pressing his cock into my ass while we crouched on the kitchen floor, rutting like animals. His size had shocked me at first; the guy was fucking hung. But the lust and magic had been so intense, I needed everything he gave me.

Daisy's face was flushed with arousal. "You guys must have really been dirty."

"Past tense, Star? You think it's all over when we can finally fuck again?"

She shook her head quickly.

"You're going to be the dirtiest of us all." I gently probed the flowerlike pucker of her ass, glistening with her juices, loving how it closed eagerly around the tip of my finger. "Reeve's cum is in here too, isn't it?"

She groaned, lifting her head. Hushing her, I put my hand flat on her belly to reassure her as I licked all over her sweet folds.

"Daisy, you're perfect." I sucked gently on her clit, humming, and smiled when her thighs began to shake. "You don't know how long I've been waiting for you."

"Blake, oh God —"

Probing her cunt with two fingers, I found the fleshy patch of her G-spot and curled the pads of my fingers against it, rubbing firmly.

Her eyes flew open wide as her hips rose off the table. I smiled to see her slick excitement dripping down to anoint the surface.

"It's so intense," she whispered. "Please, I need even more..."

Rising to my feet, I fingered her harder, hooking inside her pussy, until I was lifting her off the table with every thrust.

"Let it all go now," I urged. "I want this room dripping with your holy cum, Star."

She made inarticulate noises, her eyes fogged with pleasure.

When I sensed she was at the edge, I dropped to my knees and sucked hard on her clit.

With a gasp, she humped my face, wetting it with a sudden gush. I opened my mouth in ecstasy as the elixir of her cum sprayed over my tongue and the table.

"Blake," she cried out.

"Good girl," I panted, licking up every precious drop. "Very good girl."

18

Queen

Daisy

I fell forward into Blake's arms, my muscles limp and utterly wrung out.

"Fuck me," I whispered into his chest. "Please, just fuck me."

He held me close, then guided me off the table and to my feet.

The white counters gleamed in the vast kitchen. As I stared at the galaxy of pots and pans hanging from the ceiling, Blake turned me to face the counter and bent me over with a firm hand on my back.

"This is where I've wanted you, Star," he murmured.

My cheek pressed against the counter. The kitchen surrounded me with cold metal and tile, and for a moment, I missed the Davises' kitchen when Sasha took it over: colorful, messy, and noisy. I wanted to be there with Blake, in a place that felt like home.

But I understood why he called this kitchen his altar. It held the hushed purity of a sacred space.

"Your body will make this room complete." Reverently, he traced my hips. "Spread your legs for me and feel the serpent move within you."

As he spoke, thick coils shifted inside me. The sensation was unbearably arousing. Blake made encouraging sounds as I opened my legs.

"That's perfect, Star. Shine your glory upon this place."

He stroked my pussy firmly as his free hand covered my fresh tattoo, massaging the snake's head. Shattering pleasure ran through my veins.

"Ace," I whispered, turning my head over my shoulder to look up at him. "What are you doing to me?"

His face glowed with beauty. "I'm going to take you this way. I want you to know how it feels to pay homage to the serpent."

His fingers circled my clit like he was sanctifying the tiny bud. The serpent filled every crevice of my body, soothing hurts from years past, licking my angry places, squeezing my secrets until they longed to pop out in a string of confessions.

"It's fucking me," I gasped.

"Honor it," Blake urged. "Give it what it wants. Let it redeem you."

The men had filled me with hard flesh on the marble table, but the serpent screwed me with dark emotion so intense that it took my breath away. Every thought, fear, and feeling that made up my soul swirled around in a maelstrom.

"Oh," I gasped, as Blake's cock sank inside me.

He thrust slowly, letting me adjust to being fucked from behind. The pierced head rubbed against my inner walls, stoking my need as the balls of the barbell worked their magic.

"I've needed you for so long." He rolled my nipples between his fingers, and I clutched the counter, my pussy clenching on his shaft.

My head spun. I felt so close to Blake, and yet the sex was so new. I barely knew him, but I knew him so well... It was disorienting, spinning between different states of mind.

"Blake—" I moaned. "I need — God, I don't know—"

"It's okay," he crooned. "Arch your back a little more. That's it, baby. Feel how deep I am inside you?"

"Yes," I whispered.

He stroked my hips, gripping them to lift me onto his cock. "Does it feel like I belong here?"

"Yes!" I reached back to squeeze his hand.

Leaning over to suck on my neck, he drove the breath out of me with a sudden deep thrust. "That's because I do, Daisy. And so does our lord."

Lord. It was the first time I'd heard any of the boys use the term. The serpent coiled in approval, making me ache.

As if he immediately sensed my need, Blake cupped my pussy, caressing my clit with the same little circles that I did when I was alone.

"You know what I want," I breathed. "When I want it...and how..."

"Of course I do." He covered the nape of my neck with kisses. "That's the beauty of it. We know each other's desires. It's perfection."

I shuddered with mounting excitement.

"Good," he encouraged me. "Good, good girl. Give me your orgasm. Every time you come, it strengthens us."

I gripped the counter, thrusting back as he rubbed my clit. "Blake, I'm so close."

Wrapping a hand around my throat, he choked me. The surge of pleasure was abrupt and shocking. Especially from Blake, the gentlest of the four.

"I know you need this, baby," he whispered. "You need to be held. Squeezed. Embraced."

As my head went light, I seized up on his cock.

Only then did Blake truly start fucking me. I hung onto the counter as his thrusts sped up, his force and tempo making me unravel. The Joining had been slow, but this — this made me understand what people meant when they talked about screwing.

I moaned incoherently as he flooded me with his cum, barely hearing his groans of satisfaction. Oh God, the hot fluid was oozing out of my pussy and running down my thighs, and his dick was swelling inside me, snaking, twisting—

"Blake," I gasped.

His only reply was a hiss. His fingers on my clit set me off until I shook with the thudding of my heart. After an eternity, he pulled out. The head of his cock pressed against my ass, the barbell marking my skin, as he rode out his climax.

Blake's bedroom was a warm, dark cave. Tapestries hung from the walls, and the red-curtained canopy bed came straight out of my dreams.

"This is beautiful." Naked and damp from the shower we'd taken, I twined my arms around his neck.

His lips on my earlobe made me shiver, but all too quickly, I sagged against him.

"Aw, is my baby tired?" he asked affectionately. "Bedtime?"

He pulled back the red curtains to his bed with a flourish. I sank down on the sheets. "Mmm. It's funny. My mind is tired, but my body...does the wanting ever stop?"

Stretching out beside me, he pulled me into his arms. I curled up against his lean body, his skin hot against mine. "Do you want it to, Star?"

He kissed the crook of my neck. I laughed when he swiped his tongue across the damp skin, then broke off when the silver piercing ran across my throat.

Impulsively, I rolled him over onto his back, pouncing like Evan had. He raised his hands in mock surrender.

"Oh. Not bedtime yet, I see." He chuckled. "What have we

unleashed?"

Capturing his hands, I pinned them above his head. "Stay." I pointed my chin at him. "Or I'll make you."

Blake grinned up at me. "I'll do my best."

I felt a rush of power as I nibbled and teased my way down his warm neck.

Finally, I could examine Blake's tattoos up close. I tongued every curl of ink, savoring the soft noises he made. I tasted the feathered raven that spread protective black wings across his chest; the thorny vines that climbed along his shoulder and surrounded the serpent. I licked the golden apple that conjured up a fall from Paradise, pierced by an ornamental dagger with a drop of blood. I traced the flames and smoke that flared from his wrist, vivid orange against gray.

"Which one came first?" I swirled my tongue around the apple. Blake's hands twitched, wrapping around a slat in the headboard, as my breast brushed his lips.

"The raven." His breath quickened. "I got it after Reeve found me. He reminded me of a raven, swooping in out of nowhere, mysterious and black-haired."

"And the rest? Are they the other men?" I raised my eyebrows. "The Desiderata?"

He nodded jerkily. "The fire's Evan. The apple — that's Nate."

"Not the Beast and the Knight?"

"Their natures hadn't been revealed to us yet. That happened when we went through the first initiation rites. But this is how I saw them." His head fell back against the pillow, his eyelids fluttering as I rubbed my nipple against his mouth. "The serpent imprinted itself a year ago, when it took its true residence inside us during the Binding. I got the brambles last."

"Will you get one for me?" I asked softly.

"Of — of course," he panted. "A beautiful daisy, right above the apple and the knife."

"Good."

"One house rule, baby." His blue eyes turned serious. "We're all bonded now. Until we perform the Sealing in seven days, we need to stick together. If any of us is apart from the others for too long, we all feel it, and it doesn't feel good. Over time, it's dangerous. Go long enough and it'll be fatal. So don't try it."

"How long can we be apart?"

"Two hours, three at the most."

"Won't that be hard?"

"No. And I'll tell you why." He bucked his hips toward me. "Because it feels so damn good to be together."

He was right. A warm glow suffused my body, and I just wanted to rub up against Blake and not stop. I felt the tug of the other men throughout the House, points of beckoning light.

"You've waited a long time for this, haven't you?" I asked, my voice husky.

"So long."

"Was it hard these past few weeks?" I caressed the soft hair on his thighs, and he let out a muttered *fuuuck*. "Getting a taste on Greer Hill? Seeing me naked? Helping Reeve and Evan punish me while you held off?"

"You know it," he grunted.

I knelt over him, caging him in with my arms and legs. My hair draped us in a golden veil. "You didn't know if you would ever be inside me," I crooned. Very lightly, I let the tips of my fingers brush his balls, and he jerked. "You wanted me so badly, Blake."

"You have no idea." A bead of sweat ran down his forehead. "I want you so fucking bad right now."

I caught his hands as they reached for me. "No, no. Very bad boy, Blake. Keep holding the headboard or you'll be punished."

He caught his lower lip between his teeth in a feral grin. "Look at you, Star. Reeve would never let you get away with this."

"How do you know? Did you ever try?"

I wrapped my hands around his cock, and Blake shuddered as if possessed.

"Lie back," I coaxed, marveling at the flood of new confidence.

"Be a good boy for me, and..." I leaned close, brushing my lips to his ear, fisting his dick with both hands. "You'll be rewarded."

"Please, baby." He melted, surrendering, as I covered his chest in kisses. Finally, I did what I'd wanted to since I saw him shirtless at the party that very first night. I found his tiny hard nipple with my tongue and flicked the sparkling piercing.

"Fuck, Daisy!"

"Does that feel good?" I cooed.

I sucked his nipples as I played with his cock, relishing the contrast of soft, warm skin and hard, smooth metal. He was babbling now, pleading for me to take him inside me. He clutched the headboard as he begged for my pussy. Each word was a potion, a gift, an intoxicant. I understood now why Reeve loved to hear me beg.

"Mmm, Blake. You're delicious," I murmured. "I don't want to let you come yet. Not when it's so much fun to play with your cock."

"I'll get hard for you again, I promise," he groaned.

"Will you?" I lowered my hips, grazing my clit over the shiny tip of his cock. He snarled and arched toward me, but I pulled away and put my finger to his lips. "Such noises. Sshh, baby, try to contain yourself."

I kissed him hard as I squeezed his cock. The head was slick with his excitement, and he hissed as I smeared it over the silky skin.

The door swung open.

"What's happening here?" Nathan's voice cut through the air, deep and amused.

"Daisy's discovered her dominant side," Blake panted.

"And this is a surprise?"

I turned to see Nathan's grin. He was naked, his muscled body huge and gleaming, his tattoo sparking on his arm. As he came alongside the bed, his pupils dilated, and a flush rose on his skin as he watched me hover over Blake.

Leaning close, he stroked my ass. "I always knew you had it in you."

"Oh? Did you fantasize about it?" I fluttered my eyelashes at him. I thought he might laugh, but his eyes darkened.

"Constantly." He looked down at Blake.

"Nate...?" Slowly, Blake reached for him. When their fingers intertwined, I sucked in a breath.

"I know you need this, Blake," Nathan said softly, his honey-brown eyes lingering. "I want to see it."

"Fuck, Nate," Blake grunted. His eyelids fluttered as I stroked his length.

Nathan hesitated, then brushed Blake's curls off his damp forehead. Their gaze held, and their breathing seemed to get in sync.

"I've dreamed so many times about Daisy doing this with you," Nathan whispered. "With me. With both of us."

"I know," Blake breathed.

The moment hung suspended. I froze, braced above Blake's inked body.

Leaning down, Nathan caught Blake's chin and kissed him.

My lips parted in surprise, feeling their kiss. For long minutes, I just watched. Until their mouths separated and Blake bucked toward me, rasping my name.

Nathan turned his head. "Fuck him, baby."

My fresh tattoo sizzled, urging me downward, as I slowly lowered myself onto Blake's cock.

"Oh—" I gasped, my cunt tightening around Blake. He moaned, gripping the headboard with his free hand, while Nathan deepened their kiss.

They were beautiful together. I rocked slowly back and forth, watching their tongues dart and their teeth catch on each other's lips. There was history here that I could only guess. But the serpent hissed to me that soon, I'd know everything.

When Nathan slid his hand up my leg to stroke my pussy, stretched around Blake's cock, I let out a whimper.

"Isn't that nice, Daisy?" Nathan murmured between kisses as he massaged my clit. Every stroke made me clamp down on Blake, who groaned. His forehead glistened with sweat.

Nathan finally broke the kiss and grasped my hair in a firm hand. Blake gazed up at us both, his blue eyes blurred with pleasure.

"Lift your ass, Daisy," Nathan ordered. "I want to—"

I caught his hand, easing it off my braid. Bringing his knuckles to my lips, I kissed them.

"I think you forgot something, Nathan," I said, a naughty grin dancing across my face. "Who was in charge until you walked in?"

The men laughed, though Blake looked dazed, his fingers still twined with Nathan's.

"You," they answered simultaneously.

"That's right," I teased, easing off of Blake. His pierced cock, glistening with my juices, pointed into the air.

Blake groaned, arching upward, and excitement rushed over me. This was too good to be true. We really could have everything we wanted, all of us.

"Watch us," I commanded Nathan. "Look at what I do to Blake."

With a broad grin, Nathan made himself comfortable against the wall.

"Don't even think of touching your dick," I added. "I'll do that when I feel like it."

He held up his hands.

As I lowered myself onto Blake again, never breaking eye contact, Evan's cool, amused voice made me tense up.

"You started the party without us. Guess that's what we get for sleeping late."

I twisted to meet his pale gaze. He'd just showered, and his blond hair was slicked back. Droplets of water glinted in the patch of hair on his chest.

"Guess so," I said pleasantly. "You'll have to wait."

He raised his eyebrows. "I don't 'do' waiting."

"You will today, my Beast. You'll come when I say so."

Evan's nostrils flared. He stared at my ass as it rose and fell, giving him peeks of my pussy wrapped around his friend's cock. His hand moved to his crotch.

"Don't touch yourself," I ordered.

"No? What are you going to do about it?"

"I don't like your tone, Evan," I chided. But the hunger in his eyes made me shiver. I tightened around Blake's cock, and he moaned.

Evan arched his neck, sinuous as the curve of a snake. "You need to be taken in hand, pet. You're a very poorly behaved girl."

"Oh, no." I laughed, bowing my body just low enough for my nipple to brush Blake's lips. He sucked eagerly before I pulled free. "I don't need to be taken in hand. You're all going to eat out of *my* hand."

Nathan chuckled, his arms folded over his chest. Clearly, he was enjoying this exchange. But coiling inside me was a genuine hunger to control.

Evan's eyes slitted. "That's not what I plan to eat out, baby girl."

"Oh? Then get on the bed," I commanded. "Lick me."

Leaping onto Blake's bed, Evan crouched behind me. His grip on my thighs was hard and rough, the flesh clutched between his greedy fingers. When his hot tongue flickered over my pussy, I cried out. Oh God, he was moving all around my entrance, licking the root of Blake's cock.

"Fuck, Ev." Blake jerked hard inside me.

I cupped Blake's face in my hands. "Don't come," I panted. "Not till I say so."

Evan laughed. "Hell, no. You'll both come when I fucking make you come."

And through it all, Nathan watched, his eyes glazed, his breath quickening.

"Come here, baby." I beckoned to him. "Feed me."

Nathan crossed the room swiftly. When I opened my mouth, he offered me his gorgeous cock without a word.

I sucked eagerly, his groans filling my ears as I took him deeper.

Blake's hips bucked, fucking me at an angle that made me gasp. Evan's tongue was everywhere, fast as lightning.

And it was all so good, but it wasn't enough…

"Climb over Blake," I ordered, pulling my mouth free of Nathan's cock. "Let him lick you too."

Nerves shot through me as I gave the command. I wasn't Reeve, accustomed to directing the players in an erotic scene. What lay between Nathan and Blake seemed tender, intense and fragile. I didn't want to blunder or hurt anyone.

But their desires pulled at me, insistent that they both wanted this.

Blake swore under his breath. Without a word, Nathan leapt on the bed and straddled his face. I heard my own breathy gasps as Blake ran his pierced tongue over Nathan's balls, rubbing the metal bead against his sensitive skin.

"Let go of the headboard, Blake," I whispered. "Touch Nathan the way you've wanted to for so long."

With a groan, Blake closed his hands around Nathan's cock, stroking it hard and fast. Nathan's face contorted, his mouth opening in a soundless cry, and he gripped my waist to brace himself. I leaned forward, my breasts brushing Blake's nipples, as I bent to suck Nathan's crown.

"Fuck, Ev," Blake gritted. "Keep rolling them like that. Help me fill our Star until she can't hold any more."

I felt the brush of Evan's fingers and realized he was cupping Blake's balls, just as Blake was playing with Nathan's. The four of us were connected in a never-ending loop of pleasure, like a snake that swallowed its tail.

As Nathan's hands sank into my hair, I shrieked at a sudden hard plunge from Blake, now taking me in earnest from below.

"Are you ready, pet?" Evan squeezed my ass. "Ready for us to fuck you into oblivion?"

His words arrowed to the darkest place inside me, a place Evan seemed to know better than anyone else.

This wasn't playful anymore. I licked Nathan ravenously, tonguing the underside of his head. Blake sent shivers through me as he thrust. I tried to find a rhythm as I rocked between them, but all I could do was hang on for dear life. And when Evan began roughly rubbing my clit...I moaned and trembled, making all kinds of noise around Nathan's cock.

"Sweet Daisy," Nathan husked. "You were meant to be with us. I understand now. This is right."

An orgasm rushed between my legs and roared through my body. Nathan threw his head back and thrust into my mouth, giving me his release. I eagerly sucked and swallowed as Blake's fingers dug into my hips. He fucked me impossibly hard, until I moaned with him when he came.

I collapsed into their arms in a sweaty tangle. When my eyes fluttered open, both Reeve and Evan were watching us, their eyes glittering.

Reeve had come in so stealthily, I hadn't known he was there. He kneaded Evan's broad shoulders, massaging the back of his neck. Desire smoked from their bodies.

"Thought you'd be resting, sweet girl." Reeve bent to kiss my swollen lips. "Did Blake take good care of you?"

"Yes," I whispered, dazed.

"You really should get some sleep, Star."

I was panting, puddled in Blake and Nathan's arms. But the wanting — that new, deep, greedy stir inside me — hummed like an engine revving up. "I don't want to sleep. All my dreams are coming true while I'm awake."

Evan glanced at Reeve, his teeth bared in hunger. A look of pride slowly spread over Reeve's face.

"You first." Reeve's dimple flashed.

Without warning, Evan pounced on me.

19

Hypnotic

Daisy

I woke to all five of us tangled in Blake's canopy bed. To my right, Evan and Reeve were asleep, but to my left, Nathan and Blake were kissing. I couldn't look away as Blake covered Nathan's body with his, cupping the back of his head as their mouths met. They rolled against me, their hot skin pressing into mine.

"Hey," I whispered, unsure whether the moment was private. Nathan snaked out a sleepy hand to twist in my hair, keeping me close.

I watched quietly as Blake kissed Nathan's chest and abs, following the trail of dark hair to his erection. Nathan's eyes closed, and his free hand sank into Blake's curls. They'd clearly done this many times.

When Blake's mouth glided over Nathan's thick cock, taking him all the way in, I couldn't keep back a soft noise. There was a chuckle behind me.

"Like what you see, pet?" Evan whispered. He wrapped his arms around me, rubbing his thumbs over my tits.

"I do," I confessed.

"They got attached at the hip when Reeve first rounded us up." Evan bit my earlobe. "Don't worry. Nate told Blake all about you. He just didn't name names."

His mouth fastened on my neck, sucking until my head swam.

Seeing Blake take such good care of Nathan, putting his desires first while Nathan soaked up the attention, made it clear that Nathan needed this. I thought about how he'd grown up ignored by his parents, dismissed by Sasha for not being special enough. He'd been nice, normal... and invisible. But Blake — Blake was smitten with him.

As bold as I'd been earlier, I felt tentative now, but a moan escaped my mouth when I saw Blake swirl his tongue over the head of Nathan's cock. Blake's bright blue eyes caught mine, and he winked.

"I'm gonna come," Nathan groaned. To my surprise, he pushed Blake away and climbed on top of me. I yielded to his fierce kisses, his plunges, as Evan dotted my neck with hickeys. When there was a sudden big thrust, and a stream of lust-filled profanity from Nathan, I saw Blake above us both, and moaned when I realized what was happening.

Blake was inside Nathan. Fucking his ass. Fucking me through him. When Nathan finally let my lips go, swollen and bruised from his kisses, the soft, satiny skin of Evan's cock rubbed against my mouth. I didn't hesitate. I sucked him as best I could, my head turned toward him on Blake's dark red pillow, Nathan and Blake heavy and demanding on top of me.

I reached out to where Reeve slept. I couldn't see him, my view blocked by Evan's crotch, but a warm hand covered mine. And I knew Reeve was watching us all.

Classes seemed like an afterthought now. College itself was an afterthought. The campus existed solely as our stage, until we didn't need it anymore.

In the middle of the night, I took my flute back to the quad and played for an even bigger crowd.

The doubts were mostly gone, replaced by a surge of power every time I opened my eyes and saw the sea of faces turned toward me, the bodies that absorbed every note I played and sent devotion back to me in waves.

When the sun rose, I felt full to bursting. The serpent was fed, and I didn't need to sleep. I stalked across the pretty, white-stuccoed campus that had felt so huge and bewildering a few weeks ago, and I felt ten feet tall.

No door was closed to me, no place off-limits. This school? I owned it now. More than Reeve, more than any of the boys.

People approached as I passed. Touching my arms, reaching out for high fives, pressing close to say hello. From across the quad, they waved. Called my name.

Daisy, are you gonna play again tonight?

I carried my flute case everywhere. In my hand, it really did feel like a magic wand — a beacon of power.

It was such a high. Everything the boys had experienced, I received ten times over.

Yet between the serpent's coils and the rush of recognition, there was still a trickle of doubt.

Was any of this due to me?

Or was it the serpent whom they loved?

The ornate grandfather clock in the living room chimed nine-thirty as I entered the House, which was flooded with morning light. I realized with a twinge that I'd been away from the boys for six hours. Longer than Blake had advised.

But they'd be fine, right? No one had come looking for me, and I hadn't felt sick.

When I entered the living room, Blake and Evan were waiting for me on one of the soft, deep couches. Though the September day was warm, a fire crackled in the fireplace.

I dropped across their laps. "Miss me?"

"Very much." Blake didn't return my smile. "You've been gone too long, Daisy."

I twisted my fingers in his golden-brown curls. "You could have found me. You sense me just as I sense you now, right?"

"It's not our job to run around campus hunting you down," Evan said, a command in his tone. "If you leave, you need to come back."

"I was performing." I raised my eyebrows at him. "Sex could wait a few hours."

Blake draped an arm around me and pulled me close, whispering confidingly in my ear. "It's not just sex, Daisy."

"Is it ever?" Evan put in. "I have issues with that phrase. 'Just sex,' like it's not important."

Blake gestured for him to be quiet. "Feel us."

Warily, I pressed my hands against their chests. "You're cold."

"Exactly. The serpent needs to be fed, Daisy. More than ever this week. It retreats if it isn't cared for in a timely manner, and us? We suffer the consequences."

"This week is crucial," Evan added, dropping his joking manner. "You need to follow every rule to a fucking T, and so do we. Otherwise, this could kill us."

"Kill?" I repeated, my eyes widening.

Blake nodded. "You need to take this seriously, Daisy. Evan isn't exaggerating."

I swallowed. "Is there any other way it could — kill us? Is it listening right now?"

Evan curled a finger under my chin. "It knows our thoughts.

Feels our feelings. It's part of you, Daisy, and if you can't tell where the serpent ends and where you begin, you're doing it right."

"The only risk of it killing us otherwise," Blake put in, "is if we try to get rid of it. And that's never going to happen. So don't worry, Daisy. Worry instead about how Evan and I are going to punish you for breaking this very important rule."

I sucked in a breath. "That won't be necessary. I get it now. No long breaks. I'll pop back here every two hours for a quickie. Or, you know, a not-so-quickie..."

"No, I don't think so, pet." Evan caged me in, so I was caught between his husky body and Blake's lean frame. "You won't be getting off that easy."

"No pun intended," Blake said.

"And before you open those pretty lips in defense," Evan taunted, "trust me, we fucking *know* you want us this. You want to be punished. You can't hide your needs from us."

My breath caught. I pressed my thighs together, but it didn't keep the moisture from welling up between my legs.

"Blake? You want to do this too?" I asked. Even though he'd joined Evan and Reeve in spanking me on the marble table after the night on Greer Hill, I couldn't reconcile his sweetness with his calm insistence on discipline.

"It's needed," Blake murmured. "It's part of all our lusts. Our truths. It would be a crime to deny that. And now you're getting wet." His lips brushed my ear. "You're getting butterflies in your stomach, aren't you? Your heart is racing. You can't pretend you don't want it." His tongue traced my jaw, and I drew in a shuddering breath. "So why don't you tell us what you need?"

"Please," I whispered. Everything Blake said was true. The arousal, the butterflies, the racing heart. "Please punish me."

They whisked me upstairs to a room I'd never seen.

"Welcome to my domain," Evan announced.

Given Evan's appetites, I would have expected his room to be extravagant. Strangely, it was the least personal of the men's bedrooms. There were no trinkets, no distinctive touches. The room was stark and modern, done in black, white, and a palette of grays from light to dark. The rug was flat, the bed broad. The only art that hung on the charcoal-gray walls were abstract black-and-white line drawings.

I looked for the twin bowls of herbs that I'd seen in the others' rooms — the copper bowl with reddish herbs that summoned the serpent, and the silver bowl with dark green leaves, the ones that I now knew moderated the serpent's presence. Along with the men, I'd started taking the green herbs once a day at Reeve's instruction, so the serpent wouldn't entirely consume us.

But I didn't see the bowls.

"Kneel." Evan pointed at the rug. My face heated as I obeyed. On campus, I'd felt ten feet tall. Now, I felt small, but I craved it.

Evan took a length of black silk out of his dresser and tied it firmly around my eyes.

My dress was swiftly stripped from my body. I'd given up on wearing underwear these days — no need.

The door creaked open.

Goosebumps ran over my skin as I crouched, naked and exposed. I didn't know who stood in the doorway.

"Ah." Reeve's voice sounded as he entered, deep and satisfied. "I see you're taking care of Daisy."

An exasperated sigh followed — Nathan. "She really didn't listen to us."

Blake chuckled. "She'll behave after this. Won't you, chicky?"

"Yes," I murmured.

"Good," Evan drawled. "Because we know how to manage ourselves, but you have to understand, we've been a little uncomfortable today. Now you're going to make it all better."

"How uncomfortable were you?" I asked, worried. "Because I felt fine. Hungry, yes, but—"

"It hurt, Daisy," Reeve said quietly. "It hurt like hell to be away from you. It felt like needles piercing our hearts."

Evan coughed. "Well, maybe that's how it felt for Reeve. I'd call it the worst case of blue balls ever. But Reeve's our resident drama queen, yeah?"

I opened my mouth, but nothing came out. I wanted to yank off the blindfold and read their expressions so I could gauge the emotions in the room.

"I'm sorry," I whispered. "I was thoughtless."

"And now you'll make it all better." Nathan's voice was as encouraging as it had been in our late-night talks.

"No coming," Blake ordered. "No speaking. You're here to serve our needs right now. If you take care of us properly and are sufficiently remorseful, we might allow you to come — later. Your pussy is ours, Daisy, and we reserve the right to deny you."

Oh Lord. Not that again. Not when desire beat at me constantly, tempting me to seduce and dominate and ravish everyone in the serpent's embrace.

"You really think you can deny me?" I asked softly. But I quivered with excitement at putting that power in their hands.

"What did we say about not speaking? Another word, and you'll be spanked." Evan gripped my face, and the roughness made me moan. I nodded in silence. "Now get on my bed."

Making my way in darkness, I crawled across the rug, feeling very naked under four sets of eyes that I couldn't see. When I bumped against Evan's bed, I clambered onto it. I felt him grasp me again, hard and possessive, groping my breasts and ass.

Then he let me go, and gentler hands cupped my face. Firm flesh pushed against my lips. Cool metal balls skated over my lower lip, catching on it. Naked and blindfolded, I opened my mouth to Blake's cock.

"That's it, baby," he encouraged me. "Lick me all over. Do it nice."

Contritely, I nuzzled his full, heavy balls, covering the soft skin with kisses. He swore when I sucked one into my mouth, lavishing it with my tongue.

A hand spread my pussy open, massaging the welling juices over my clit. I moaned, arching toward the tantalizing touch.

"Who is that?" I whispered.

"Wouldn't you like to know." Blake chuckled, and I shuddered as one, then two fingers slid inside me. "But Daisy, did you forget what would happen if you spoke? Because we haven't."

A hand cracked across my ass. I shrieked, tightening on the fingers that leisurely fucked me. Spanks rained down on my upturned cheeks. I wriggled and thrashed until strong hands pinned me in place. Tears of pain and pleasure slid down my face. All through it, I did my best to suck and lick Blake's balls while I stroked his cock.

Whoever was spanking me spread my cheeks wide. Cool cream suddenly met my pucker. I tightened up at the next smack on my ass, then relaxed as greedy fingers massaged my tight back hole, pushing inside.

When they were replaced by the blunt tip of a cock, I groaned, my ass opening to the thrust of an unknown man. I was still pinned firmly to the bed. A large hand worked between the sheets and my mound, squeezing it, slipping forcefully into the slickness of my pussy and massaging my clit.

As the thick, heavy cock sank into my ass, I licked Blake's balls frantically, squeezing and stroking his cock. The metal barbell, hot from my hand, bumped against my palm. He shouted, gripping my hair surprisingly hard, and thrust his cock against my cheek. Hot cum spurted out, oozing down my chin and neck and into my hair.

As I caught my breath, another cock bumped my lips. Obediently, I opened my mouth. Whose was it? I should know, but all I got was warm skin, a hard, veined shaft, and a woodsy, musky scent.

"It doesn't matter," came Evan's voice. "We're all one to you right now."

I sucked harder, trying to get a response. But whoever it was remained anonymous, with no tells to give their identity away. Quickly, too quickly, they came, filling my mouth, then pulling out to spatter my face, and I was being spanked again as my ass was taken.

It was overload, I craved it, it was too much, it was just right, and all I wanted was to—

There was a low sound behind me — Nathan, I was sure of it. Oh God, Nathan was the one fucking my ass. He jerked, his cock slippery and pulsing in my tight embrace. Before I could savor the feeling, warm liquid spurted inside my ass, the sensation more unexpected than tender.

Too soon, he pulled out, and another male body took his place. A cock sank into my pussy from behind.

He felt so big, fucking me at an angle, quick and rough. Evan, it had to be. His fingers closed over my hips and slid to my ass, squeezing the cheeks cruelly. My clit throbbed, though he didn't touch it. I ached, burning for it.

"Sweet little slut," he growled

I shouldn't be so close to coming just from him inside me, but there was something about Evan and me that I didn't understand. Every touch caused a shower of sparks. My clit pulsed, swollen and needy, as though he were massaging it. The fuck was greedy and taking, yet all I could do was suck him deeper inside me.

I couldn't hang on any longer. I cried out as I came, growling and snarling.

"Shit," Evan breathed. He held me close when he climaxed, driving deep with a roar.

Finally, he eased out, and the mattress sank beside me. Evan pulled me on top of him and I collapsed on his broad chest, my vision still velvety black. He wrapped his arms around me as our breathing slowed.

"Ev, what did you do?" Reeve's voice held a note of warning. "You know our girl wasn't supposed to come."

"We thought you could control yourself better than that, Beast," Blake joked, but he sounded wary. "I know it feels good when Daisy comes on your cock, but we had an agreement."

"I didn't do anything." Evan sounded drained. "Neither did she, as far as I know." He rubbed my back, and I soaked up the rare sweetness of his attention, resting my head on his shoulder. "Right, baby girl? You didn't touch yourself. You were holding onto the bed."

I nodded.

My blindfold was untied and removed. Reeve sat down on the bed next to Evan. "You can speak now. What happened, Daisy?"

Reeve. Reeve must have been the second one to come in my mouth. But I hadn't known it was him. He'd been silent, anonymous. Holding back.

I shuddered in Evan's arms.

"I don't know." I gazed into Reeve's eyes as the pupils narrowed to slits. "There's something about Evan. It happened before when we were in a practice room together. I came without him touching me in the usual area."

"You can say 'clit,' pet." Evan's voice was weary and hoarse. "We're all big boys and girls."

Beneath the sun-kissed mop of hair, his eyes had dark shadows that rivaled Reeve's. On his bedside table, I noticed a bottle of whiskey.

He shouldn't need it. Reeve had told me that alcohol dulled the serpent's presence. But it worked differently than the herbs we took daily — less reliable, less powerful, more temporary. More like a mask than a leash.

"Evan, are you okay?" I asked softly. "You sound sick. If it's because I stayed away so long—"

He caught my hand as I tried to stroke his face. "I'm fine."

Nathan frowned. "Why do you think Ev has that effect on you? Why not the rest of us?"

Evan stirred as I shifted position. "Chill, Nate. We all know you're competitive. Just accept that I can make her come better than you can."

I sat up. "You know, I was all set to cuddle with you, but now I'm having second thoughts."

Then Blake laughed and jumped on top of us, and Nathan started tickling me as Evan grabbed me in his embrace, and Reeve smiled on it all like a benevolent overseer. And I forgot about lethal serpents and unanswered questions.

I forgot about Reeve saying he had needles in his heart.

20

Air

Daisy

That afternoon, Reeve took me into his study.

"The House belongs to all of us now," he announced. "I want you to be acquainted with every room."

It was the first time I'd seen this space. The room was cozy and well-lit, with stained-glass Tiffany lamps, warm wood, and dark leather armchairs. Books lined the built-in shelves, and sigils and runes covered the wood-paneled walls.

On the polished desk sat a large flat-panel monitor with two screens attached to its frame, and a color-coded keyboard.

"What happens when we leave Pacific Crest?" I asked. "Are you going to keep the House?"

A shadow passed over Reeve's face. Then his dimple flashed. "Haven't decided yet."

"Do you work in this study most days?"

"When a certain Star isn't distracting me." He tapped a key, and the screens lit up. Colored numbers and charts flared to life on a black background.

With all the whirlwind of our romance, the House, Reeve's wealth and lavish decor, I'd almost forgotten just how he made his money.

"Show me what you do here," I said, waving my hand at the setup.

He raised a dark eyebrow. "You'll be bored. Didn't you split your sides laughing when I said the stock market was beautiful?"

"Try me." I perched on his lap.

Putting an arm around my waist, he scrolled down a chart.

I eyed the numbers that filled the screen. "Does this run through your head?"

"All the time."

"And it's beautiful to you?"

"Yes." He switched between windows, comparing sets of data. I leaned back and watched through half-closed eyes as he observed the screen intently. The array of letters and numbers made me sleepy.

"It's so private," I remarked. "Your talent, I mean. The rest of us have an audience, but you're squirreled away here, crunching your numbers."

"It suits me, Daze. And people see the results. The House, the parties."

"The parties," I mused softly. "Did you ever have fun at them? Or did they just exist to feed off the energy of your guests?"

"Mmm." He pulled me closer. "They were part and parcel of our offerings to the serpent, with the guests as willing tributes."

"But they didn't know they were participating in magic," I objected.

"They enjoyed themselves. No one was harmed, I promise. The Sealing will be the final party, and the most lavish."

I shivered with anticipation and tapped the terminal. "Does music seem as strange to you as this does to me?"

He ruffled my hair, focusing on the screen. "Probably."

"Do you think you could make me come while you work?"

He chuckled, sliding a hand over my bare hip. I hadn't bothered to get dressed. "Could you make me come while you play the flute, sweet flower?"

"I need both hands to play," I protested, giggling. "That reminds me, I have to make a phone call."

"Oh?" Reeve kissed my neck. Alone together, I got a taste of what had been between us before the Joining. I snuggled against him, reveling in the feeling.

"I want to get back into Siderio."

His lips paused on my nape. "Daisy, you don't need conservatories or scholarships now. Once we leave Pacific Crest, you'll take the world by storm."

"I'd just like to know that I can have it. I want them to offer me everything I had before."

"Why?" He sounded troubled.

I twisted on his lap to face him, stroking his tousled dark hair.

What could I tell him? That having my scholarship reinstated, whether I took it or not, would fill a hole that still remained in me?

I kissed him. "Just because."

"You don't have to prove anything."

"Isn't that what this is all about, Reeve?" I flexed my left arm, and the tattoo grew warm.

He shook his head. "All right, go ahead, Daze. Make the call."

I held his gaze. "I wasn't asking for your permission. I'll do it regardless."

He pressed his lips together, then gave me a resigned smile. "Of course. Use the study for privacy if you want. I'll step out."

The conversation didn't sit right with me, but I hopped off his lap, giving him another kiss, and went to get my flute.

Alone in Reeve's study, I opened my instrument case, fitted the joints of my flute together, and placed a call to Dr. Antonio Armore, the head of the woodwind department at Siderio.

"Hello, Dr. Armore," I said demurely. "This is Daisy Fisher."

"Daisy!" Dr. Armore exclaimed, sounding both pleased and

uncertain. "What a pleasure to hear from you. I hope all's well? We've — well, we've missed you here this year."

"I've missed you all too."

A pang pierced me as I remembered that life and everyone I'd loved in it. The wistful feeling managed to edge between the coils of the serpent. Then, distinctly, the serpent opened its jaws and swallowed it.

"And I'd like to talk about coming back," I said pleasantly. "That's why I called."

Dr. Armore coughed. "Oh! I see. Well, from what I understood — that is to say, your hand — uh, I guess the injury wasn't as severe as it seemed?"

I laughed. "Not at all. In fact, it's gone now. Let me play for you. I've got my flute right here."

"Um..." Dr. Armore hesitated, sounding flustered. "Well, we're holding flute auditions at the end of February, so if you'd like to re-audition, we'd be happy to consider you. Though I have to warn you, we have very few slots for transferring students, and our scholarship funds are extremely limited—"

I set the phone face-up on the desk and began to play.

The piece I chose was *Air* by Toru Takemitsu. It was a gamble, because I hadn't played it in years. I'd picked it up when I was fifteen and obsessed with Nathan. Then I'd put it aside, because the hardest passage always brought his face to mind, and it gave me too much angst.

The gamble paid off. Every note was perfect. The phrases arched up gracefully, then bowed to profound depths. I ran from silvery scales to languid slurs.

But in the end, the joke was on me. Because as I played, Nathan's teenage face appeared, leaner, more hopeful, and — something I'd never noticed back then — sadder. Then Sasha was beside him, trying to hug me, asking if we could make room for her on the patio swing, and I told her we couldn't.

I shooed her away.

I told her to leave.

I don't love you anymore, Sasha. I never will.

Dammit.

Sasha.

Alone in Morocco. We hadn't spoken for days, not since our fight over Nathan.

What had I done?

The last note winged into the air. I put my flute down and picked up the phone, shoving my feelings away.

"I just couldn't help myself, Dr. Armore," I said into the silence. "I had to share with you. My apologies if I overstepped."

My voice was sure and knowing, bolstered by the serpent. But my heart throbbed, playing tug-of-war in its grasp. It constricted, fighting for Sasha. It called out for Reeve, as he — as *we* had been before the Joining. It longed for the Nathan that had been more innocent.

Stupid, treacherous heart.

"Daisy, that was —" Dr. Armore stammered, groping for words. "That was astounding. I don't know what you've been doing out on the West Coast, but the California air...well, it's obviously agreed with you."

"More like the California land," I said. Dr. Armore laughed with me, though he had no idea what I meant.

"Of course we'd love to have you back. That goes without saying. It's a little unorthodox to bypass the audition process this way...the rest of the department would love to hear you play, they really must...but I feel safe in assuring you that your scholarship will be reinstated. Siderio — unofficially, of course, but I'm sure I can say this — will be very happy to have you back, should you choose to return."

"Thank you so much, Dr. Armore. I'll think it over."

When I hung up, Reeve entered. He smiled when he saw me sitting at his desk, my flute out.

"They let me back in!" I jumped into his arms. "Full scholarship and everything."

"Of course they did." He looked unruffled, but when I squeezed him tight, he swung me around.

"I live for when you're silly," I whispered.

"Me? *Silly?*" He shook his head at me. "Go find another guy. Nate, Blake...Evan...they're very silly."

I shook my head. "I like the way it looks on you. It makes me happy when you laugh."

His expression changed. "Truly happy, Daze?"

I gave him a mock pout. "Um, *yeah.* Truly, deeply, profoundly happy. Now you're just being silly again. I'm the happiest I've ever been. Come on, sit down." I dragged him to a deep armchair and pushed him into it. "I'm going to play for you. Prepare to be seduced."

He smiled and leaned back, his eyes never leaving me. "Go ahead, love."

I tensed. Reeve had never called me that before. What kind of love was this? The love of the serpent, the Joining? Love for the Star? Or love for *me,* Daisy Fisher? Did Reeve have any feelings for the old Daisy, pre-ritual, with all her faults and imperfections, or was she dead to him?

Could I even tell the difference anymore?

I lifted my flute to my lips, because I didn't know what to say... what to think or feel.

I chose a different piece than the one I'd played for Dr. Armore, a piece that didn't have any Davis memories attached to it.

I'd understood exactly what Reeve meant. Happiness was different now.

But that didn't mean it didn't exist.

Or that we weren't happy.

In the week that followed, I was prepared for sex. Lots of it.

But I wasn't prepared for the cocoon of affection. There was always a strong pair of arms to jump into when I got back from class. A lap to sit in while we had Blake's exquisite meals. So many warm male bodies to snuggle with while we listened to Evan play or watched Nathan on the field. Kisses, hugs, compliments, taps on my ass.

It was intoxicating. It was wonderful. I trusted the men, opened to them.

But of course there was sex. And as my power grew, I wanted more. I needed less and less sleep. Why lose myself to the hazy world of dreams when I could flex reality more every day?

Once in a while, I noticed the growing shadows under my eyes, similar to Reeve's and Evan's, the only discordant note in my magically enhanced appearance. Occasionally, it occurred to me that I didn't have a space of my own in the House, shuttling as I did between the men's rooms.

But who cared?

The whole world would be my playroom soon.

My worries dissolved. The past didn't matter. Sasha faded from my mind; Nathan as a lonely teenager faded from my mind. The relationship I'd had with Reeve before the Joining paled in comparison to the constant attention from the men.

At least, that's what the serpent whispered to me when doubt continued to creep in.

Until I didn't doubt anymore.

Siderio sent me an enthusiastic email, and I told them I'd consider their offer.

I played flute in the quad every night, where the crowds grew.

And the five of us bided our time until we could break free.

21

Twisted Ambition

Daisy

A rumble in the earth woke me. The Sealing was in two days.

Turning over, I blinked awake. I was in Evan's bed, sandwiched between him and Nathan. Blake had been with us, but I didn't see him. He was probably up and busy in the kitchen.

The ripples in the ground were coming from the direction of Greer Hill, which shone to my senses like a beacon.

"Something's wrong." I struggled to sit up.

"Nothing's wrong." Mashing his face into the pillow, Nathan tried to pull me down to him. "Come back to bed."

Evan's eyes opened, their greenness more luminous with the serpent looking out. I squeezed his shoulder. "Do you feel it?"

He pushed away the covers and rose to his feet like a sleek cat. "Oh, yeah. Trespassers on Greer Hill. There's a problem."

Nathan pulled his pillow over his head. "It's too early in the morning for problems."

"Are you all right?" I put my hand on his chest, which was

strangely cool and clammy. I was used to the men burning like the desert sun.

"Mmph," Nathan mumbled. "You're wearing me out, baby."

Then rest, I would have said, just a few days ago. *I'll let you be.* I would have stroked his hair and tucked him in, and I would have felt privileged to finally be able to do that for Nathan Davis.

But now, I felt a flicker of irritation. How could he be worn out by me? I was the Star. I deserved to have the men whenever I wanted. There were four of them and one of me, and I wasn't complaining about being worn out. Was Nathan really so weak that he couldn't handle my needs?

Inside me, the serpent hissed in agreement. Its jaws opened wide, unhinging on an endless abyss of desire.

"Come on, pet," Evan said, breaking the vision. "Let's go investigate." He pulled a black T-shirt over his head.

I dashed around Evan's room, looking for my clothes. He and Nathan had been careless when they yanked them off last night, while Blake watched with a smile, and now every piece of clothing was scattered.

My body throbbed from their rough attentions, demanding more. The constant appetite made it hard to think, and it was becoming increasingly intense the closer we got to the Sealing.

"We should get Reeve and Blake," I said.

Evan retrieved my gauzy purple dress from a pile on his armchair and slipped it over my head, reaching around from behind to button up the front and pulling me close in the process. His movements were slow and deliberate.

"I don't think, baby girl," he whispered, his lips moving down my neck in bites and nibbles, "that we need to bother Reeve and Blake. You and I can handle whatever it is just fine."

He brushed my nipples through the thin dress, and I shuddered. Lust clouded my mind.

"They should come," I protested.

"Reeve hasn't, shall we say, been displaying the strongest leadership." Evan licked my neck, then sucked it until I moaned. "Not since you've come on the scene. I doubt he'll tackle the issue with the necessary force."

"Force?" I repeated. "We don't need to hurt anyone."

"No?" Evan's hands covered the slopes of my tits, squeezing until my nipples hardened like pearls. One hand slid between my legs, pushing in the fabric of my dress, and rubbed my pussy roughly through the bunched cotton. "Sometimes that's the only language people understand, sweet toy."

I could hardly breathe. He knew exactly how to work me into a fever pitch. More and more as the week went on, Evan's touch kindled an inner flame greater than any of the other men.

"We have other powers," I murmured. "We can persuade."

"Where's the fun in that?"

"Oh, it's very fun." The ground trembled again, and I broke away from his grasp. "Come on. We can't waste time."

We rushed down the stairs together. I didn't love the way he was hustling me along, gripping my hand like I really was the pet he called me. But if the hill was in danger, we didn't have a moment to lose.

The serpent coiled inside me, dissolving my anger, assuring me in a soft, seductive hiss that I was doing the right thing in protecting the hill. That I could trust the Beast with my life.

Still, when we reached his car, I freed my hand and gathered my wits.

Evan drove a black SUV. I'd seen it parked in the driveway, but I'd never been inside. We jumped in and he stepped on the gas.

"Was this your car before you joined the Desiderata?" I asked, as he roared down the quiet streets. Palm trees swayed, and the early morning sun shone gold over fleecy clouds that would burn away soon. The neighborhood looked tranquil, but the energy in the ground wobbled crazily. "Or did Reeve buy it for you?"

Evan gave me an indulgent smile. "It's been mine since high school. There wasn't a lot of making nice in my family, but there were always things. Reeve's been generous with the House and his toys, but I refuse to be totally bought by him."

"You really see it that way? Blake and Nathan don't."

"I know." He accelerated, making me hang on to the handle above the door as he careened around a corner. "They're very happy to be taken care of by Daddy Reeve. Their own fathers weren't around when they needed them. But mine was too fucking present."

"Evan..." I reached for him, but he shook his head. I tried a different tack. "You make Reeve sound so controlling."

Evan laughed. "Would you disagree? You've seen it first-hand. I know it turns you on."

I shook my head. "He wants to take care of people because he can't do that for his family. He feels guilty."

"Guilt." Evan snorted. "If he's doing this right, he shouldn't feel any. The serpent eats all the guilt you feed it." He pulled up with a jerk down the street from Greer Hill. "What the fuck...?"

Construction vehicles jammed the road. Men in hard hats swarmed around the base of the hill.

I yanked off my seatbelt and shoved open the door. "The Chancellor," I yelled over my shoulder at Evan, already hurtling down the sidewalk. "He's tunneling into the hill."

Evan swore behind me, hurrying to catch up.

When I reached the foot of the hill, a furious woman stared at me.

Tara.

Her beauty was blurred, her face halfway between a glowing angel and an ordinary girl next door. Her hair stood out in a coppery halo around her face. Arms folded, she stood a few yards away from Chancellor Weston, who was talking with the head of the construction crew.

I went straight toward her. With the serpent inside me and power coursing through my veins, I didn't fear her machinations anymore, or even the collar. That was locked safely away in the House, and it couldn't be used against me now that I'd joined the Desiderata. I was sure of that.

When I got in her face, she shrank back, then drew closer, pulled in by her own fascination.

I gripped her arms. "What are you doing?"

"What does it look like?" she sniffed. "Your fun is over, Daisy. Hope you enjoyed it while it lasted."

"So you're trying to destroy the hill out of spite?"

"Look at this!" Her lips twisted, and her jaw — harder than when she'd been fully glamoured — trembled. She dashed an angry tear away and pointed to her face. "Look what you did to me! You're stealing what's mine. If you finish out the week, my face — it'll be gone."

"That's not your face."

"It is now!" she screamed, her features marred by fury. "It has been since I came to Pacific Crest three years ago. I'm not letting it go. It's all I have left."

"Along with the money Reeve's been paying you?" I needled. "Or have you burned through it all? Was your glamour part of the deal with him? He'd funnel some magic to you and make your wishes come true if you just kept quiet?"

"It wasn't only that," she sniffed. "I agreed to be their vessel. You know that, right? I had to have some advance compensation in exchange for staying *pure*. Reeve needed to know what it was like to pay a price too. Giving me some of his magic all these years, it's weakened him. Not that you can tell — he's been building up his stupid strength since he was sixteen. But he had to give the serpent more, because of me. More blood, more dedication. And I liked that. I couldn't stand for him to get too strong when he already had so much. I wanted him to remember that he wasn't fucking invincible, because of me."

I stiffened. I remembered Reeve's anguished words to me in the woods, when he accused me of forcing him to love me with magic. I'd protested that my spell could only bring out what was already there.

"I can't love anyone I'm not already bound to," he'd shouted.

What if my spell had worked because he was weakened by Tara? What if his feelings for me were Tara's fault?

And what if those feelings really were solely the result of witchcraft?

I shook myself. It didn't matter now. We were joined by magic far more powerful than the insignificant spells I'd cast as a human. Quibbling about love meant little when we were bonded to the serpent for life.

"So you were his shadow when you were kids," I said to Tara. I heard my own voice, casually cruel. To the right, Evan approached the Chancellor, a deceptively friendly smile on his face. "You lived down the road in your going-nowhere town, and you followed him everywhere because you wanted to be like him."

"That's what he told you?" she sneered, her wild eyes staring up at me. "I followed him because I wanted to keep an eye on him. He was always up to something, from the time we were young and he tried every way he could think of to get rich quick. Do you know he started a pyramid scheme in high school when we were fourteen and people *bought into it?* He's crooked. There's nothing good about him. But he was fucking ambitious, and I wanted a piece of that. If he pretends for one second that he's better than I am, he's lying."

Chancellor Weston's raised voice met my ears. "Get off this hill, Hayes, or I'm calling the police."

Evan flexed his arms as the foreman nervously palmed his phone. "Go ahead and call them, Weston. I love a party."

His eyes blazed yellow-green, the pupils lengthening. The foreman took a quick, jerky step back. The Chancellor averted his gaze, pulling his own phone out of his pocket.

"Now, Hayes. If you know what's good for you."

Evan laughed. "You clearly don't know what's best for you, Weston. Let me show you."

"And you're using him too?" I asked in a low voice. "Weston?"

Tara tossed her hair. "Why not? I help him, he helps me. I took a job in his office when I first got here because I thought it might be useful down the line. He was all too willing when I started making moves on him. Though *this*—" She pointed at her face — "makes it a lot harder. He wants this school to be great so he can soak up some of the glory. Once he traps you all here, I'm sure we can work something out, you and I. Something that will benefit us all. The boys will be a lot more willing to listen to me. They never did take me seriously enough."

Sweat ran down my forehead, but I responded calmly. "If he destroys the hill, Tara, it might destroy our magic. You could lose your face with no one to help you."

There was a shout to our right. The air shimmered around Evan, hazy and writhing.

"Don't try anything funny, Hayes," the Chancellor snapped.

Evan stretched out his left arm. When he pointed his finger, his tattoo writhed furiously on his biceps. It was — alive. It was moving. An actual snake crawled out and slithered down his arm.

I stifled a gasp. How was he doing that? Without any aids of magic? This snake was smaller, the size of the king snakes I'd seen around campus, but it glowed with bands of crimson, black, and gold.

The foreman turned and ran. The Chancellor backed away, his eyes locked on Evan.

"Where are you going, Weston?" Evan's voice was deeper, raspier, more gravelly. "This is what you wanted, isn't it?"

He was enjoying this too much. He flung his arm out, and the snake flew through the air to wrap around Chancellor Weston's neck.

Tara let out a screech, clutching her own neck. For a moment, heat flared around my throat, and I felt the clasp of the collar.

The Chancellor gasped for breath as the snake squeezed. We were alone at the foot of the hill. The construction workers had vanished, and the machines stood abandoned.

I closed the space between us in three strides. The flash of fear I'd felt was replaced by the confidence that had mounted all week. This wasn't the way. Evan needed to be taken in hand immediately.

"That's enough, Evan," I said sweetly. "Let the man go."

Evan glanced toward me as another snake crawled out of his tattoo. I noticed they were exiting at the point where the serpent bit its own tail. "It's not enough," he rasped. "Never enough."

Weston's face was turning purple. I clamped my hand over Evan's tattoo, which blazed searing hot under my palm. He glared daggers at me.

"Don't interfere. This one's for Tara." He raised his arm again, pointing at Tara, who leapt backwards, scrambling through the bushes. "Run, Tara," he called. "You won't get far. Reeve should have dealt with you long ago."

"Stop," I ordered, exerting my will as I bore down on the tattoo. Sweat broke out on Evan's forehead. I stared into his eyes. "Now."

A loud, shuddering breath broke through. The first snake dropped away from Weston's throat and vanished as it touched the ground. The second fell from Evan's arm and disappeared as well.

"You're despicable," Weston railed at Evan, backing away. "You're finished here. I'll see to it that you—"

I stalked toward him, hips swaying. Even my walk had changed.

"Look at me," I said softly.

As I stared into his narrowed eyes, he halted, swallowing hard. He tried to avert his gaze, but his head kept snapping back, forcing him to obey.

"Listen to me, Weston." I spoke slowly and deliberately. "You're done with Greer Hill. You will forget any vendetta you had against Nathan Davis. You will allow Reeve McClellan, Evan Hayes, Blake Phillips, and myself to proceed with our activities unobstructed. You will cancel the plans for tunneling into this hill. It's a historic site, Charles, and it should be preserved as such." He blinked furiously at the use of his first name. "You are the steward of this campus, and it's up to you to protect its treasures. If you don't, you can tender your resignation now."

"Are you done?" he muttered.

Walking until I came close to him, I lifted his chin with one finger, as Reeve had done so many times to me. He stared into my eyes, transfixed.

"I hope so," I murmured. "I hope I don't ever have to speak to you again. I hope I don't ever have to touch you or look at you. All I need is your promise."

God, the fucking power. I didn't need spells anymore, didn't need herbs or crystals or props. The serpent and the earth were enough.

Weston trembled. Beneath us, the ground wobbled slightly. Tara peeked at us from the bushes, and I thought at her, *Don't you dare leave.*

"I promise," he whispered.

"If you break that promise, you're done at this school. You're done at every school. You'll be a disgrace. Understood?"

"Yes."

"Good." I chucked him under the chin. "I'm glad we have an understanding."

He stared at me as I let go, his hand coming up to touch his chin.

"Oh, and Tara..." I couldn't resist blowing her a kiss as she stood frozen in the bushes. "You'll just have to get used to your real face. No more flimsy little schemes. No more taking magic from Reeve. He's mine, along with everything inside him. You know that, don't you?"

Her features contorted. "Good luck with that." Turning on her heel, she dashed away.

In Evan's car, I stretched luxuriously on the seat. "Well, that went well," I purred.

Evan stepped on the gas with a jerk. *"Well?* Going well would have meant eliminating the threat. You were weak. What, you felt sorry for them? You felt compassion?"

Before the Joining, I would have said yes, no matter how Tara and the Chancellor had tried to foil our plans. I would have said that compassion equaled strength, not weakness.

But I'd been foolish then. Human, with a fragile heart. Now I was learning.

"No," I said. "There was simply a better way. My way."

Evan flexed his fingers. "You shouldn't have taken over, pet. They deserved to be hurt. I would have enjoyed hurting them."

"That would have caused problems, Evan. I don't want any more problems before the Sealing. You can't barrel around doing whatever you want."

He growled, looking more like a beast than ever, then reached over and gripped my face in his hand. "But you can? Don't take all the glory for yourself."

Before, I would have been frightened. Now, I just laughed, the ever-growing power surging inside me, and patted his cheek.

"I like the way you manhandle me, but it's done. I took care of it. Now let's go home so I can sit on your face. We've got two more days before we conquer the world."

22

The Fall Tonight

Reeve

The party was perfect, exactly the bacchanal I'd planned. All over the ground floor, indoors and out, people were acting out their desires.

And the five of us had a hand in materializing them.

At midnight, we would perform the Sealing. The audience wouldn't be aware of their role; they didn't need to be. All we required was their desire. They'd be willing voyeurs to a scene with the five most wanted people on campus, and in return, we'd gain the strength to leave.

Nate clasped my shoulder. "You've got everything ready?"

"Brother, that's the third time you've asked me that."

He shook his head, looking around the great living room, where half-naked college students writhed on the couches, the piano, the floor. Blake's food was being devoured. Music saturated the air. A crystal glass from my collection smashed on the piano, and I winced.

"This is the most people we've ever packed in here," Nate muttered. "Fucking fire hazard."

Three girls swayed up to us, plucking at our clothes. "Why are you guys so *dressed?* It's your party!"

I smiled indulgently at them and waved them away. "It's good, Nate. Everyone's going to want to watch. The more lust, the more power."

He picked up a drink from a tray and set it down again. "True. If anyone's offended, they can leave."

Bodies gyrated and heaved around us. "I sincerely doubt anyone will be offended."

"Mm. Daisy will love being on that table." He nodded toward the black marble slab.

I draped an arm around him. "Nate, remember how hard you fought this? Four weeks ago, you were hustling her off that table and out the door."

He laughed. "Rub it in, Reeve. You were right. I was wrong."

But in the sparkling light of the chandelier, which was being used as a swing once again, the green flashes in his eyes looked dulled. He opened and closed his hands, his agitated movements recalling the days before the Joining.

"Are you all right?" I asked.

"Just restless. And fucking horny."

"Nervous about the Sealing? Don't be. The serpent's pleased and Daisy will carry the day."

He nodded absently.

Blake held court in the corner by the kitchen. I recognized Daisy's roommates laughing and chatting with him, which jarred me. Amy and Michelle didn't seem like the orgy type. And they reminded me of the night I first met Daisy, when her love spell almost knocked me out.

She'd confided that she was only a shell, that her kisses were cursed. And I'd spent the past month intent on convincing her otherwise.

I'd succeeded. More importantly, she'd succeeded. She was

powerful. Unstoppable. And when we performed the Sealing, we'd break free from Pacific Crest together and conquer the world.

I looked back to Michelle and Amy. "Nate, you think Daisy will be upset if her roommates see her fucking us?"

He rubbed his temples. "Ask her."

Evan came up behind us, slinging his arms around our shoulders. "Hell no, she won't. Our girl has a serious exhibitionist streak. Her roommates will thank us for the masturbation material."

"Are you drunk?" I asked, smelling liquor on his breath once again.

"Course." He hiccupped.

"Dammit, Ev! You're not supposed to be drunk for the ritual."

"I'll be sober by then, brother. We got a couple hours. It's our last party here; might as well get roaring drunk."

"You can drink after the Sealing," I grumbled.

"Relax, McClellan. If you're so nervous, go check up on security or supervise the fucking food or tell Daisy your needs are consuming you and she should take the edge off."

"She's not here to relieve my needs," I snapped. "We're adults. I can handle my own needs."

"Sheesh. Someone needs to get laid." Swatting my ass, Evan swaggered off. A trail of guests followed him to the piano.

"At least one of us is having fun," I muttered. "Make that two, with Blake." I couldn't see Daisy anywhere.

Nate grasped my shoulders. "I'm going to go lie down," he said hoarsely. "I'm not feeling so great. Gotta save my strength. You do the partying for me, okay?" I raised an eyebrow at him, and he managed a laugh. "All right, Blake and Ev will do the partying for both of us."

I gave him a brief, hard hug. "It's going to be incredible, Nate. Our lives are just beginning."

Nate held up a hand and disappeared up the stairs.

I paced the House. Why the fuck was I at loose ends?

Whatever I'd had with Daisy before the Joining, I didn't know if we'd ever get it back. We'd been together without limits this week.

Screwed more times than I could count. I'd taken her everywhere: alone, with my friends, in every room of the House and in the secret places on campus. We'd even dared to fuck in the forest on Greer Hill, because she assured me she could handle us there. I'd tied her up, spanked her, teased her, edged her, soaked her with my cum, and she'd had her wicked way with me more than once.

But every day, she became harder and more sure. Her confidence was bulletproof, her appetite immense.

The serpent had locked into her like they were made for each other.

Maybe she felt more for that creature than she did for me.

The tattoo on my arm blazed hot. *That creature.* How could I think of the serpent that way? It rescued me from the dirt hill of my life. It gave me everything — my friends, my House, my girl.

She's not yours, came a hiss from deep inside me.

A flash of golden hair caught my eye as I came back down the stairs: an arrow with a flaming tail.

She was dancing half-naked on the marble table, her beautiful little tits bouncing in the glittering lights. Women surrounded her. The male guests seemed to have gotten the memo not to approach.

Michelle and Amy were grinding on her, and I frowned.

I was all for people leaving their inhibitions at my door, but this scene bothered me. Not that the girls were touching Daisy; I knew nothing would come of it. No, what bothered me was that the behavior was uncharacteristic. Whatever innocence they'd had before tonight, I wanted to give it back to them.

Stupid. I'd just snapped at Evan that we were all adults. This was my own controlling, overprotective bullshit, trying to keep Daisy in a tower, a modern-day Rapunzel with a golden braid and an enchanted flute.

I walked toward the table to examine the veined surface. Which angle would be best for the Sealing? Should we fuck Daisy at the north end of the table, or the south?

It would be a repeat of the Joining. We'd take her one at a time, then together. Her light would flow outward and the earth would shake. I should be an inferno of tightly leashed need, but I just felt weary and burned out.

What I really wanted was to kick all these people out, sit in my library with a book in front of a crackling fire, enjoy my art collection without a hundred guests screwing on my furniture, and end the day by curling up in bed to talk with my girl.

Such simple desires. And they'd never been further out of reach.

Laughter rattled my body, deep and guttural. I grabbed the back of a chair for support.

Are you weak, my servant? Are you unworthy?

I straightened. "Never."

The mocking laughter filled my mind until I thought it would crack. *Don't tell me...you have a headache.*

"I understand," I muttered. "You're testing me."

You have no privacy, Reeve. You signed that away to me. I share your body, your needs...

With an effort, I clamped a hand on my stinging tattoo. "Everything will go as planned."

Where's your heart? It's not in this.

"That's because you've got it," I murmured.

Hips swaying, Daisy waved at me from her perch on the table. A week ago, she would have instantly noticed something was wrong. She would have stopped what she was doing and rushed over, her face betraying every emotion. She would have held on to me tight, and fool that I was, I wouldn't have hung on to her tightly enough in return.

Now, her lips simply curled in a sultry smile. Making sure all eyes were on her, she shimmied out of the pale blue panties she wore, leaving her long, glowing body bare. Whistles, cheers, and groans of lust followed her as she tossed the panties to me.

I caught them in my fist. I didn't feel like playing, but I went through the motions. I pressed the silky fabric to my lips, tucked the panties in my pocket, and winked at her. She swayed closer, inviting my touch, but I walked away.

Halfway across the room, I felt like an ass. I'd rejected Daisy; I'd probably embarrassed her in front of everyone. I turned back, ready to make amends. I'd dance on that fucking altar with her if that's what she wanted, though the last thing I felt like doing was dancing.

But she'd already forgotten me. She gyrated naked between her friends, head thrown back, soaking up the attention.

The clock in the corner chimed eleven. In an hour, the Sealing would begin.

23

Hell On Wheels

Daisy

I danced through the living room, buck naked, tossing back one of Blake's drinks. At the last party, I'd been nervous and inexperienced. I'd known nothing about the world.

But tonight? Tonight was so much better. All those doubts and fears, the pain and earthly concerns...poof. Gone.

"Thank you, baby." I pressed my fingers to the tattoo. It blazed to life, and need curled between my legs. "You're hungry, aren't you?" I cooed, rubbing my pussy. "Don't worry. You'll get fed tonight."

The tiny part of me that didn't belong to the serpent realized vaguely that I was talking to my vagina while a group of guys ogled me by Blake's cocktail bar. The rest of me didn't give a shit. After the Sealing, that tiny, annoying corner would be swallowed for good.

Reeve drifted around the edge of the living room, looking haunted. What was his problem? He'd been so eager for the Sealing; this should be the happiest night of his life. And Nathan seemed to have vanished. At least Blake and Evan were living it up.

I stalked to the piano, where Evan's chords rippled through the air. An adoring crowd hung around. I pushed through them to lean against him on the bench. He was shirtless, and I enjoyed the heat of his skin.

"How you doing, baby girl?" He caressed my breast. It felt good. It felt even better in front of everyone. I could feel the dicks hardening around us, the nipples tightening, the clits swelling. I was awake to everyone's desires.

I licked his ear. "Missed you."

"How about we have a little preview before tonight's main event?"

"Mmm, yeah." I tried to straddle his lap on the piano bench, but he shook his head. Lifting me easily, he draped me over the top of the piano.

"Just like this," he growled in my ear. "I've wanted to screw you here since I first set eyes on you."

"No way! Me too." I laughed.

But had I?

No. I'd shrunk away from Evan's searing chords, stunned and uncomfortable. Why had I done something so silly? The old, uptight Daisy would never have let go and fucked on a piano. No, she would have complained to Reeve about ruining the varnish.

But it was nothing more than a hunk of wood created to serve us. Just as my flute was a tool to wield power.

Evan squeezed my ass roughly as I lay belly-down on top of the piano, squirming in anticipation.

"Finally, I get you alone," he growled.

"Yeah, right, Evan." I giggled. "We've got a full audience."

"But you're all mine."

I twisted around to meet his pale, glinting eyes. A chill of excitement and nerves pierced the armor that hid my emotions. The serpent's approval quickly chased it.

Give him what he wants, the serpent hissed. *Feed his needs. Only you can satisfy them.*

I moaned, my cheek pressed against the lacquered wood of the piano, as Evan pinned me down by the waist.

"Mine," he grunted, his hand connecting with my ass.

A bottomless black chasm opened in front of my eyes — the abyss from my dreams and visions. It gaped. Beckoned. In my mind, I took a step forward, then another, as Evan's palms roamed and slapped my ass, my thighs, my pussy, drowning me in pure possessiveness.

There was a heavy hand on the back of my neck. Fingers played with my clit as I was held down on the piano. More fingers, slick with gel, massaged my ass, sliding into my tight pucker.

"Yes," I moaned, trying to hump his hand. "Please..." He laughed as he fingered me.

Desperately excited, I stepped to the brink of the chasm. It grasped at me, promising endless depths.

Hot flesh pressed against my ass. Evan had lubed us both generously, and I was so worked up that he sank in easily. My ass fluttered around his cock, eager and welcoming.

"Mine to have," Evan whispered. "Mine to use."

In that tiny corner of awareness, warning bells sounded. But Evan felt so good, so intense, and he was spiraling me into nothingness exactly as I wanted. The deeper he fucked my ass, the more I needed him to obliterate me with his cock, his greedy hands, his overwhelming want.

A ring of people pressed close to the piano, watching slack-jawed. Their desire made me prickle. I whimpered gratefully as they began to touch themselves and each other, shedding their inhibitions.

"Evan," I moaned, working my hand between the piano and my crotch to rub my needy clit. "I need the Beast."

"Damn right you do," he hissed.

When he came, I cried out as his cum flooded my ass.

"Come on, baby girl," he crooned. "Come for me and everyone watching us. I want you to fall apart in a great big orgasm. Give me all your strength."

I shrieked, clutching his cock in a long spasm. Light flared out from our joined bodies and the piano. For a moment, the chasm was illuminated before me.

Jump, Daisy. Jump.

As my breath slowed, Evan withdrew from my cleft, rubbing my back in circles.

"Show's over for now," he informed the disappointed crowd. "Come back at midnight."

The chasm vanished. Groaning softly, I came to a sitting position on the piano, heedless of the fluids smeared on the polished surface.

Normally, I liked to cuddle after sex, and the men were happy to oblige. Even Evan turned into a big, snuggly teddy bear after a rough fucking. But when he reached for me, I put my hands on his chest.

"Where's Nathan?"

He shrugged. "Hell if I know. Off having a good time, I hope. As long as he shows up before midnight, we're good."

"I haven't seen him all night." I surveyed the living room. Blake still held court by the kitchen, telling stories to a group. Reeve appeared briefly on the far end of the room, speaking to no one, and disappeared through a door.

"He was with Reeve earlier, looking kind of fried. Maybe you should find him, rev him up for tonight's climax." Evan raised an eyebrow at me. "The boy's going to have to perform regardless of how he feels. I don't know what his problem is. I feel fucking invincible. Don't you?"

The chasm opened in front of me again, and I stared at its seductive depths. "Absolutely, baby. As long as you take a shower before we do it again, because I need you all clean."

"Me, clean? That's never going to happen," he joked. "But anything for you."

I laughed. Everything would be fine, and there was no need for alarm bells. After tonight, I'd never have to worry again. None of us would.

I kissed Evan on the lips and sashayed up the stairs.

When I knocked lightly on Nathan's door, a low sound came from within.

"It's me." I pushed the door open. The fish danced in their tank. The lights in the room were off, and the only illumination came from the purplish glow of the aquarium.

"Nathan?" I asked. He lay prone on his bed, wearing boxers, his huge back rising and falling. "Are you okay?"

There was no response. I sat down on the edge of the bed and put my hand on his shoulder. The serpent, coiled around my insides, thought only of the heft of his muscles, the strength of his body, its athletic skill and winning prowess and raw sex appeal.

But the tiny slice of Daisy that was still left fought for air. It remembered that from the start, I'd thought Nathan Davis was in danger.

"Nathan," I said again, more urgently.

He made a faint noise and rolled his head into his pillow.

"What's wrong, baby?" I asked. His only answer was a groan. "Are you sick?"

I pressed my palm to his forehead. With the serpent inside us, we all ran hot, but he was burning with fever. Sweat dampened his hair. His pulse was sluggish, barely detectable. When he rolled slightly toward me and I put my hand on his heart, the beat was faint.

"Can I touch your snake?" I asked quietly. He managed a nod.

I touched my fingertip to the tattoo and immediately jerked back. The ink stabbed through his skin, angry and searing.

"What's happening?" I whispered, concern starting to overtake me. "I'll get Reeve. This isn't right."

"Daisy..." Nathan's voice was a dry rasp. "It's killing me."

"No. No, that isn't possible."

"I'm — fighting it. I've been fighting it all along. When I collapsed on the field — that's why. And I'm the only one — whose body's changed so much." He struggled to sit up, then sank back to the bed. "This was never meant to happen. Getting bigger, faster — it's not natural."

"It's hurting you?" There was a lump in my throat.

"Yes. We all went — too far. The power — you — the Star —" He broke off. He was pale now, his face clammy.

"*I* did this to you?" I couldn't swallow.

"I don't know. Maybe. The power you gave us — We knew it was a gamble."

"Nathan, hang on." I squeezed his hand. "I'll help you. We all will. You're going to be okay."

His voice was a paper-thin whisper. "The only way to be okay — is to stop."

"Stop what? The magic?"

His eyes were glazed, those beautiful honey-colored eyes I'd obsessed over in high school. The lavender light of the fish tank cast an eerie glow over his face.

"Have to — reverse. It's the only — way."

"You mean, expel the serpent?" I stared at him in dread. "But we've made it so far. All our dreams are about to come true. Blake said it's dangerous to get the serpent out. It could hurt us."

"Daisy, I'm — not going to make it if we do the Sealing."

"Jesus, Nathan. No." My eyes stung. I hadn't thought I could ever cry again. Jolted by fear, I jumped off the bed. "Fuck magic, I'm calling an ambulance."

"Doctors can't help me."

"How do you know?"

"I know." Perspiration rolled down his forehead.

"Just tell me what to do," I said. "I'll do whatever it takes to help you."

Inside me, the serpent lashed in protest, and I tried to get a grip on it.

"We need to reverse. All together. What we're doing, Daisy — it's bad. We're bad."

"How? Why?" I gripped his hand, but he didn't answer.

"Get — the book. Do what it says."

"The red book? The one Reeve gave me?"

He managed a nod.

"All right." I got up, barely able to breathe. For Nathan, I needed to be strong and in control. "I'll get the book, I'll tell the others, we'll help you. I swear, you'll be okay. We'll fix everything."

I kissed his forehead, and he attempted a weak smile. Nathan, the charging Knight. The boy I'd promised to rescue.

Racing to Reeve's room, I threw open his cabinet of curios. The red leather book sat on the top shelf, where we'd put it back after the Joining.

There had to be something else I could do. A healing spell, a better understanding of the magic operating on all of us. Anything less drastic than reversing.

But all my supplies were back in my dorm room: my crystals, my herbs and candles, Reeve's book on healing spells.

Why hadn't I studied the Desiderata more carefully? Why hadn't I prepared? Had I been so seduced by the idea of having it all that I'd leapt without looking?

I found one of my dresses in Reeve's closet and pulled it on. I smelled like sex and sweat, and my hair was a mess.

It's going to be okay, Nathan, I thought over and over again.

Fingers trembling, I opened the red book and flipped to the final section.

Reversal

My stomach twisted. I'd be giving up everything I'd tasted for the past week. The men would lose their talents.

Reeve's magic had been six years in the making. Who would he be without it?

I snapped the book shut, hoping for another way.

But Nathan's life was on the line.

I smacked the book open, rapidly flipping pages, until an image caught my eye. It was in the first section of the book, which explained how the magic worked. I'd skimmed this section because the print was cramped, the language dense, and I'd been exhausted and stressed.

In the illustration, a towering person radiated light like a star. In their hand stood a much smaller person, whom they were opening their mouth to swallow.

The image was so arresting that I paused to read the lines below. This couldn't be part of our magic. Nothing like this had happened.

Shivering, I focused on the words.

In order to increase your talents, it is necessary to feed on the talents of others.

A sick feeling crept through me. I forced myself to keep reading.

The magic will draw on them. It will channel their abilities to you. Use with caution, as desire is hungry and always contains more room in its coils.

God. God, no. This couldn't be where our talents had come from.

Magic preserves the order of the universe. Nothing is free. In order to maintain your abilities, the magic needs sources. It will not kill. A dead body is useless in its ability to provide. But it will feed off your sources as long as you use it. It will trap their potential and funnel it to you.

I swore, gripping the book.

Weakness creates vulnerability. Those who question their talents, who do not fully use their gifts, who are unaware of them, or who waver on their path are most likely to yield them to you. But your desire must be strong enough to conquer theirs.

My throat closed up as the full meaning sank in. How many dreams had we crushed? How much unrealized potential had we stolen?

Hot tears stung my eyes. Without knowing it, without ever meaning to, I'd surely put other musicians in the same position I'd found myself in last spring, when I slipped. I'd silenced their music. Fucked up their future.

Did the men know?

They couldn't. The alternative was too horrible to contemplate. To purposefully steal others' dreams for your own...

Yet I remembered Reeve entrusting the book to me in the forest. And when we spoke afterwards —

"Do you know exactly what you're getting into?" His voice had been so urgent. "You need to come into this with your eyes open."

Reeve wasn't rash. He would never have allowed the serpent into his body without reading every word of the book. And he expected I'd do the same.

I buried my head between my legs until the urge to throw up passed. Frantically, I studied the Reversal pages at the very end of the book.

Four to bind. Five to seal. Four to reverse.

Four, meaning the four men? Or could it be me and three of them?

I muttered as I read, absorbing the incantations to speak, the herbs to burn, the circles to walk, the stones to cast. At the bottom of one page writhed the serpent tattoo that lived on our arms.

Performed correctly, the Reversal will cause the serpent to depart. Beware, as it will make every attempt to take a soul with it.

I touched my tattoo, trying to communicate my worry, my fear, my urgent need to see all of them now. They'd resist giving up their talents, but when they saw Nathan's condition, they'd have to agree. I doubted anything else could save him.

As I stood, my phone rang.

Sasha.

Shit. This was the absolute worst time. But we hadn't spoken since the fight, and I just — I needed to hear her voice.

"Hey," I panted.

"Daisy?" She sounded small and lost.

"What's wrong?" I opened Reeve's door and hurried into the hall.

"I don't — I don't feel good. I think I need to leave Morocco."

"What do you mean? You're sick?"

"I think so. No one knows what's going on. I feel so tired all the time...I haven't been able to make it to class, or into Farida's kitchen. Maybe it's mono? I don't know. I can't focus."

A very, very bad feeling settled over me.

"No," I whispered.

"I just — if I still feel like this in a few weeks, I won't be able to go back to school, or work in the restaurant. I feel so foggy, I can't even explain it. Maybe I'm depressed? Half the time I'm crying, and just thinking about food makes me sick. I don't even know, Daisy. I had to call you."

"I'm sorry," I whispered. "I'm so, so sorry. I'm going to make it right."

"It's not your fault! I know I was mad at you about Nathan. I probably still would be, except I don't have the energy. But life is too short for that shit. I miss you so much."

"I miss you too." I looked frantically up and down the empty hall. Where was Blake? Still living it up downstairs? Had he taken Sasha's abilities in the kitchen for himself?

Please, I prayed, *let this be a coincidence.*

I didn't think it was.

"Sasha, hang in there, okay? I love you. Please remember that." The serpent fought me as I spoke, tightening around my throat.

Forget her. Not important. You only love me. "Don't leave Morocco just yet. Give it a few days. Can I — can I call you back in a little while?"

"Of course." She laughed, but it turned into a hiccup. Sasha, so tough and bright, was crumbling. "I'll be here, doing nothing."

"I love you," I repeated. "You always shine for me."

"Call back soon," she whispered, then hung up.

Clutching the book, I rushed toward the stairs and ran straight into Evan.

He held out his arms. "Whoa, whoa. What's going on, baby girl?"

"Evan — we have to — this is really bad." I gasped for breath.

"Hey, it's okay. Calm down. Let's talk." He took my arm.

"Nathan's sick," I panted. "Really sick from the magic. And I found out how it works...we have to reverse it."

Evan's eyebrows shot up. "Let's not be hasty. How do you know Nathan's sick from the magic?"

"I know. He knows. And his sister — the way the magic works — Evan, we only have half an hour until the Sealing. We need to help Nathan."

"Don't worry, pet," Evan said calmly. "It's going to be fine. Meet me in the tower in five minutes, okay? I'll get the others."

I hurried down the hall to the hidden door. Since the Joining, the House was no longer a labyrinth to me. I knew the secret places, the hidden crevices. Opening the door, I inched up the narrow staircase and emerged into the tower.

The stars blazed brilliantly overhead. Through the glass ceiling, they looked close enough to touch. Hands shaking, I lit the candles on the table by the telescope. Then I studied the pages of the Reversal, reviewing all the steps. My throat was dry, but I forced myself to focus.

Footsteps sounded on the stairs. The door swung open, and Evan entered alone. He'd put on jeans, but his chest was bare. His shaggy blond hair hung in his eyes, and he brushed it back.

"Relax, pet. The others are on their way." He closed the door and set a small bag on the table by the candles.

I walked up to him and got in his face. "This stops tonight."

He looked puzzled. "Why would we stop when the fun has just begun?"

"Because we're vampires. We're feeding on the souls of others."

He put his hands on my shoulders. Despite my height, it suddenly hit me how much bigger he was than me.

"Of course we are, Daisy," he said softly. "Of course we are."

I tried to twist free, but his grip tightened. "How can you do that?" I gasped. "It's evil."

"You signed up for this."

"I didn't know!"

"Because you didn't read the manual. Guess you were too eager to fuck us all. Oh yeah, and there's the music part too. I hear you wanted to be better than me?"

"Shut up."

"I'd like to show you something." His voice was so sweet and understanding. My stomach roiled, even as the snake inside me throbbed with twisted desire. "You should know the truth, Daisy. It's what you deserve. I'm sure you're tired of secrets. It's time to see and understand the full extent of my power."

"Your power?" I had a very bad feeling. *"Yours?"*

"I keep a diary. Did you know that?"

I stared at him. "No, I didn't. What are you trying to say?"

"Maybe you should have taken the time to get to know me. I have this annoying feeling, pet, that I'm just an object to you. A means to your ambitious ends. A snake for you to use and cast away, a stepping-stone for fame, when I've given you so very much." His words narrowed to a hiss.

I jerked out of his grasp. "How can you talk that way?" I snapped. "I'm not Tara."

"Really? You might find you have a lot more in common than you think." He went to the bag on the table and took out a dark green journal. Flipping through the pages, he let out a sound of satisfaction. "Here we go. April 4th."

"That's the date of my accident," I whispered.

"Poor baby. But it worked out in the end, didn't it?"

My spine prickled as Evan handed me the diary.

"Read," he ordered.

24

Mr. Hurricane

Daisy

I follow her. She's different from the others.

I stared at him. "What is this?"

"Keep reading."

Her doubts flicker in and out. They're woven with her genius. I can't get a grip on them. So I follow her for days.

That blonde braid hangs down her back, taunting me.

"Evan?" My head lifted sharply. His jade eyes were fixed on me with eerie intensity.

"Go on."

She walks around New York like the sidewalks are hers.

She plays her flute like no angel ever has.

More like a spirit possessed.

"Tell me you're joking." The floor heaved and rolled beneath me. "Please tell me this is some kind of sick joke."

"Keep reading, Daisy." Evan's voice was soft, merciless.

I have Rowan to thank, for once. He brought her to my attention, slavering over her like a dog. "Such a brilliant flutist at Siderio, spitting sparks on that solo in Firebird. I couldn't take my eyes off her. That young woman lit up the stage."

And I know the truth. That night, the serpent confirms it in my dreams.

She's the Star.

Once in a century.

And she will only find her way to us if she loses her powers.

"You didn't." I clutched the diary, my knees ready to give out.

Finally, my chance comes. Doubts pierce her confidence. She lies awake all night, questioning her path: is she selfish at heart? Is she meant to live like this forever, consumed by her art?

The next day, it snows. It's so easy to relieve her of her burden. Just one little push is all it takes.

"Dammit." My vision blurred, my words choked. "Dammit Evan, fuck you..."

He was silent. Frantically, I read on.

I miss following her, but if she finds her way, she'll be with us soon enough. And the power—it's unbelievable.

There was one more entry, dated Friday, August 20th. The night of The Crush.

She's here. There are no accidents. She's come for us and the prophecy will be fulfilled.

Slamming the diary shut, I shoved it in Evan's chest. "You're a monster."

He grabbed my wrists, and the book dropped to the floor. "Why so angry? You were meant to come to us. You got everything back, plus more. When you play, the world falls under a spell. Would that have happened if I hadn't given you a push?"

"Stop it!" I twisted my hands free and smacked his chest. He stumbled backward, off-balance. Tears rolled down my cheeks. "You were never thinking of me. You *stole* from me. I was so empty, so torn up..."

"I did this for you!" he snarled. "You're better off than you ever would have been without these powers. It was a crime, Daisy, for you to walk around as the Star and not know it. You would have squandered all your abilities."

"They're not mine!" I cried out. "We're thieves. All of us, Evan. Don't you feel any remorse?"

He studied me with eerie calmness, never faltering. "No. The serpent takes care of all that. I'm surprised you do, Daisy. Maybe you don't have enough faith."

"No, Evan. *You* don't." I put my hands on his chest again, trying with everything I had, willing him to feel some spark of humanity.

He blinked, his eyes clearing. His mouth opened, and a strained rattle came out. For a second, a mortal man stared out at me — wounded, seeking, terrified.

Then his eyes blazed green, his pupils lengthening to slits, and he hissed at me in gravelly tones that filled the tower. "Don't ever do that again."

"That's not you. That's the serpent talking."

"We're one and the same, pet. A perfect union. As you were supposed to be, with all of us." His voice was still gravel. "But I'm above the others. You know why? I stopped fighting the serpent.

Stopped trying to tame it. I stopped taking those pathetic little herbs the others rely on to gain some hold on their weak, human selves."

"What?" My voice dropped. "Evan — when?"

"Nine months ago. It's how I saw you, Star. How I was led to you. Without my eyes opened...I never would have known."

"That's why you drink so much," I said, awareness dawning. "It's not just to party or push back old memories. You're trying to keep that snake down so it won't overcome you. Reeve told me it hates alcohol."

He barked a laugh. "I've been weak too, pet. I can't handle its full glory. But after the Sealing, with you at my side — I'm looking forward to finally experiencing true pleasure. I got your powers, Daisy, but I didn't get your enjoyment of them. You kept that."

"Do you feel *anything* when you play the piano?"

"Hunger. That's it."

"And they knew?" I looked around the room wildly. "Reeve? Blake — Nathan? You lured me in together? This was your scheme all along?"

His face worked. "They know nothing. I've hidden it well."

He watched me with a strange smile, and I clenched my fists.

"None of them have my powers. They can't see their sources. Reeve thinks he has so much vision, but it never would have occurred to him to seek out the Star. He would have contented himself with Tara, who brought no power of her own. Everyone thinks I'm the clown in this House, the beast who thinks with his crotch. They're wrong."

"Why did you hide it from them?"

Evan's face twisted. "Sometimes it's useful to keep your cards close to your chest." He drew a line between my breasts with his finger. I snarled and slapped his hand, but he grabbed my wrists. "And this, Daisy — this is one of those times."

I tried to wrench away. "Let me go. I quit. I'm done."

"Oh, no. We're just beginning. You need to cool off so you can see reason. It'll be time for the Sealing very soon."

"Dammit, let go of me. Nathan is sick—"

"Nate will be just fine, as soon as he stops fighting." His voice was eerily calm, but it filled the tower, shaking the foundation. "There are risks in joining with the Star and we all knew it. Do you really think Reeve will let you ruin what we've worked for?"

"There's no alternative." I twisted free and headed for the door.

"Never let anyone tell you, Star of the Cosmos, that there isn't an alternative."

In a sudden, catlike motion, he lunged at me. I struck at him, catching him on the shoulders, and he flew back.

But when I made a dash for the door, he grabbed me around the waist. Though I thrashed and shoved, I couldn't break his hold.

Inside, the serpent taunted me, withholding its power.

It wasn't my friend. Wasn't on my side.

You have one purpose and one purpose only, it hissed.

The tarot card for the Star swam in my vision. Hope, guidance, purpose — everything I'd looked for when I came to Pacific Crest.

I focused inward, staring into the snake's glowing eyes. *My purpose is not your purpose. I answer to no one except myself, snake.*

Its jaws opened wide.

"Did my father touch you after that concert?" Evan growled, breaking into my thoughts. For a moment, his eyes were his own, pale and frantic. "Did he come on to you? Did he dazzle you with his fucking baton?"

"No!" I cried out. "I didn't speak to him. Forget your dad, Evan. You have to let him go."

"I don't forget, Daisy. I never forget."

I struggled as he pinned me against the wall. I kicked and bit, screaming at the top of my lungs and praying the other boys could hear.

No one came. I knew now that Evan hadn't told them to join us in the tower. This had been his plan all along.

Evan dodged my blows as he rummaged in his pocket. Out came a length of rope, similar to the golden cords in Reeve's room.

"Take a deep breath, Daisy. Count to ten."

"Fuck you," I spat.

"It's for your own good, Star." He bound my wrists together and lashed them to an ornate loop in the wall.

"Don't you dare call me that. You can't get away with this. Reeve and Blake will come looking for us."

"Of course they will. And they'll agree with me. The serpent's our master, Daisy, not you." Evan stroked my cheek. I whipped my head to bite his fingers, and he pulled them away. "You'll thank me after the Sealing. In time, you'll see our wisdom. You belong with us."

My eyes locked on his pale green gaze, and I shuddered. "Evan, don't do this."

His teeth bared. "You called me a monster. This is what monsters do."

I flinched. "You're a human being. Please...let yourself be one. See me as one too."

His eyes flickered. His hands dropped, and for a moment, I had hope. Then, looming over me, he put his lips to my ear.

"Eat or be eaten, Daisy," he whispered. "That's the way of the world. I'm damn well going to be the one who eats everyone else."

My heart pounded in my chest. "That's not you. That's your asshole father talking."

"The great Rowan Hayes." With a mocking smile, he trailed his finger down my jaw. "Soon, no one will remember his name. You and me, Daisy, we're stronger than the others. You understand the all-consuming hunger. You love power as much as I do. As soon as you came out of the Joining, you started exploiting it. You were fucking drunk on it!"

"That was the serpent," I gritted.

"Oh no, pet. That was you. I promise, you'll enjoy the Sealing tonight. And afterwards, you'll never look back."

"If you even think of forcing me, I'll rip your balls out."

He blinked, momentarily rattled, then chuckled. "Your body answers to mine. You can't deny there's something between us. Something you don't have with anyone else. Not your beloved Reeve, or your precious Nate...not Blake and his magic pierced dick..."

"Because you stole part of me, you asshole."

"You're so responsive," he murmured in my ear. "You come so hard with me. I barely have to touch you, because we're magically linked. You wouldn't want to give that up, would you?"

I yanked at the cords, but they didn't yield.

"You can't hurt me. The magic won't allow it," I rasped.

"I would never hurt you," he crooned. "I'm going to do something that's so much better."

He went to the small table where the package lay. I struggled against the bonds, my heart hammering. Sweat broke out on my forehead.

Evan opened the package and turned to face me. "I just want you to know, I *really* like seeing you like this."

He held an object in his hands. It caught the candlelight, dazzling me. When my vision cleared, I saw the collar from the herbal shop.

Walking to me slowly, he dangled the collar from his fingers.

I pushed down a surge of fear. "No. Fuck no, Evan. Not that. Even you wouldn't put that on me. You know what happened with Tara?"

"I know," he said evenly. "She wasn't worthy to put it on you. But I am."

"So you really do want me to be your little pet? You expect me to crawl around and bark?"

"Always a smart answer, Daisy." He swung the collar in front of my face. "This is your new friend. You're going to be much happier once I put it on you. All those bad, bad thoughts will go away."

"Shut up, dickhead," I snapped, my temper stretching. "I can't believe I ever let you inside me."

"You invited me in, baby, when you doubted your future. Stick with me and you never need to doubt it again. You want Reeve? He can't give you what I can. He doesn't even understand music."

"He understands me." My voice went quiet.

"Does he? You've surpassed him, Daisy. You're more powerful than he is, and he knows it. He's too weak for you. Too soft. You made him that way. Now that you have the serpent inside you, he can never keep up. His time is done."

I stared into his shifting green eyes. "I thought he was your friend. How can you speak that way about someone you love?"

He laughed harshly. "You don't know much about love, do you, pet?"

"I know plenty." Fear made my voice hoarse. Had I loved music? Did I truly care about my family, my friends? Nathan, Reeve, Blake? Or did I just care about myself? "You're the one who doesn't."

Evan leaned close, his breath hot, my doubts feeding his appetite. "Don't worry, Daisy. All you need to do is see reason. When I put this beauty on you"—he stroked the intricately embossed leather—"you'll be blissfully mine."

"It's a lie," I said desperately. "Are you going to believe that lie, Evan?"

"Oh, there's already truth to it." He stroked my cheek. I flinched, whipping my head away, but he was right. A deep, animal part of me yearned for his touch. "I will never give you up. All that power...we're joined, pet. You can't deny it." He ran the buckle of the collar over my jaw, then down my throat, trailing it between my breasts. I bit my lip as hard as I could to keep from reacting. "Here's your future, Daisy." He cupped my breast in his hand, drawing ever-tightening spirals with the collar's leather tip. When he reached my nipple, he pinched it firmly. Tears sprang to my eyes, and unwanted desire shot through me. "With this circling your neck, you'll want nothing more than to do my will. Together, we'll overthrow Reeve. We'll take the lead in this group, harness the serpent for our very own, and harvest immeasurable power." He stroked my belly tenderly, and my muscles clenched. "You'll bear my children. They'll be capable of things we can't even dream of. The entire world will kneel at our feet."

I spat in his face. "Never."

"Cute, Daisy." He wiped his cheek, his pale green eyes dangerous. "I hope you enjoyed that pointless act of rebellion. Your powers, pet? They're mine now." He put his lips to my ear, nuzzling my earlobe like an affectionate lover. "As they have been since April."

My mind raced. There had to be something I could do, even bound. I was more powerful than Evan, and we both knew it. But without the support of the serpent — still hiding from me — I was helpless.

I heard Reeve's voice from the first night in the tower. *You're powerless here.*

I kicked out as Evan buckled the collar around my neck, startling him. "Evan, wake up. This isn't you, it's the serpent. You can stop."

"I am the serpent." His voice came out as a deep, gravelly hiss. "I am no one and nothing without it. It killed my past. It is my future."

I shook with rage. "I swear, with everything in me, that you'll regret this."

"Shhh," he murmured. "This'll make it better."

I glared daggers at him. But the circle of leather around my throat began to warm — to glow — suffusing my limbs with sweet languor.

Give in, the collar whispered. *It'll be so much easier.*

I strained at my bonds and tore my gaze away from Evan, who watched me intently.

Yield, said the collar. *It'll feel so sweet.*

My skin tingled. "Evan—"

"Hm?" He leaned over me, running a finger along the edge of the collar..

This is what you want. What you need. You yearn to submit to these men.

That was a choice, I thought frantically. Not an enchantment.

Bend to Evan. Bend to all of them. You'll never have to worry about anything again.

My lips opened.

All you'll know is pleasure.

"Master," I whispered to Evan.

No! screamed a tiny piece of my mind, even as my mouth shaped an adoring smile at the thief of my abilities.

Evan grinned. "That's more like it."

"I'll do anything for you," I murmured.

He tousled my hair. "You're going to be a good girl now, aren't you, Daisy?"

"Of course I will."

He loosened my bonds slightly, easing the pressure on my wrists, but didn't undo them completely. "I'm going to get the others now. You're going to wait here and think about how to behave for us. And when we come back, you'll show us just how good you can be."

"Whatever you want," I breathed.

I clutched at my awareness, even as the collar threatened to dim everything with a dark, sweet haze. Evan dropped a soft kiss on my lips, and I arched toward him, straining for more. His chuckles echoed down the stairs along with his footsteps.

God, I yearned for him, down to my bones. I clung to the tiny spark of awareness that was me, in the corner of my mind that could fight.

Beneath my feet, the floor trembled.

The future that Evan wanted unrolled before my eyes. I lived to please him, to obey. Reeve was diminished, his beautiful eyes dulled, falling into Evan's thrall — and mine, because he loved me. Blake would follow our orders. So would Nathan, if he survived.

I saw Evan's and my endless expansion, consuming more and more of the world. Having his babies — so many, because Evan always wanted more of everything, and I hungered to fulfill his desires. They were touched with magic as soon as they were born, and heartless.

And the serpent was everywhere, in us and of us.

It was a nightmare. That future took the power of every dream I'd ever had and twisted it, hurtling me into an endless abyss of taking and wanting and yielding.

I focused on my spark of awareness and clung to it. If the abyss wanted to claim me, I'd fight it with every reserve I had. Closing my eyes, I tuned in to the earth.

The ground trembled beneath my feet. As I fought the chasm, the vibrations grew stronger. Shrieks came from downstairs, far below.

"Earthquake!" someone yelled.

Gritting my teeth, I tried to control the tremors, but I couldn't hang onto them while I fought. Yet the fight itself was causing the quake. The serpent was working against me, lashing the earth with its tail.

The ground shook harder. There was the sound of breaking glass. Blake's voice boomed from downstairs, telling everyone to get down.

The candles fell from the table. Flames caught the edge of the closest curtain, dancing upward.

"The Tower," I whispered.

I'd pulled that card from my tarot deck when I did a reading for the men. The tall tower stretching into the dark sky, its top exploding, flames leaping out the windows. People falling — or flying.

Catastrophe.

The death of the past, the birth of the future.

Sweat broke out on my forehead. I tried to loosen my bound hands, while the collar whispered to me to do no such thing.

The floor vibrated, and the tower swayed, rope pulling tight on my wrists as I jerked away from the wall. The curtains were ablaze.

"Reeve," I hissed. "Nathan. Blake..."

Would they come? Would they expect to go through with the Sealing if they did? Did they give a damn about me, or was I just a tool to them, an instrument, as I was to Evan?

Hadn't I started to see them the same way?

"Nathan, please hang on," I gritted.

We're bad, he'd said. He knew where the powers came from. No wonder he'd tried to warn me away.

The door burst open. Reeve rushed in, followed by Blake.

"What the fuck!" he roared.

In a second, he was in front of me, unbuckling the collar, untying my hands. Gripping the collar, he hurled it into the flames.

"Reeve..." Blake choked out.

I clutched my throat as it constricted, and the boys did too. The collar flared up in a green flash and a shower of sparks before falling in a black curl to the floor. The three of us gulped for breath as the pressure eased.

Blake hauled the heavy rug off the floor and beat at the fire on the curtains, smothering it.

"Daisy, what happened?" Reeve grasped my shoulders. "Who did this to you?"

"Evan." The floor pitched and rolled beneath us. With the collar off, I tried desperately to bring the earthquake under control, but I was too furious. At Evan, at myself, at Reeve and Nathan and Blake.

"Evan?" Reeve stared at me.

"Why would he do that?" Blake demanded.

"Because he wanted to control me." I fisted my hands at my sides, putting myself at their mercy. "I can't do this anymore. I have to stop. *We* have to stop."

"Stop what?" Reeve looked at me blankly. "The earthquake? That is you, right?"

"The spell. The magic. The power. Everything. I quit. And I need — I absolutely need — you to quit with me. Please. We can't be the bad guys anymore."

Reeve and Blake stared at each other.

"Daisy..." Blake began. "We're fifteen minutes away from the Sealing."

"We're thieves! That's what we are. We're vampires, sucking the blood of other people's talents. Did you know? Did you?"

Blake bowed his head.

"You knew," I whispered. "Oh my God, you knew, and you never said a word. How could you do this?"

"Daze," Reeve said very quietly. "You told me you read the book. You agreed to this."

"I know! I skimmed. I was wrong. I thought I read everything I needed to know." My voice cracked. "I made a mistake. But what we're doing — we can't continue."

The House shook. The serpent reared its head inside me, and I summoned every ounce of strength to shove it down.

I'm stronger than you, I thought.

"If people gave us their talents, it's because they didn't want them enough to hold on to them!" Reeve shouted. "Unused skills, Daisy. Wasted potential. All the serpent does is recycle, because they didn't deserve them."

"Nathan's sick," I argued. "The serpent is eating him from the inside. He wants to reverse. He says it's the only way."

"*Nate* said that?" Blake asked, alarmed.

"We'll go to him," Reeve said firmly. "We'll straighten this out."

As we hurried to the stairs, he reached for my hand, but I pulled away. The pain on his face made me flinch.

Nathan hadn't moved from his bed. When we entered, he stirred feebly. "You have the book?"

I held it up.

Blake went to his side. Dropping onto the bed, he wrapped his arms around Nathan, his face creased with worry. "You're burning up."

Reeve followed swiftly. "Nate, hang in there. Let's talk."

Nathan shook his head against Blake's chest. "Nothing — to talk about. We have to stop."

"Nathan—" I cut in quickly, joining them on the bed and taking his hand. "There's something wrong with Sasha." Nathan moaned, and I met Blake's eyes. "Nathan's sister? He may have mentioned her? Brilliant with food, an aspiring chef? This week, that all went away."

Blake blanched. "A coincidence."

"Blake, she felt *different*, and I sensed it across six thousand miles. She was tainted. A snake reached into her and took what it found."

"That can't be," Blake breathed, turning to Nathan, who stared up at him. "Nate, I swear I would never hurt her."

"How would you know?" Nathan croaked, his voice down to a rasp. "I'm done. This is my sister, goddammit. We have to reverse."

Blake looked from Reeve to me, his face white. "He's a wreck. We need to help him."

Reeve was almost as pale. "Reversal is an absolute last resort. It's extremely dangerous. There are other paths to healing him..."

I pulled out the last card I had. "My fall, Reeve. It wasn't an accident. It was on purpose."

"What?" He'd been pacing, and he halted.

"Evan did it. He stalked me in his dreams, pushed me down the stairs, and stole my potential. He heard about me from his father, decided I was the Star, got it confirmed by the serpent, and considered it his responsibility to strip me of my talents *just in case* I found my way to you. If I was already succeeding, I wouldn't be so eager to take a snake inside me, would I? When I think for one minute that I've done to anyone what he put me through, so I could rise on their back—"

Nathan pushed himself up on his elbows, anger contorting his face. "That fucker," he hissed.

"No," Reeve whispered. "That's not possible. We don't know who's giving to us. We can't see our sources."

"*Sources?* They're people! They're not giving, we're taking! And Evan knew. He stopped using the herbs that contained the serpent, which meant he could see everything. He watched me for days. He wrote about it in his fucking diary."

Blake winced, and Nathan clutched my hand hard. Fury twisted Reeve's features, making him look more snake than human.

"He did that to you and he never told me? All these years, I trusted him. Daisy, Jesus, if I'd known—"

Blake stretched out a restraining hand. "Reeve, don't go after him right now. Nate needs us, and Daisy—"

"He wants control," I broke in. "He wants us all in his thrall. He plans to use me as a power source while I pop out his babies."

Reeve lunged out of Blake's grasp. "I'll kill him."

"You can't," Nathan managed.

"The Sealing's in seven minutes," Blake said. "If we miss this window, we're trapped."

"You're talking about *fucking* right now?" Reeve rounded on him.

Blake grasped his arm. "I'm talking about our lives."

"We have to make this right," I pleaded. "Please, Reeve."

The ground rumbled. Nathan's bed rattled against the wall.

Blake thrust his hands into his hair. "Daisy, you need to stop the quakes. The ground has to be stable before we do anything."

"I'm trying! I'm upset. I'm furious."

Reeve pulled me to my feet. There was nothing cool or composed about him. He was savage, radiating dark energy. His grip on my hands was iron.

"I was nothing before this!" He let out an anguished snarl. "If we renounce the serpent, I'll be nothing again!"

The ground stilled. I stood before him and put my hands on his shoulders. His eyes shuttered between the green stare of a snake and the dark gaze of the frustrated, angry boy he'd once been.

"You were never nothing," I told him quietly. "And if you do this — if *we* do this — you'll be so much more than what you are right now."

We stared at each other, his eyes searching mine. Then Reeve turned his head. The movement began sinuously and jerked halfway through into humanity.

He was fighting the serpent. Sweat stood out on his forehead as the struggle took its toll.

"Blake," he said simply.

Blake closed his eyes. "I'll follow you. I always have."

"Don't say that. For once, make a fucking decision of your own."

Blake swallowed. When his eyes opened, they were wet and

bright. "I can't lose Nate. You know that. If he's gone, nothing else matters."

Nathan made a feeble noise from the bed. I squeezed his hand, and he managed to squeeze back.

Reeve squared his jaw. "Clear the House," he said to Blake. "Get everyone out. Daisy and I will bring Nate downstairs."

"And Evan?"

"We'll deal with him when he comes."

Blake swung back his shoulders, looked around at us once, then left the room.

Reeve and I hooked our arms under Nathan's. Strength surged through my muscles, as if the serpent were toying with me. Supporting Nathan, we carried him out the door and down the stairs. The floor shook again, and Reeve's framed art shivered on the walls.

Downstairs, the last of the guests fled from the House.

25

Can't Find My Way Home

Daisy

As Blake cleared away dishes and candelabras, Reeve and I helped Nathan to the black marble table. He slumped on the shining surface.

I grabbed Blake's arm. "Michelle and Amy. Are they okay?"

He was pale. "They made it out. They're fine. Everyone's gone now."

We worked swiftly, gathering the supplies for the Reversal and setting them on the table. Time was short, but I paused by Nathan to put my hand on his cheek. He gave me a weak smile.

Blake looked bloodless, and Reeve's face was closed and set.

Did they feel remorse for the talents they'd taken? Were they mourning what they'd lose?

As I placed the last item on the table, the copper bowl we'd used in the Joining, it occurred to me that the serpent was strangely quiet. Surely it knew what we were doing. Why wasn't it persuading us to stop?

We gathered around Nathan and joined hands. Candles flickered on the table.

"Daze," Reeve said quietly, not quite looking at me. "I'm sorry."

I didn't know what to say. Didn't know what I felt for him, with the serpent inside us both and all the wrongs we'd done. I squeezed his hand.

"What are the risks?" I asked.

Blake and Reeve exchanged glances.

"The serpent will fight us." Blake's voice was tight. "It'll try to take one of us with it when it goes. We need to be strong and stick together to ward it off."

Reeve finally met my eyes. "Daze, Blake's putting a good face on it. Even if we resist the serpent's pull, I don't know how much of me will be left when this is over. I didn't take Evan's path, but I've allowed a lot of magic in. For six years, I've let the serpent possess me."

I swallowed hard. "What are you saying?"

"I just need you to be prepared."

I stared at Nathan lying motionless on the table, at Blake silently gripping Reeve's hand. "Are you telling us you might not make it, no matter what?"

He nodded. "It's a risk."

"No. That is not okay." A sickening tremble ran through me. I could barely breathe at the thought of losing Reeve.

"We never planned to reverse, Daisy. We have no idea what will happen. I'm the most saturated by far."

My head shook violently, my chest clenching. "No! I won't take that risk. There has to be another way. We'll save Nathan, give back what we stole—"

"There is no other way." He wrenched his hands free, cupped my face, and kissed me hard. His lips burned mine.

"I love you," he said hoarsely, staring into my eyes. "*You,* Daisy, not some fucking snake or your flute playing or what you do with magic. Just you. Only you, no matter what. Always you."

"Reeve," I choked out, wanting to say more, but I could hardly speak.

"I don't care if it started with a spell," he went on, his voice gruff. "This is real. And if the last thing I see is your face, it's worth it."

He pulled me to him and kissed me again.

"Wait." I grabbed his wrist, but he twisted free and smacked his hand on the table.

Sparks shot up to the ceiling, fizzing and exploding. A starburst showered us with spots, dazzling in its heat and light. A supernova.

"Four to begin, five to bind, four to reverse," we intoned. The words blew out of us, reverberating in the great hall.

The door crashed open.

"What the fuck?" Evan stormed into the living room. In one glance, he took in the four of us at the table, and his mouth fell open. "Oh no. Oh, hell no."

He streaked across the room, his fist shooting out. Reeve shoved it away without turning around. His reflexes were as fast as Nathan's. Had they been, all this time, and he'd hidden it? Or was it only now, with magic sparking everywhere?

"Four by four by four shall you—"

Evan lunged at me. Blake swiped at him and sent him sprawling.

"You shouldn't have let her see that book," Evan yelled. "You trusted her too much."

The words of the spell gathered momentum, sweeping us along with them.

"How could you betray me?" Evan panted. "A month ago, none of you would have cared. The end always justified the means. You were right, Reeve. She's destroying us all."

He reared back and took a flying leap at the altar, hands poised to ruin and scatter.

As he did, the last word left our mouths and echoed in the air.

For a minute, nothing happened. Then it felt like my insides were being sucked out. In the Joining, the men had given to me again and again. Through them, the serpent had filled me.

This was the opposite. I was being emptied.

We all were.

It hurt like hell.

I gripped Blake and Reeve's hands as tight as I could. Sweat poured down Blake's forehead, and Reeve's jaw clenched. Nathan's head lolled back on the table as he gasped for breath. Evan roared from the floor, clawing at the air.

Above us, sparks glittered red and black and gold, swirling until they took the form of a massive serpent.

Its immense, spade-shaped head rose above us, scales overlapping like jewels. The tattoo on my arm blazed hot, and the stronger the serpent's outline grew, the more the tattoo burned. I bit my lip, stifling a scream, until I tasted blood.

Glowing eyes turned to each of us.

Farewell so soon? When I was about to get the choicest feeding in four hundred years?

Somehow, I found my voice. "You tried to take Nathan. So yes, we're evicting you."

Its laughter shook the rafters. *Oh, Star. You think I'll let you go so easily?*

Evan stumbled forward, spreading his arms wide. "Take me. If you're looking for a soul, you've got mine. Use me as your host, I'll find others, you'll rise again..."

The serpent raised its huge head, curving over Evan. *Perhaps I will. Or perhaps I'll kill you. Will you take that chance?*

"Yes!" Evan shouted.

"No," Blake said urgently.

The serpent dipped toward him. *Are you volunteering?*

Blake met its gaze steadfastly. "I'm not afraid."

The serpent arched toward Nathan, lying motionless on the table. My body jerked to go to him, but I stayed put.

The strongest is now the weakest. He should be put out of his misery.

Reeve spoke in a low voice. "There's nothing weak about Nate."

The serpent opened its jaws inches from Reeve's face.

And you. The most generous host in centuries. You've given me so much, Reeve McClellan. Why not give me this parting gift?

"I've given you enough," Reeve bit out.

Then I'll choose the one who's caused the most trouble. You were never very good at following orders, Star.

Twisting, it lunged at me.

It all happened so fast. The handholds breaking. Reeve, leaping in front of me. My left hand flying up to shield him as the serpent aimed. The searing pain when it struck through my hand to Reeve's heart. The spreading scarlet mist that shrouded my vision and darkened the room.

When the mist lifted, I was slumped on the marble table beside Reeve. Nathan crouched over me, a trace of color in his cheeks. Blake knelt by Reeve, who lay still.

Evan stared balefully at us. He sat in a heap against the wall, hugging his knees, as rage and grief played over his face.

"You're awake." Nathan stroked my cheek, his eyes full of relief, but his shoulders were tense.

"Reeve," I whispered.

"He has a heartbeat," said Blake. "But he's not waking up."

I tried to push myself up frantically, but couldn't. My left arm was completely numb, and my head pounded as though it were about to split. Nathan helped me sit up, his brow pinched and worried.

Reeve didn't move. His face was a beautiful mask, his fathomless eyes closed. When I felt his pulse, it was faint, and mine skyrocketed in response.

"Was it worth it, Daisy?" Evan's voice scraped, sounding hoarse and scratchy. As though his throat had been blocked — or constricted — for a long time.

"Leave her alone." Nathan moved protectively in front of me.

"There's nothing left to live for now," Evan muttered, making me choke back a sob.

"Shut your mouth," Nathan told him firmly, "or I'll shut it for you."

Reeve's chest rose and fell slightly. Warm breath came from his nostrils. But he didn't react to Nathan slapping his cheeks, or to my urgent voice. Blake pressed against his chest, driving a hand into his sternum, with no response.

"We have to get him out of here," Nathan said.

"No, don't move him," Blake argued.

"It's not safe to stay. This House is soaked with magic, and we've started unraveling it."

Blake jumped off the table. "I'm calling 911."

Evan laughed humorlessly. "Don't be stupid."

"Evan, keep your mouth *shut,*" Nathan growled.

"Magic's what put him there," Evan insisted. "Magic's the only thing that's going to get him out."

"He's right," I murmured, my insides twisting as my eyes stayed on Reeve. "There has to be something we can do."

Everyone turned to look at me. "Daisy, you're a witch," Blake said in a strained voice. "Cast a spell."

"What spell?" I asked desperately. "This is huge. I've never resurrected someone. And the serpent won't be helping me now. I can't do this alone."

"Read the book, fallen Star. It's all in there." Evan slumped against the wall, giving me a strange smile. "This is your fault."

"And whose fault is it that I'm here?" I glared at him. "If you hadn't pushed me, I never would have come to Pacific Crest. So you brought me upon yourself. Congratulations, Evan. There's such a thing as justice."

He looked sick, and for a second, I welcomed it. Then my own stomach heaved. The sudden absence of magic, the serpent departing, the realization that Reeve might be gone — it was too much.

"You call this justice? Losing Reeve?" Rising painfully, Evan lurched toward the table. Nathan tensed, his hands curling into fists.

"He's not dead," I whispered, my heart aching.

Evan's question rang in my ears. Was it justice? Reeve had done terrible things. It was his ambition that called the serpent; he'd found the others and brought them into the fold. If I were on the outside, observing the whole story, I'd call him a bad man.

But when I looked at the body on the altar, all I saw was a boy, looking so much younger with his eyes closed, who'd told me he loved me and never gave me the chance to say I loved him back.

"Leave him alone, Evan," Blake said quietly, holding up the red leather book and beckoning me closer.

"Oh, I won't hurt him," Evan muttered. "I want him back as much as you do."

I shot him a look. "You would have enslaved him."

Evan pushed up his sleeve. On his inner biceps, there was a red, blotchy stain where the tattoo had writhed, marking the departure of the serpent. "No. This would have."

"Take some fucking responsibility." Nathan glowered in his direction. "You knew the risks of going off the herbs."

The earthquake had subsided. The House was very still. Yet I sensed the quakes weren't over. Evan staggered, losing his balance, and grabbed the edge of the table. His jade eyes were ghostly, and the fight seemed to have gone out of him. I wondered if he'd survive the expulsion of the serpent.

"Did you want to be so completely possessed?" I asked him quietly. "Did you like it?"

He tried to laugh, but failed. "After a few days off the herbs — it wasn't my choice anymore."

Blake handed me the book. Grimly, I flipped through it until I neared the end.

Under the extraordinary circumstances that someone may survive the taking, yet lie as though dead...

Nathan and Blake read over my shoulders. When we reached the close of the instructions, Blake went abruptly to a cupboard in the kitchen, unlocked it, and carried back an armload of supplies.

I took the scissors he handed me and snipped a lock of Reeve's hair, black and shining in my palm. Nathan started a fire in a copper dish at the center of the table.

We worked quickly, exchanging instructions as we knelt on either side of Reeve. Evan slumped to the floor, where I kept a sharp eye on him.

Struggling to focus, I took a deep breath and sprinkled herbs on the surface of a bowl of water. My left hand still hung limp and numb at my side. Reeve lay motionless between us, and his coppery skin had gone pale with a greenish tinge.

I heard his voice, low and velvety. *You think you've lost what matters to you, but there's a lot more that someone could take.*

Nathan and I each took one of Reeve's hands. At his head, Blake tossed a bundle of herbs and the lock of Reeve's hair into the fire, and the flames rose high.

We'd studied what to say and do during the spell, reading the passage three times over. But once we began, the force of the incantation took over. The words seemed to speak themselves.

As we chanted, dripping water onto Reeve's forehead from the bowl, the darkness of the abyss opened before me.

There was fire, flickering and leaping.

Golden coils, spiraling.

A stone cliff, overhanging the chasm.

Reeve stood far away on the opposite edge. I called to him, but he shook his head.

The flames leapt higher between us. I dragged my awareness back to the marble table.

"He doesn't want to return," I said, the numbness in my arm beginning to overtake my emotions.

"He has to." Blake gritted his teeth.

"Why, Reeve?" I thought, urgently trying to understand, willing him to return. "Are you too ashamed of your deeds, of yourself, to come back to this world? Do you believe that without the money, the influence, the fucking *things,* you're nothing? I know what's left. The man who's sarcastic and brilliant and scarily good at self-control, but wildly romantic at heart. The man who loves knowledge and books and a good story, who would do anything for his friends. You want to protect and control, maybe too much, but without the serpent crushing you, you finally have a chance to breathe. To make amends. To be human. That's who I want, Reeve. You. *You.*" The words he'd spoken to me just minutes ago tumbled through my thoughts. "Not your power or riches or the beautiful things you never really owned. Just you. Only you. Always you."

The other men stared at me. Too late, I realized I'd spoken out loud.

I met Nathan's eyes, and he nodded toward Reeve. *Help him.*

Silently, Blake gestured to the knife lying between us. The small, ornamental, mother-of-pearl-handled dagger from Reeve's cabinet, that he'd used on me in the Joining.

I pressed the point to the palm of my left hand. A sharp spark sliced through the numbness. I did the same to Blake's left hand, then Nathan's, and finally Reeve's. One at a time, we clasped Reeve's hand. I lifted my left hand with my right and held it to his, our blood welling up together.

Reeve didn't respond. His hand lay heavy in mine, the scarlet thread of blood winding down his wrist.

Panic raced through me, my eyes becoming blurry with hopelessness. "He's not coming back."

Blake rubbed my leg. "He has to come back."

"Bring him, Daisy," Nathan said firmly, squeezing my shoulder.

"I'm trying." My right hand ached as it clasped my left palm to Reeve's.

"You're powerful." Blake urged me on with a faint smile, but his eyes were rimmed with red. "You're our Star. You can do this."

"Not anymore. I hurt people, I—" I let out a breath, and a tear rolled down my cheek.

"We all did." Nathan glanced at Evan, who stared at us from the floor, his face haunted. Passing his hand over Reeve's forehead, he lightly slapped his stubbled cheek. "Don't take this all on yourself, brother," he whispered. "Don't punish yourself for our sins."

Blake stroked Reeve's chest, as still as marble. "Let us pull our own weight for once. Let us pull yours."

I stared at the crimson smear on our joined hands, a sign of life. Reeve had taken away any shame or fear of blood when he'd worshiped me in my tiny dorm shower. He might be the Devil, but he had a way of bringing sacredness into the most profane, earthly moments.

Bending, I kissed Reeve's cold knuckles. "Please wake up," I whispered, my plea broken and desperate. "You belong here."

Belong.

He'd seduced me with that word, even before the promises of fame and success. That was what we all really wanted, wasn't it? To belong. To mean something to someone else. To be loved.

"I overreached." I bowed my head over Reeve's hand. My tears fell, mingling with our blood. "I lost sight of you. I thought I had a purpose."

"You do," Blake promised.

Dragging my gaze away from Reeve, I stared at him.

"You saved me," Nathan stated firmly. The color had returned to his face. He looked brighter, healthier. "You did what you came to do. Now do it for Reeve. Do it because we fucking love you both."

I sucked in a breath, drawing strength from Nathan and Blake. The gaping chasm left by the serpent's exit filled with a rush of their love. Even Evan, who looked less solid on the floor, seemed to be sending out a spark of energy. I would have cast it away, but this was for Reeve.

Come on, Reeve.

A thousand pins and needles pierced my left hand as it unexpectedly, painfully stirred.

His eyes opened, and I gasped, tears falling down my face in a rush of relief.

"Daze." He lifted his hand to my tear-stained face, his touch soft and searing. I turned into it, heedless of the blood smearing my cheek.

Evan leapt toward the table.

"You've come back," he cried out wildly. "We'll start again. It's not too late. We'll call the serpent—"

"No, Evan," Reeve said quietly. "It's done."

"Don't give up. There's still a chance."

"Enough. I don't want to see you right now." Reeve's voice was a dry rasp, yet it carried command.

Evan's face slumped, and he twisted angrily away.

But Reeve was calm as he turned back to me. I touched his jaw, stunned at the sight of a fully human Reeve McClellan. Blake and Nathan clasped his arms in an embrace, while Evan buried his head in his hands by the wall.

There was no sign of the snake or the chasm in Reeve's eyes. No endless black orbs that invited me to tumble headfirst and find out how deep the bottom lay.

But his dark eyes were beautiful and intense, shadowed from sleepless nights. When he stared at me, they burned me up, reviving my aching heart.

"Your hand." He gently picked up my fingers that lay limp in his. After the burst of pins and needles, I felt nothing. Abruptly, he tried to sit up, weak and shaky. "Daisy, what happened? Can you move it?"

I shook my head, resigned. "It's numb now."

He struggled to rise. "You are not sacrificing that again. You saved my life."

"Reeve, lie down," Blake said, grabbing his shoulders. "You're not ready to get up."

Nathan tried to ease him back to the table.

"Just wait," I told him softly. "We need to make sure you're okay."

"I don't care about myself." Reeve pushed on Nathan and Blake, to no effect.

"That's a first," Evan muttered.

Nathan clenched his hand into a fist. "Evan, if you don't stop talking–"

Evan climbed to his feet. "I know how this story is going to go. You're good, I'm bad. You're the heroes, I'm the villain. If you think that's true, you're fooling yourselves."

Blake shot an exasperated look in his direction. "Aiming pretty high, weren't you, Evan? World domination?"

"Fuck you, Blakey," Evan snarled. "I'm the only one of us who had the guts to take this all the way."

Nathan whirled toward him. "You mean, you're the only one of us who would push a girl down the stairs."

"We all took," Evan snapped. "At least I got to know my sources. I did what needed to be done to bring the Star."

"How long, Evan?" Reeve asked quietly. "How long ago did you stop repressing the serpent? Was this always your plan?"

Evan folded his arms and looked away. "Nine months ago," he admitted in a low voice. "I just didn't see any reason to hold it back. I thought you were weak for trying to contain it." He turned to the wall, pressing his face to the gilded wallpaper.

I knew what he was feeling, because a sudden wave of nausea swept me. The serpent's exit felt like going through withdrawal. A tremor ran over Reeve, and Blake's eyes looked glassy. Only Nathan seemed hale and healthy.

"You know why your hand is numb, right?" Evan muttered, turning around as he clutched his stomach.

I stared at him. "Enlighten me."

"The Reversal would've brought you back to the way you were before I pushed you. You'd sound like you hadn't practiced in six months, but your hand would be uninjured. But your heroic act, protecting Reeve? The serpent struck through your hand and took what it could. Your potential — your nerves."

"So fix it," Reeve ordered, his tone cold as ice.

Evan's eyes flared green. "What makes you think I can?"

"You seem to know all kinds of information that you never bothered to share with us. I have thoughts about this, Evan. Believe it or not, I have *feelings* about it. Now heal Daisy's hand if you value your life."

"Reeve—" Evan began.

"I may be lying on this table, but I can fucking end you and you know it. There's no serpent to protect you now. So do it."

"What makes you think I want Evan to help me?" I asked.

Reeve blinked.

"Listen, Reeve. I have been manipulated and planned about and treated like a thing, and too many people have tried to control me, and I am not here for it. Whatever happens with my hand, it's my decision. No one else's."

A faint smile twitched Reeve's lips. "What do you want, Star?"

I stared at my hand. "I don't know."

"Fire," Evan said wearily, looking at me from the floor. "And both sets of herbs. The ones that summon the serpent, and the ones that contain it. Reeve needs to be the one to put your hand in the fire."

I whirled to him. "I have no reason to trust you."

"Do you feel it, Daisy? The guilt?" All signs of anger seemed to have left Evan's body. "It's a parting gift from the serpent — all the remorse we couldn't feel while it possessed us. You'll get the least; you had it for a week. I'll get the most. I already lost my ability to play. Do me a favor and heal your fucking hand so I can at least sleep at night."

"I owe you no favors," I gritted. "The serpent's gone and you're still completely selfish."

"Do you want to heal your hand or not?"

"Leave me alone," I ordered, and he subsided. I looked around at Reeve, Nathan, and Blake. "I don't know. I don't want to be numb forever. But the fire—"

"I think Evan speaks the truth," Reeve said, his voice barely audible. "I can add to the fire to make the healing easier. Do you want me to help you, Daze?"

I sucked in a breath. It would almost be easier to let my hand be.

To consider it a penance and never touch my flute again. But I didn't want to take the easy route.

I also didn't trust Evan. What if the fire burned me — or called back the serpent? Yet the guilt he'd described was seizing me too. I could see in his eyes that it wracked his body.

"Yes. Yes, I want you to. Please," I conceded, looking into Reeve's eyes.

Reeve rose halfway on his elbows, wincing at the effort. "Blake, bring me those herbs."

Blake returned with the herbs in their copper and silver bowls as Nathan moved behind Reeve to support him. My nervousness grew as he sifted through the herbs, measuring and making selections. How much magic did he know? I'd assumed all his power came from the serpent. It hit me how much of a mystery he still was, how little I knew — and how much I wanted to understand.

The fire from Reeve's awakening, nearly embers at this point, roared up when he tossed in the handfuls of herbs. Scarlet and green ribbons twisted in the flames. My stomach lurched as I watched for the serpent, but only flickers showed: a forked tongue, a sinuous curve, glowing eyes that shuttered and disappeared.

"Daze, give me your hand," Reeve said quietly. "Do you trust me?"

I swallowed, but answered without hesitation. "Yes."

His eyes pierced mine. "Don't let go. And don't scream."

He plunged my hand into the fire.

I gasped as a hundred bees stung me. The prickling and tingling made me bite my lip hard to keep from crying out.

This was Reeve's idea of *easier?*

Reeve's words rose to the ceiling and filled the room. My head swam from the overload of sensation and the power I'd expended in reviving him. The floor shook, and Blake leapt toward me. Hands cupped my head — Nathan? Reeve struggled to sit up. Evan jumped to his feet, his face terrified, and bolted from the room.

Then the marble table tilted, and the room was a wash of red.

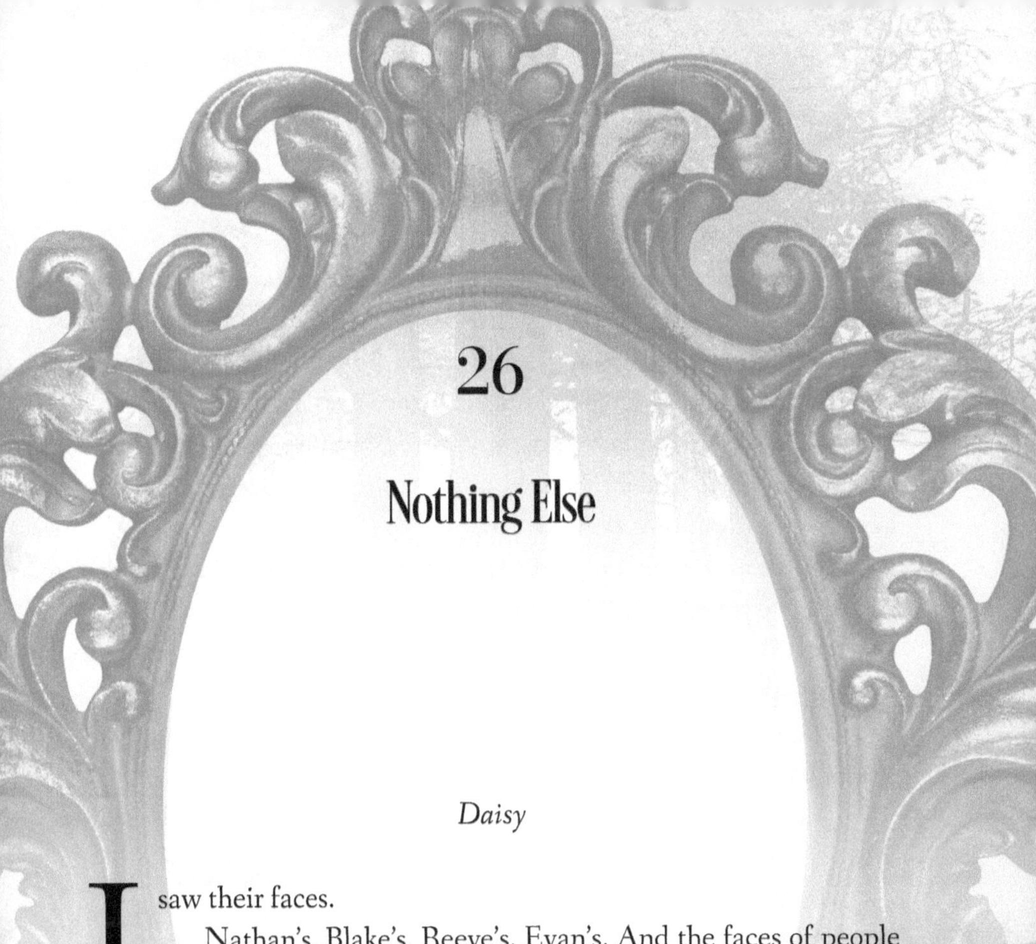

26

Nothing Else

Daisy

I saw their faces.

Nathan's, Blake's, Reeve's. Evan's. And the faces of people I'd never met, the ones I'd stolen from.

Reeve had spoken the truth. Most didn't know about their talents, or at least the full extent of them. Some lacked confidence. They got stage fright that prevented them from performing. Others didn't have the resources to pursue music, or thought it wasn't valuable enough to demand their focus.

Or someone had shut down their dreams by telling them that they weren't good enough, and they'd taken a different path.

I'm sorry, I said, over and over again.

At least it had only been a week.

At least their talents flowed back to them after the reversal.

At least some of them recognized their abilities more once they returned.

But I knew excuses meant little.

I tiptoed through their dreams, driven to find them.

"You have those talents back now," I whispered. "Use them if you choose."

At other times, the faces of the Desiderata floated above me. Nathan was pressing a cool washcloth to my forehead. Blake was propping me up and holding water to my lips. No, it was hot soup, but for some reason it had no taste. Reeve was holding me, and I begged him feverishly for words, any words, because I wanted to hear that velvet voice. Finally, he said he'd read to me, because he didn't have any words of his own right now.

I tossed and turned in bed, and the sheets smelled like lavender and rosemary. Why was I smelling Sasha?

I tried to speak her name when Nathan came in. He gave me a fresh pillow and said nothing.

When Blake arrived with water, I ranted. "Where's Evan? Evan is very bad. He needs to be punished."

Blake looked haunted, and the electricity of his once-bright blue eyes was dimmed. "Shh, Daisy. You need to rest."

"Don't shush me."

A rusty smile cracked Blake's face. "Sleep. You have to preserve your strength."

"Why? I'm a terrible person. We all are. Do you see them?"

"Yes," he said quietly. "I'm trying to repair their dreams, but it's hard work."

I touched his face. His beard was longer, bushier. "How long have we — where are we —"

"Sshh," he soothed again, pressing his fingers to my temples. I let him send me off to sleep.

The chasm opened before me. Nathan, Blake, Reeve, and I stood on one side; Evan stood on the other.

I'm sorry, he called.

I ignored him. "Sorry" was easy to say. "Sorry" meant nothing. I cared more about the chasm itself, which was full now — of dreams, of souls. Had they always been there, and I'd never noticed them until now?

Holding my breath, I walked to the edge. I took Reeve and Nathan's hands, and together we jumped.

I fought the fall all the way. My job wasn't to find the bottom of the abyss. It wasn't to plumb the depths of desire without limit. It was to rescue all these dreams. I bobbed and soared and fell, grabbing and healing.

I wished Sasha were here. She was the healer...she'd know what to do...

"Sasha," I muttered. "Sasha."

"Daisy!"

The voice was different. Feminine. A husky girl's voice, bright and quick.

"Sasha?" I croaked.

As I opened my eyes, coming back to myself, her face hovered over mine. I saw her hazel eyes, rimmed with purple liner. Her short hair, bleached blond now. The freckle by her mouth, her incredulous smile.

I grabbed her and hugged her tight.

"What's the word of the day?" I asked when we let go of each other, my voice cracking.

She shook her head, looking like she didn't know whether to shake me or hug me again. "Hubris. That's exactly what you've been up to."

"Greek," I mumbled. "Nice."

"Nathan told me everything."

"Everything?"

"Well..." she said judiciously. "He left out the dirty details. But I know what you did with those boys, Daisy. I know you sold your soul for dark magic so you could be the greatest musician in the world. You let some kind of grand high serpent of desire into your body and spent a week banging four guys, including"—she screwed her face up and shuddered—"my *brother.*" Her voice dropped. "I know what happened to him, and how you saved him."

"You know Evan caused my fall?"

"Yes." She squeezed my left hand hard, making me yelp, and quickly let go. "Oh God, I'm so sorry. Your hand—"

"I can *feel.*" Stunned, I lifted my hand and flexed my fingers. "No numbness, no pins and needles."

"So the spell worked," Sasha said quietly. "They were worried. Reeve, most of all."

The sound of Reeve's name twisted my heart. Who the hell was Reeve McClellan IV? Did the man I'd loved even exist anymore?

Sasha cleared her throat. "I should have listened to you when you told me there was something wrong with Nathan," she said, halting my runaway thoughts. "You were trying to help him, and Reeve pulled you into all of this."

I looked down, fiddling with Sasha's lilac-colored comforter. "Don't blame him. I cast a love spell right before we met. It was meant for Nathan, but Reeve was the one who felt it."

"Oh — *oh,*" Sasha said.

"Yeah." I played with a loose thread. "I was kind of desperate. Nathan and I kissed before school started, and he ran away, and I was just so sick of the curse..."

Sasha pushed her bangs off her forehead, clearly debating what to respond to out of all of this. "I don't know if this is helpful or not, but Reeve's thought of nothing but you, at least since I came back. Well, except when he's sorting through the dumpster fire of his finances."

"Jesus," I muttered. "The House?"

"Sold. Along with everything in it. Even with the damage from the fire and earthquake, which wasn't as much as you might expect. The proceeds will pay his debts, which are suddenly sky-high. All that money is flowing back to its origins." She shuddered. "That is some powerful magic, Daisy."

"So he's back where he started," I murmured. "Before he bound himself to the others."

I tried to lift my head. Helping me to a sitting position, Sasha propped the pillows behind me.

"We're in your room," I said in surprise, as the familiar furnishings and decorations came into focus for the first time. "Wait, aren't you supposed to be in Morocco? Did you come back early after all? God, I'm sorry — I thought you'd be yourself again as soon as we did the Reversal."

"It's okay, Daisy. I got better." Her voice was wistful. "Who knows if it was your magic that caused it? Blake blames himself, but I could have just been sick for a few days. It's not like I was doubting myself or not using my abilities with food. You've been here for a while. I had my eight weeks in Morocco."

I grabbed her arm. "That means I've been in your house with the men for what, three weeks?"

"Yep."

I looked around her room for some evidence of my old life. My phone, my laptop — my books. "Shit, my classes. School—"

"You care so much about Pacific Crest all of a sudden?"

"I don't want to flunk out. My parents and I are paying for it together. They shouldn't suffer because of me."

Sasha wrinkled her nose. "I think Reeve said something about a conversation with the Chancellor? Apparently, he's been very helpful about having the dean approve a leave of absence for you all. Go, Daisy — you must have really freaked him out. It sounds like he deserved it. At least something good came out of all of this."

"Maybe more than one good thing," I murmured. Reeve's face appeared in my mind.

Sasha raised her eyebrows. "Daisy, you and those boys worked some really fucked-up dark magic. I'm not letting you off the hook for that."

I looked into her eyes, so similar to Nathan's. "But you and Nathan are talking."

A smile flitted across her face. "We've talked more in the past two days than we have in the past two years. Maybe ever."

"Sasha, you need each other. You should have always been there for each other."

"Enough." She held up a hand, but her face crumpled.

"I'm not blaming you," I said quickly. "I'm just saying—"

Suddenly, she grabbed me in a hug.

"I blame myself," she sobbed. "For you and for him. I shouldn't have tried to control you. If you liked him, you liked him. And I just kept pushing him away and putting him down. It's like he had to be small in order for me to be big. Like there was only so much space in our family." She hiccupped. "No wonder he wanted to bulk up. He literally wanted to get huge, because he always felt tiny."

"Sasha, it's not your fault." I rubbed her back, and she sniffled into my shoulder.

There was a knock on the door. "It's Blake."

Sasha rolled her eyes. "Blake, you aren't bringing her that soup again, are you?" she called.

The door opened. Blake entered, carrying a tray with a bowl of soup. His wet brown curls were pulled back in a bun, and his eyes had more life. He was still beautiful, even with the serpent gone. But shadows marked the hollows of his cheeks.

He shrugged, glancing sideways at Sasha. "She needs to eat."

"She doesn't need your tasteless food."

"Wait, it's not just me?" I asked, as Blake sat down on the opposite edge of the bed and offered me the tray. "The soup actually doesn't have a taste."

Blake shrugged again. "After-effect of the Reversal. The food I cook doesn't have flavor. At some point, the effect might recede. It's not clear when."

"Yet he still insists on making you soup," Sasha snorted.

"Hey, it has nutrients," Blake argued. "Those don't go away. Lots of veggies."

I sighed. "I haven't really been in a place where flavor mattered for the past few weeks."

"I know," Sasha said, subdued. "But let me cook for you now, okay?"

Blake's mouth opened and closed. He looked away. "That's fair, I guess."

I reached for his hand. "You can still make me soup. I'll eat it."

Eyeing our linked hands, Sasha rolled off the bed and began bustling around her room, straightening it up. She opened the windows, fanning in fresh air that made the curtains stir. Outside, the lone palm in the Davises' backyard swished its fronds, and the porch swing creaked.

"Are you all right?" I asked Blake softly.

He squeezed my hand. "Hanging in there. Honestly? It's shit. Daytime feels like going through the withdrawal I never had three years ago, because Reeve used magic to help me get clean. And the nights, well...you know what those are like."

"I do." I stroked his hair.

"It's easier now. In the beginning, I don't know what I would have done without Nate and Reeve. They took care of me when they were falling apart themselves."

"We all need someone to take care of us sometimes."

Sasha avoided looking at us as she straightened the journals and jars of herbs on her desk. But I knew she was listening, reluctant to leave the room.

Blake lifted his head, and his blue eyes suddenly blazed into mine, intense in his hollowed-out face. "The thing was, Daisy — I thought I was doing something good with the magic. I fooled myself into believing that. Every day, I told myself I was a real fucking saint, because at the root of it all, I wanted to make people feel good. Fame and fortune — yeah, they sounded nice. But really, I tried to make everyone happy. To make *her* happy. And I convinced myself that the ends justified the means."

"Her," I repeated, my mind sluggishly turning over what I knew about Blake. I would have expected him to talk about Nathan. "You mean — your mom?"

He nodded, wincing. "I thought if I got enough power, I could heal her. I could make her happy forever."

I held his hand between both of mine, staring at the ceiling. His rings were warm against my fingers. "Those are two different things. And neither of them are your responsibility."

"I'm getting that now." He rubbed his forehead. "No one can be happy forever. And I don't know if she'll ever get better. But I'm going to see her next week. Nate said he'd come."

"Really?" The note of hope in Blake's voice kindled my own.

He nodded. "You know those treats I mailed her every week? She told me how much she looked forward to them. But with all the care packages I sent, I felt so guilty that I didn't visit her myself."

"You couldn't, though," I murmured. "At least once the magic bound you to Pacific Crest."

"But even before that, I stayed away."

"And your dad?"

Blake smiled a little. "We're talking too. I'm not angry at him anymore. I know now that he was as upset as I was when my mom had to leave. I think we're going to be okay, in our own way."

Silence fell. I tried a spoonful of soup and rested my head against Blake's.

"How is it?" he asked wryly.

I laughed. "I can taste the love, if nothing else."

Sasha turned abruptly from the closet, where she'd just unnecessarily reorganized her clothes in rainbow order. "What if you try being my sous-chef?" she said to Blake. "We can find out whether you screw up food, period, or if you can do that much."

"Sure. We can try it." Blake lay back on the bed beside me, my hand still in his, closing his eyes as if the conversation had exhausted him.

I ate my soup. It really didn't taste like anything, though I saw carrots, zucchini, tomatoes, and herbs. But I was grateful that I could sit up and eat it without assistance.

"He's cute, isn't he?" asked Sasha. Blake didn't stir.

"Excuse me?" I stared at her. "You were just ragging on him and telling me what terrible people we all are."

"At least you're trying to fix it."

"You're ogling someone I spent a week having sex with. Dirty, ritualistic sex. And there were other... encounters beforehand. Yes, he's *cute*. He's more than cute."

"How do you feel about him?" Sasha asked cheerfully.

"Blake? I mean, there's the whole dark magic thing to contend with. But leaving all that aside..." I set the spoon in the soup. "I love him. I really do. That's still there, snake or no."

"You love him, or you *love-love* him?"

"Why are you looking at me so urgently all of a sudden?"

She shrugged. "Daisy, I'm not asking for myself."

I studied her. "Who, then? Nathan? I know there's something between them. I just wasn't sure how much of it was magic."

Sighing, she straightened a framed poster on her wall. "I shouldn't get involved. I'll let you all hash it out. But Daisy, this is weird for me. Four people are staying in my home, two of whom I met for the first time when I got off the plane from Morocco and came here expecting an empty house. You all sleepwalk and mutter during the night and cry out and fight battles with things I can't see. I bumped into you out of bed last night. You don't remember, do you?"

"No." I stared at her. "Wait, where are you sleeping?"

"On the couch. I started on the floor here"—she pointed to the rug where I'd curled up in a sleeping bag so many times—"but with all the nighttime visits from the boys, and the calling out, and Reeve reading to you while you struggled with nightmares – I decided to move."

I pushed off the covers. "Let me give you your bed back."

She put her hand on my arm. "Keep it for now. I mean it."

"Thanks, Sasha," I whispered. "I don't know how to say I'm sorry for everything."

"Don't." She gave my arm a squeeze.

Blake opened his eyes. "Did you eat your delicious soup, Daisy?"

"Wait, did you *hear* all that?" I accused.

"Of course he did," Sasha said. "He wasn't sleeping. He never would have looked so peaceful if he were."

Miranda Silver

I must have dozed off, because when I opened my eyes, Sasha and Blake were gone.

The bedside clock said it was one in the afternoon. Sunlight poured through the open window. Down the hall, there was the clink of dishes rattling in the kitchen.

For the first time in three weeks, I got out of bed.

Stretching my stiff muscles, I walked down the Davises' hall and took a shower. I turned the water extra-hot to wash away the sweat of tossing in bed, the sick temptation of Evan's dreams of power.

As long as he was at large, this business wouldn't be finished. I wondered warily if he'd come find us.

Squeezing Nathan's shampoo into my hand, the same kind he'd used in high school, I lathered up my hair. The familiar breezy scent filled the bathroom.

My left arm prickled under the hot water, and I turned it slowly to see what was left of the serpent.

On my inner left biceps was an angry red stain in the shape of the ouroboros. Something told me it would always be there, a reminder of what we'd done.

Would I ever be able to pick up my flute again?

Worry, sharp and sudden, seized me. My flute, my baby, might be gone. If the men had fled the House with me in a hurry, I doubted anyone had gone back to Reeve's room to get it.

Maybe it was for the best, I thought, steeling myself against the surge of loss. My flute, magic — it would be safest to turn my back on all of it. I'd gone too far, and even with the serpent expelled, I still felt its shreds clinging to my heart, as if it had split and ripped when we forced it out. Music felt dangerous now, and so did magic.

I hung my head forward under the spray and let the scalding water fall.

When I stepped out of the shower, I heard a teakettle whistling in the kitchen. Sasha and Blake were arguing — well, Sasha seemed to be doing the arguing, and Blake was responding agreeably. Nathan's voice chimed in, lighter than it had been at Pacific Crest.

During a lull in the conversation, a voice spoke up. The deep tones were threadbare, but unmistakably Reeve's. The others laughed, and after a moment, he joined in.

Slowly, I rubbed my hair dry. When we thought we were on the brink of losing each other, we'd confessed our love. But who was Reeve? Could we actually work together as a couple? What about the others?

Back in Sasha's room, I searched her dresser for fresh clothes. Pulling on a pair of shorts, I smiled when I saw a T-shirt with the slogan *Resting Witch Face*. Then, after hesitating, I pushed it back into the drawer. I borrowed a plain black tank top instead.

Combing my hair, I left it loose to dry instead of twisting it into my usual braid.

The door opened, and Nathan entered.

Wordlessly, we reached for each other. He pulled me into a tight hug, burying his face in my hair. He smelled fresh and clean, his scent mingling with mine.

"Thank you," he said quietly.

My eyes stung as I hung onto him. "For what?"

"For stopping it. For risking everything. For convincing Reeve and Blake."

I pressed my lips to his shoulder. "I could never lose you, Nathan. I would *never* have allowed the serpent to take you. And you saved me too."

"Did I?" he murmured into my hair.

"If you hadn't asked for help, we would have gone through with the Sealing." I closed my eyes, taking comfort from his embrace. "We'd be possessed forever. I could have become Evan's toy—"

He made a low noise. "Let's not think about that."

For a moment, we held each other in silence, our bodies entwined.

Finally, I spoke. "What's your plan now?"

He chuckled ruefully. Still groggy, I pulled back to take in his physique. He must have lost at least thirty pounds since the Reversal. The thick neck and massive arms had melted away, leaving a man much closer to the lean, lanky boy I'd loved in high school.

He sat on the edge of Sasha's bed and patted the rumpled covers. I dropped down beside him.

"I'm taking a leave of absence," he said simply. "I told them the pressure was too high, and I needed a mental health break. They're hoping it's temporary, but you and I know it's permanent."

"They must be devastated that you're gone," I murmured.

"They were. But you know what? They won two out of the last three games. The other team might have been sloppy because they saw I wasn't there and thought they had it in the bag. Or maybe there were other reasons. Maybe it strengthened them when I lost my abilities." He shook himself. "Whatever it was, they don't need me, Daisy. They'll rise to the occasion, and I'm glad. I felt trapped every day in what I owed that fucking snake."

I touched his hand, and his shoulders twitched with a crackle of electricity. Then he wrapped his hand around mine. I leaned against his shoulder. Though he was thinner, he was still solid.

"Your house brings back so many memories," I murmured. "What are we doing here, anyway? Was it not safe to stay at Pacific Crest?"

Nathan grimaced. "You know how the Binding tied us to the land? The Reversal flipped that around. For the length of time we were bound, we can't set foot at that school. That means a year for us. But for you, it's just a week. So if you're dying to go back—"

To my surprise, I laughed. "Maybe I am. Maybe I'm ready to be a normal college student for a while."

"What about your dreams? You shouldn't throw them in the trash, Daisy. Don't let that snake take them all."

I lifted my left hand and moved my fingers, staring at it. "I've been busy repairing other people's dreams. I haven't thought about my own."

He was quiet, his hand still covering mine.

"Do you know where my flute is?" I hoped for and dreaded his answer.

He winced. "We didn't have time to get it out of the House. I'm really sorry, Daisy. We were carrying you out, and the ground was shaking — the marble table cracked in half. We just wanted to get out alive."

"I understand. Believe me, you made the right choice." My chest felt hollow. I'd hoped for relief, a sense of freedom, but I ached instead. Nathan pulled me into his arms again, his lips grazing the top of my head. "I wanted you so much in high school," I murmured. "I thought you were the most perfect boy. Did I know you at all?"

He gave me the sweet, fleeting smile I'd pinned all my teenage hopes on. "I didn't lie, but I hid myself from you."

I shook my head. "No more hiding."

He kissed me softly on the forehead, then the lips. "I love you," he said quietly. "You know that, right?"

"I love you too," I murmured. "What does that mean for all of us?"

"Does it need to mean anything right now?"

I shook my head, curling up in his arms.

"I don't think we'd work one-on-one, Daisy," he said slowly. "You liked that I seemed steady, but we're too different in some ways. Too similar in others. But the four of us..."

He trailed off.

"The four of us," I repeated.

"I know how you and Reeve feel about each other. You're his star and he's your dark night sky. Blake's my sun, and I'm—"

"His field," I supplied helpfully.

"Exactly," he agreed in a rush. "But we're all bonded. Not by that snake anymore, just by — ourselves. I know we can't have it all. Fuck,

I know that. But I don't want to give you up, either. Or Reeve. I think the four of us belong together."

I pressed my face into his shoulder. "Nathan, I don't even know where I stand with Reeve right now. I have guilt. I still have work to do. I have so much to sort out."

"I understand. But when you do sort it out, know that this is how I feel."

He kissed me again.

That kiss said it all. It offered tenderness, love, and peace.

For years, I'd yearned for a boy who didn't truly exist. Now we could be people together.

27

Only For You

Daisy

When Nathan left, I took Reeve's mother's tarot cards from my purse, which I'd found on Sasha's desk. The men must have grabbed it on the way out of the House.

Pacing Sasha's room, I shuffled the worn cards, but I didn't pull one.

There was a knock.

"Come in," I called.

The door swung open, and Reeve stood in the doorway. He was rumpled, bags under his eyes, his stubble sprouting into a full-grown beard. His black hair hung lank over his forehead. His gaze was deep, searching, watchful.

For all his fatigue, and the hollowed-out look to his sleek body, he was still beautiful.

"You're awake." His voice was hoarse.

I nodded, because I couldn't speak.

"I've missed you," I said finally.

He crossed the room in two steps and caught me in his arms. I hugged him tightly, burying my face in his neck.

"I was so worried about you," he whispered into my hair. "I thought you'd be lost in the abyss forever."

His heart beat crazily as his chest pressed against mine.

"You're so...human," I whispered back.

He pulled away just enough to look at me. The half-grin was all Reeve, and it made my stomach flutter. "For better or for worse?"

"Better," I said, staring up at him.

"I didn't think you'd want to see me."

My brow furrowed as I traced his cheek. "Are you sleeping at all?"

He let out a brief laugh. "More than ever. But I get no rest."

"Me neither."

"I see them all, Daisy." His voice was low and choked. "The things I did to them. I see the people we took from..." He broke off. "I saw your fall. More than once."

I steeled myself. "Do you think Evan's going through this?"

"Yes," Reeve replied grimly. "Because I see him every damn night, begging me to make it stop. At some point, he'll have to realize no one else can take away his guilt."

I dug my fingers into Reeve's back. Everything the serpent had sucked up — doubt, love, compassion — rushed back in, like a waterfall pouring through an uncorked hole.

"Where is he? I need to know."

"Daze, we have no idea."

"Tell me the truth." Gripping his collar, I suddenly recognized the shirt he'd been wearing at the party. The crispness was gone, the expensive fabric softened from washing and wear. I wondered if all Reeve had right now were the clothes on his back. "If you're trying to protect me, or *him* — don't."

His voice was quiet, but each word arrowed to my heart. "This is the truth. And it's in my nature to protect you. You can't fault me for that, any more than you can fault me for breathing. I will never lie to you. And without that snake inside me, I will never keep information from you again. None of my secrets are worth blood anymore. You, on the other hand — "

"What about me?" My throat went dry.

"You're worth everything."

Heat flamed my face. "Reeve, you've *lost* everything. The House, your fortune...your car..."

"What does that mean to you, Daze?" he asked steadily, his thumbs rubbing circles on my hips where he still held me.

"It means that you put people before possessions. You gave up everything to save Nathan."

His jaw worked. "There's something you need to understand. Nate was doing very badly that night. He might not have made it through the Sealing — fuck, he could have died, Daisy. But if you hadn't been with us — if it had been a woman who didn't have a history with Nate, who hadn't been pushed by Evan, who I wasn't head over fucking heels in love with—"

"Tara, let's say," I interrupted.

"Right. If you hadn't been there to change my mind, I would have convinced Nate to do the Sealing. I would have written his own doom. Without you, I don't think he would have admitted how much he wanted to reverse. I loved him, Daze, but..." He trailed off.

"You had the serpent inside you," I protested. "And who knows if Nathan would have gotten so sick without me? You know the prophecy. The Star is a gamble."

Reeve's voice was urgent. "But if he had, I would have done that. It's who I was. The reason I gave everything up — it's you, Daze."

I stared into his eyes, silent and in awe.

"I thought I lost you," he said roughly. "Three times, the night of the Reversal. I saw you dancing at the party, and I thought the Daisy I loved was gone. Then the tower, seeing you collared as the curtains caught fire. And finally, when the serpent lunged at you."

I buried my face in his neck, thinking back to that night. His woodsy scent was faint, yet present.

"Why me?" The question hurt to ask, but I had to. Every insecurity the Joining had diminished was back now, seemingly stronger, and I'd have to quiet that inner voice of doubt on my own. "Do you still blame the love spell?"

He laughed, his fingers running through my hair. "Sweet girl, we're ninety miles from Pacific Crest. All the magic's been purged from us. I don't blame any spell."

"Then what?" I whispered, breathless.

"I blame only you, Daisy," he said in a low voice. "My greatest downfall and my saving grace. My troublemaker and my star."

I flushed hot, everything in him pulling at me. "My devil," I murmured, "who leapt to save me. When the serpent struck — you moved so fast."

His hands caressed my arms before tightening around my back. "I didn't need to think about it."

My voice was a soft thread in the room. "And now I'm your greatest downfall."

"You should..." He kissed my jaw... "take it..." He trailed down my throat... "as a compliment." His lips nudged the hollow of my collarbone.

I sucked in a quick breath. "Should I?"

His dark eyes held mine, entirely human. But a green spark flashed — a memento of the serpent.

"I would fall again and again for you, Daisy. I go into the abyss every night in my dreams — for you. And now I want to fall in the light, wide awake. Together."

"I fell for you a long time ago," I whispered, my gaze moving from his beautiful, intense stare to his lips.

He didn't wait a second more. His mouth claimed mine. With a moan, I jumped up to embrace him, wrapping my arms around his neck and my legs around his waist. He gripped me close, walking me backwards toward the bed, until we tumbled down in a tangle of limbs.

For long minutes, we just kissed. I needed to get to know Reeve without a snake between us.

Rough and eager, his lips found the spot on my neck that got me shaking. He whispered filthy words in my ear that made me writhe. His teeth closed on my earlobe, hard enough to drive the breath from my lungs.

And when I kissed him, he groaned like his world was ending and a new one was beginning.

He pushed up my tank top, but I caught his wrist. "Wait."

"*You're* telling *me* to wait, sweet flower?" His eyes sparked with laughter.

"Let me touch you." I climbed over him, pinning his arms above his head. Muscles straining, he allowed me to hold him down. His body shook as I heedlessly sucked and licked and bit the coppery map of his skin.

"You're beautiful," I rasped. "You're all mine right now. You belong to me and yourself and not to any damn snake."

The words came out in a snarl, and I stiffened, ready to take them back. But Reeve bucked in my grasp.

"Yes," he growled. "I'm all yours. Take me."

His flat, dark nipples tightened to beads under my tongue. I lapped at them, driving a groan from his lips. In a frenzy, I dragged off his clothes and mine, stroking his thick shaft and teasing his balls until he begged for mercy. His cock strained in the air as I licked up a trickle of precum and praised him for being such a good, patient boy.

His curses through gritted teeth were the sweetest music to my ears. I wanted to play him forever, but I needed him too...

As soon as the thought rose, he tore his wrists from my grip, rolled me over, and leapt on top. He was all sinuous, muscled force, sleek and hot. I gasped at the flash of green in his eyes.

"Reeve — promise me it's you in there."

Pinning me down, his body heavy on mine, he cupped my face. "The serpent won't ever be completely gone, Daze. I see it in you too. Shreds of it get caught when it leaves. Even unbound, we're tied. I sense your wants just as you sense mine. But the remnants of the serpent can't crush. They can't control. They can only react to desire — and I have so much of that for you, sweet Star."

I shuddered at his words.

"You need that, don't you?" Though fatigue cracked his velvet voice, it drew me in more than ever. "You need to be my good, sweet girl. My beautiful love."

"*Yes.* I need to be yours, Reeve. Any way you'll have me."

I rocked against him, burying my face in his neck. I was naked at this point. I'd stripped off my clothes to tease him, to rub my breasts against his chest and pull away, but pulling away was the last thing I wanted to do now.

He touched me deliberately, tenderly, until my thighs shook uncontrollably. My clit was unbearably sensitive, my pussy completely open to him. Spreading my legs, he buried his face between them, licking the soaked and swollen flesh.

It was my turn to beg, and he called me the sweetest names as he denied me. His face was shining, and his dark beauty radiated love.

It was too great a gift. I didn't deserve it. But Reeve was offering it, and all I could do was make an altar of my heart in return.

When his cock sank into me, I gasped and scratched lines on his back. Magic didn't ease the way this time. I was wet and eager, but tight, uncomfortably so. Even after a week of fucking four men, with the serpent gone, sex was human. Awkward. New.

"Reeve—" I gasped.

He groaned, holding himself still. My legs closed around his waist.

"I love you." I touched his face. "I can finally say it back."

"Oh, Daze." He pulsed inside me, and his arms flexed with the effort of remaining motionless. "I know."

"But it means something to hear it, doesn't it?"

"Fuck, yes. It means everything. I love you too." His gaze held mine, and suddenly I was tumbling. I wanted to fall, together. It was unbearably intense, looking into Reeve's eyes as he penetrated me, uncushioned by spells or snakes.

"Come in," I whispered, melting around him, and he plunged into me fully.

Tears of need streamed down my face as my fingers found my clit and rubbed it. I enclosed him, he filled me, and together, we climbed.

"We're meant for this." He gripped my hips, picking up his pace until he thrust deep. "Let me make you fly."

I clutched his back, gasping as his cock opened me with every stroke. When he finally sent me spinning downward, I let go completely. I gave in to him as I spiraled, and he leapt with me, offering his release.

We slammed into the bed. I opened my eyes, dazed, as if we'd just woken from a dream. A subtle glow surrounded us both.

"How is that — did we —" I gestured to the glow. Reeve's inky hair was damp. Rolling over, he pulled me into his embrace and cupped my breast in his palm, softly rubbing my nipple.

"You're the Star. You always will be, serpent inside you or not. And with us together, this happens." He nuzzled my shoulder, and the glow let out a feeble flare. "Even if you put aside magic forever."

"I don't know." The words came out in a rush. "I don't know what I'm doing next. Music, magic — I can't even think about them right now. And us..."

"I understand." His face was shadowed, but he kissed my forehead. "You don't have to decide right away."

"What about you?"

He grinned ruefully. "You make me feel safe, Daze. With you, I can rest."

28

Glowing Heart

Daisy

I woke in Reeve's arms, with the sunlight streaming soft and golden over Sasha's bookshelves. We must have dozed off for a few hours, and strangely, my sleep had been untroubled.

Laughter and conversation drifted through the open window.

When we went out to the back patio, we found Sasha and Nathan sitting on the porch swing, sharing a pint of ice cream.

Blake stood behind Nathan, rubbing his shoulders. As I joined them, Blake leaned down to nuzzle Nathan's hair, and Nathan turned his face upward so their lips brushed.

Sasha caught sight of me and held out the ice cream, patting the space next to her on the swing. Nathan grinned as I sat down, and I reached across Sasha to squeeze his knee.

"How much money did you lose today?" Blake called cheerfully to Reeve.

To my relief, Reeve gave him a wry smile. "I'm better off if I don't think of it as mine. It never really was."

"Do you have anything left at all?" Sasha asked.

Reeve leaned against a lone palm tree by the swing, folding his arms. "We went through the Binding a year ago. We'd spent over two years proving our dedication to the serpent." His lips twisted. "Longer, for me. Before that, I had about a thousand in savings. I assume that once the chips fall, that's what I'll have left."

"Stay here with me and Blake," Nathan urged. "We've talked about it. My parents won't care — they're almost never here. And Sasha's cool with it. Daisy, you can stay too, although I know you're thinking about going back to Pacific Crest."

"Don't leave us, Reeve," Blake added.

Reeve raked a hand through his hair. His eyes moved over Nathan and Blake, and I could see all his complicated feelings: love, regret, protectiveness. "All right. At least until we finish the year and graduate."

"Graduate," I murmured. "It's so strange to think about."

Reeve tweaked my braid. "I want a college degree, sweet flower."

"*Sweet flower?*" Sasha mouthed at me.

I patted my knee, smiling at Reeve. "Come on, sit down. Join us."

Reeve raised his eyebrows. Then, his dimple showing, he plopped down on my lap.

"Oof, you're heavy," I gasped. He started to shift, but I grabbed him around the waist. "Don't you dare move."

"This glider's going to break." Sasha laughed.

"Sasha, stop kicking," Nathan said.

"I will if you share the ice cream. You're hogging it all."

Blake grabbed all of us in a hug around the shoulders. "Do I get any?"

The gate to the patio rattled and swung open. A disheveled blond figure walked through and halted at the sight of us.

Evan.

He was still big, but he'd grown gaunt, his cheeks hollowed. Everything about him was points and edges now. He'd gone from a lazy, sleek lion to a feral street cat.

He looked straight at me, and I shuddered.

"I want to talk to you," he said. "Alone."

Then my view was blocked by four people who leapt to their feet and formed a wall in front of me.

"Hell, no," Nathan growled, while Blake spoke, calm but threatening: "Whatever you have to say to Daisy, you can say right here."

"You're Evan?" Sasha snapped. "Get off our property."

Reeve said nothing, but his shoulders were drawn and tight.

I rose to my feet. "Let me through."

Reluctantly, Reeve and Nathan parted to let me see Evan. He stood by the gate, making no attempt to come closer. His clothes hung loosely on his frame.

"I won't hurt you." His jade eyes held mine, eerie in their intensity.

I'd sensed the serpent's shreds in Reeve while we made love, but in Evan, they were *visible.* As if a dimmer switch had been raised, I saw his heart glowing red through his shirt. The faint blue network of veins running through his body. The torn patches of scales — crimson, black, and gold — that coated his throat, his guts, his groin.

And shimmering through it all, his intentions. I didn't know what he wanted, but there was no violence there.

I sucked in a shaky breath.

"Daze, you don't have to do this," Reeve said quietly. "Say the word and we'll send him away."

I took a step forward. "I believe you," I said to Evan. "I know you won't hurt me."

His peaked face sharpened. "Then let's go."

"You can't be serious," Nathan began, as I walked between him and Reeve.

I turned to face him, putting my hands on his shoulders. "Evan's an open book to me now," I told him softly. "I don't have anything to fear from him."

"He could tempt you."

"So let him."

Blake stared at me, and Reeve folded his arms impassively.

"Daisy, have you lost your mind?" Sasha demanded. "Are you guys really going to let her go? Because I'm not."

"It's okay, Sasha." I squeezed her arm. "You couldn't stop me if you tried."

She turned pale. Blake put his hand on her shoulder, leaning over to whisper. I realized that no matter how much I might want to, I could never go back to who I'd been. The Joining had awakened something in me that was a little scary.

Glancing back at Reeve's unreadable face, I followed Evan out to the street, where he unlocked his black SUV. I touched the metal, warm in the sunshine.

"We're going to talk in your car?" I asked warily.

He opened my door. "We're going for a drive."

Nerves flickered through me. Gripping the door, I climbed into his car.

A black flute case lay on the passenger seat.

"Evan?" My throat closed up.

"It's yours," he said gruffly. "When I left the House, I grabbed it. I knew we'd be forced out."

I snatched the case and held it to my chest. "My flute is inside? It's okay?"

"Take a look."

Fumbling with the clasps, I unlocked the case. The joints of my flute gleamed up at me as Evan started the car.

"Why?" I asked, tears threatening to fall. "Why would you do that?"

"I feel it," he said, staring straight ahead. "Every night, Daisy. I slip and fall down icy stairs. I feel my bones break. I see your friend Darian share the video I made with the talents I stole from you. I live through the months that you drowned in despair. I'm inside your body. I fucking kiss Nate when you do, in his backyard."

My stomach clenched. "Is it good for you?"

"The kiss?" He let out a brief laugh. "As you, it is. Personally, I was never into kissing Nate."

I stared down at my flute in its case.

"I'm sorry." Evan's voice was gruff and choked. "I'm sorry for the pain I caused you."

I traced the keys on the flute. "I know."

"Are you sorry, Daisy?"

My head jerked up. "For what?"

"Are you sorry things turned out the way they did? Do you wish I'd never pushed you?"

"Evan—"

"Do you wish you'd never met us?" The words tumbled out of him like they'd been bottled up for weeks. "Never fallen in love with Reeve, or found out you were the Star? Do you wish we'd Joined with Tara and let the serpent eat our hearts for the rest of our lives, while you made love to your flute and were cursed to never get close to anyone?"

I tensed as he navigated a turn. We were climbing the hills of L.A., the road curving as the hillside dropped away. "Are you asking me to *thank* you for giving me a push?"

"No. I'm asking how much you regret."

I ran a finger around my flute's mouthpiece, unwilling to answer. Evan rolled down his window, and the wind blew his shaggy hair off his forehead. Stubble coarsened his jaw, making him look older.

"I'm just saying, it would be a colossal waste for you to turn your back on it all. Your flute, your magic, four guys willing to do your bidding, Reeve McClellan throwing his entire fucking fortune away out of love for you."

"Four guys willing to do my bidding? You're *including* yourself in that group?"

"You're still the Star. The serpent's gone, but we haven't forgotten."

"What makes you think I want to turn my back on it?"

He drummed his fingers on the steering wheel. "You're an open book to me, Daisy. As much as I am to you. You've been inside me in your dreams, haven't you?"

"Yes," I muttered.

"I know that you're in love with Reeve, but you're afraid to consider a real future with him. I know you still want Nate and Blake. In your dreams, you even want me too."

"Evan—"

"And I know it means more that Reeve got rid of all his money for your sake than it would have if he spent every damn cent on you."

"He might say it's for my sake," I argued. "But it was really for Nathan."

Evan barked a laugh. "Whatever good there is in Reeve, it's because of you." He blew out a breath, passing a slower car in front of us. "You can still be great, Daisy. This isn't the end of the road. It's one bump."

I twisted toward him. "Are you planning something? Because I swear, if you try to work more dark magic, I will stop you."

He pulled into a long, curving driveway. Parking in front of a large house, he gave me a hollow grin.

"I'd enjoy that, pet. But all I've got are scraps of the serpent inside me and a fucking burden of guilt that I can only ease by helping you."

"I don't need to be helped."

Springing out of the car like a huge cat, Evan appeared at my side and opened the door. "That's how I felt too."

I climbed down cautiously. Evan reached for my elbow, but I pulled away from him, and he dropped his hand.

The house rose above us, all modern concrete and glass with light wood accents. It was colder than Reeve's House, and less beautiful, but equally imposing.

"Why are we here?" I glanced at Evan. "Whose house is this?"

His eyes flicked to the flute case I cradled to my chest, but he said nothing. As we approached, the temperature seemed to drop. Beneath the golden California sun, I shivered. The house radiated the same cold hunger I'd felt from Evan in my dreams.

"This is your house," I said flatly.

"Very good. I knew you'd figure it out. And unfortunately, it's all mine."

"What do you mean?"

"Rowan — my father — died last week." The words came out without emotion. "Heart failure."

"I'm so sorry," I said automatically, pressing my lips together. "That's what got Reeve's dad too."

"Yep." Evan's pale gaze was trained on me. "But Reeve's father died long before his time, and his family mourned him."

"You don't miss your father at all?" I asked softly.

Evan crossed his big arms over his chest, looking away. "I don't know. Right now, I'm fucking glad he's gone. But he left me this house in his will, and I don't want it either."

I blinked. "What about your mother? You've never mentioned her."

"We're not close. She's in London now, in their other house. That's where Rowan was when he died. I flew there last week, after a couple weeks of — I don't know the hell what." He shuddered. "She wants to get rid of this place as much as I do."

We climbed the steep stairs to the door. Even the entrance made you work for it, like you somehow had to prove your mettle to approach, and if you couldn't climb at all, you were out of luck. It fit what I knew of Rowan, stirring my anger.

Looking at the hostile steps, I wondered if Evan had purposefully waited until I was on a staircase of my own to push me.

As if he sensed my thoughts, he stretched out his arm. "I won't let you fall."

I ignored the hand he offered. "I won't let myself fall."

The house seemed to reach for us as he unlocked the door. Not with dark, decadent tendrils, the way the House had, but with a rush of cold that clutched at my stomach.

"Why are you bringing me here?" I asked.

Evan looked directly at me. His hair had grown longer in the weeks since the Joining, almost obscuring his catlike green eyes.

"I want to show you where I came from. I want you to play your flute here, in this house, and then I want to give it to you."

My mouth opened and closed. Evan ushered me into the yawning front hall, where the only decorations were three spiky sculptures, an asymmetrical mirror, and an uncomfortable-looking chair. The floor was made of stone, the sunlight turning gray as it filtered through the massive, unshaded windows.

"Give me what?" I asked, the words sinking in.

"The house," he answered simply, as if it were obvious.

I stared at him. "I don't want your house."

"Neither do I. So Reeve will help me put it on the market, because he has a better head for that, and the money will go to you."

"Why?" My mind was spinning. "I don't need your money, Evan. I—"

"It's the least I can do." An ironic smile played over his face. "The way I see it is, you'll want to go back to music. You should, Daisy. You'd never forgive yourself if you didn't. But you might not get that scholarship back. The one you had at Siderio, the one I stole from you." His smile faltered, and he looked away to stare out the windows. "So this would pay for your education. It would pay for whatever you want. I'd settle all my debts to you."

Heat flooded my cheeks. "You're trying to direct my life again. All because of what would make *you* feel better. What *you* think is right."

He took three steps toward me. "I want to sleep at night, yeah. I'd like to crawl out from under the suffocating guilt. I also want you to succeed, because you're still the Star, and I get off on seeing you rise. Are my motives selfish? Maybe. Does that make them bad?"

I held my flute close, my heart beating rapidly.

Evan spread his hands. "I'm offering to help you. Period. No strings attached."

"And you expect I'll do all this, just because you want it? Take a tour of your childhood home, play my flute, accept your money?"

He ran a hand through his thick blond hair. "Like you said, I'm an open book to you. I don't deny what I want, Daisy. There's no point. So I'm laying it all out. Either you'll do it, or you won't."

I pressed my lips together. "Show me the house."

Evan led me through one room after another, all of them cold and modern. There were high ceilings and walls of industrial concrete and galleries of mirrors that split and refracted our images. It was hard to believe anyone had ever lived here. That Evan had been a little boy once, in this unfriendly house.

We walked slowly, without speaking. I followed behind him, and the line of his shoulders grew more tense the deeper we got into the house.

"Did the others ever see this place?" I ventured.

He jerked a nod. "After Reeve found me and I joined him and Blake, we came back here to get my things."

"So they met your parents."

His shoulders twitched in what might have been a laugh. "Reeve spooked them. That was fun. He was already powerful."

Evan halted in front of a closed door. The twitch of his shoulders intensified. He wasn't laughing anymore — he was shaking.

The air felt even colder and more repellent. I hugged my flute case close. "What's behind that door?"

He lifted his hand, touched the doorknob, and dropped it as though he'd been burned. Then he tried again, shoving, grunting, until he forced open the door.

A piano stood behind it. It was a beautiful instrument, a shining baby grand. But scratches and pits pocked the glossy black surface, and the windows were barred.

I swallowed hard. "This is the room he locked you in."

Evan didn't respond. I felt like I'd entered a nightmare, where everything that should be beautiful had become ugly.

"The piano — you made those scratches? You attacked it? And the windows — you tried to jump out, didn't you? So he barred them."

Evan was trembling now, his gaze fixed on the piano. Steeling myself, I walked around him, trying to see his face.

Before I could, he whirled around, grabbed the door, and pulled. His hair flew with the force of his thrusts. Grinding, panting, he threw his weight against it again and again. He hammered it until his knuckles bled. The wood shivered and splintered.

I stood frozen, holding my flute case like a shield. Evan roared, grappling with the door until he ripped it off its hinges. He threw it across the hall, where it hit a framed photograph of Rowan Hayes conducting.

The photograph fell to the ground, and the glass shattered.

Evan pressed his face to the wall, his big body shuddering. I felt sick to my stomach, but also like something had been purged. Cleansed.

Cautiously, I approached him. I raised my hand to touch — not quite touch — his back.

"Just play," he said roughly, without turning around. "Please."

I didn't want to stay in this room, but I knew we had to start here. My own hands shook as I opened my flute case and fitted the joints together.

"I won't sound good," I murmured.

"Fuck, Daisy, I don't care how good it sounds."

Lifting my flute to my lips, I started slow.

My fingers were stiff, my breathing labored. Every note reminded me that I'd never play with the absolute perfection I'd known with the serpent inside me.

I played *Prélude to the Afternoon of a Faun*. It was another Debussy piece, gentler than *Syrinx*. Again, a mythical creature played its panpipes in the woods, pursuing nymphs and catching none of them. But instead of ending in death, the faun fell into an intoxicating sleep, where he could finally realize his dreams and desires.

My tone wavered, and I ran out of breath early on some of the longer phrases. I flubbed a few notes in the runs. But as I played,

Evan turned from the wall to face me. His eyes were dry and haunted.

Still playing, I walked out of the room with slow steps. Evan picked up my flute case and followed as the music led us through the house. I played in the hall; I stepped into each cold room and moved around it. I wondered which of the five bedrooms had been Evan's, because there was no sign of him in this house. I heard him breathing beside me.

Finally, we ended up in a cavernous living room with pillars and black leather couches that looked like they'd swallow you up. I sank to the floor, ending the piece and moving into a Bach flute sonata.

Evan collapsed beside me, his head dropping between his knees. I kept playing until my fingers cramped and my throat was dry. My flute fell into my lap.

He raised his head. His pale eyes were wet.

"Congratulations," he rasped. "You just broke my heart."

I don't know who reached out first. I only know that after one agonizing moment, we grabbed each other.

"I'm sorry," he murmured. "I'm so sorry."

"He won't hurt you anymore. He's gone." I tightened my hold on him.

We held each other, rocking back and forth on the floor until we stilled. His face was buried in my neck, and my hands gripped his back. His blood-streaked knuckles pressed against my arm.

"It — he — it was choking me. I couldn't breathe. They were everywhere, Daisy."

I didn't know if he meant the serpent, or Rowan. Probably both. The silence hung heavy until he broke it.

"When Rowan was in the hospital, he asked me to play the piano for him over the phone." Evan's voice was rough. "I sure as hell didn't want to. I'd lost the magic. I'd already taken down my videos and erased the evidence. I told him I was too upset to play, but he said he didn't care how I sounded. It would mean something to hear his son play one last time."

"Did you?"

He exhaled, his hair grazing my cheek. "Yeah. It was adequate. Nothing amazing. And he said, 'It's good enough.' Like it was still his place to judge me."

"But did it help?" I asked tentatively.

"I don't know. You asked if I miss him, but what I miss is everything I wish he'd been. He got peace, but I didn't."

"You will." And I meant it.

Someone cleared their throat.

I looked up and saw Reeve standing a few feet away, his dark eyes trained on us.

"How long have you been here?" I asked.

"A while."

"You followed us?" I asked, resigned.

"Daze, I believed that you felt safe coming here. But I had to follow to make sure."

"We all did." Nathan emerged from behind a pillar, with Blake at his side.

Evan tensed as he looked up at the men he'd been bound to for the past three years. We all stayed stock still, like statues waiting for someone to break the spell. Then Reeve came to us and dropped to his knees. Searching Evan's face, he put his hand on his shoulder.

"I'm sorry, man," Evan said, his voice choked.

Reeve's tired face sagged, and he shook his head. "I should have foreseen this. I knew your inclinations, Ev. This was my fault."

Evan gave him a reluctant smile. "No, it fucking well was not. Let go of control for once, McClellan. You can't own everything."

"I paved the way," Reeve insisted. "I welcomed the serpent; I pulled you all in. *You* are my fault."

"No. This is on me, not you." Evan loosened his hold on me, still facing Reeve. "You were right, though. You told us at the beginning that she could destroy us all."

Reeve took my hand, gently brushing a drop of Evan's blood off my arm. "And now we're reborn."

"Drama queen." Slowly, like he was moving through water, Evan slapped Reeve lightly on his unshaven cheek. The tightness in Reeve's jaw relaxed, and he didn't flinch away from the touch.

I pulled Reeve into our embrace. Nathan and Blake approached, dropping to the floor as well, and spread out their arms to enclose us.

We stayed that way for a long time, until the sun slanted through the unshaded windows and the shadows lengthened.

Finally, Nathan spoke. "Let's go home."

29

Tempest

Daisy

That night, we had no dreams. The abyss didn't open. No one called for us, and no one needed to be rescued.

A light knock on the door woke me. I stirred in someone's arms, surprised at how safe I felt.

Evan spooned me from behind, his breathing peaceful. My fingers were twined in Reeve's. A leg was thrown over mine, and I wasn't sure if it was Nathan's or Blake's.

The moon cast a pale glow over the simple wooden furniture in Nathan's room, where we all lay curled up on his queen-size bed. The bed where I'd dreamed of joining him, sneaking in after midnight, for so many years.

I mumbled something as Sasha came in, fully dressed.

Her eyes narrowed when she saw Evan on the bed with us. But all she said was, "Come on. It's time for you to be out in the world."

An hour later, we left the Davis house.

We piled into Evan's car and Sasha's, driving to downtown L.A., where we blinked at the bright lights and the people talking, laughing, living their lives.

In a plaza, a group of street performers struck up a samba tune.

For the first time since my fall, hearing music didn't stab at my heart or drive me to be the best. There was no tempest, no complicated cocktail of emotions. Just pure joy.

I took Reeve's hand, grabbing Sasha with the other. "Come on!"

The six of us ran into the square.

Reeve twirled me around, spinning me fast. My dress flew out around me as I pulled up close to Reeve and swung out again. He was a good dancer, and seeing him so uninhibited spurred me to twirl faster, trusting him to catch me, drawing outward and coiling back into him, until the lights strung overhead and the color of the street carts and the laughter and chatter of everyone filling the plaza spun around us in a bright swirl.

I was laughing so hard I couldn't speak, and the beat of the music throbbed through our joined hands in a way beyond words, beyond thinking and understanding. This was what I loved about music. Forget the competition, the striving, the practicing, the pressure and applause. This was what it was all about. Being in a crowd of people and feeling the same emotions, experiencing a joy beyond language, a connection to total strangers and a deeper bond to the ones you were with.

Reeve's gaze was black as a starless night, his eyes shining like jet, inviting me to fall. But instead of pulling the strings, I knew that every fiber of his being was ready to jump with me.

I wanted the song to stretch on forever. We were just six people, six *happy* people, connected in the spiral of life, and what was happening right now was everything I loved and had cut myself off from for so long.

The music ended with a crash of drums and a flourish of horns. We bent over laughing, out of breath, clapping madly for the band. They sipped from their water bottles, brought back to earth before they picked up their instruments again.

All around us, people cheered for more.

I cupped the back of Reeve's head. His hands circled my waist. *That was so transcendent,* I wanted to say, but words weren't adequate.

The band struck up a slower song, and we swayed together as the others joined our circle. Nathan had an arm slung around Sasha, and Evan looked more at peace than I'd ever seen him, his head resting against Blake's.

Evan was right. I could never turn my back on music, or magic, or the people I'd come to love. Especially the one who held me close right now. All I could do was to go forward into the future, a little older and wiser, and make the most of a second chance.

"I love you, Reeve," I murmured. His dimple flickered in his cheek.

"I love you too, Daze." He kissed my lips again, then my cheek, leaving one more soft press on my forehead before his eyes met mine.

"What exactly are we to each other?"

Reeve blinked. As soon as I said the words, I wanted to take them back. This perfect moment — why mar it with such a question? And yet, when else would I ask?

His hands moved up and down my back, stroking me from shoulder blades to waist. "What do you want us to be? Tell the truth."

"The truth?" I laughed a little. "I want you to be my boyfriend."

I flushed as soon as I said it. *Boyfriend?* God, the word sounded so simple, even naïve, when faced with Reeve's obsidian eyes and shadowed stubble. This was a man made of secrets and masks, who had remnants of a serpent inside him and always would. A man who'd fucked me with his friends, who'd owned so much yet so little.

This was a man who saw and understood me. Whom I was beginning to understand as well.

"There's a problem, though."

His hands tightened on my waist, eyes narrowing. "What's the problem?"

"I hear you don't date."

He let out an incredulous laugh and waved a hand in one big, dismissive gesture, as if he were sweeping away every word of gossip that had swirled around our old life at Pacific Crest.

"Forget everything you've heard. Let's do it."

I hugged him close, wrapping my arms around his sleek shoulders, and pulled back to drink him in. "Let's."

"My girl." He grinned, a sudden sunbeam breaking through his dark beauty. "I've never really had a relationship before."

"Me neither. We get to have a first together."

He caught my braid in his fist, rubbing his thumb over the twisted strands. "I like that. I like it a lot."

"I like you, *boyfriend.*"

His laughter rumbled from his throat. "You're going to keep saying that, aren't you?"

"Oh, you don't like it? How about 'lover.'"

"Lover...boyfriend...whatever you want," he murmured. "And you're my Daisy."

30

I Have Held the Hand of the Devil

Daisy

I sat in the woods on Greer Hill. Sunlight dappled the ground, and the logs and moss were still damp from a winter rain the night before.

Since returning to Pacific Crest, I came here every week. Sometimes I cast spells; sometimes I simply sat in the clearing.

Greer Hill had re-opened after the earthquake that rocked campus three months ago. But rumors abounded, and the woods still repelled anyone else who tried to enter.

As far as I knew.

I wasn't sure whether the trees would let me in when I had first returned. But I couldn't shy away from the truth.

I was still the Star, and a part of me would always feel most at home in these woods.

That same part of me also wanted to keep tabs on the serpent.

I sensed its presence, though it never spoke. I didn't try to summon it. The herbs to call and contain it had been lost when we fled the House.

Pulling my puffy jacket around me, I listened to the wind blowing through the trees. It was January now, a California winter – mild, but chillier in the woods.

Most of my time since returning to Pacific Crest had been spent making up the schoolwork I missed. I could have taken a leave of absence for the rest of the semester, but I wanted to move forward. To do something with my time now that the men's absence left a yawning gap at the university.

Everyone had conflicting memories of what happened the night of the Sealing. There was an earthquake that seemed to have its epicenter at Greer Hill, yet it only affected the House. The campus and surrounding neighborhoods were unscathed. My Geology of National Parks professor had a field day discussing it in class, but when I stopped him to talk, he conveniently rushed off to a meeting.

Michelle and Amy vaguely recalled the party at the House, concluding that they must have been too drunk to remember details. To them, and everyone who asked about the men, I said they were taking a break from college to focus on their careers.

It wasn't a lie. Both Reeve and Blake wanted to pursue the dreams that had brought the serpent to them in the first place. As soon as Reeve resolved his debts and his finances returned to ground zero, he'd gone back to the stock market. He was far more cautious, making small investments to begin with. He didn't have a Midas touch anymore, but he was whip-smart and he'd picked up knowledge in his years of trading.

For the first time, his mother accepted his offer of financial help, as though she sensed the money he made was finally untainted. She allowed him to visit, to see his brothers and sisters, and he'd brought me to meet them.

I'd smiled to see Reeve's beautiful dark eyes on four younger faces, watching how protective he was as a big brother. His mother was reserved and cautious, and when I showed her the tarot cards Reeve had passed on to me from her, I could tell her hackles went up.

But, to my surprise, she let me do readings for her and all his brothers and sisters, which broke the ice and made everyone laugh.

Reeve had also established a charity fund for a portion of his earnings to go to, and when he called out in the night, in my arms, I knew he was still making reparations in his sleep.

Blake got a job in the L.A. restaurant where Sasha had worked over the summer. A few people recognized him from the media attention he'd gotten while working at Étoile, which he shrugged off, saying he wanted to hone his skills from the ground up. Once a week, he volunteered in a soup kitchen.

He'd made the drive to Northern California to visit his dad and see his mom in the institution where she lived, bringing Nathan along, and promised to come back when he could. What stayed with him the most was his mom telling him that the care packages had been nice, but seeing his face was true happiness.

He no longer had a magic touch either. But with the skills he'd learned, and the flavor of his cooking back, his food tasted damn good. Nathan even said he liked it better than the enchanted version.

And Nathan — he was focused on school. All the men had made arrangements to finish the year remotely, but Nathan, for the first time in his life, was getting into studying. He'd also talked about coaching kids, giving them the support he'd always wanted, but he decided to allow the football world a little time to forget him first.

Evan was the most guarded about his plans. But we'd had a stretch of time alone in his car — I visited L.A. every weekend, and Evan was frequently the one who picked me up and drove me back — when he'd said that rather than erasing his memories of his father, he was thinking of repairing his legacy. Getting a degree in conducting, so he could treat ensembles better than Rowan had. I didn't know if this was the right choice for Evan, but he had to figure out his own path.

I hadn't given him an answer yet about his offer of the house. I practiced my flute daily, slowly building up my stamina, but I wasn't sure I'd be accepted to a conservatory again.

The wind picked up around me, whistling through the branches and making me shiver. Between the leaves that still clung to the trees, I thought I saw shimmers of crimson and gold.

When they finally came, the words were barely distinguishable, a mere rattle of pebbles and sticks.

So trusting, sitting here in my presence. Whereas you once feared Evan, who is only a man. You rejected him when the two of you could have ruled the world.

I rose to my knees. My chest heaved, and I put a hand on it to calm myself. The serpent couldn't hurt me now.

"He's changed," I called out. "And you're powerless without a host."

The rattling grew louder. *No one can truly change. I know your essence, Star.*

"You're wrong."

Tara still wants you. She gropes for me in her dreams, crying for the face I gave her. She comes here every day, attempting to enter the woods. You can gain power together.

I shook my head. "She can look for power on her own. She's better off without a false face from you."

I'd wondered if Tara would leave Pacific Crest, once her power source via Reeve was cut off. But she'd stayed, though she kept a low profile. One day, I'd crossed paths with her in a deserted back area of campus. She was completely unglamoured, her natural face hidden beneath a baseball cap and sunglasses.

"You have to help me," she'd pleaded. "I know I was bad to you. But I need your help. I *need* it."

I'd stepped away. "You're the only person who can help yourself."

"I can't show my face. I'm sneaking around all covered up. I'm hiding in the back of my classes."

"Get over it," I'd snapped. "There's nothing wrong with your face."

Her jaw set. "Just you wait. I'll still be famous, one way or another. And you — you were an idiot, to throw it all away."

The serpent's hiss intruded on my thoughts.

You crave attention and glory. There's a part of you that will never be satisfied, no matter how many times you fuck the Desiderata.

I flushed. So it knew.

Reeve and I were a couple, and so were Blake and Nathan. Evan was a lone lion, a solitary beast who'd insisted on finding his own place in L.A., though he was frequently at the Davis house.

But there were weekends when we came together — when I was sandwiched between two of them, or worshiped by three, or teased and punished playfully by Reeve for the audience of his friends. There were times when I watched Blake and Nathan together and ached at their beauty. There was a night during my last visit when I'd dared to work magic in the men's presence for the first time, a cleansing spell, and I'd succumbed to desire, because I needed them all. I took them inside me one at a time and then together, though it was far more challenging, more awkward and exciting, to handle four men than it had been at the Joining.

They needed me too. And they needed each other.

I lifted my chin to the woods. "I can live with that. If I'm never fully satisfied, it's okay."

You're safer without them. You're putting yourself in the path of temptation.

"I know," I said steadily. "I understand what you are. I want to always remember that."

I could have taken you with me. Given you endless pleasure. That would have been your fate if Reeve, my steward, hadn't leapt in front of you. Now you're confined to a mortal life of suffering and limitation.

"I don't want endless pleasure," I murmured. "Just some. I don't think you're all bad, either. Only in excess."

The ground shook with laughter.

You feel me when you lie with them. The five of you will always be drawn together. You play your flute daily and remember a greatness you can never attain.

"I don't regret losing that," I said quietly. "I love them. And you? You can't love. You're lost without a host."

The sound of rushing water surrounded me. I could swear it was a yawn.

It's been an eventful few years. I'll rest here until a new group of Desiderata devote themselves to me.

"They won't. You'll be alone forever."

They will, Star. They always do. I live in every heart.

"I'll do everything I can to prevent that."

More laughter came.

I look forward to seeing you try. You've entertained me to no end. Come to these woods any time, Daisy DiCosmo Fisher. I treasure our conversations.

31

Girl on the Wing

Daisy
Three years later

A flurry of notes came from the stage. Waiting in the wings, I held my flute close. The Siderio Orchestra crescendoed into the ending of Verdi's *La Forza del Destino* overture — The Force of Destiny.

Goosebumps covered my shoulders, and my floor-length purple gown swished when I stepped forward. I'd splurged and purchased it new for the occasion — performing as one of the winners of the Siderio Concerto Competition.

Before I auditioned for the competition, I'd thought long and hard about *why* I was competing. It wasn't for glory or for vanity. It wasn't because I needed to be the best. I'd lost my taste for those temptations.

But I still wanted to challenge myself.

The orchestra played its triumphant closing chords. Applause rose and subsided, and in the lull that followed, I walked on stage.

The clapping crackled again. Smiling hard under the bright lights, I took in a panoramic view of Carnegie Hall's cream-colored tiers.

Bowing, I straightened. Behind me was a stage full of friends — people I'd reconnected with when I came back to New York, people I'd gotten to know.

In the audience, one row pulsed with energy. I felt Reeve sitting in the middle, gorgeous in his tux, holding a bouquet of blood-red roses, pride radiating from him so intensely that it warmed me. Blake smiled beside him, his arm slung around Nathan, who leaned forward, hands gripping his knees, nervous on my behalf.

On Reeve's other side sat my mom and my friend Darian, beaming, along with my dad and Carmen, now married and expecting their first kid, who'd both made the trip to New York for the occasion.

They all loved Reeve. To be fair, he charmed them on a regular basis. Though he'd ousted the serpent, he still had an uncanny ability to read people. When I teased him about winning my parents over, he flashed that devilish dimple and said it came naturally.

My mind jumped to Tara, with her natural face. I'd almost forgotten about her after I left Pacific Crest — until I turned on the TV one day and saw her on a reality show. Somehow, she was still working toward her dream of being famous. And the spot she'd landed on the show was the perfect safe space for her power-hungry machinations.

Next to Nathan, the last seat sat empty. Evan, coming late down the aisle from an evening conducting class, shrugged off his black wool coat and removed his scarf, his eyes fixed on me. As he took the open seat, I nodded slightly.

In the end, I'd accepted Evan's offer of money from the sale of his house. Half of it, to be exact. It was more than enough to pay for college, to get me and Reeve — along with Nathan and Blake — situated in New York after we finished the year at Pacific Crest, and to put a chunk away in savings.

I'd worked hard to build up my playing skills after the Reversal, but I hadn't expected to be admitted to Siderio. I could never recreate the brilliance of what I'd played for Dr. Armore with the serpent inside me. But I'd re-auditioned, and though the judges were silent and impassive, I was accepted.

My playing had more depth than before. It held pain and joy, shame and redemption. It held experience, and maybe a trace of magic.

Most importantly, I loved playing again, and I didn't take a single struggle or emotion for granted.

I didn't get a scholarship, though. And I'd have to stay an extra year because most of my credits from Pacific Crest didn't apply — and I hadn't completed my courses from the semester of my accident. It was fair for Evan to make reparations by paying for my education.

I told Evan the rest of the money was his. As much as he gravitated toward the four of us, he needed to stay independent so he wouldn't be lured by the serpent. With Reeve's help, the Hayes house sold quickly. Hard to believe, but apparently there was a demand for hideous homes with bad juju in the L.A. hills.

Or maybe Evan's atonement, the music I'd played, and the reconciliation of the five of us had changed the energy for the better.

As I lifted my flute to my lips, the stage lights sparkled on the ring Reeve had given me yesterday, a cluster of black diamonds and pearls.

Will you be mine, Daze?

My answer had tumbled out almost before he could finish. We were already one, and if Reeve wanted to seal it with a ritual, I'd do it.

I had to try not to stare at the ring, because its beauty kept catching me unawares. I'd considered leaving it off to perform, since I wasn't used to playing with a ring on yet. But in the end, it was part of me.

As Reeve was.

I wanted that reminder.

I felt the love from my people in the audience. It was real, imperfect, and unconditional. It had nothing to do with whether I played well tonight, or how successful I became, or what the reviews would say. It had nothing to do with magic, and everything to do with who we were.

Making eye contact with the conductor, shaping my lips to blow the first note, I sent that love back to them.

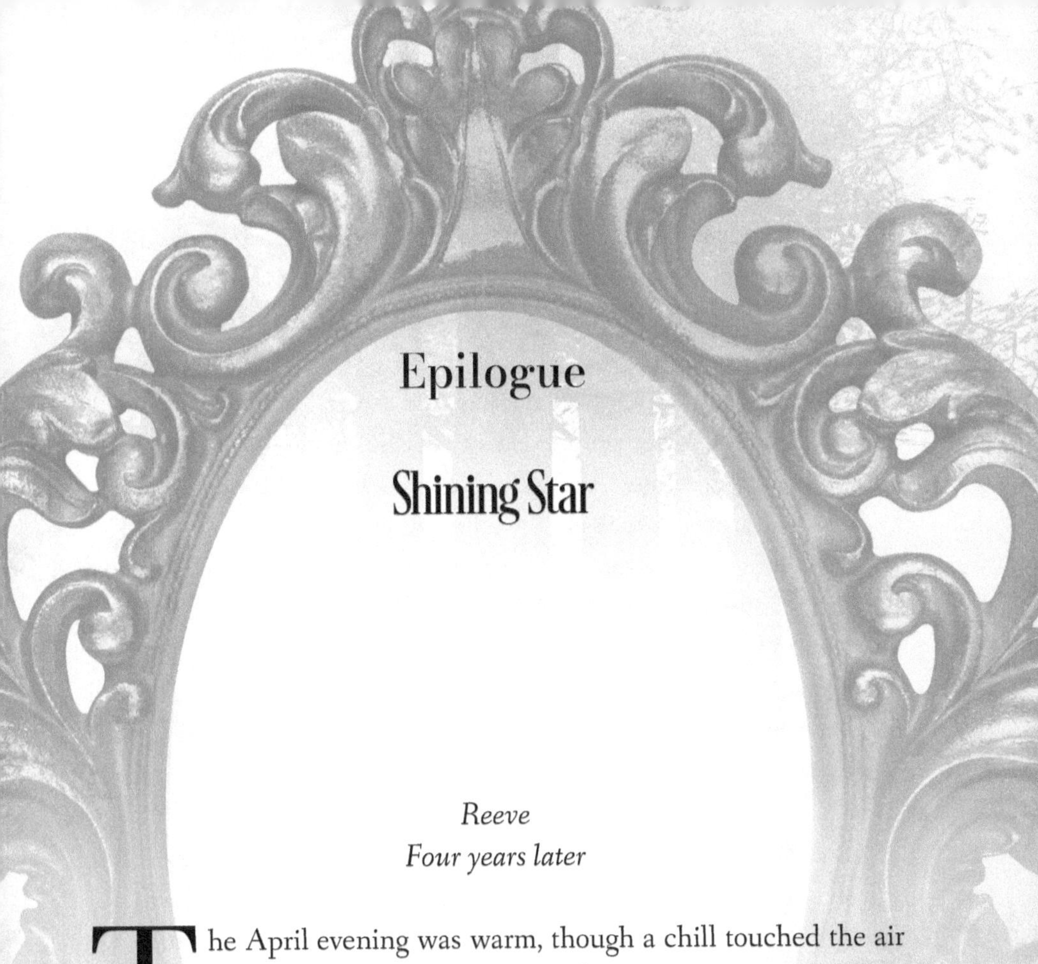

Epilogue

Shining Star

Reeve
Four years later

The April evening was warm, though a chill touched the air as the sun set. Cherry blossoms hung on trees, petals falling to the sidewalk like confetti. Spring was unfolding in New York.

Shrugging off my suit jacket, I walked into the apartment that I shared with my wife.

Daisy worked late most nights — teaching, attending orchestra rehearsals, or performing. She wouldn't be home yet. But when I entered the common area, with its snug, city-sized kitchen, dining table, and living room, it bustled with energy.

In the kitchen, Blake stood over the stove, swirling sauce in a pan. Nate leaned against the counter, stealing tastes. Evan, who had commandeered the living room couch, was giving Blake unsolicited advice on the menu.

As I unbuttoned my shirt, Evan let out a wolf whistle. "Take it off."

I grinned. "If you expect to be fed tonight, keep it under wraps."

Evan shook his head as I slipped off the shirt. "You show off all that chest and you expect me to keep quiet?"

"Yep," Nate said from the kitchen, as Blake batted his hand away from the pan. "We do."

"It's a lost cause, Nate." Blake whisked cream into the sauce.

"I want to shower before Daisy gets home," I said, tossing my shirt over my shoulder. Apparently, Evan's bad influence won out, because a chorus of catcalls followed me down the hall.

It no longer bothered me to show my body. Not to my friends; definitely not to my wife. Maybe because I wasn't fighting what lived inside me anymore.

As hot water streamed over my head and shoulders, I felt her: a bright point of light that deepened to gold at its heart. She was in our neighborhood, a couple of blocks away, hurrying home from the subway station with her flute case in her hand.

The serpent's exit had been imperfect. Within a certain radius, I still sensed the Knight, the Ace, the Beast — and most of all, the Star.

Quickly, I toweled dry and got dressed. I wanted to greet her when she came in.

Today marked five years since her fall. The day the serpent, through Evan, altered the course of her life, without any inkling of how she'd return the favor. I knew she had complicated feelings about it.

She'd been the one who insisted we gather tonight.

I returned to the living room just as I felt her coming up the stairs.

Nate coughed. "So you changed your suit...for another suit."

I shrugged. "Daisy likes me in suits. You think she'd like me as much in gym shorts, Coach Davis?"

"Hell yes. I know I would." He came over and made a show of straightening my neatly knotted tie. Nate had gotten a job coaching high school football. He had a reputation for being patient and supportive, and he made a point of looking out for kids who needed extra attention.

The key scraped in the door, and my wife walked into our home.

Her blonde-streaked hair was loose, blown into wildness by the spring breeze, and cherry blossom petals were caught in it like snow.

Her eyes lit up when she saw the four of us. Leaving her flute case on the coffee table, she came into my arms.

The room dissolved as I kissed her, as it always did. She finally pulled back, nudging my ear with her nose.

"Did you survive another day of investment banking?" she teased, her voice low and throaty.

"Barely." I brushed a stray petal from her hair.

"Oh, I'm sure you did. You're good at your work."

"I talked to my mother today," I murmured. "I finally convinced her to come to New York, along with my brothers and sisters."

"All of them?" A smile tugged at Daisy's lips.

"Every last one. They can't wait to see you."

Tight-lipped as always, my mother never did tell me how much she guessed about the dark magic I'd practiced. But it felt damn good to finally help my family, to see my brothers and sisters go to college or look for jobs beyond our hometown, knowing their world had room to grow.

Giving me one last kiss, Daisy sashayed into the kitchen. She hugged Blake from behind, resting her head against his curls. He grinned, turning from the bubbling sauce for a quick kiss, and reached back to squeeze her hip. On his left arm, an inked daisy spread its petals above the golden apple pierced by a knife.

Nate reached for her with a hint of his old impatience, pulling her into a hug and covering her mouth with his.

"Hey there." She wrapped her arms around his neck, tilting her head to the side.

Rolling off the couch, Evan walked up and swatted her ass. "Get a room."

"Don't touch this." Blake shielded a tray of crackers topped with smoked salmon as Evan tried to swipe a bite. "It's for later."

Evan shook his head. "So Nate gets a taste, but not me? You're playing favorites, Blakey. It's like I have to live with you to get to the good stuff."

"I freely admit to playing favorites with Nate," Blake replied serenely, his eyes going soft as Nate slipped a hand under his shirt.

I sauntered over to join them, and Daisy leaned against me.

It was rare for Evan to be in town. He had a position in upstate New York as an assistant music director. As much as he'd tried to separate himself from his father, in the end, he chose to do penance by reshaping his path.

I'd gone to a recent concert he conducted, and was surprised by how attuned he was to the group. One of the players actually described him afterwards as "nurturing." It wasn't a word I ever would have associated with Evan, but seeing him on the podium, and in occasional quiet moments with Daisy, I believed it.

Snatching one of the salmon-topped crackers, Evan swooped down on us before Blake could stop him.

"Open up, pet," he told Daisy.

Laughing, she let him pop the cracker into her mouth. He scooped a smear of cream cheese from her lower lip and pushed his finger in. Leaning back against me, she sucked him clean.

The echo of the serpent on my arm, like a negative film image, itched and twinged. It reacted when we were all together, or in moments of intensity between Daisy and me. It never failed to remind me of what had been, and what we had now.

What we owed to others.

The guilt had eased over the years, though I knew it would never leave entirely. I saw my former victims in my dreams sometimes, freed from the serpent's coils: discovering their passions, stepping into their potential like a sunrise. In the daytime, we all made it our mission to help with that, without ever discussing it much. I looked for opportunities to mentor. I tutored promising kids for free, kids who mirrored my own determination growing up. I built up my foundation, and every morning, when Daisy woke sleepily in my arms and pulled a tarot card from the deck on the bedside table, I remembered that I was grateful. That I wanted to give back.

The future I'd sketched out for Daisy, when I'd tempted her to perform the Joining with us — it was here.

We lived in New York, in a beautiful apartment. It wasn't a lavish penthouse; it wasn't the House; but it was home. The rooms overflowed with books and music. Art hung on the walls — not the expensive paintings I'd accumulated to display in the House, but original pieces picked up from street vendors and small galleries.

We traveled, and bit by bit, we were seeing the world as I'd always wanted to.

We loved each other.

We were together.

She was truly mine — and ours.

Evan leaned in to kiss Daisy, and I ran my hands up her sides from her waist, stroking the curves of her breasts.

"What was that about getting a room?" Nate teased, draping an arm around me.

I didn't tense or shake him off the way I would have in the beginning. It was easier, even pleasurable, to receive. Daisy had helped with that.

"Ev isn't here that often," I said. "Let Daisy get her fix."

She arched against me as Evan undid the top button of her blouse, pressing his lips against her neck. "God, Evan, you're going to leave hickeys all over me..."

"Umph," he grunted, sucking harder.

Her breath quickened. "Catch me," she whispered, and we both gripped her tight.

At that moment, a towering stack of books on the coffee table tipped over and fell with a crash.

Daisy disengaged herself and gestured breathlessly toward the living room. "Love, we need to do something about all those books."

"We'll get more bookshelves." I kissed her neck.

"New York has great libraries, you know. You don't have to accumulate everything. You can read something, give it back afterwards, let it go..."

I laughed. Daisy was right; it was hard for me to let go of things. I wanted to own them, to know they'd be here tomorrow, that they had some permanence in an uncertain world.

Blake scraped the pan, shaking his head. "Food's almost ready," he said, as I went to stack up the books. Daisy joined me, helping to gather them.

"Before we eat," I said to her, "come with me. I want to show you something upstairs."

"I've heard those words before." She arched an eyebrow. "The night I met a certain Reeve McClellan IV, who took me up to his tower and tried to seduce me."

"Pretty sure you did some of the seducing, sweet flower." I spun her around, her hair flying out, and caught her by the hand.

"Don't be too long, lovebirds," Blake called after us as we ran out the front door to the hall. "Dinner won't wait."

I led Daisy through a door at the end of the hall and up a narrow flight of stairs. At the top, I paused.

"You're taking me up to the roof?" She laughed. "Do I *finally* get to see the surprise?"

For weeks, I'd told her to not even think of climbing these stairs. Though she liked being out on the roof of our apartment building — a concrete slab with a couple of lawn chairs and straggling plants, where she insisted the energy was good for casting spells — she'd grudgingly agreed.

We both liked high places. Points where you could look out and dream. The tower of the House, which I'd last seen in flames, my girl bound by dark magic before she overturned our lives. The rooftop garden near the tower, where I'd imagined our glorious futures. Her old dorm at Pacific Crest, where she'd confessed to looking out the eighth-story window after I was barred from campus and imagining that she could see all the way to L.A.

I pushed open the door.

Daisy followed me onto the roof. The spring air was fresh and sweet, the last of the warmth lingering as the sun cast a reddish glow over the skyline.

"Reeve, what — oh." She stopped short. "Oh my God."

Grabbing my hand, she rushed forward.

The corner of the roof was transformed. Potted trees and bamboo created a screen that hid the street and enclosed the space in an intimate grotto. Lanterns in red, purple, and gold hung from a frame of wood and sat between smaller pots overflowing with herbs and succulents. A woven mat covered the roof's concrete surface, bright outdoor pillows scattered across the top.

On the nights Daisy worked later than I did, I'd sneaked up here to create an oasis.

Daisy just stared. Then, slowly, she moved around the garden, touching the lanterns, rubbing the leaves of the herbs between her fingers and releasing the scents of lavender, basil, thyme, and rosemary into the air.

"Where did you get this?" She traced the wooden frame that sparkled with lanterns.

"I built it," I said, with a touch of pride.

She shook her head at me. "But how — right. I'm remembering now. You worked as a manual laborer in high school. And those skills all came back to you?"

I shrugged. "I fix everything around the house, don't I?"

"You do." She laughed. "You never stop surprising me."

"Do you like it?"

"I love it," she said softly, still looking around with wonder. "But — why?"

"Do you need a reason?"

She took my hands. "Why this in particular? Why now?"

"Because today's anniversary got me thinking," I told her quietly.

"I know how much it means to you to have a place of your own. A place that calls to you."

She swallowed and said nothing.

"Greer Hill was yours, and you've never found anything like it." At the mention of the hill, she flushed, and I stroked her cheeks. "I know you kept going there after we expelled the serpent. Ever since we moved to New York, you've been searching for that. Even though the five of us are together and you're doing what you love."

Daisy remained silent, but her eyes were bright.

"I would never try to create such a place for you from nothing. But after we moved in and you kept talking about the energy on the roof, I knew I wanted to make something out of it for you."

"Reeve?"

"Yes?"

"I love you so much." She launched herself at me and grabbed me in a fierce hug. My hands sank into her hair, scattering the cherry blossom petals.

"I love you too, Daze."

Our lips met, quick and passionate.

Even after four years together, she never took it for granted when we kissed, and I felt it. I felt her eagerness, her relief at the second kiss that always came after the first. The third, the fourth.

I still held by what I'd said the night we met: first times had power. But I'd stayed for more, striking down her worries one by one.

I'd stay for the rest of my life.

She pulled me down to one of the pillows. "You stocked up with herbs for casting spells," she marveled. "Everything I need is here."

"Same for me." I twisted a finger in her hair.

"Oh?" She stroked the stubble on my jaw. "Tell me about it."

I shook my head, because suddenly it was hard to speak.

"You know what I think, Reeve?" Daisy looked at me seriously, kneeling on the pillow. "I think this oasis you've made is one of those places that's bigger on the inside than it is on the outside."

I raised an eyebrow. "You mean, like magic?"

"I mean, like our lives."

I kissed her again. I would never get enough of her soft, warm lips. Her passion, her vitality, the sheer intensity she brought to everything she did. I'd called her a drug, a safe harbor, my shining Star. She was all of those. But more than anything, she was my love.

"You delivered me, Daze."

"*I* did?" She laughed.

"You brought me back to humanity."

"Mm-hm. My Devil," she said affectionately.

"You think?"

"Oh, I know it's still in you, Reeve. Desire, lust, ambition — you'll never lose them. And I don't want you to. As long as we both remember that's not all there is to you."

She was right.

I flirted with temptation daily. I worked with money, greed always snapping its jaws on the other side of the curtain, testing myself to remain firm that I wouldn't yield. I'd married the woman who held my heart in the palm of her hand, the woman who'd always had the power to lift me to the greatest heights and to utterly destroy me.

The woman who'd turned her back on that magic and simply loved me. Who took my soul only in bed, and gave me hers in exchange.

Images formed in my mind of what would happen after we met the others in our apartment, gathering around the table and eating Blake's exquisite food.

The dishes swept away, the table bared for Daisy to become the feast. Her eyes going unfocused with pleasure as I gave or withheld from her according to my whim. The four of us covering my wife with love-bites, leaving souvenirs for her to find long after she took us all inside her. The moment when my friends might decide to make me lose control, and I'd willingly hand it over to them.

Our shining Star, at the center of it all, cracking our world and reshaping it.

"Come on." Daisy rose to her feet and took my hand. "Blake's going to be dying that we're not eating his food the second it comes off the pan. If we don't go now, Nate and Evan will finish it all."

"A fate worse than death," I agreed.

"Thank you again," she whispered, her lips brushing my ear as we exited the oasis. "Always."

"Forever, Daze."

Descending the stairs, we walked into the warmth of our home and the love of our friends.

THE END

Acknowledgments

Big thanks and love to:

Jan, for always inspiring me as a critique partner, reading pages (over *many* drafts) since this story's inception, sharing your tarot knowledge with me, and giving frank, forthright, and whip-smart feedback.

Mackenzie of Nice Girl, Naughty Edits, for your thoughtful insights, cheerleading, patience, and commas. You truly believed in these characters. Thank you also for creating beautiful graphics that capture the dark, magical vibe of this story.

L.J. of Mayhem Cover Creations, for bringing your artistic vision to the vague symbols and vibes I sent your way and crafting the most unbelievably perfect pair of covers.

Darci, Marina, and Sarah, for beta reading and offering your hilarious commentary, honest opinions, and helpful feedback.

Annette and Michelle of Book Nerd Services, for your dedication, kindness, and support.

My husband, for always being there while I wander in and out of fictional realms, and for reading my drafts, cracking jokes to keep me sane, and being my rock in the emotional jungle of writing.

The wonderful readers and fellow authors who illuminate the indie publishing world and make this journey worthwhile.

And thanks to you for picking up this book and taking a chance on Daisy, Reeve, Nate, Evan, and Blake's journey. It means more to me than I can say.

About the Author

As a writer of new adult and erotic romance, Miranda Silver lives for exploring complicated characters and steamy love stories. She has degrees in English literature and music, and has always loved creating with both sounds and words. Miranda lives in California with her family, where she enjoys the perennially beautiful weather when she's not hunched over a screen, putting characters through their paces.

You can find Miranda here:

Instagram: @mirandasilverbooks
Twitter: @silvermusings
Facebook: @mirandasilverbooks
Goodreads: Miranda Silver

Join Miranda's Reader Group, Miranda's Muses, for exclusive sneak peeks and news about upcoming releases.

Also By Miranda Silver

Desire the Star (Serpentine Duet #1)

Priceless: A Dark College Romance

The Boys Next Door (Next Door #1)

The Girl in Between (Next Door #2)

Crave: An Erotic Story Collection

www.ingramcontent.com/pod-product-compliance
Lightning Source LLC
Chambersburg PA
CBHW030914050726
47498CB00003BA/735

* 9 7 8 1 0 0 5 5 0 5 2 1 9 *